— AN ASSASSIN'S CREED SERIES —

LAST DESCENDANTS

— AN ASSASSIN'S CREED SERIES —

LAST DESCENDANTS

FATE OF THE GODS

BY

MATTHEW J. KIRBY

SCHOLASTIC INC.

In bringing this trilogy to a close, I feel grateful for the continued support of this project by an amazing team of fellow storytellers and bookmakers. At Scholastic, Michael Petranek, Samantha Schutz, Debra Dorfman, Charisse Meloto, Monica Palenzuela, Lynn Smith, Jane Ashley, Ed Masessa, and Rick DeMonico have all worked tirelessly to bring readers the best story possible. At Ubisoft, Aymar Azaïzia, Anouk Bachman, Richard Farrese, Caroline Lamache, and Andrew Heitz continue to make me feel at home in the world of Assassin's Creed. Finally, my family and friends, especially Jaime, remain at my side, cheering me on as I begin each new project, and each new adventure. Thank you, all.

ISBN 978-1-338-16395-7

10 9 8 7 6 5 4 3 2 1 18 19 20 21 22

Printed in the U.S.A. 40
First printing 2018

Book design by Rick DeMonico
Map created by Matthew Kirby and Joshua Kirby

To my nephew, Will, a fellow adventurer.

Uppsala
SVEALAND
Västerås
GÖTALAND
Aros
JUTLAND
Jómsborg

CHAPTER ONE

Sean had grown accustomed to violence, but he didn't yet enjoy it the way his Viking ancestor did. Styrbjörn gloried in the sights, sounds, and smells of battle: the feel of a shield shattering under a blow from his bearded axe, Randgríð; the cleaving of limbs by his Ingelrii sword; the cackle of ravens flocking over corpses.

In fact, Styrbjörn privately felt glad that the Danish king, Harald Bluetooth, had rejected the terms of peace. It meant the battle could begin at last. Even though Sean did not look forward to the violence of the memory, he could admit to himself that he did enjoy the strength and power he felt in his ancestor's body.

Styrbjörn's fleet waited off the coast of Jutland, at Aros, as Harald's longships rowed out to meet him. The Dane-king's fortress would never hold against a land assault by Styrbjörn's force of Jomsvikings, and he no doubt believed his larger fleet could easily win an engagement at sea. It was also possible that Harald suspected that Gyrid, his wife—and Styrbjörn's sister—would commit some treachery unless she was kept far from the battle. Regardless of the reason, Styrbjörn smiled at the oncoming ships.

Sean could taste salt in the air as cormorants and pelicans dove into the sunlit waters around him. The journey to this moment had taken him weeks in the Animus, traversing years of Styrbjörn's life, seeking the moment when his ancestor would finally gain possession of Harald Bluetooth's dagger, the third prong of the separated Trident of Eden. But to find its modern resting place, Sean still had to learn what Styrbjörn had done with it before his death.

The simulation is holding very well, Isaiah said in Sean's ear. *It appears another battle is imminent. Are you ready?*

"I'm ready," Sean said.

Isaiah had removed Sean from the Aerie facility ten days ago, after it was compromised. Sean still hadn't heard from Grace or David or Natalya, or even learned what happened to them. Isaiah said they had gone rogue, and that Victoria was helping them, possibly even working with the Assassin Brotherhood. It was up to Sean to find the Piece of Eden before it fell into the wrong hands.

Your fortitude continues to impress me, Isaiah said.

"Thank you, sir."

The world owes you a debt of gratitude.

Sean smiled within the current of Styrbjörn's mind. "I'm glad I can help."

Let's get to it.

Sean returned his attention to the simulation, focusing on the flexing of the ship's timbers beneath his feet, and the shouts rolling toward Styrbjörn across the water from Harald's advancing ships. He turned toward his own men, his dreaded Jomsvikings. At the heart of his fleet, he'd ordered two dozen ships lashed together into a floating fortress from which his men could cast spears and arrows. His other ships would engage the enemy in close battle, ramming, grappling, and boarding. Styrbjörn planned to find Harald's ship so that he might engage the Danish king in single combat and end the battle quickly. It wouldn't help Styrbjörn's cause for his men to kill off the very warriors he hoped to command.

"I count at least two hundred ships," Palnatoke said beside him, hardened and gray. In the years since Styrbjörn had defeated the chieftain and assumed leadership of the Jomsvikings, the two men had arrived at a grudging respect for each other. "No, more than two hundred ships. Are you sure about this?"

"I am. But if it comforts you, last night several of the men made an offering to Thor. One claimed he was shown a vision in which I reached the coast of my home country with Harald Bluetooth tied to the mast of my ship like a dog." Styrbjörn removed his outer fur, then pulled his axe, Randgríð, free of his belt. "Harald's fleet will be mine."

Palnatoke grunted. "I wonder if the Bluetooth has made offerings to his White Christ."

Styrbjörn gestured across the water toward the oncoming ships. "And if he has, does that worry you?"

"No," Palnatoke said. "The Christ is not a god of war."

Styrbjörn scoffed. "Then what good is he?"

"To which god do you make offerings?"

Styrbjörn looked down at his axe. "I need no god."

The beating of Harald Bluetooth's drums grew louder, the rhythm by which his long ships heaved across the waves, and Sean let himself be swept up in the current of Styrbjörn's fury. He raised his axe and roared a battle cry with his ancestor's voice, and the Jomsvikings echoed his terrifying eagerness for battle. He gave the order, and his fleet charged ahead, their dragon prows clawing through the waves, sea spray salting Styrbjörn's lips.

The distance between his ships and Harald's collapsed quickly, until the enemy came within range. Styrbjörn waited until the precise moment, and then he gave the order. The forward ships dove to the side, cutting across the waves, opening a corridor to the fortress at the center of his fleet, and the archers and spearmen there loosed their missiles. The surprise barrage fell hard upon Harald's fleet, causing havoc, breaking up the rhythm of his oarsmen and the direction of his ships. Some of his vessels collided with one another, rocking and tossing men over.

Styrbjörn held his satisfaction in check and gave the second command. His forward ships surged back into the breach without breaking stride and rammed into the disorganized enemy at full speed. Harald's vessels, still struggling to recover from the rain of spears and arrows, took the impact broadside, splintering shields and capsizing a few ships. Within moments, the sea roiled with the violence of a battle storm, the cries of drowning men, and breaking wood.

Amid the chaos, Styrbjörn searched the horizon for Harald's banner, and when he found it, he ordered his vanguard into action. Two ships to either side of his formed a wedge and broke the enemy line, allowing his oarsmen to muscle his ship deep into Harald's ranks. Styrbjörn had to reach the king quickly, seizing the remaining moments of confusion before the Danes regrouped and found a Swedish ship at the heart of their fleet.

The Jomsvikings behind Styrbjörn plowed the waves silently, without chanting or drums, their red vision honed. Styrbjörn gripped his axe with one hand and leaned against his ship's dragon figurehead with the other, bracing himself. He drew nearer to Harald's ship, but before he reached it, shouts of alarm flew among the Danes. Then arrows and spears fell on Styrbjörn's ship. Their iron teeth sank into wood and flesh, and though some of his oarsmen were hit, none cried out, and the rest of them kept rowing. Styrbjörn stepped backward, away from the prow, readying himself.

He saw Harald now.

Then Harald saw him.

But a Danish vessel leapt between them, protecting the king and blocking the way.

Unable to stop, Styrbjörn's ship rammed into the new enemy, and the eruption of wood and waves tossed Styrbjörn into the sea. Sean tasted briny seawater that burned his lungs. He choked and coughed, the water around him black and cold.

The simulation went blurry.

Steady, now, Isaiah said. *You're fine. We know your ancestor didn't drown.*

Right. Sean dove back into the memory, letting the waves overtake him, and clawed with Styrbjörn toward the surface. His armor and weapons dragged at him, pulling him down, but he managed to breach the waves and hook the rail of a passing ship with Randgríð's fang. He then used his axe to heave himself out of the sea onto the deck of the ship, where he rolled to his feet, heavy with water.

Harald's ship still lay within reach, but Styrbjörn would have to cross the decks of two Danish vessels to reach him. He had lost his shield in the water, but had his axe and pulled his dagger from its sheath just as the first two Danes rushed him.

He ducked and parried, throwing them both off-balance, and managed to stab one of them in the back as he stumbled past. In a different battle, on a different day, he would have stayed to finish them, but he could not waste the time. He rushed down the deck of the ship, shouldering men aside, blocking and dodging their blows, letting Randgríð taste their blood when he could.

As he reached the stern, he slashed the man at the rudder with his knife and vaulted over several yards of ocean to the deck of the next ship. The Danes there were ready for him, and a mass of them blocked his path. Beyond them, Harald's vessel had already started to retreat. Styrbjörn sheathed his weapons. Then he wrenched a heavy oar from its spur and, holding it across his chest, he charged at his enemies, using the oar as a bull uses its horns.

He smashed into their line, dug his heels into the deck, and drove the enemy backward. Some went overboard, and some fell and were trampled by Styrbjörn and their own kinsmen. Those that managed to stay on their feet tried to strike at him with their weapons, but he kept them in retreat and none of their blows landed. His back and arms and legs strained, the heat of his muscles turning the seawater in his clothing to steam, until he'd pressed the enemy line all the way to the bow.

Within the power of Styrbjörn's memory, Sean found

the feat he was experiencing almost unbelievable, and if he'd read about it he would have dismissed it as an exaggerated legend. But the strength he experienced in his ancestor's body was very real.

Styrbjörn now stood at the bow and realized Harald's ship had already rowed too far away to make the leap. But he couldn't let the king escape. This battle had to end with Harald's defeat at Styrbjörn's hand, and no other way.

Styrbjörn tossed the oar aside, and before any of the Danes he had plowed under could rouse themselves, he dove into the sea. The cold snapped at him, and the waves shoved him, and the depths reached for him, but he surged through the water toward Harald's vessel, and soon arrows and spears split the water around him. Before he had reached the king's ship, an arrow bit deep into the back of his thigh.

Sean and Styrbjörn let out a roar of pain, but the Viking kept swimming. Moments later, he pulled Randgríð free and used her once again to pull himself onto the ship.

He landed hard on the deck, exhausted, soaked, and bleeding, but still he towered over the shocked Danes. They gaped as Styrbjörn wrenched the arrow from his leg and tossed it into the sea, but after the shock of that moment had passed, two of them attacked. Styrbjörn felled them both before he charged at Harald.

"You are neither man nor king!" he roared.

The intent of those words could not be mistaken. Harald, shorter than Styrbjörn by two hands, flinched and faltered, giving ground before combat had even begun, and in that moment Styrbjörn knew he had won. But Harald had to know it, too. The Danes had to know it.

Styrbjörn did not wait for his opponent to recover his footing before attacking. The first blow from Randgríð cracked Harald's shield, and the second shattered it. Harald raised his sword in a meager posture of defense, but his arm had no strength, and fear filled his eyes.

Styrbjörn laughed so that it filled the ship. "Do you yield?"

"I yield!" Harald said. His sword clanged against the deck. "I yield to you, Bjorn, son of Olof."

Styrbjörn nodded. "Then give the signal before any more of your Danes die."

Harald stared up at him for a moment before nodding to one of his men, who raised a large horn, and then the order of surrender sounded across the waves, picked up, and carried to the edge of the fleet. Several minutes later, the clamor of battle had ceased, Dane and Jomsviking ships rising and falling with the waves.

"It didn't have to come to this," Harald said.

Styrbjörn let out a heavy sigh. "You would prefer I go on raiding your villages?"

"We could have reached an agreement."

"I tried to reach an agreement with you. My sister, your wife, tried to persuade you—"

"You asked for too much, Styrbjörn."

"But now I have everything," he said.

"You want my crown? Is that it?"

"My sister already has your crown. I came for your fleet."

"To attack your uncle? You would take my men to Svealand?"

"Yes," Styrbjörn said. "And you will come with them."

Sean felt the rush of his ancestor's victory, in spite of the pain in his thigh, but he also noticed the dagger at Harald

Bluetooth's belt. It had an odd curve to it, and it obviously wasn't an ordinary blade, but Harald clearly had no idea what it was, or how to use it. That dagger was the entire reason for this simulation, and at some point, it would come into Styrbjörn's possession. A part of Sean wanted to simply reach out and grab the Piece of Eden now, but doing so would desynchronize him from the memory and throw him violently out of the Animus. Instead, he had to wait, as patiently as he could, and let the memory unfold just as it had happened. There wasn't anything Sean could do to change the past.

But the past could change the present. And the future.

CHAPTER TWO

Owen leaned against the third-floor glass railing, overlooking the open atrium below. The Aerie's glass walls admitted a pale green light from the mountain forest that engulfed the facility. Griffin stood next to him, and together they watched three Templars in dark suits, two men and a woman, as they marched across the atrium floor toward the elevator, their footsteps echoing up the vaulted space.

"Who are they?" Owen asked the Assassin.

"I don't know," Griffin said. "But I assume at least one of them is a member of the Inner Sanctum."

"Inner Sanctum?"

"The Templar governing body." Griffin's posture had tensed up, and Owen knew what that meant. It was how Griffin looked in the moment before he struck, hidden blade no longer hidden.

"This bothers you, doesn't it?" Owen nodded toward the elevators right as one of them dinged, and the Templars stepped inside. "Just watching them come and go."

"Templars have killed friends of mine. People I thought of as brothers and sisters. So, yeah, it bothers me." Griffin flexed one of his hands in and out of a fist. "Doesn't matter. The only thing that matters is stopping Isaiah. That means letting them come and go."

"Are you worried Victoria might turn you in?"

"Yes. But I've decided to trust her."

"I wonder what the Templars would do to you if they knew you were here."

"What they would *try* and do, you mean."

Owen shrugged. "Sure."

"Victoria has it under control. And my alliance is with her, not the Order."

"What would they do to her if they knew?" Owen asked.

Back in Mongolia, Victoria had seen that it was necessary to join with Griffin against a common enemy. Now that Isaiah possessed two of the three daggers, the prongs of the Trident of Eden, he had already become too powerful for either the Assassins or the Templars to stop on their own. If he found the third, he would be all-powerful. A conqueror and god-king unlike any the world had seen since Alexander the Great. Humanity didn't have time for ancient rivalries and politics. Victoria and Griffin had kept their alliance a secret from their masters because they couldn't risk any interference in their plan.

"Victoria has already betrayed the Order once before," Griffin said. "They forgave her then. I don't think they'd forgive her a second time. Of course, if we don't stop Isaiah, none of that will matter."

"What about after we stop Isaiah?"

"I hope for her sake the Templars recognize that all of this was necessary."

"What about you?" Owen asked. "What will the Brotherhood do to you?"

"Me?" Griffin looked up at the ceiling of the atrium, a glass dome filled with blue sky and two crisscrossing contrails. "There's no going back for me."

Owen balked. "Never?"

Griffin shook his head.

"Why?"

Griffin said nothing and Owen frowned. This was his first moment alone with the Assassin since they'd left Mongolia, and he still had serious questions about the Brotherhood.

"The last time I was in the Animus," Owen said, "my ancestor killed Möngke Khan. After that, the Mongol army retreated and never recovered. My ancestor literally changed the history of the world, all on her own, but because of an injury to her knee, the Brotherhood just abandoned her. They even took away her father's hidden blade." Owen still shook a little with the pain and confusion of that memory. He raged against the cold and ruthless calculation to leave someone behind. "Her mentor said she wasn't 'useful' anymore."

"She *wasn't* useful anymore. Her knee would never be the same. She couldn't—"

"So? It isn't fair. She was a hero."

"No one said she wasn't."

"But you're saying the Brotherhood would do the same thing to you just for working with Victoria?"

"The last time a Templar spy infiltrated the Brotherhood, we were almost wiped out. So, yes, I'm saying that working with a Templar means that my life as an Assassin is over. I don't regret my choice, and I don't blame anyone else for it."

Owen found that difficult to believe. "You're telling me that you're really okay with them kicking you out?"

Griffin's posture softened. His shoulders relaxed. "Yes," he said.

"But that's not right. It's not fair—"

"Or maybe you're just a kid and you don't get it," Griffin said, his voice harsh. "To serve humanity and the Creed, you have to let go of what you think is true. You have to let go of your ideas of fairness. Even your ideas of right and wrong. One day, you may have to do things that you can't imagine yourself doing right now. You have to realize that in any given moment, what is best for the world may not fit neatly inside your comfortable box."

Owen looked away from him, back toward the floor of the atrium. "I don't know if I want to be a part of something like that."

"No one is forcing you."

Owen turned his back to the open atrium and leaned against the railing. No matter what Griffin said, right and wrong were important. Fairness was important. They had to be, or else it didn't matter whether Owen's father was guilty of robbing a bank and shooting a security guard or not. It didn't matter that he had died in prison for a crime he didn't commit. Owen couldn't accept that, because those things mattered to him more than anything else.

"Isaiah showed me a memory in the Animus," Owen said. "My dad's memory."

Griffin nodded. "Monroe mentioned that."

"Did he tell you about the Assassin? The Brotherhood forced my dad to rob that bank, and then they framed him for that murder."

"He told me that's what Isaiah showed you."

"Are you going to deny it?"

Griffin gestured his arm in a wide circle. "Look where you are. Look what Isaiah has done. And you need me to deny that?"

"Yes," Owen said. "If it's not true, deny it."

"What if I don't?" Griffin said. "What if I refuse to, because it offends me that you would even think about taking Isaiah's word for anything. What would you do then?"

Owen looked away, scowling, and the two of them stood there until the three Templar suits came back down the elevator, crossed the atrium floor, and left the Aerie.

"When we first met," Owen said, "you told me that my dad wasn't an Assassin. But you said he might be involved somehow. You have never explained that. So, no. I'm not taking Isaiah's word for anything, but I'm also not taking yours."

Griffin sighed. "Look, the bank your dad robbed—sorry, was accused of robbing—was a Malta bank. They're a financial arm of Abstergo. That's all I meant." He went quiet. "We'd better go check in with Victoria."

So they walked to the elevator and rode it the rest of the way to the top floor, to the office that had belonged to Isaiah before his defection. The setup reminded Owen of a chapel, with rows of benches, and a large desk-like altar at the front. The others had come, too, and Owen took a seat next to his best friend, Javier. Nearby, Natalya looked exhausted, with dark circles under her eyes, and a somewhat vacant stare. She still blamed herself for the death of the Assassin Yanmei even though everyone else knew it wasn't her fault. The last simulation had been rough on her, too. Her ancestor had shot the arrow that had ruined Owen's knee. Or his ancestor's knee. Sometimes it was hard to keep that straight.

Grace and David sat across from them, next to Monroe, and Victoria stood at the front of the room before the desk, clutching her tablet to her chest.

"I doubt we'll receive another visit like that for at least a week," she said. "Perhaps two. I think it's safe to resume our work in earnest."

"What'd they say?" Monroe asked, leaning forward, his hands joined by interlocking fingers.

"They are focusing the majority of their tactical efforts on finding Isaiah, and they have a few leads. In the meantime, they want me to continue searching for the third prong of the Trident in the Animus. With all of you."

"Will they be sending more agents here?" Griffin asked.

"They're trying to keep this situation contained," she said. "The fewer Templars who know that one of our own has turned, the better. For the time being, the Aerie is ours."

"What about our parents?" Grace asked.

"They remain unaware of what has happened. If they want to visit you as they usually do, they are welcome." Victoria closed her eyes and rubbed her temples with her fingertips. "Which brings me to something I feel I must say."

"What's that?" David asked.

"I will not force you to remain here. After what has happened, here and in Mongolia, I cannot in good conscience keep you against your will. If you wish to leave, I will call your parents to come get you, and you have my word that Abstergo and the Templars will leave you alone."

The silence that followed led Owen to think that some of them might actually be considering her offer. And why wouldn't they? Their lives were in danger if they stayed. But so was the rest of the world, now that Isaiah had two-thirds of a weapon of mass destruction. Owen could leave the Aerie, and he might even be safe from the Templars, but that didn't mean he was safe. It didn't mean his mom and his grandparents were safe. The only way to protect them would be to stop Isaiah, and to do that, Owen had to work with Victoria.

"I'm still in," he said.

"Me too," Javier said.

Grace and David looked at each other, communicating in that wordless brother-sister way. Ever since Mongolia, something had changed in their sibling rivalry, and Owen had noticed that they seemed to be more in tune with each other.

"We're in," Grace said.

Victoria nodded. "That leaves you, Natalya."

Natalya stared at the floor a moment longer, and then looked up. "Where is Sean?"

"Security footage shows that he left with Isaiah," Victoria said. "I assume he is working with Isaiah to locate the third Piece of Eden."

"Willingly?" Javier asked.

"I'm not sure that word applies anymore," Monroe said. "Not when Isaiah has two prongs of the Trident."

"I'm staying," Natalya said, and everyone turned to look at her. "I'm staying for Sean. We have to save him from Isaiah."

"I understand," Victoria said.

"What if he doesn't want to be saved?" David asked. "He already chose to stay behind once before."

"We have to give him the chance," Natalya said.

"I agree." Victoria stepped away from the desk toward them. "And if we're going to help Sean and stop Isaiah, we don't have any time to lose."

"What's the plan?" Griffin asked.

Victoria swiped and tapped her tablet, and a holographic display appeared over her desk. It showed the double helix sequences of all their DNA, with sections of concordance marked, the places where their genetic memories intersected and overlapped. In the beginning of all of this, it had seemed an almost impossible coincidence that Owen and the others had ancestors present at so many of the same historical events, but Monroe's research had revealed there wasn't anything coincidental or accidental about it.

Something had bound their ancestors to the history of the Trident. That same influence, or force, had brought the six of them together at this moment in time. Monroe had learned that each of them carried in their DNA a piece of the collective unconscious, mankind's deepest and oldest memories and myths. Monroe had called that phenomenon an Ascendance Event, but he still didn't understand what caused it, or what it meant.

"We believe Sean and Isaiah have a lead on the third prong

of the Trident," Victoria said. She tapped the screen of her tablet, and the display switched to an image of the earth, with an area circled that included Sweden. "Sean's last simulation took place in the memories of Styrbjörn the Strong, a Viking warrior who fought his uncle for control of the Swedish throne in the late tenth century. Based on my analysis, some of you had ancestors present at their final battle in the year 985."

"Some of us?" Owen said.

"Yes," Victoria said. "Javier, Grace, and David."

"What?" Grace said. "Vikings? Really?"

"That's unexpected," Javier said, his tone dry.

"Perhaps." Victoria switched the image back to their DNA. "But it shouldn't be surprising, really. The Vikings were some of the most widely traveled people in the world during the Middle Ages. They left their mark, from the Middle East to Canada."

"What about us?" Owen nodded toward Natalya. "We don't have ancestors there?"

"No," Victoria said.

Natalya sighed, and Owen realized she was probably grateful for the break. But he wasn't. He didn't like the idea of waiting around outside the Animus. He wanted to go back in with the others.

"You two can always help me," Monroe said. "I've got a lot more work to do."

"Okay," Natalya said.

Owen nodded. At least that was something. And if he couldn't be in the Animus trying to stop Isaiah, maybe he could at least use the time to find out the truth about his father.

"The Viking simulation is almost ready," Victoria said.

"David and Grace, you'll be in your usual Animus rooms. Javier can use one of the spares. Why don't you all go downstairs and find something to eat before we begin."

"I'm not really hungry," Javier said.

"Then go downstairs to rest," she said. "The simulation will be taxing."

Her directive had a clear purpose. Victoria had things she wanted to discuss with Monroe and Griffin alone, and Owen didn't like that. It meant they were still keeping secrets, and he was tired of secrets. But it didn't seem like the right time to push it, so he left the office with the others, and they made their way toward the elevator.

"It's strange to see this place so empty," Grace said.

"I don't know what we'll find to eat," David said. "There's no one left to cook the food."

"There are always snacks down there," Grace said.

Owen pushed the button to call the elevator, and a moment later the doors opened. He watched Natalya as they got inside, wishing he could do something to make her feel better. She kept her head down during the elevator ride, and then lagged behind Grace and David as they led Javier toward the Animus wing of the Aerie facility.

Owen decided to stop and wait for her. "You okay?"

"I'm fine," she said.

"Really? Doesn't seem like you're—"

She stopped and turned to face him. "Are you okay?" she asked, and he felt a spark of anger in her voice. "Are you? With everything that's happening, tell me how you would answer a question like that."

"I—I guess . . . I don't know."

"I'm not okay, Owen. But if I say I'm not okay, you're going to want to talk about it, and I don't want to talk about it."

"We don't have to talk about it."

"Good."

"I guess I just want you to know I'm worried about you."

"Then just say that."

"Okay. I'm worried about you."

"I appreciate that," Natalya said. "I'm worried about you, too. I'm worried about Sean. I'm worried about all of us."

"You don't have to worry about me."

"No? I shot you in the knee with an arrow."

"No, you didn't. That was my ancestor. And your ancestor."

"So? I experienced it. Like it happened to me. But I couldn't change it. I didn't have a choice, and that almost makes it worse. You and Sean and the others, you think the Animus gives you freedom, but to me it's a prison. The past is a prison, where you have no choices, and I don't want to live there."

She walked away from him, and he followed after her. They entered a warm glass corridor that stretched through the woods until it reached another building, and before Owen could think of anything to say to her, they entered the common room, where the others had already found some food, mostly bagged chips and granola bars, but the fridge still held quite a bit of yogurt, milk, and juice. After they had each found what they wanted, they sat down at the same table to eat.

"Do you guys trust Victoria?" Javier asked.

Grace peeled the top off her pink strawberry yogurt. "Do you trust Griffin?"

"I don't think we can really trust either of them." Owen opened up a granola bar and broke off a bite. Javier had spent time with Assassins, and Grace had spent time with the Templars. Loyalties had already begun to form, but not for Owen. "They're both hiding things from us," he said.

David took his glasses off and used his shirt to clean them. "Victoria could have turned us over to the Templars, but she didn't. Griffin could have done his Assassin thing and killed us if he wanted to, but he hasn't. Just because they have secrets doesn't mean we can't trust them."

"That's true," Grace said.

"I still think we need to be careful of Victoria," Javier said. "Try not to tell her anything—"

"I tried that," Natalya said. She hadn't brought any food to the table. She just sat there, looking around at each of them. "I tried not to tell them what I knew. And Yanmei ended up dead because of it."

"That wasn't your fault." David put his glasses back on and looked directly at Natalya. "Remember what Griffin told you? This is war, and Isaiah is the enemy."

"It's actually not that easy for me to just blame Isaiah for my mistakes," Natalya said.

Javier folded his arms and leaned back in his chair. "All I'm saying is, with Victoria, we need to be careful."

"And I agree with you," Natalya said. "I'm still worried about what happens after we find the third piece. Even if we can stop Isaiah, what happens after that? The Templars and the Assassins will just go back to fighting over the Trident, and I don't think either of them should have it."

"So what are you saying?" Grace asked.

“I don’t know,” Natalya said. “I don’t know what to do. For now, we need to save Sean. Or at least give him the chance. After that, I just hope we can figure something out.”

A few minutes later, Victoria entered the common room with Monroe and Griffin.

“The simulation is complete,” she said. “It’s time to begin.”

CHAPTER THREE

David wondered how this time in the Animus would work. He and Grace would have the same ancestor, but they couldn't both be in those memories at the same time. During the Draft Riots simulation, he had only experienced an indirect memory, a reconstruction from extrapolated data, while Grace got the full dose. It was the only way they could be in the simulation together, but it also meant David could die at the hands of racist thugs, or at least his ancestor could, a frightening experience he never wanted to think about, let alone repeat.

"Javier," Victoria said.

Next to David, Javier sat upright. "Yes, ma'am?"

"We've prepared your Animus. Monroe will take you there and get you situated."

"Are we all going into the same simulation?" Javier asked.

"No." Victoria looked down at her tablet. "You'll be in separate simulations, though you might interact with the other's ancestor."

"Why keep us separate?" David asked.

"To reduce the risk of desynchronization," Victoria said. "Shared simulations are less stable, and we don't have time to troubleshoot problems. We'll run this operation as cleanly as we can."

"Okay, then." Javier rose to his feet, and he and Monroe left the common room.

"How will that work with us?" Grace asked, nodding toward David. She'd apparently already wondered the same thing he had. "We have the same ancestor."

"You will take turns," Victoria said. "Each of you will get to experience your genetic memories. If it becomes clear that one of you is better suited to this simulation, we might stop switching you out."

David looked at Grace. There was a time that they might've turned this into a competition, because of course he wanted to be the one to go into the Animus. Not that long ago, he'd almost looked at this whole situation like a virtual reality game, back when his ancestor flew planes in World War II. But things had changed since then, and he knew now how important it was that they find the last Piece of Eden. If that meant Grace got to be a Viking instead of him, he was all right with that.

"You can go first," Grace said.

"I was about to say the same thing."

"Sure you were."

He gave her a smile, and then Victoria asked them to follow her.

They left Owen and Natalya in the common room with Griffin and walked with Victoria down the glass Aerie hallways to the Animus room where David had spent a lot of time in the last few weeks. The coppery scent of electricity and the subtle but insistent hum of machinery charged the air, while several computer monitors blinked from the sterile white walls. David crossed to the Animus and stepped inside the waist-high metal ring. He clipped his feet into their mobile platforms, giving his legs almost complete freedom of movement, and then Victoria helped him climb into the full body framework that supported every joint, allowing even the slightest motions. Within that ring, David could walk, run, jump, and climb as the simulation demanded, all without going anywhere.

Victoria tightened the last of the clamps and straps. "Secure?"

"Secure," David said.

"Let me double-check the calibration before we put the helmet on." Victoria stepped away to one of the nearby computer consoles.

"You're going to look pretty stupid in those horns," Grace said.

"Vikings didn't really have horns on their helmets," David said. "In a real battle horns would—"

"I know that." Grace shook her head. "Just be careful, okay?"

Her voice had the same tone as when she used to tell him not to talk to the gangbangers, and which streets to avoid on the way home from school. But he wasn't that kid anymore. "You don't have to take care of me. I'm good."

"Tell that to Dad. Maybe then he'll leave me alone about you."

"I'll be careful."

Victoria returned to the Animus. "Everything looks optimal. Are you ready?"

David nodded, and Grace stepped back and away.

Victoria brought the helmet down from its nest of wires above. "Okay, here we go." She placed the helmet over David's head, and the whole world went black. No sights. No sounds. Like getting smothered with nothing.

Can you hear me? Victoria asked through the helmet.

"Yes."

Good. We're all set out here.

"Whenever you're ready."

Loading the Memory Corridor in three, two, one . . .

A flash of light shredded the black nothing inside David's helmet, and he closed his eyes. When he opened them, he saw gray. A shifting, billowing void of shadow and haze surrounded him. The Memory Corridor was supposed to make the transition to the full simulation smoother, and David thought it probably accomplished that, except nothing could make the next part easier.

Parietal insertion in three, two, one . . .

David took a deep breath, and then his head took an electromagnetic beating. The energy pulses were supposed to quiet the part of his brain that kept him grounded in time and space, but for several moments he couldn't think of anything else except the hammer inside his skull.

Loading genetic identity in three, two, one . . .

The pain receded. David gave it a moment, then opened his eyes and looked down at himself, blinking away the last of his disorientation, only to feel a new type of confusion set in.

He was a giant.

Or as close to a giant as a man could get.

David raised his ancestor's hands and studied them, fascinated. It wasn't their white skin, although that was weird, but the sheer size of them. They were somehow more than just hands, as if David were wearing leather baseball mitts. His arms and his legs were huge, too, but not like he'd been going to the gym. He didn't look like a bodybuilder. He was just big. Tall and wide and strong.

David? Victoria asked. *How are you doing?*

"Good," David said. "But it feels weird for you to call me that when I feel like Goliath."

Victoria laughed in his ear. *Written records from this time period are scarce, and extremely unreliable. We know very little about who your ancestor is, or how he will be involved with the Piece of Eden. I can't even tell you his name.*

"I should be able to figure all that out once I settle into his memories."

Good. But it might be a bit of a rough transition until you do.

"If I can't get it to work, Grace can try."

That's the idea. Are you ready for me to load the full simulation?

"Give me a second."

Of course.

David turned his thoughts inward, searching for the mind of his ancestor within his own, digging deep for a voice that wasn't his, listening closely. When he finally heard it, he engaged that voice in a conversation. Not of words, but the thoughts and memories of his ancestor, a farmer and warrior named Östen Jorundsson.

Östen owned his own land, a modest holding at the base of

a round hill not far from a lake, with pastures, a small woodland of spruce and oak, and a spring that bubbled water cold enough to crack teeth. Östen took far more pride in his land than he did his many victories in battle. He fought when called upon by his king, or when honor demanded it, but would rather be at home, sharing a warm fire next to his wife, or fishing with his son, or singing with his daughters. It was a life David could want for himself.

"I think I'm ready," he said.

Excellent. Loading the full simulation in three, two, one . . .

The Memory Corridor shattered into a blinding, crystalline dust, which ebbed and swirled, then gradually massed together into sturdier forms, assuming the vague shapes of buildings, trees, and ships. David's eyes adjusted to this new reality forcing its way into his mind. But it wasn't really a new reality. It was an old reality and an old voice speaking for the first time in centuries, and soon David stood fully in Östen's world.

Before him, rich green grass covered the main pasture, grazed by his twenty-six head of cattle. They were sturdy mountain stock, mostly white with black spots, and he hadn't polled them, because horns made bears and wolves doubt themselves. The sun had begun to dip low, spreading a golden patina over his farm and the land below, all the way to the shores of Mälaren to the south.

David knew, through Östen, that it was time to bring the herd in. So he gave Östen his voice, and then cupped his hands to his mouth. The cows looked up at his call, but went back to grazing, more interested in the summer grass at their hooves than anything he had to offer. Östen glanced down at Stone

Dog, who lay at his feet, perfectly still, eager, waiting for a nod from his master to shoot him out into the field.

David hadn't seen Stone Dog's breed before. He was like a cross between a stubby-legged corgi and a wolf, but he could run, and he knew just how to round up the herd, circling, barking, pressing the cattle together, and driving them toward Östen. They came mooing and bellowing, and with Stone Dog's help, Östen pushed the herd into its fenced enclosure for the night, a small paddock near enough to keep watch against predators.

"Well done," Östen said once the cows had been secured.

Stone Dog's tongue flapped from one side of his mouth, and his eyes shone.

"Let's go see how Tørgils is getting on, eh?"

Östen turned from the cattle in the paddock toward the large byre that stood next to the stable, near the hall, and on the far side of it he found his son chopping wood. At fifteen, Tørgils stood as tall as Östen had at his age, but he had his mother's almost-black hair, the color of wet soil. Arne the Dane labored next to him in his breeches and loose-hanging tunic, and as Östen surveyed the results of their splitting work, an ugly awareness crept over David and then seized him by the neck.

Arne was a slave.

Östen used a different word in his thoughts and memories. He called Arne a *thrall*. But the word didn't matter. What mattered was that David's ancestor owned a *slave*.

"Father?" Tørgils had stopped swinging his axe. "Are you well?"

David didn't know what to say. He felt too shocked and angry to listen to Östen's voice. He didn't want to hear it. To think of what slavery had done to African Americans, and to the world, only to find out that his own ancestor had enslaved someone else . . . David wanted to shout back at Östen, but he couldn't, because he was supposed to *be* Östen.

At his side, Stone Dog growled at him suddenly, his hackles high and head low as he backed away from the strange boy wearing his master's body.

"Father?" Tørgils asked again.

Arne the Dane, slender and hard as a nail, looked at David now. "Östen?"

David shook his head. No, he was *not* Östen.

The simulation trembled, distorting the farm with ripples and seams, and the quake only worsened with each moment that David refused to synchronize.

What's going on? Victoria asked. *You were doing great, but now we're losing stability. Are you okay?*

"No," David said.

The simulation is about to collapse.

"I know!"

David, whatever is happening, you need to rein it in.

His anger did not feel like something he could control.

I can pull you out and put Grace in—

"No." David didn't want that. He didn't need Grace to protect him or rescue him anymore. Besides, she'd probably have a harder time with their slave-owning ancestor than he did. "Just hang on," he said and took a deep breath.

Tørgils, Arne the Dane, and Stone Dog had all been caught in the glitch storm, frozen in place. David focused on the dog first, and listened to Östen's memory of how Stone Dog had been trampled by a two-year-old cow when he was a pup, but jumped up and shook it off as if nothing had happened. "That dog's head must be made of stone," Arne had said, and the name planted itself.

David smiled at that memory, and the simulation jolted back to life, still uneven and jerky, but moving again.

Excellent, David. Keep doing what you're doing.

David turned to Östen's son next, remembering a time from his toddling when he had lost a perfectly good axe trying to hunt fish with it. The water had claimed the weapon, and Tørgils had splashed and shouted at the fish, enraged. Östen had laughed and taught his son how to use a hook and handline, and Tørgils had taken to it like an heir to the god Njörðr. Not long ago, at the age of fourteen winters, he had pulled in a salmon the length of Östen's leg, and the pride of that moment still lingered.

These were memories David could listen to. These were moments he could want to be a part of, and they made synchronization possible.

You're almost there. Simulation stabilizing . . .

But when David looked at Arne, his anger flared again, and his grip on synchronization slipped. This wasn't something he could reconcile. It wasn't possible to identify with this. It went against everything David knew to be right.

He remembered how many winters ago, before Tørgils was born, Östen had joined a raid against the Danes, from which he'd brought Arne back in chains as his prisoner and thrall. It didn't matter that Östen had since removed those chains, or that he wasn't a cruel master.

It was still wrong.

When David tried to convince himself it was right, or tried to see slavery how Östen saw it, his anger sent the simulation reeling again.

We're wasting time, Victoria said. *I need to know if you can do this.*

David didn't want to admit that he couldn't. He just needed time and perspective to figure out a way to get his mind in agreement with Östen's. He didn't need Grace.

David, the simulation is—

"I know." He could see for himself that he was desynchronizing. "Just wait."

For what?

He didn't know. He took one more look at Arne, and tried to force himself to believe it was right to enslave the Dane. But no amount of will could ram something into his head that wouldn't fit.

David—

The world fell into a blender, taking his mind and body with it. For several moments, he felt only pain that radiated from every point in his body, all at once, as though layers of him were being sliced away, exposing nerves, until the last shred of him vanished, and only his mind remained, spinning around and around in a maelstrom, detached from any place or point in time, or even a sense of who he was.

David.

He heard the voice, but it wasn't holding still, and he didn't know where it was coming from.

David, I'm going to take your helmet off.

The voice sounded familiar, but before he could figure out

who was speaking to him, a white-hot light burned his eyes back into his head, and then the fire raged from his mind down his spine, into his stomach and his arms and legs.

"David, can you hear me?" the first voice asked.

"David?" came another.

He knew the second voice better than the first, and he opened his eyes. Grace stood in front of him. Grace, his sister. David blinked, and it all rushed back at once. Who he was. Where he was. Why he was there. Like someone had opened the floodgates, and it was enough to drown him. A swell of nausea climbed up his throat.

"I'm gonna throw up," he said.

Victoria lifted a small bucket to his mouth just in time. His stomach convulsed, painfully, and he lost the food he'd eaten. Grace stood by until he was finished, and then she helped him out of the harness, and the Animus, onto his wobbly legs.

"And that's why you don't desynchronize," she said.

"Now you tell me."

She put her arm around him. "What happened in there?"

David shook his head. "Give me a minute."

Grace helped him over to a swivel chair, and he fell into it, hard enough to send it rolling backward a couple of feet. Victoria walked over to him, jabbing at her tablet.

"Your neurovitals looked good during the simulation," she said. "Elevated blood pressure, though."

"I was angry."

"Angry at what?" Grace asked.

"Angry at him. Our ancestor."

Grace frowned. "Why?"

"He—" David's head still throbbed, making it hard to form a sentence longer than a few words, and it would take a lot of words to explain. "Can we . . . talk about this later?"

Grace looked at Victoria. "Yes."

Victoria paused a moment, and then offered an abrupt nod. "Fine. We'll take a break. Then we can debrief and plan the next step. Perhaps you can help prepare your sister for her attempt. In the meantime, I'm going to go check on Javier."

She left the room, seeming irritated, and Grace looked hard at David, not saying anything.

"What?" he finally asked.

"Are you okay?"

"You don't need to take care of me. I'm okay. I just need to rest."

"Fine." Now she was the one who seemed irritated. "But then I want an explanation."

David nodded, hoping that Javier's ancestor would turn out to be the one with access to the Piece of Eden. That way, it wouldn't matter who David's ancestor had been, or what he had done.

CHAPTER FOUR

Javier waited, suspended in a structural body harness as Monroe initiated the machine's core. He had never been in an Animus like this. The previous two had kept him reclined, but this one allowed complete stationary mobility, and it felt good to think about getting back in a simulation. Javier had tried to make himself useful while Owen explored the memories of his Chinese ancestor. He'd even broken into a police warehouse and stolen the evidence used at the trial of Owen's father. But that wasn't the same as chasing a Piece of Eden through history. Nothing was as important as finding the rest of the Trident before Isaiah did.

"They've made some upgrades to the Parietal Suppressor," Monroe said.

"The what?"

"The Parietal—never mind. It'll take too long to explain. The point is, this will feel different than my Animus, or Griffin's."

"Different how?"

"Hard to describe."

"You can run it, though, right?"

"Of course I can." Monroe stood. "Are you ready?"

Javier nodded. "Yes."

Monroe checked each of the straps, clips, and buckles one more time, making sure Javier was secure. "So are you an Assassin now, or what?" he asked almost casually as he pulled the Animus helmet down from the nest of wires overhead.

Javier hesitated before answering. "No."

"You sure about that?"

"Why?"

Monroe shrugged. "Just try to remember what I've told you."

Javier may not have become a member of the Brotherhood, but he had definitely thought about it. "I believe in free will."

"So do I. That's why I don't want to see any of you giving it over to the Templars. Or the Assassins." He lifted the helmet. "Here we go."

Javier let him place the helmet over his head, surprised at the totality of the barrier it created between him and the outside world. He heard nothing and saw nothing. But then something buzzed in his ear, and Monroe spoke.

You reading me?

Monroe's voice had guided him through Mexico in the sixteenth century, and New York City during the Draft Riots of 1863. "Just like old times."

This part won't feel like old times. I'm going to engage the Parietal Suppressor. You'll notice it, but it will pass quickly. Okay?

That didn't sound pleasant. "Okay . . ."

This is it. In three, two, one . . .

The Animus shoved an ice pick down through the top of Javier's head. At least, that was how it felt. He gasped and clenched his teeth against the shock and the pain, which only got worse when someone stirred the ice pick. Javier lost track of everything except that agony.

Hang on. Almost there.

Another excruciating moment passed, and then the pain vanished as quickly as it had come. Javier opened his eyes and saw the undulating void of the Memory Corridor.

You all right? Monroe asked.

"Yeah." Javier took a deep breath. "Does it do that every time?"

They say it gets easier.

"I can't imagine it getting worse."

I'm about to load your ancestor's identity. This will feel more like what you're used to. Are you ready?

"Sure."

I'll count you down again. Three, two, one . . .

Javier felt an invader in his mind, an occupying force marching through his thoughts, trying to replace them. Monroe was right. This felt familiar. Javier would soon have to surrender his own mind to synchronize with the simulation. He looked down at who he would become and saw a lean frame, perhaps early twenties, with white, pale skin, and freckles on the backs of his hands. He wore close-fitting wool and leather armor, with a short beard and a shaved head.

We don't have any information on this guy. You'll have to get to know him.

"Then let's do this."

You got it. Loading full simulation in three, two, one . . .

The Memory Corridor darkened, turning to night. Black shadows emerged, and stars sparked to life overhead. A moment later, Javier stood on a narrow forest path, listening to the wind shake the trees to either side. He smelled wood smoke on the air, coming from the east, which meant the camp lay nearby.

But what camp, Javier didn't know. That thought had come unbidden, an advance scout ahead of the main force. Javier let down his guard to admit an army of thoughts like that, surrendering his mind to that of his ancestor, and Thorvald Hjaltason took the field. The Svear crouched and slipped away into the cover of the trees, following the trail of smoke, creeping toward the camp, and Javier became aware of the completely silent way in which Thorvald moved. The way his ancestor extended his senses into the almost total darkness of the woods. The hidden blade strapped to his wrist.

"He's an Assassin," Javier said.

So it would seem.

That wasn't Monroe. That was Victoria.

"So you're watching me now?"

Yes. Monroe has important work to do.

Javier felt uneasy with the idea of a Templar managing his simulation, even though his ancestor in New York City had been an Assassin hunter, Cudgel Cormac, the grandson of the Templar Shay Cormac.

It seems you have both Assassin and Templar ancestors.

But Javier knew which one he preferred and settled back into formation behind Thorvald, allowing the Assassin freedom to pursue his objective, whatever that might be. Though summer had come, winter still had its sword drawn, and the night air carried its cold edge. The aroma of wood smoke grew stronger, and Thorvald kept to the thick of it, downwind, in case his targets had dogs that might scent his approach, while the wind covered the sounds of an owl he disturbed with his passing.

Soon, he saw the distant flicker of firelight through the trees, and at that point, he went up. The canopy of the trees concealed his approach as he climbed, leapt, and swung his way toward the encampment, free-running through the branches and trunks in the same way Javier's Templar ancestor had traversed the rooftops of Manhattan.

When he reached the camp, he came to a stop, high in the shadows, and settled down to listen. The fire popped below him, sending up sparks and smoke nearby. Five men sat around a stone ring, sucking on the heads of the fish they'd had for dinner. They were bondsmen who had fled their masters before settling their debts, and had been living in the wilds, which their faces and clothing spoke plainly. Thorvald supported their freedom, but something had brought them back to the Uppland, something worth risking capture over, and he needed to discover what it was.

For a long while, the bondsmen said little.

But Thorvald knew patience. And he waited.

When the fire burned low and needed more wood, one of the men, with a nose like a raven's beak, ordered another to fetch it.

"Fetch it yourself," the other said. "For the last time, I don't take orders from you, Heine."

"And you best mind your tongue, Boe Björnsson," Heine said. "My memory is as long and sharp as my spear."

"And yet, you forget that I broke your nose." Boe stared at the first man from across the red coals. The other three hadn't moved, but seemed to be watching the exchange with mild amusement.

"I haven't forgotten." Heine paused. "You'll know that, before the end."

"So you've told me," Boe said. "Many times."

"You doubt me?"

Boe laughed. "Have I fetched the wood?"

"No. But you'll wish you had when I gut you—"

"That's enough, Heine," one of the other men finally said, having apparently grown impatient. "Save it for the real battle. After that, you can kill each other at your leisure."

The real battle? Thorvald didn't know what that meant, but it seemed that these bondsmen had come back to Uppland expecting a fight. But over what? And against which enemy? These questions needed answers before Thorvald could leave.

Heine rose to his feet, glowered at Boe with a look Thorvald knew well, and then stormed away from the camp into the woods. The others settled down to sleep, and Thorvald watched and waited some more.

The fire turned to embers, filling the camp with the red light of Muspelheim, and the men began to snore. Then Thorvald saw Heine returning, but not as a comrade. He came slinking through the shadows, staying just over the firelight's border, until he stood near Boe. Thorvald knew what he intended before the bondsman had even pulled out his knife.

A breath later, Boe's eyes shot open as Heine pounced on him, smothering the man's mouth with one hand as he drove the blade into Boe's throat with the other.

"You see now, don't you?" Heine whispered like a snake.

Boe thrashed weakly, silently, but he was already a dead man, and Heine held him down until the life went out of his still-open eyes. The murderer pulled his knife free, wiped its blade and his hands on Boe's cloak, then snatched up his pack. The other three men slept on as Heine vanished into the woods.

Thorvald left them with the corpse and pursued Heine, but without overtaking him right away. Instead, he simply kept pace until Heine had put enough distance between himself and the camp to avoid rousing the others. Then Thorvald surged ahead through the branches to lie in wait, and as Heine scurried below, Thorvald fell upon him, driving him hard into the ground.

Heine buckled with a crack and a whimper, and before he could make another sound or fight back, Thorvald touched his hidden blade to Heine's throat.

"Struggle and you'll drown in your own blood," he said, crouching over him.

Heine swallowed and the apple of his throat moved the tip of the blade. "Who are you?"

"You haven't realized it yet, but your back is broken. You think you're in a position to question me?"

A moment of night-silence passed in which Heine looked down at his legs, but they didn't move. His face paled against the darkness.

"You see now, don't you?" Thorvald said. "Answer my questions, and I might give you a swift death."

Heine's nod was slight and full of fear.

"You're an escaped bondsman, but you've come back. Why?"

"I heard I could earn my freedom. My own land."

"How?"

"By fighting the king."

Thorvald had not expected that answer. Eric had enemies, but none who would be foolish enough to rise in rebellion. "Why?"

"Because he is a usurper," Heine said, almost spitting the last word.

"So it is for Styrbjörn that you fight?"

Heine shook his head. "I don't know. We were simply told to be battle ready."

"Your fighting days are over."

"Then finish me."

Thorvald held the hidden blade to Heine's throat for a moment longer, but then he pulled it away, and with a flick it disappeared, back inside his leather gauntlet. "No," he said, still crouching. "I need you to give the other bondsmen a message."

"What message?"

"That I will be hunting them. I stand for their freedom, but if they return to the Uppland in treachery, I will find them and kill them. If they are already in the Uppland, or pretending loyalty, I will root them out. If Styrbjörn is returning, there will be war, and if the bondsmen will not fight for their king, they will fight for no one. Do you understand?"

"How—how do you expect me to deliver this message?"

Thorvald rose to his feet and looked down at the wreck of a man, his useless legs bent at wrong angles. "In the morning, when your former companions discover your treachery against Boe, they will come looking for you."

Heine's mouth opened. "No. Please—"

"You will tell them exactly what I have just told you, and in that act perhaps you will reclaim a small amount of honor. Then I expect you'll plead with them for mercy."

"They will show me none."

"As you showed none to Boe."

Thorvald turned his back on the murderer and strode away, back down the forest paths along which he had come. He wondered if Heine would call after him to beg, but he didn't. Thorvald didn't know whether the man would convey the message, but the words didn't actually matter. Heine's body would be message enough. His fellow bondsmen would want to know what had happened to him, and even if he told them nothing, they would know they were in danger. For their cowardly lot, perhaps that would be enough to send them back into hiding. The larger problem would be Styrbjörn, if he was indeed preparing to attack.

Thorvald needed to return to the Lawspeaker with this, and he didn't think it could wait until morning.

He hurried through the forest, back to the clearing where he had tied his horse, Gyllir. The brown stallion, like the rest of his northern brethren, stood only fifteen hands tall, but he was agile, and strong, and never tired. Thorvald mounted and spurred him toward Uppsala, where the king of Svealand had his hall and the gods had their temple, galloping through the night along lonely roads.

Toward dawn, as the sun reached over the hillocks to the east, Thorvald reached the line of posts that led to the holy place. Each stood twenty feet tall, hewn from the straightest pine, placed upright every fifteen feet in beds of stone. He followed this line of pillars, each carved with images honoring the gods and the heroes who had risen to live with the gods, past the mounded barrows and graves of kings, until he came to the temple itself.

The morning light glinted off the shields that adorned its walls and roof and the golden paint that gilded its pillars. The temple's size also distinguished it from other noble halls, standing twice as long and half again as wide as that of King Eric. But that was as it should be. This place housed the gods.

Thorvald dismounted before its great doors and led Gyllir around to one of the outbuildings near the temple, a small hut with walls of clay and a turf roof. He tied his horse outside it and pounded on the door.

"The gods aren't awake yet, and neither am I!" came a shout from within.

"It's me," Thorvald said.

Footsteps approached, and then the door opened. "Thorvald, come in. I didn't expect you back so soon."

Torgny the Lawspeaker waved him inside. From behind Thorvald's mind, Javier studied the old man, who might have been the most ancient human being he had ever seen, and certainly the closest thing to a wizard. Torgny wore a long tunic, belted loosely at his waist, that gave the impression of a robe, and his hair and beard were both flowing and white. His milky eyes, and the way he held his head up without fixing his gaze on anything, let Javier know the Lawspeaker was blind.

Thorvald stepped into his hut and shut the door behind him. The single room contained little light, save the few slanted beams that cut their way in through cracks and gaps in the walls. Torgny also possessed few pieces of furniture, but the two men took seats on opposite sides of a wooden table near the old man's bed.

"Are you hungry?" the Lawspeaker asked.

"That can wait."

"When food can wait, the Valkyries ride." Torgny leaned

closer, over the table, and lowered his voice. "Tell me what you have learned."

"It's Styrbjörn."

"What about that upstart?"

"The bondsmen you sent me to find. They had come back for war."

"Styrbjörn means to make war against Eric?"

"I'm not certain, but I believe so."

Torgny pushed back from the table, rapping on its edge with the fingers of both hands. "I have heard rumors, of course. He took command of the Jomsvikings. But he's been raiding against the Danes. I thought he was the Bluetooth's problem."

"Perhaps he was."

"But perhaps not any longer."

"What would you have me do?"

Torgny looked down into his lap, his head bowed, a posture he adopted when deep in thought. Back when Thorvald had first met the Lawspeaker and had seen this habit, he'd thought that the old man might be dozing off. Though that might occasionally happen, in spite of Torgny's denials, Thorvald had nevertheless learned it was foolish to ever assume the Lawspeaker wasn't listening.

"Go east, to the sea," Torgny finally said. "If Styrbjörn is coming, he will bring his fleet through Mälaren."

"Yes, Lawspeaker."

Torgny looked up, and his eyes found Thorvald's, as if the old man could see him, and it felt as if he had more to say.

"Yes, Lawspeaker?"

"Why now?" the old man asked, almost to himself.

"Pardon me?"

Torgny spoke louder. "Our Brotherhood has so far been successful in keeping the Order from infecting this land, but our enemy is out there, and we must remain vigilant."

Javier realized then that both of these men were Assassins, one the mentor, one the student. It seemed that Thorvald did what Torgny no longer could.

"Why do you mention the Order?" Thorvald asked.

"I am worried about what Styrbjörn brings with him. His sister married the Bluetooth, who has had traffic with the Franks and with Rome. It is possible that Styrbjörn, whether he is aware of it or not, has become a tool of the Order. He must be stopped, Thorvald. Even if I am wrong and he does not serve the Order, he does not bring freedom to Svealand. We must keep Eric in power."

"I understand."

"Go," the Lawspeaker said. "Watch the seas. I believe you will see Styrbjörn's ships before long, and when you do, report back to me."

"Yes, Lawspeaker." Thorvald bowed his head. "And what will you do?"

"I will speak with the king," the old man said. "I will tell him that war may be upon us. Then I will eat my breakfast."

CHAPTER FIVE

Natalya sat in the common room with Owen, and things were still a bit tense between them after the confrontation they'd had in the corridor. For a long time, neither of them spoke.

She hadn't meant to unload on him like she had, but it was getting hard to feel so alone. It didn't seem like any of the others thought the way she did about any of this. It didn't seem like Yanmei's death upset them the way it should. The way it still upset her. It didn't seem like they worried about what would happen to the Trident after they found it, or more important, who would control it. Natalya found it exhausting to be the only one who seemed to really see what was going on.

"At least you don't have to worry about going into the Animus this time," Owen said, breaking the silence in the room.

Natalya nodded. "I guess."

"I thought you said the past was a prison."

"It is."

"Then why—"

"I don't *like* going into the Animus, but at least if I do, I can try to do something to stop the Assassins and the Templars from finding the Trident."

Owen looked at her for a moment. "I guess that's true."

Natalya knew that both times Owen had been in the Animus, he'd experienced the memories of Assassin ancestors. But he didn't seem to be committed to the Brotherhood like Javier already appeared to be. "Which side are you on?" she asked him.

He fumbled with the zipper on the Assassin-issued leather jacket he still wore. "I don't know. My own side, I guess. Like Monroe."

"Isaiah showed you a simulation of your father's memories, didn't he?"

"Yeah. Before he went all megalomaniac."

"Did you learn anything from it?"

"Nothing I can trust. Monroe is right. It would be pretty easy for the Templars to manipulate a simulation so I see what they want me to see." He paused. "But I don't trust the Assassins, either."

Maybe Owen did see some things the same way Natalya did. "So what are we going to do?"

"Like you said, we need to save Sean. So I'm planning to play along for now. Stopping Isaiah is what's most important. At least Griffin and Victoria both know that."

"Their truce won't last forever."

"No," Monroe said behind them, "it won't."

Natalya and Owen both spun around, and Monroe, standing in the doorway, held up his hands.

"Relax, I wasn't spying on you. I just got here. You two ready?"

Natalya nodded and rose to her feet. Owen joined her, and they followed Monroe from the common room and back down the glass corridor to the Aerie's main hub. From there, they crossed to a wing of the facility where Abstergo scientists had been doing research prior to Isaiah's defection. They passed several darkened laboratories filled with equipment and surrounded by glass walls. Natalya saw what looked like artificial arm and leg prosthetics, as well as different pieces and types of Animus technology.

"It's been a long time since I was here," Monroe said, leading them into one of the labs.

Automatic lights switched on at their presence, illuminating the long room and filling it with a barely audible buzzing. There were several wide workstations and cubicles along the walls and also down the middle of the room, each with its own white desk, a bank of computer monitors, and other tools and instruments. Natalya recognized the centrifuges, but didn't know what most of the other devices were.

Monroe walked to a computer terminal near a very large wall-mounted screen, and switched it on. Natalya and Owen waited as he navigated through the Aerie's database.

"Let's see what they've done with all my work," he said.

Several minutes went by, until Monroe seemed to find what he was looking for. He switched the image from his computer monitor over to the big screen.

"There it is," he said. "And they've added all the current data."

Natalya studied the images in front of her. On the left, she saw representations of DNA fragments, one next to her name and picture, and another next to Owen's. Each of the teens Monroe had brought together possessed a link in a larger chain displayed on the screen. To the right of that, Natalya saw a timeline of world history that traced the appearances of the Trident and its prongs.

"This is the Ascendance Event," Monroe said. "There are two dimensions to it. On the left, you see the results of my work studying the DNA from humanity's collective unconscious."

"The what?" Natalya asked.

"She wasn't there when you explained that," Owen said.

"Oh." Monroe looked in her direction. "Right. So, psychologists have theorized that human beings all have an ancient, shared collection of memories, which explains why so many people are automatically afraid of snakes and spiders, and why stories of heroes are so similar all over the world. We call it the collective unconscious."

Natalya looked at the screen again. "And you found DNA for it?"

"Yes," Monroe said. "You can think of it as an embedded signal in our genome. But in the present day, it only survives in fragments. I've been trying to put together the complete sequence for years, without success. Then I found you two and the others." He pointed at the screen. "Between the six of you, I now have all of it."

"Wait." Natalya looked again at the images, evaluating the meaning of what he was saying. "What are the chances of that?" she asked.

"Not tremendously unlikely." Monroe smiled. "But it doesn't

stop there." He pointed at the second half of the screen. "The six of you also happen to be connected to the history of the Trident through your ancestors, across time and even continents. And to answer your question, the odds of that, combined with the collective unconscious, are so low, it might as well be impossible. Yet here we are. Which means that all of this can't be due to chance."

"If it's not due to chance," Natalya said, "that means . . . are you saying it's intentional?" Even as she asked that question, she wondered who, or what, could bring something like this about.

"Intentional is a tricky word," Monroe said. "It implies consciousness, for one thing, which is not what I'm saying. I don't think anyone or anything is steering this ship. But it might be that the autopilot has kicked in."

"But that means someone had to program the autopilot in the first place, right?" Owen asked.

Monroe sighed. "Let's not overextend the metaphor. I'm a scientist. I stick to what is observable and measurable, and that's what you're going to do while you help me."

"What can we do?" Natalya asked.

"We have two questions." Monroe moved to a whiteboard and grabbed a dry-erase marker. He pulled the cap and started writing, the tip of the pen squeaking, and Natalya smelled the light fumes of the chemical ink. "First," Monroe said, "what is the nature of the collective unconscious DNA? Isaiah thought of it in terms of power and control. He wanted to know how he could use it as a weapon. But I don't think that's its purpose. Second, how does the collective unconscious relate to the Trident? As we've discussed, it can't be a coincidence that both of these dimensions have emerged at the same time. I believe they're part of a larger event. In fact, I think the collective unconscious might even hold the key to stopping the Trident."

"How?" Natalya said.

"I'm not sure," Monroe said. "But if you look at the history of this weapon with your ancestors, it's almost like the ascendance of the collective unconscious has taken place in *response* to the Trident. But we need to understand the collective unconscious before we can conclude that."

"Okay," Owen said, and took a seat at one of the workstations. "So how do we understand it?"

"That's where things get interesting," Monroe said.

"Interesting how?" Owen asked.

"Now that I have the complete sequence for the collective unconscious, I can use the Animus to create a simulation of it." Monroe snapped the cap back on the marker.

Owen leaned forward in his chair and looked over at Natalya. She took a seat of her own in an ergonomic chair made of white mesh and plastic. She was trying to imagine what a simulation of the collective unconscious would look like, but couldn't.

"How would that work?" she asked.

"Well, it's really just memory," Monroe said. "Old memory. The oldest memory, actually. This DNA goes back to the beginning of humanity. But it's still memory, which means the Animus can use it."

Owen pointed back and forth between himself and Natalya. "And you want us to go into this simulation?"

"Yes," Monroe said. "And to answer your next question, no, I don't have any idea what it will be like. It could make no sense at all, or it might be full of archetypes."

"Archetypes?" Natalya said. "Like from stories?"

"Basically," Monroe said. "Archetypes are images found around the world that have a shared meaning. Like the way most everyone can recognize the figure of the wise old mentor, or the fact that just about every culture in the world has its own version of a dragon. The collective unconscious is made up of archetypes and instincts."

"Will it be safe?" Natalya asked.

Owen frowned at her. "Why wouldn't it be?"

"No, she's right," Monroe said, and nodded for her to continue.

Natalya looked at Owen. "Think about synchronization. How is that even going to work with this simulation? What about desynchronization? And then there are the Bleeding Effects. What will those be in a simulation like this?"

"Exactly," Monroe said. "This simulation comes with risks because we don't know how your minds will receive it or cope with it. If I'm being candid with you, it could be extremely dangerous."

"Dangerous how?" Owen asked.

"You won't be going into this simulation in the memories of an ancestor. You'll be taking your own mind fully into it. If you get lost in the simulation, or too deeply traumatized by it, you could do irreparable damage to your psyche. Your mind could break."

Those were the very things Natalya feared, though she wouldn't have necessarily put it into those words. A broken mind sounded terrifying.

"And you want us to go in there anyway?" Owen asked.

"The decision is yours," Monroe said. "It always is. But no,

I don't *want* you to go in there. I don't want any of this. But our situation is dire, and this is the best way to understand what the collective unconscious really is. Maybe the only way."

"Why don't you go in?" Natalya asked.

"That's a fair question," Monroe said. "One answer is that I can't. You might have heard something about it from Isaiah and Victoria. When I was a kid, my father was . . ." He bowed his head, and the skin around his eyes tightened, as if he felt pain. "Well, let's just say he left marks. Deep scars. Physical and emotional. I tried to use the Animus as a way to go back and confront my father. All that did was open up old wounds. And it created new ones." He paused. "Bottom line, you can't change the past. Now a normal Animus simulation can be dangerous for my mind, but a simulation like this would be impossible."

In that moment, the way Natalya looked at Monroe changed. He had his own past and his own secret pains, which she had never deeply considered. But he had also said that was only one answer to why he couldn't go into the collective unconscious. "Is there another answer?" she asked.

"I also have very little of the collective unconscious DNA," he said. "They're not my memories. Same with Griffin and Victoria. For the simulation to remain stable and make synchronization possible, whoever goes in there needs to have as much of that DNA as possible. That means you six are the best candidates, and of the six, you happen to be the two here working with me."

"Lucky us," Owen said.

Natalya felt some pretty fierce apprehension about this, but she had also become intensely curious about what she would experience in the simulation. What would she see if it worked? This would be like going back in time to the beginning of mankind. These would be the memories that every person on earth shared, to some degree. Regardless of who you were or where you came from, these were the memories everyone had in common. Natalya wasn't going to pass up an opportunity to catch a glimpse of them. If she got in there, and things seemed dangerous or harmful, she could always quit. But until then, she planned to try.

"I'll go," she said.

Monroe nodded. "I admire your bravery."

"I'm in, too," Owen said. "But I want you to do something for me."

Natalya wasn't surprised by that, and Monroe didn't seem to be, either.

"I think I can guess what that might be," Monroe said.

Natalya could guess, too.

Owen stood up and folded his arms. "I want you to let me see the real simulation of my father's memories. You couldn't before, because you didn't have the right kind of Animus in your bus." He looked around. "Now you do. I don't trust what Isaiah showed me. But I trust you."

Monroe looked at Owen for a moment, and then nodded. "Okay. You do this for me, and I'll do that for you."

"Deal," Owen said.

Monroe turned back to the workstation, and the images vanished from the large screen. "I've got some more extraction and calculation to do, and then the Animus has to render the simulation. I don't need you here for that, so if you want to wander, you can. Just don't go far. We'll start the minute the simulation is ready."

Natalya and Owen looked at each other, and then both turned toward the lab door. Before they had exited, Monroe called to them.

"Thanks, you two," he said.

Natalya nodded, and they left.

Out in the hallway, Owen asked her, "Where do you want to go?"

They could always go back to the common room, but there wasn't much to do there, other than just sit and stare at each other. "Let's just walk around," she said. "Maybe get some fresh air."

He pointed in the direction of an outside door down the hallway.

They walked toward it, and found that it led to one of the Aerie's many patios and balconies. Two benches there formed an *L* and faced the forest that covered the mountain and surrounded the facility with the scent of pine. The tops of the oldest, tallest trees swayed back and forth in a breeze, their arthritic branches creaking.

Natalya took one of the benches, and Owen took the other. The warm sunlight felt good on her cheeks, and she lifted her face toward it, her eyes closed.

"Are you worried at all?" Owen asked. "If this simulation is as dangerous as Monroe made it sound . . ."

"I think we have to take the risk," Natalya said. "The stakes are too high."

"You're probably right." He paused. "What did the Piece of Eden show you?"

She opened her eyes and looked at him. He was asking about

the effect of the fear prong that Isaiah had used against them back in Mongolia. Each piece of the Trident had a different power and effect. The prong they had searched for in New York caused others to put blind faith in the person who wielded it. Natalya hadn't experienced the power of that first relic, but she had felt the fear caused by the second.

"You don't have to answer if it's too personal," Owen said, then paused and stared off into the trees. "I saw my dad. He confessed to everything. Even killing that guard. And he didn't feel guilty about it. He was smiling."

It made sense that would be his fear, and Natalya nodded. "I'm sorry."

"It's hard to get that out of my head, you know?" he said.

She did know. The Piece of Eden had shown her something, too. A nightmare she'd had for a few years now. Not every night, but often, and it always played out the same: she was walking to visit her grandparents after school.

Natalya loved their tidy, plain apartment with its old wooden floors, so full of her grandfather's jokes and her grandmother's cooking. After school, she was supposed to go straight there, but instead she stopped in a park to use a swing set. Laughing, she tucked her legs, then stretched out her toes as far as they would go, over and over, back and forth, trying to get as high on the swing as she could. After what felt like several minutes had passed, she got off the swing to be on her way, and that's when she noticed it. The sun had almost set. Somehow, she'd been swinging for hours, not minutes, and now she was very, very late. Her grandparents would be so worried about her. So she sprinted all the way from the park to her grandparents' apartment, but when she finally got there, ready to blurt out her rehearsed apology, lungs burning and out of breath, she noticed their door was ajar. But not by much.

That dark gap, only an inch wide, looked and felt all wrong.

She didn't want to open the door the rest of the way. But she had to. So she pushed on it, cold with fear, widening the utter silence beyond, and then stepped through.

The first thing she always noticed in her nightmare was the blood. It was everywhere, tracks of it splattered up the walls and even on the ceiling. Then she noticed the bodies of her murdered grandparents. She saw what the killer had done to them, and she wanted to look away, but she couldn't, and even if she did, the image would remain in her eyes.

The police and her parents always arrived shortly after that, with sirens and screaming. Her mom shouted at her, shaking her, asking her why she hadn't been there. Natalya *should* have been there. That's when she always woke up.

And that's what the Piece of Eden had shown her, though it had felt more real than her nightmare ever did.

"It's okay," Owen said, bringing her back to the mountain, the Aerie, and the patio. "You don't have to tell me. Sorry I asked."

"Don't be sorry," Natalya said. "I don't—"

The door opened behind them, and Monroe waved them inside. "It's ready," he said.

CHAPTER SIX

After he'd recovered from the effects of his desynchronization, Grace listened as David explained that his ancestor, Grace's ancestor, owned a slave. Grace wasn't surprised. Vikings enslaved other Vikings. Grace had known that, but she hadn't stopped to think their ancestor might have been a part of that system, and she could understand why it made David so angry.

"I don't know how to synchronize with that," he said, still sounding rattled.

Victoria lowered her tablet. "What do you mean?"

"For me—" David put both his hands out in front of him. "Okay, when I'm in the Animus, I have to find common ground with my ancestor so I can relate to them. If I can't see things the way they see them, I can't synchronize with them."

"Interesting." Victoria folded her arms and tapped her index finger against her lips. "So you need agreement with your ancestor. And this is something you can't see the way a Viking would see it."

David nodded.

That wasn't how synchronization felt to Grace. For her, it was like letting someone come into her house. She didn't have to accept everything about them to do that, but then, she hadn't ever tried inviting in a slave owner before.

Victoria turned to her. "Do you want to give it a try?"

Grace didn't think she had a choice if she wanted to find the Piece of Eden before Isaiah did. "I'll give it a try," she said.

David slumped down lower in the chair and sighed, and she couldn't tell if he felt relieved or annoyed. Maybe a bit of both. He'd made it pretty clear that he didn't need her to protect him anymore, or bail him out of trouble. But the piece of the Trident in Mongolia had shown her that he did. This needed to be done, regardless of how David felt about it.

"Stay out of trouble," she told him.

Then she walked over to the Animus, and Victoria helped her climb in and suit up. When Grace was strapped and secured, Victoria brought the helmet down and placed it over her head, plunging her into emptiness.

Are you ready? Victoria asked.

Grace took a deep breath, preparing herself for the hard part. "As ready as I can be."

Good. In three, two, one . . .

Grace endured the painful intrusion of the Parietal Suppression, traversed the momentary disorientation of the Memory Corridor, and emerged into the Viking world of Scandinavia.

She stood in the doorway of her home, watching a man approach, carrying some kind of thick staff across her land.

Grace sensed her ancestor waiting outside the walls of her mind, ready to inhabit her with his memories. She didn't find his presence aggressive, or combative, but rather patient and strong. She felt in him a gruff kindness that probably wasn't obvious to everyone who knew him, and in that way he reminded her of her father.

But then she thought about his thrall. His slave.

Sudden anger reinforced her walls against him. In the face of that evil, what did it matter how patient or kind he was? He wasn't anything like her father.

Grace? How are you doing?

"I'm okay."

You haven't locked in yet.

"I know."

The simulation won't stabilize until—

"I know."

Grace didn't need Victoria to tell her that. What Grace needed was to figure this out, and quickly, because this was for David. She faced this challenge so that he wouldn't have to, because that was what she'd always done. Like the times she'd hurried him out of the store before he noticed the security guard following them around, or the times she told him not to speak back to the gangbangers as she walked him past the corner where they hung out. She always placed herself between him and trouble.

One little push. That's all it would take to send David down the wrong road. Why should he have to reconcile himself to this if Grace could do it for him?

Her ancestor's name was Östen, and she tried to learn what she could about him from the other side of the wall. She felt his love for his wife and children. She felt the pride he took in his land, crops, and livestock, and because of that, she allowed herself to watch him laboring alongside Arne the Dane, ignoring her anger as best she could. She observed the two men sweating and laughing through the summer shearing of Östen's sheep, wool clinging to their forearms, tickling their noses, and drifting into their food as they took their midday meal together, eating the same cheese and thin barley bread.

Slavery this might be, both unjust and wrong, but at least Östen was not cruel. Perhaps that was enough for Grace to permit him entrance.

Though wary, she opened the gates of her mind, and Östen came in with the warm strength of a boulder that had been sitting in the sun. As Grace allowed him nearer, she realized she could not and would not justify him, but she didn't need to. She only needed to accept that this was who her ancestor was, instead of fighting it, for synchronization to happen.

We're looking better out here, Victoria said. *Excellent work. Continue doing what you're doing.*

That woman really had no idea what she was asking of Grace, or David. Victoria could acknowledge all she wanted how hard it must be, but she would never know. Neither had Monroe known when he'd sent them back to experience the atrocities of the Draft Riots. And for what she needed to do, Grace didn't need them to know. She wasn't doing it for them.

Almost there.

Grace allowed Östen to settle in, planting his feet as if her mind was his farm, and at last she felt fully synchronized with his memories.

The man approaching his home with the staff drew nearer, and Östen recognized him as his neighbor, Olof, whose fields and pastures bordered his, and with whom he had never had a disagreement. The staff he carried was the Bidding Stick, and Östen felt a heaviness in his arms at the sight of it. His son, Tørgils, came around from the cowshed.

"Father?" he asked, squinting into the distance.

"Go inside and tell your mother we have a guest."

Tørgils did as he was asked, and Östen waited until Olof drew near enough to greet.

"I wish I came to you bringing a fairer wind," his neighbor replied.

"Do you summon me to the Thing?" Östen asked, though he already knew the answer by the shape of the Bidding Stick.

Olof shook his head. "We are summoned under the *ledung*. Eric calls us not to counsel, but to war."

"Against?"

"Styrbjörn."

Östen nodded, unsurprised. Years ago, after the death of Styrbjörn's father, it had been decided by the Thing, under counsel from the Lawspeaker, that until the unruly Styrbjörn was of age, his uncle, Eric, should rule in his stead. That judgment had angered the prince, and he had departed his country with the fury of a storm. At the time, Östen had pitied those who might lie in the path of that storm, wherever it made landfall. Now it seemed the howling maelstrom had returned home, and there was to be a reckoning.

"Come inside," Östen said. "Eat with us."

With a shake of his head, Olof handed Östen the Bidding Stick. "I wish I could accept the honor, but time is scarce, and I need to make my own preparations."

Östen nodded, accepting the heavy summons. This Bidding Stick was a thick length of knotted oak, charred on one end with a cord tied to the other.

"Where?" Östen asked.

"Uppsala," he said. "We gather at Fyrisfield."

Östen nodded, and Olof bade him farewell, returning the way he had come toward his own land. Östen watched his neighbor's departure for a few moments, and then turned to go inside.

Within the central hall of his home, he found that Hilla had laid out cheese, smoked fish, bread, and ale. As Östen came inside, she looked past him, over his shoulder, as though for their guest.

"He could not stay," Östen said, setting the heavy Bidding Stick in the middle of the table.

Hilla and Tørgils stared at it without speaking. Östen's daughters, Agnes and Greta, drew closer to see what had brought such silence into the room.

"It's a piece of oak," Greta said, looking up at Östen.

She had been too young to remember the last time such a summons had taken place. "It's a Bidding Stick," Östen said. "The king has summoned me."

"What for?" Agnes asked.

Hilla turned away from the table and went to her loom in the corner, where she resumed her weaving. Östen watched her, but even without the help of his memories, Grace could read the angry way Hilla pulled and beat the thread. But there wasn't anything Östen could do or say to appease her. To refuse the Bidding Stick would mean death and the burning of their farm, but that was not what angered his wife. She knew that a part of him wanted to go, not for the sake of battle and bloodshed, but for his honor.

"Father?" Agnes asked.

"It summons all the men to war," Tørgils said, not yet considered a man by the Bidding Stick.

Östen laid a hand on his son's shoulder. "Carry it to the next farm. As quick as you can, so that you can return before nightfall."

Tørgils picked up the Bidding Stick. "Yes, Father." And he left with it.

After that, the rattle of the loom sounded even louder and more agitated in the small hall.

Östen turned to his daughters. "Agnes, why don't you take Greta outside for a little while."

"What should we do?" Greta asked.

"Go fetch Arne. I think he's milking the cows."

"Yes, Father," they said in unison.

A moment later, Östen and Hilla were alone, and he crossed the room to the corner where she attacked her weaving, saying nothing to her at first, simply watching the way her strong arms moved the shuttle and beater. He smiled at her careless braid, loose and uneven in places as it always was. As long as he had known her, she had never tried to lighten the color of her dark hair with lye as other women did, and he loved and admired that about her.

"What do you want, Östen?" she asked without turning around.

From within a corner of her mind, Grace smiled at her ancestor's predicament, wondering if he understood its precariousness, and how he would answer.

"I want a skein from you," he said.

Hilla ceased weaving and turned around to face him, frowning. "You want a piece of thread," she said, sounding unamused.

"Yes."

She raised an eyebrow at him, and then turned to pick up a skein of gray yarn. She stretched out a length of it, cut it off with her knife, and handed it to Östen. He shook his head, and extended his wrist.

"Tie it," he said.

Still frowning, but now also shaking her head in confusion, Hilla wrapped the thread around his wrist.

"Make it tight, and tie it fast," he said.

"What is this for?" she asked.

He nodded toward the loom. "Watching you just now with your weaving, I fell in love with you again."

She finished tying and shifted her stance, placing one hand on her hip. "Did you, now?"

"I did." He looked down at his wrist. "And now I will carry that moment with me into battle. This is the thread of my life, and only you can cut it off. When I return home."

His answer seemed to disarm her, and her posture lost some of its hardness. "You fight for yourself, Östen. For your own glory and—"

"Styrbjörn has returned," he said.

Her frown vanished.

"This isn't a petty squabble between Eric and a Geat chieftain," he continued. "Styrbjörn must not be king, or we will all suffer under his rule."

She reached down and touched the thread at his wrist. "I see."

"I don't like the thought of leaving you—"

"I know." She laid her other hand against his chest. "But don't worry about us. I have Tørgils and Arne. All will be well here until your return."

"Hilla, you are—"

"And you *will* return." She looked directly into his eyes. "Won't you?"

"Yes." It was the only vow Östen ever made knowing he might break it. "Only you," he said, holding up his wrist.

Just then a shadow fell across them as a figure stepped through the door, blocking the sunlight. It was Arne the Dane, reminding Grace that no matter how good a husband and father Östen was, no matter how honorable in the other aspects of his life, in this he would always be dishonorable. But she reminded herself she didn't need to justify him, and even though she felt some of her anger returning, the memory continued.

"You asked for me?" Arne said.

"Yes," Östen said. "Olof brought the Bidding Stick just now. Styrbjörn has returned."

"I see." Arne stepped farther into the small hall. "When do we leave?"

"I will leave tomorrow. You will stay here."

"Yes, Östen." The Dane bowed his head. "Then I am not to fight?"

"I need you to look after the farm with Hilla and Tørgils."

"Very well." Arne gave Hilla a nod. "We'll manage."

"I am relying on you," Östen said. Then he and Hilla glanced at each other, and she nodded her approval for what he was about to say. They had been discussing it for some weeks now. "When I return, if you have served my family well in my absence, we will talk about the terms of your freedom."

Arne bowed his head even lower. "Thank you, Östen."

"You have earned it," Hilla said.

With that, Arne the Dane left the hall to return to his work, and Östen set about gathering and packing what he would need for the journey to Uppsala. Throughout that process, Grace considered what had just occurred, searching through her ancestor's mind for a better understanding of it. Thralls, it seemed, could be freed, and while the promise made to Arne had the appearance of generosity, Grace couldn't forget the fact that the Dane should never have been enslaved in the first place.

Hilla helped Östen prepare his food stores of dried fish, cheese, and hard bread, along with some smoked mutton. He gathered his knives and other tools, extra clothing, and bundled it all into his cloak.

After the evening meal, surrounded by his family, he sharpened his spear, his sword, and his axe by the light of a sun that would set but little at this time of year. He accompanied the grinding of the whetstone with stories, some his, some those of other people, and some those of the gods. After Agnes and Greta had fallen asleep, he gave instructions to Tørgils for the managing of the farm. Even though Hilla and Arne would be there, it was time for his son to take on more responsibilities. After Tørgils had gone to bed, Hilla nestled up to Östen by the fire until it was time to sleep.

The next morning, Östen bade his family good-bye and departed while the ghost moon still haunted the sky. The journey to Uppsala would take several days by foot, and he set himself a hard pace, following the old roads to the great temple. Grace, almost a passenger on this journey, took in the countryside of lakes, rivers, forests, and hills, while her ancestor marched to war.

CHAPTER SEVEN

Sean lay in bed, and even though the sun hadn't risen yet, he had been awake for hours. He couldn't sleep with the room bobbing and swaying, as if he were still aboard the ship in Styrbjörn's mind. Even though Viking vessels were far more flexible than Sean would have thought, bending with the currents and waves to a frightening degree, they were still relatively small and easily tossed about by the sea. For a while now, that sensation had been following him from the Animus. Some kind of Bleeding Effect. Sean wondered if he would ever enjoy eating again. The only thing that brought relief was to get back into the simulation.

A bird chirped outside the high window in his room, signaling that morning wasn't far away. Isaiah would be coming for him soon. He knew he'd never get back to sleep, so he sat up, and then leveraged himself easily from his bed into his wheelchair. The strength in his upper body was one thing the accident hadn't taken from him.

Through his window he saw the yew tree that had been his view each morning for the past several days. They'd moved from the Aerie facility and flown here, an old monastery out in the middle of nowhere, surrounded by rugged green mountains crisscrossed by stone walls. It looked like England or Scotland to Sean, but when he'd asked about it, Isaiah had told him he didn't need to worry.

Sean was safe.

His parents knew where he was, and they were proud of the work he was doing.

Isaiah was proud of the work he was doing.

That was all he needed to know.

And Sean had faith in Isaiah. He believed in the mission. Sean's work in the simulation would lead them to the final piece of the Trident, and when they found it, they would have the power to end the war between the Templars and the Assassins forever. They would have the power to set things right for the whole world.

Sean looked around his small room, imagining the devout monks who had occupied this chamber through the centuries, and what they might have experienced before the modern world had brought in heat and electricity.

The bird sang again, sounding somewhat farther away, and then someone knocked at the door.

"Sean?" Isaiah asked. "Are you awake?"

"Yes, sir," Sean said.

"May I enter?"

"Yes, sir."

The door opened, and Isaiah ducked into the room, his presence seeming too large for its close walls. "I see you are ready. Excellent. We have much to do."

"Yes, sir."

Isaiah strode around to stand behind his wheelchair. Sean normally hated it when people pushed him, ever since he'd gotten the hang of wheeling himself. There was nothing wrong with his upper body, and it was important for him to know he could go where he wanted to go. But it didn't bother him to let Isaiah push him.

"Off we go, then," Isaiah said, reaching around to hand Sean an energy bar.

Sean accepted it, and the wheelchair moved.

They exited his room and moved down the monastery's silent corridors, past stained glass windows only dimly lit by the sunrise, and past a courtyard dotted with weedy flower beds.

"How are you feeling?" Isaiah asked.

"I'm tired," Sean said, taking a bite out of the bar. In fact, he had never felt tired in the way he did now. The exhaustion reached into the deepest recess of his mind, but left him upright, awake, but not quite himself.

"I know you're tired," Isaiah said. "But your efforts will be rewarded. I need you to be strong. I need you to tell me the moment you think the Piece of Eden might come into your ancestor's possession."

"Yes, sir."

They came to the monastery's front gate, where one of the Abstergo vehicles waited for them, idling. It was painted white, and looked a bit like a Humvee, if that Humvee had gone back to school for a double PhD in aerospace engineering and computer science. It was a prototype that Isaiah had commandeered, and Sean called it Poindexter, just to keep it from getting too full of itself. Since coming here, it had been his regular means of transportation, because the only space in the monastery complex large enough for the Animus was the chapel, which sat at the top of a hill. A very cumbersome climb with a wheelchair.

Isaiah rolled Sean up to Poindexter, and at his approach, a rear door opened and a ramp lowered to the ground automatically.

"Welcome, Sean," Poindexter said, with its precisely enunciated robot voice.

Isaiah wheeled Sean up the ramp and secured him inside the back of the vehicle. Then he hopped into the front passenger seat.

As always, no one sat in the driver's seat.

"Are we going to the chapel again this morning?" Poindexter asked.

"Yes," Isaiah said.

"Very well," the vehicle said. "We will arrive in approximately four minutes and thirty-two seconds."

"Thank you, Poindexter," Sean said.

"You are welcome, Sean."

The vehicle rolled out, moving along a course it had calculated to the inch.

Isaiah shook his head. "I can think of nothing more unnecessary than manners with a machine."

"Maybe," Sean said. "But when that machine is controlling the steering wheel, I'll play it safe."

As they reached the top of the hill and came to a gentle stop, several Abstergo agents greeted them and helped Sean out of the vehicle. Isaiah had brought dozens of men and women from the Aerie, and more had joined him since then. They acted as guards, technicians, and labor.

"Is everything ready?" Isaiah asked Cole as he pushed Sean toward the chapel.

"Yes, sir," she said, her manner somewhat severe. She had been head of security back at the Aerie. "I believe they finished calibrating a few minutes ago."

At the chapel entrance, one of the other agents opened and held its heavy wooden door, and Isaiah wheeled Sean through. Inside, the old pews had been stacked against one wall to make room for the Animus in the middle of the floor. The air smelled damp and earthy, but not unpleasant. Thick wooden rafters stretched overhead, much of the vaulted space beyond them kept in shadow. This church wasn't like the bright cathedrals Sean had seen in movies, with all their stained glass. This place felt more like a fortress, with narrow windows that let in little light, keeping the edges of the chapel in darkness.

Technicians circled the Animus beneath the only real source of light, a broad chandelier made of iron with bare bulbs, stepping over the wires and cables that snaked across the flagstones. Isaiah wheeled Sean up to the device and then helped him out of his chair and into the harness, strapping him to the frame. Then Isaiah brought the helmet down and placed it over Sean's head.

He'd almost grown accustomed to the trauma of the Parietal Suppressor and the transition into his ancestor's memories. Almost. But it was over quickly, and it had become both easy and natural for him to synchronize with the familiar currents of Styrbjörn's mind.

He sat in the hall of Harald Bluetooth, at a table with the Dane-king. Styrbjörn's sister, Gyrid, sat next to them, and it seemed she had settled well into her title as queen. But before she was Harald's wife, she was a princess of the Svear, as wise and cunning as Styrbjörn was strong.

"You must sail the fleet up the coast of Götaland," she said. "Then west through the lake of Mälaren. There are many who loved our father, and some of them silently oppose Eric, even now. If our allies see you sailing along the coast and through the very heart of Svealand, they will be emboldened to join the battle in the name of Styrbjörn the Strong."

"The Strong?" Styrbjörn asked.

"Have you not heard?" Gyrid looked from her brother to Harald, whose face had reddened. "Word of your battle with my husband has spread. They say you possess the strength of ten men—"

Harald slammed his mug of ale on the table. "This plan is too risky. My men and my ships are yours to command, but I won't let you send them to the bottom of the sea. Mälaren is a trap. There is only one way in and out of that lake, and if Eric orders it blocked—"

"You speak as if you are already planning your retreat," Styrbjörn said.

"I plan how I enter my battles," Harald said. "And I plan how I leave them."

"Perhaps that is why you lose," Gyrid said, and the Dane-king flushed even deeper.

"I like the queen's plan," Styrbjörn said. "We'll sail through Mälaren, then up the Fyriswater, and then march on Uppsala."

Harald shook his head, his jaw grinding hard enough, it

seemed, to crush rocks. But he said nothing in objection, for what could he say? He had lost the battle to Styrbjörn and surrendered in front of his men. But Styrbjörn saw fire in his brother-in-law's eyes, and noted the way his hand was never far from the curious dagger he wore at his side. Sean noted it, too, as the memory swept him along, but until that prong of the Trident came into Styrbjörn's possession, noting it was all Sean could do.

Harald's anger amused Styrbjörn, and he decided to blow across its embers. "Something vexes you, Harald?"

The Dane-king stared at Styrbjörn for a moment, and then smiled, revealing his rotten tooth. "To what god are you devoted?"

"To no god," Styrbjörn said. "They are all the same to me."

"Do you not fear them?"

"No."

"To what are you devoted, then? To a woman?"

"Not until I have my crown, for I would marry a queen."

"Have you found no woman worthy of you?" Harald asked. "There is a shield-maiden in my hall named Thyra. She is both beautiful and strong. Perhaps—"

"No," Styrbjörn said.

Harald pulled at a loose thread in the embroidery of his tunic. "You are devoted to your men, surely."

"I am glad to fight alongside the Jomsvikings, but I have not sworn to them, nor they to me. They follow Palnatoke, who met me at the crossroads in single combat, with honor, even in defeat." His statement was intended to shame Harald for his quick surrender.

"The old rituals are coming to an end," Harald said. "Their honor is fading."

Styrbjörn shrugged. "Among the Danes, perhaps. After all, it would seem your men remain devoted to you."

"There is much more to a king than his victories." Harald paused a moment, and then looked over at Gyrid. "You are devoted to your sister, perhaps?"

Styrbjörn had once been devoted to his sister, and she to him. But she had come into her power, and now possessed her own crown. Harald Bluetooth would never rule her, for she was the master of both her fate and her honor. Now it was Styrbjörn's time.

"I am devoted to myself," he said, "and none other."

Harald's eyebrows went up, and he nodded, as though he had just realized something. "I think I understand."

"I doubt that." Styrbjörn drained the last of the ale from his mug. "The matter is settled. We sail through Mälaren. Word will spread. Men will flock to my banner. Eric will fall." He spoke as if his words had the power to reshape the world by their utterance.

In memories like this, Sean felt almost overpowered by the strength of Styrbjörn's mind, and that to synchronize with his ancestor's fearlessness and force of will, he needed to become stronger himself. He had experienced something similar in New York City and London as he had followed the memories of another ancestor, Tommy Greyling.

"My ships are yours to command, Styrbjörn," Harald said. "As are my men. I will await news of your victory—"

"Await?" Styrbjörn glanced at Gyrid.

She looked hard at Harald. "Surely, husband, you will fight at my brother's side."

It was obvious to Styrbjörn, and likely to Gyrid, that Harald had not intended to sail to Svealand. In truth, Styrbjörn didn't want Harald to sail with him, but he knew the Danes would fight better if led by their king, even though their king took his orders from a Svear who had defeated him in battle.

Harald Bluetooth touched his dagger again, the Piece of Eden, fixing his stare upon Sean's ancestor for several moments. Then he looked away, appearing both frustrated and perplexed.

"I will sail with you," Harald said.

Styrbjörn nodded, but Sean had become aware of something. He was pretty sure that Harald had just tried to use the power of the dagger on Styrbjörn, and upon reflection, he realized this was the second time it had happened. Sean raised his head above the waterline of Styrbjörn's mind and spoke to Isaiah.

"Harald knows what he has."

That makes sense, Isaiah said. *Sources from this time period tell us that Harald managed to unite all of Denmark and Norway under his rule. He was a very powerful man.*

"If that's true, then why didn't the dagger work on Styrbjörn?" Sean asked.

Harald attempted to use it?

"Yeah."

Are you certain?

"I think so."

If your ancestor was able to resist the power of a Piece of Eden, it is essential that I understand how. Did Styrbjörn do something to shield himself?

"No. It seemed automatic. Like he was immune."

Stand by, Isaiah said. *I'm going to terminate the simulation so I can analyze the—*

"No."

Isaiah paused. *What did you say?*

"Do not terminate. Leave me in here." Sean sounded more forceful than he meant to, which surprised him, but he wasn't ready to return to his own body and mind yet.

I make those decisions, Sean. Isaiah spoke with a low and even voice. *You do not tell me what to do.*

"Then I'm asking. Leave me in the simulation. Please."

No. I have other priorities—

"What about my priorities?"

Your priorities?

"Yes." Sean didn't know where this confrontation was coming from.

Sean, my priorities are your priorities. You don't have priorities of your own.

"Yes, I do."

If that is the case, I would suggest you rid yourself of them quickly. Principles and priorities come at a price that I doubt you are prepared to pay.

"I think I can judge that for myself." Sean felt as if he were in a simulation of his own mind, listening to another person talk, wanting to shut them up. Almost as though Styrbjörn were speaking through him. "This is my simulation, and if I want to stay in it, then I—"

Something smashed through Sean's skull, seized his mind with its fist, and then wrenched it from his body. The simulation shredded around him, and he felt himself shredding, strips and layers of him torn away by the raking of claws until there was almost nothing left that he recognized as himself. He was but a single thought floating in an endless nothing. Then a blinding light replaced the nothing, and he opened his scorched eyes.

A tall man with green eyes stood in front of him. Sean blinked, and then recognized him.

Isaiah held a bucket up to Sean's face. "Vomit," he said.

Sean obeyed, hanging like a doll from the Animus framework, his mind still reeling.

"That was foolish of you."

"Which part?" Sean asked. He thought back to what he had said, and still couldn't explain where it had come from. He also wasn't sure he regretted it, in spite of the violent desynchronization.

"It is foolish to provoke me, Sean." Isaiah leaned in closer. "I know you want the Animus. You want it desperately, but I think you've forgotten that I control your access to the Animus, as I have just demonstrated."

"But you won't cut me off," Sean said, not quite as confidently as he had spoken in the Animus. "You need me to find the dagger."

Isaiah leaned away from him. "You still don't understand."

Sean noticed then that all the other Abstergo technicians had left the chapel. He and Isaiah were alone, their voices echoing against the stone.

"What don't I understand?" Sean asked.

Isaiah walked away from the light, into the dark recesses at the far end of the chapel. A few moments later, he returned, carrying something long and thin, like a spear.

No. Not a spear.

It was a trident with two prongs, its third prong missing. Until now, Sean had only seen the relics as daggers, but with their leather grips removed, they now looked like what they were: two parts of a larger deadly weapon. Isaiah had combined them and mounted them on the head of a staff.

The Trident of Eden.

He carried it toward Sean with authority. "Now," he said, "I will make you understand."

CHAPTER EIGHT

Owen followed Monroe and Natalya back down the hallway to the lab, and Monroe led them into an adjacent room with three different Animus rings that looked similar to what he'd seen elsewhere in the Aerie, but not as polished. They seemed more industrial and skeletal, with exposed wires and components.

"Will these do the job?" Owen asked.

"Of course." Monroe walked over to one of them and gave it a solid pat. "These are mostly used for research. They were built as workhorses. They're not as pretty as the others, but they'll perform."

Owen glanced at Natalya and shrugged. "If you say so."

Monroe looked at both of them, sighed, and nodded. "Let's get you situated."

"You seem nervous," Natalya said.

"I've been researching the collective unconscious for a long time," Monroe said, "hoping to one day get a look at it. But now that it's here, I . . . Just try to be safe in there, okay?"

Owen would have liked more reassurance than that. "Okay."

Monroe directed him and Natalya toward two of the Animus rings that he had networked together, allowing them to share the simulation. Owen stepped inside his ring and climbed up into the framework of his exosuit, which did feel more sturdy and solid than it looked. Monroe helped Natalya buckle in, then did the same for Owen, and they were ready to go inside.

"Another couple of notes," Monroe said. "First, I've been looking at the Animus code for this simulation, and it's significantly atypical. This isn't a memory of an experience in the way you're used to. It's not a sequence of events, with cause and effect. It's more holistic than that. More organized. Almost like it was written with the end in mind."

"That should make synchronization easier, right?" Owen asked. "We won't be tied to a certain memory. We don't have to worry about making the right choices."

"Maybe," Monroe said. "But that's the other thing. This simulation is old. The data is intact, but we're talking dawn of humanity here. This is actually an incredible moment. I mean, I know we're doing this to stop Isaiah, but it's so much more than that. You two are about to step inside a place that makes us who we are as human beings."

"We'll take notes," Owen said.

"You'd better." Monroe pulled Owen's helmet over his head, and after a few moments of complete silence, he heard Monroe's voice in his ear. *Are you both reading me?*

"Yes," Natalya said.

"Yes," Owen said.

Excellent. Are you ready to begin?

They both said yes.

Hold tight. Initiating Parietal Suppressor in three, two, one . . .

Owen grimaced through the intense pressure, the sensation of his skull bones grinding together, until the weight lifted away, and he opened his eyes upon the boundless gray. Natalya stood next to him, rubbing her temples, and she appeared as herself. He looked around, waiting for shapes to materialize out of the nothing.

How are you two doing?

"Good," Owen said. He was wearing his favorite jeans, the comfortable ones with holes in them that he pulled out on lazy Sundays, and a T-shirt. Somehow the Animus must have pulled that from his own memories. Natalya wore jeans and a loose, button-down navy blouse.

"I'm fine," Natalya said, her eyelids pinched shut.

You ready for the next step? This is the big one. Neil Armstrong big.

Owen watched Natalya and waited until she opened her eyes, blinked a few times, and then gave him a nod.

"I think we're ready," he said.

Okay. One giant leap for mankind in three, two, one . . .

Instead of resolving itself into shapes, the Memory Corridor darkened. It turned from gray to black, as black as the inside of the Animus helmet. For a moment, Owen wondered if something had gone wrong, and he was about to ask Monroe, but then a faint speck of light flickered ahead. At first, it only sparkled weakly, like a distant star, but gradually it grew brighter, and nearer, until it caused Owen to squint.

"What is that?" he asked Natalya. "Some kind of—"

LISTEN TO ME. A woman's voice rang in Owen's head like a bell, resonating through his whole mind. **THE WAY OF THE PATH IS THROUGH FEAR, DEVOTION, AND FAITH. FIND THE WAY THROUGH EACH OF THESE, AND I SHALL BE WAITING FOR YOU AT THE SUMMIT.**

Then the light slowly diminished, but as it shrank it also changed, gaining hard, square edges. When it finally settled firmly into place, Owen realized they were now standing in a tunnel, and the light had become an open doorway at the far end of it. Behind them lay only blackness, which left them one direction in which to go.

"Did you hear that?" Natalya asked.

"Yes," Owen said.

Is everything okay? Monroe asked. *The Animus is having a really hard time converting this data into an image on my end. You're going to have to tell me what you see.*

"There was a light," Natalya said.

"A talking light," Owen added. "Now we're in a tunnel."

A talking light? What did it say?

"The way of the path is through fear, devotion, and faith," Natalya said. "And something about waiting for us at the summit."

Well, that is certainly interesting. It means we're on the right track.

"How so?" Owen asked.

Because the prongs of the Trident each have a different effect on human minds. One causes fear, one causes devotion, and one causes faith. That can't be coincidence, which means the simulation you're in is connected to the Trident somehow, just like we'd hoped.

"I guess we keep going," Natalya said. "To the summit."

Owen nodded. "I guess so."

They set off toward the distant doorway, the echoes of their footsteps filling the tunnel. The walls to either side seemed to be made of dry stone, hewn rough and uneven, and the air smelled of dust. Eventually, they reached a point where the light coming in through the doorway no longer blinded Owen's view of what lay beyond, and he caught glimpses of huge tree trunks.

"It's a forest," Natalya said.

A forest? Monroe asked.

"We're almost there," Owen said.

They approached the end of the tunnel, but stopped and stood at the threshold for a moment, peering out into the deep, dark woodland, very different from the one that surrounded the Aerie. These trees were unlike any Owen knew of. They stood close together, with wide trunks, worm-eaten bark, expansive branches, and exposed roots that seemed ready to pull up so the trees could go walking. Very little sunlight made it down through the dense canopy of leaves and needles, but where it fell, fine grass grew like hair, and where the sunlight could not reach, a soft black soil covered the ground.

"You could get lost in there," Natalya said.

Owen agreed. Not too deep into the woods, a hazy and impenetrable shadow consumed everything. But more than that, just at the edge of that darkness, where the forest swallowed itself, the trees appeared to be distorted, or moving. Owen blinked and squinted, wondering if he only imagined it, along with the faint and distant sounds of wood cracking and groaning. It was almost like the simulation had glitches.

"Monroe?"

Yeah?

"Is the simulation stable?"

Yeah, it looks good.

"Are you sure?" Natalya asked, which meant that she had noticed it, too.

Hang on.

Owen and Natalya both breathed in at the same time.

"I don't want to go in there," she said.

"I don't, either."

But if they didn't enter the forest, where else were they supposed to go? They couldn't go back through the tunnel. Owen saw no light at the other end.

Okay. Monroe had returned. *I've checked everything. The simulation is stable, so whatever you're seeing, that's how it's supposed to be. That's the memory.*

"That's disconcerting," Natalya said.

Maybe not. I told you, this DNA is different. It's not going to behave like a normal simulation. It's more . . . primordial.

"It's the forest that's disconcerting," Owen said. "The only way forward is through it."

Maybe it—maybe it's not a normal forest.

Owen peered again at the shifting woods. "Uh, yeah, it's definitely not a normal forest."

No, I mean, maybe it's not just a forest. Maybe it's the *forest. The archetypal Forest.*

"The Forest is an archetype?" Natalya asked. "How does that work?"

Archetypes aren't just people. They can be places and objects, too. The Forest appears in numerous myths.

The air just outside the tunnel felt heavy and smelled of

something Owen couldn't quite identify, a scent that was green and rank. Something about it tensed his body and tingled his neck, but he couldn't recognize it, and didn't know why it unsettled him. Regardless, their situation hadn't changed. "So what you're saying is, we *do* have to go through the Forest."

"Unless we just stand here," Natalya said. "Or we leave the simulation."

Owen nodded and sighed. "Right."

I'll be right here, Monroe said. *I can pull you out if things go south. But remember why we're doing this. The collective unconscious DNA that you all carry is connected to the Trident.*

"Understood." Owen took a step forward, crossing the boundary. The soft, rich soil gave way a half an inch beneath his foot, and he noticed mushrooms growing all around. He took another step, and another. When he and Natalya stood some yards away from the tunnel, they turned to look back at it.

From this side, the opening through which they'd entered the Forest wasn't a tunnel, but a stone portal. Two rough and massive stone slabs had been set upright on their edges, parallel with each other, and a third slab had been laid on top of them, forming a doorway with nothing but forest on the other side. The gray rock from which the slabs were made bore weather scars and blooms of lichen. The lonely monument stood there among the trees of the Forest, silent and imposing, and Owen couldn't tell whether it or the woods had been there first.

"No going back that way," Natalya said. "The tunnel is gone."

"This memory isn't stable," Owen said. "I don't like this."

"Monroe said it's fine. Let's just keep going for a little while and see what happens."

Owen looked around them. The Forest in each direction appeared endless. "Which way?"

"I don't think it matters." Natalya looked to her left and her right, and then gestured to her right. "Let's keep going that way, I guess."

Owen resumed walking in that direction, and when he reached the first spot of sunlight and grass, he paused to look up. A seam of empty sky looked back at him, and from the perspective of the Forest, the break in the canopy was a wound full of blue blood. He and Natalya left that light behind and ventured deeper, trying to walk in as straight a line as they could, winding their way without a path through the trees. Their journey seemed to drive the distortion's edge before them, as if they traveled in a pocket of reality they created as they went.

Owen heard birds singing and knocking at the trees. He heard insects thrumming and chittering. He smelled leaves, and flowers, and dirt, and occasionally, that disturbing and rank odor, as on they walked.

It was impossible to say how far they traveled, and Owen had only a vague sense of the passage of time, but he eventually reached a point in the Forest that stopped him against his will. He looked down at his feet, and then his mind became aware of the terror his body already felt.

"We're not alone," he whispered, trembling.

Natalya froze and peered off into the trees. "We're not?"

"No." His eyes widened and his heart thumped. "Do you feel that?"

"Feel what?"

"There's something in the Forest with us." He couldn't see it, but he could feel it as surely as he felt the soil beneath his feet.

"What is it?"

"I don't know." But Owen knew that whatever it was, he had been smelling it all along. "Let's keep moving. Quietly."

So they resumed their journey, taking care with their steps to avoid twigs and roots, neither of them speaking. Tree after tree they rounded and passed. Hundreds of them. Thousands, perhaps. And then Owen glimpsed something up ahead. A difference in the unending pattern of the Forest. He couldn't see what it was, but it was large, and it lay on the ground.

He stopped and whispered to Natalya, "Should we go around?"

"No. Let's see what it is."

He nodded, and they crept closer, using the trees to hide behind, until they were near enough to see it wasn't a living thing, or even a moving thing. Owen stepped out into the open and approached it, still confused. It seemed to be made of some kind of translucent material, all folded and twisted, about six feet wide. But then Owen saw how long it was, stretching off in either direction through the trees.

"What is that?" Natalya asked.

"I don't kn—"

But then Owen noticed a subtle repeating pattern in the material. And he realized how he knew that foul odor. It was a smell from his third-grade teacher's classroom. She had a terrarium, and on the first day of school that year she had introduced the class to its occupant. Until then, Owen hadn't thought that snakes would smell, and most of the time they didn't. But sometimes they did, and so did the terrarium.

Natalya leaned closer. "Wait, is that skin?"

"Yeah," Owen said. "It's a shed skin."

Natalya turned to look at him. "From a snake?"

"Looks that way." Owen took in the size of it again, recalculating. "It's huge. Not just anaconda huge. It's *huge* huge." Owen wondered where the previous owner of the skin might have gone. "I want to see just how long it is. Should we find the head? Or the tail?"

"I guess."

Owen decided to turn to the left this time, and they followed the snakeskin as it curled and wound away into the Forest. They walked a few yards, and then a few more, expecting it to stop, but the skin kept going, and going, until they'd walked several hundred feet without reaching the end of it. The skin behind them seemed to vanish with the trees in the shadows, and Owen wondered if this was another distortion in the simulation that Monroe claimed was stable. An endless loop of snake.

"This has to be another archetype, right?" Natalya said.

Owen nodded. This was the presence he had sensed. "Let's try to get out of this Forest before it finds us."

But they still didn't know exactly how to get out, other than to just keep walking. So that's what they did, but much more cautiously now. Owen jumped at every rustle along the ground and every snap above him in the branches, and over time, his unrelenting dread burned off the edges of his senses so that he started hearing and seeing things that weren't there. Figures darted just out of view. Voices whispered unintelligible speech. The Forest had swallowed him.

How are you two doing? Monroe asked. *I'm showing spikes in your adrenaline and cortisol levels. Both of you. Increased blood pressure and heart rate, too.*

"Snakes will do that," Natalya said.

A snake?

"I think you would probably say *the* Snake," Owen said.

You found the Serpent.

"Just its skin," Owen said. "The Serpent is still out here."

"Maybe it's a good archetype," Natalya said. "Like the snakes on that medical staff."

The caduceus? Monroe said. *I doubt that. The snake is almost always a symbol of fear and death. Exceptions to that usually mean we've tried to take control of that fear by inverting the meaning of the symbol. Even worshiping it.*

"I'm sorry, are you trying to help?" Owen asked.

Yes, I am. Just remember, this is a memory. Probably from a time when our ancestors were smaller and the snakes were bigger. But this memory isn't literal. It's symbolic. Symbols can't hurt you.

"Are you sure about that?" Owen asked.

Yes. Just keep a firm grip on your fear and your mind.

"What if we can't?" Natalya's face looked pale in the dim light. "What if—?"

"Shh!" Owen said.

A sound had found its way into his mind. A quiet sound, a sinuous sigh along the ground, from somewhere in the Forest nearby. Owen held still and waited, listening, watching the trees.

Nothing made a noise.

Nothing stirred.

And then he saw the Serpent.

Its head emerged first from the woodland depths, the size of a leather sofa. Black and crimson scales gleamed around its mouth and nostrils, and framed its copper eyes, which seemed to shimmer. Its slender tongue whipped the air as it slithered directly toward them, bringing more and more of its endless body out of the shadows. The sight of it immobilized Owen, as if he were a panicked rodent.

"Run," he whispered, as much to himself as to Natalya.

CHAPTER NINE

David sat deep in his chair, alone in the common room, facing the windows. He stared out into the trees, and thought about the Viking simulation. The fact that Östen owned a thrall hadn't stopped Grace from synchronizing with the memory, but the process was apparently different for her. So she had stepped in and taken over, rescuing him like she always did. But this time, it also kind of felt as though she'd left him behind, so David had left her in the Animus and come here to be by himself.

He wanted to call his dad. But he'd be at work right now, and as a welder, he couldn't exactly drop everything and answer his phone whenever his son called. Even if David could talk to his dad, he wasn't sure what he'd say or ask.

David had to deal with this on his own.

Back in Mongolia, he and Grace had come together in a way they never had before. She'd finally treated him like he was more than just a little child. She'd trusted him. But then Isaiah had used that dagger. The fear prong of the Trident. David would never forget the vision that had invaded his mind.

He was walking home from school and he was alone, even though Grace had told him not to do that. But Kemal and Oscar hadn't waited for him, so what else was he supposed to do? He'd made it about halfway to his house when he saw Damion standing on a corner up ahead. Everyone in the neighborhood knew Damion. Everyone knew to stay clear of him. So David ducked into a drugstore to wait it out for a bit.

He bought a Coke, and then he flipped through some magazines, until someone bumped into him from behind.

"Watch it," David said, turning around.

A huge white man stood over him. He wore a ball cap backward, and had a blond goatee on his chin. "What'd you say to me?"

David swallowed, but he wasn't about to back down. "I said watch it."

The man stepped closer, eyes narrowed, smelling like mildew and bad cologne. "You threatening me, boy?"

"No." David's heart beat hard enough to make his T-shirt quiver. "And don't call me boy."

"You threatened me." The man reached under his shirt. "Everyone in here will say you threatened me."

David ran, scrambling down the aisle, and then out the drugstore door, where he crashed right into Damion and dropped his Coke. The brown soda splashed all over Damion's shoes and pants. David didn't wait around to see what would happen next. He knew what Damion would do, so he kept running.

He heard shouting and swearing behind him, and he knew Damion was chasing him. But when he looked back, it was both of them. The white guy was chasing him, too, and both men had guns. If they caught him, they would kill him.

David had to get home. If he made it home, he'd be safe.

So he took every shortcut he knew, and ran faster than he ever had, but he couldn't escape his attackers, who were always there. Always behind him.

Somehow, it was dark by the time he reached his block, but when he got to his house, the lights were out. He leapt over the gate and raced up the porch steps, then frantically unlocked the door and burst inside.

"Grace!" He closed and bolted the door behind him. "Dad!"

No answer.

"Mom?"

Through the blurry window in the door, he could see the wavy figures of Damion and the white guy approaching his gate, the streetlight behind them turning their shadows into giants climbing David's front steps. There wasn't anywhere else he could go. No other place to hide.

"Grace!" he shouted. "Dad!"

The dark house ignored him. The two men stepped through the gate and walked toward the door.

David was alone. He wasn't safe. The door wouldn't stop them. The windows wouldn't stop them—

That was where the vision had ended. That was David's greatest fear. Not Damion and the white guy.

The empty house.

David was on his own.

But he didn't want to be afraid of that. He didn't need his older sister to come in and save him. Right now, the only thing he wanted was to get back inside the Animus, but he still had to figure out a way to synchronize with his ancestor. How was Grace able to do it? Why wasn't she as angry as he was? She'd probably say that she *was* just as angry as him. And yet she was in the Animus right now and he wasn't, because it was different for her, apparently.

Could it be different for him? It was all a mind game anyway. Did he need to agree with his ancestor on everything? He'd always assumed so. But maybe not. Maybe that assumption was actually the thing blocking him. Maybe it wasn't the anger, after all, but the belief that his anger had to be a barrier.

There was only one way to know.

He rose from his chair and left the common room, then returned to the Animus room, where he found Grace still harnessed inside the ring. He'd never really watched someone using the Animus from the outside. His sister looked a little goofy, walking in place with the helmet on her head. Victoria sat at the computer terminal nearby wearing a headset with a delicate microphone, monitoring multiple screens that displayed information on the simulation and Grace's biodata.

"How is she doing?" David asked.

Victoria glanced at him, and then went back to watching Grace. "She's good. Good physiological response. Strong synchronization."

David nodded. Then he pulled up a chair next to Victoria and sat down.

"How are you doing?" she asked.

"I'm fine," David said. "But I want to try again."

"You want to go back into the Animus?"

"Yes."

She looked at him and cocked her head. "To be candid, I don't think that's a good idea. We can't afford to waste time—"

"I can do it," David said.

"But why bother? Grace is in, and she's locked. We don't need anyone else."

"Maybe she needs a break. She'll need one eventually, right?"

Victoria gestured up at the screens. "She seems to be doing well."

"Could you ask her?"

Victoria leaned away from David, her elbow on the armrest of her rolling chair, and didn't answer for several moments. "I suppose," she finally said. Then she touched a button on the side of her headset. "Grace, how are you doing?"

Pause.

"Good to hear," Victoria said. "Do you need a break?"

Pause.

"Okay, then, let's keep you—"

"Can I talk to her?" David asked.

He received a sigh of apparent irritation, and then Victoria spoke into the microphone. "Grace, I have David here with me. He'd like to speak with you and . . . yes. Hang on a moment." She pulled the headset off and held it toward David, her eyebrows raised.

After he'd taken the headset and put it on, he adjusted the microphone and said, "Grace?"

Hey, she said. *You feeling better?*

"Yeah," he said. "But this is weird. You're right here, looking like an idiot with that helmet on, but you're also there. In Viking land."

Sweden, actually. Or Svealand. Östen would clarify.

"Right. Speaking of that guy, I think I want to try again. So if you ever need a break or anything—"

You want to try the simulation again?

"Yeah."

You don't have to. I got this.

"I know you do. But you don't need to do that for me. I want to do this."

You sure?

"I'm sure," he said. "It's okay. I'm good."

His sister went quiet.

"Grace?"

Put Victoria back on.

"Sure."

David handed the headset over, and then waited as Victoria put it back in place, tugging the microphone toward her lips.

"Grace, it's me," she said. "Yes, I—what's that?"

Pause.

"I see." Victoria looked over at David, and he caught a hint of a smile on her face. "You need a break, do you? Very well. Stand by."

David sat down and waited while Victoria took Grace through the extraction procedures and pulled her out of the simulation. After the helmet came off, Grace blinked and shook her head, her hair a little wild, as Victoria undid some of the clamps and straps.

"Could you give us a hand?" Grace asked.

"Oh, sure." David jumped up and went over to help his sister out of the harness and the ring. Then it was his turn to climb in, and Grace worked with Victoria to secure him in the Animus framework.

"I need to switch over to your profile and biodata," Victoria said. "It'll just be a moment."

David watched Grace take the chair he'd been using. She sat down and wiped some sweat from her forehead with the heel of her palm. Then she pulled out her ponytail, and with the elastic held between her teeth, she ran her fingers through her hair, pulled it smooth and tight toward the back of her head, and then stretched the elastic back around it.

"So what's going on in Sweden?" David asked her.

"Östen is at Uppsala, where an army is gathering. They're expecting a battle."

David nodded. "Okay."

"What if you desynchronize?" she asked. "You want to go through that again?"

He was trying not to think about that. "I won't."

Grace rose from the chair and walked over to him. "Just remember, you don't have to justify him. You don't have to agree with him or make excuses for him. You don't have to explain him or apologize for him. You don't even need to accept what he did. All you need to do is accept that he did it."

"Okay," he said. "Thanks."

She nodded and backed away, and a moment later, Victoria stood up and said they were ready. She brought the helmet down and placed it over David's head, and then she spoke in his ear. David felt impatient, already looking past the process of entering the simulation, to the simulation itself. He just wanted to be inside the memory.

Minutes later, that's where he was, standing in a large encampment on a marshy plain, inhabiting the body of a giant. David immediately turned his mind inward, toward Östen's, facing his ancestor in all his human successes and failures. His family, his stubbornness, his hard work and honor, his stoniness, his victories in battle.

His thrall.

David felt his anger rising at the thought of Arne the Dane, but this time he didn't try to extinguish it or ignore it. He didn't try to force himself to agree with something that he never could. Instead, he reminded himself that he could still synchronize with his ancestor in spite of it. David could still converse with him. He could find other common ground with him. And he could stay angry with him.

Like Grace had said, it wasn't David's job to justify Östen as a man of his time and his people. David didn't have to excuse him at all.

You're doing well, Victoria said. *Much better than last time. You're almost there.*

David needed only to talk with his ancestor, and so he opened his mind to Östen's thoughts, and he listened, accepting what he heard not as truth, but as Östen's truth, however wrong it might be. Gradually, he felt himself synchronizing, not because he saw things the same way Östen did, but because he understood Östen without forcing himself to agree.

That's it. You have it.

David sighed and gave Östen his voice.

Before him in twilight lay the Fyrisfield, a great plain that followed the course of a marshy river from Uppsala south to the lake Mälaren. Hundreds of campfires burned across its breadth, like the sparks of Muspelheim fallen to the earth from the firmament. Large tracts of its sodden expanse never dried out during the year, and it was not a place Östen would have picked for a battle. But it lay in Styrbjörn's path to Eric's hall, and the army of the true king would make its stand here.

Östen turned back to the fire he shared with a dozen other men, including Olof, his neighbor back home. Most in this circle were farmers and herders who had likewise answered the call of the Bidding Stick. Some of them were seasoned fighters, others only barely come into their beards, but each of them knew they might not leave this place except in the winged company of Odin's warrior women.

As Östen took his place and sat down, a shadowy figure neared their camp.

"Who approaches?" called Alferth, a man whose right hand possessed only three fingers.

The figure came into the firelight, and Östen recognized Skarpe, a freeman from West Aros. Mud covered his legs from his boots to his thighs, the rest of his clothing wet through. It looked as though he'd suffered a mishap in the marsh, and some of the other men laughed at the sight of him.

"Skarpe, you fool," said Alferth. "There isn't any gold on this plain."

"So you've said." The soggy man took a seat close to the heat of the fire.

"Then why are you out there rooting around in the marsh like a pig after mast?" asked another.

"You know the story as well as I," Skarpe said. "The difference between us is that I believe it."

Alferth pointed off into the darkness. "You believe that Hrólf scattered his gold out there, and that Eadgils stopped to collect that gold instead of pursue his enemy?"

Skarpe shrugged. "Eadgils was a greedy king. And I think there's a good chance he didn't find every piece of gold on this plain."

"Bah!" Alferth said. "You know what I think? I think you're a raven starver, and one of these days you plan to run off—"

"I'm no coward," Skarpe said. His hand had gone to the knife at his side. "I'm certainly not afraid to fight you, Alferth. Nor any man here who—"

"There will be no fighting under the *ledung*," Östen said.

Every man around that fire turned to look at him.

He continued. "Or have you forgotten? Until Eric dismisses you, the only men you'll fight and kill will be Styrbjörn's men. When the battle is over, if the gods have kept you alive, then you can kill each other if that is how you wish to spend your good fortune. But not before. Am I understood?"

Östen wasn't in command of these men, but they nodded toward him nevertheless, and he looked each of them in the eye before returning his gaze to the thread tied around his wrist. He yearned for his wife and his bed. It had never bothered him before to sleep in a war camp and listen to the bluster of frightened men facing their deaths. He had never complained against the rough ground he lay upon or the biting flies that found his neck. Perhaps he was getting old, or a bit white in his liver.

Olof leaned in toward him. "That was well-spoken."

"But perhaps not well-heard." Östen nodded toward Skarpe,

who glowered at the fire in his sodden clothes, his eyes full of flames.

"Let every man wait for battle in his way," Olof said.

Östen nodded, and David nodded with him. Östen looked up into the sky and saw the Great Wagon in the stars. He was about to lie down to sleep under his cloak when a commotion rose up out on the plain. Men called and shouted in the distance, and some carrying torches ran between camps. Östen rose to his feet.

"What is this?" Olof asked.

Some moments later, one of the runners passed by them, but paused long enough to tell them that Styrbjörn's fleet had entered Mälaren, and he brought not only the Jomsvikings with him, but Dane ships as well.

"How many ships?" Östen asked.

"I don't know," the runner said. "You can count them when they land in two days' time." With that, he moved on toward the next camp.

"Two days," Olof said. "Two days until we fight."

Östen sat himself back down. He wasn't counting the days until the battle. He was counting the days until he went home.

CHAPTER TEN

Thorvald and Torgny approached Eric's long hall. Though not as impressive and imposing as the temple, it was large and fitting for a mortal king, ornamented with carvings of gods, warriors, and beasts that fought endlessly along its walls and pillars. At its wide doors, the marshal of Eric's personal war band met them and blocked their entrance with five of his men. Javier sensed within Thorvald that this was unusual, but not necessarily unexpected.

"Hail, Lawspeaker," the marshal said. "And to you, skald."

Thorvald nodded a reply, but remained poised and alert.

"Hail, *stallari*," Torgny said. "We would speak with the king."

"The king is in war council," the marshal said.

He offered no further answer, and neither he nor his men moved aside, making their full intention known. Thorvald then looked each of them over, assessing stance, size, arms, and armor. If necessary, he could mortally wound three of them before the remaining two had drawn their weapons.

"The council is why I have come," Torgny said.

"The king has counsel enough, Lawspeaker," the marshal said, without meeting Torgny's blind gaze. "Your time would be better spent at the temple, appealing to the gods on Eric's behalf."

"You should guard your words more carefully," Thorvald said, "lest the gods take a dark interest in you."

The marshal's jaw hardened. "And you should—"

"At all times the gods take interest in courage and honor," Torgny said. "Which they reward. Or punish when found lacking." He stepped closer to the marshal and looked up at him with his clouded eyes. "The king has never refused my counsel before, *stallari*. On whose order do you stand here before me?"

The marshal recoiled as far from Torgny as he could without physically giving ground, appearing unnerved by the Lawspeaker's words and gaze. "I take no orders from any but the king."

"But the king did not command you to bar me. We both know that." Torgny took another step toward him. "But someone did, so tell me, how much did your honor cost? Was it cheap? Perhaps I might wish to buy it at some point in the future."

"Watch yourself, Lawspeaker," the marshal said, but his voice had no strength behind it.

"I am watching *you*," Torgny said.

The marshal blanched, by a degree, and Thorvald seized the moment.

"The king awaits his Lawspeaker," he said. "We will keep him waiting no longer."

Then he led Torgny around the unmoving marshal and through his confused men, who looked to their leader for guidance. But the Lawspeaker had disarmed the marshal and rendered him harmless, all without Thorvald needing to lay a hand on him.

Inside the hall, dozens of members of Eric's court gathered in clusters at tables and along the two middle hearths that ran nearly the length of the room. Banners hung from the heavy beams above, and the air smelled of roasting pork and red wine. Some of the nobles looked up at the Lawspeaker's entrance, and some of them bowed their heads in deference as he passed. Some of them simply glared, for jealousy and rivalry could be stronger than a fear of the gods.

"Someone here does not want us influencing the king," Thorvald said in a low voice.

"Is that not always the case?" Torgny said.

"I worry the Order might have already found a way in."

"That is unlikely." But Torgny nodded. "Let me deal with it."

They strode the length of the hall to the king's throne at the far end, and behind it, they reached the king's private chambers, rooms appointed with Saxon silver and tapestries from Persia. This time, no one denied them entrance, and within the council room they found Eric leaning over a table, surrounded by his highest jarls and closest kinsmen. Thorvald studied their reactions upon seeing the Lawspeaker, hoping to discern which of them might be the enemy, but none of the faces betrayed their wearers.

Torgny bowed his head. "Greetings, my king. May the gods grant you victory."

"I look to you in that matter, Lawspeaker," Eric said. He wore a blue tunic embroidered with red and gold, his hair and beard in braids. Two wolves snarled at each other from the ends of a silver torc around his neck, and numerous finger rings from all corners of the world glinted on his hands. "Why are you late?"

"A delay that proved inconsequential," Torgny said, his response clearly designed to provoke their enemy. "I beg your forgiveness."

Again, Thorvald searched the reactions of those present, but their enemy remained hidden. He and Torgny drew closer to the king, and, upon his table, Thorvald saw a map of the country and its borders.

"We're discussing how best to make our stand." Eric pointed at the mouth of the Fyriswater, where it poured into Mälaren. "Some, like Jarl Frida, argue for a confrontation farther south, here."

Frida nodded. "Styrbjörn aims his spear at the heart of Svealand," she said. "I say we place our shield so that he cannot reach it."

Eric pointed at another place on the map. "Others believe we should wait for Styrbjörn here at Uppsala, where we are strongest."

Torgny nodded, but said nothing, and Thorvald waited. So did the rest of the room.

A moment later, Eric looked up, his brow creased. "Does the Lawspeaker wish to speak on this matter?"

"Not yet," Torgny said. "There is another matter I wish to speak of first."

"What matter?" the king asked.

"A dream," Torgny said. "A vision. For you alone, Eric."

That sent a rustle and grumble through the nobles, which the king silenced with a raise of his hand.

"Time is short, Lawspeaker."

Thorvald spoke up then. "All the reason to give each moment its due."

Eric frowned at Thorvald, tugging on his beard, but then nodded. "Out, all of you."

Now the faces of the nobles were indistinguishable from one another for their shared ire, each of them an enemy in that moment. But they obeyed their king and filed out of the chamber, and after they'd gone, Eric went to his chair and sat down.

Now Thorvald and Torgny stood alone before the king, the only other being in the room the king's house-bear, a brown sow he had raised from a cub and named Astrid. Unconcerned with the affairs of men, she slept chained in a corner of the room, against a wall, and the rumblings of her breathing sent tremors through the bones of the hall. The sight of her surprised Javier, but not Thorvald.

"We both know you've had no vision," Eric said. "So tell me what your blind eyes see. What would you see done?"

The Lawspeaker dropped his empty gaze to the floor, where it stayed until Thorvald could sense the king growing impatient. "May I speak freely?" Torgny asked.

"You are the Lawspeaker," Eric said. "Of all men, you may speak freely."

"I wish to bring something into the light," Torgny said. "You know of what I speak, though you have been content to pretend you do not see it moving in the shadows."

The king's guarded expression held its ground. "Go on."

"You have never asked the name of my Brotherhood, and I have never offered it. But we have watched and supported you, as you have ruled with wisdom and justice. We have advised you. As skalds, we have shaped the stories that are told, to inspire our people. We have fought and killed your enemies, at times with your knowledge, and other times without it."

Eric shifted in his chair. "There are some things better left unsaid, Lawspeaker."

"I agree," Torgny said.

"Then why bring this to me now? Why not leave your work and your Brotherhood in the shadows?"

"Because my Brotherhood has an enemy. We oppose an Order that has gained tremendous power among the Franks, and their influence is spreading. They have had dealings with Harald of Denmark, who sails with Styrbjörn."

"I see." Eric rose to his feet and paced around his chamber. "You believe my nephew, Styrbjörn, has brought your enemy Order to our lands?"

Torgny nodded. "I fear that is so."

Eric stopped pacing near Astrid the house-bear, who raised her great head to sniff his hand, her huge nostrils flaring with each powerful breath. "This is your fight," the king said. "Is it not?"

"It is," Torgny said. "But it is also your fight. If the Order establishes a foothold here, they will seek to control you, and failing that, they will seek your downfall."

That seemed to finally catch the king's ear. "Do you believe Styrbjörn has entered into a compact with this Order?"

"No," Torgny said. "Styrbjörn is far too willful and unpredictable to serve their purposes. But I assure you the Order is taking an interest in the outcome of this conflict."

Eric returned to his seat. "What does this mean for the battle?"

"Styrbjörn cannot simply be defeated. His army must be annihilated. We must destroy any agents of the Order who lurk among his or Harald's men. Not one seedling can take root."

Eric nodded. "Done."

"No," Torgny said. "Styrbjörn fights with his pride above all. He will seek to challenge you, as he did before you banished him."

"He was a boy then. If he seeks to challenge me now, my honor will demand that I accept."

"I know, my king. Which is why he must not be allowed to reach you. You must not meet his army on any open field of battle, either here or to the south. Not yet."

"Then what are you suggesting?"

Torgny turned to Thorvald. "Here I turn to my apprentice, Thorvald. You will find him to be even more cunning than I am."

Eric looked at Thorvald. "Speak," he commanded, and waited.

Astrid stirred in the corner, awakening. With a deep huffing, she rose and lumbered across the room on her heavy paws, dragging her chain, to stand beside Eric's throne. The king reached out and scratched her neck as if she were a hunting hound. Javier felt very small under the power of that moment. It was like staring a legend in the face. But Thorvald did not shrink.

"We must harry Styrbjörn relentlessly," he said. "He must pay dearly with the lives of his men for every foot of ground he gains on his way to Uppsala, so that when he arrives, his force will be small enough to crush."

"How?" Eric asked. "He will simply row his ships up the river, which will bring him almost to my doors."

"Jarl Frida's plan showed wisdom, but not cunning." Thorvald turned to the map, and Eric left his seat to join him. Astrid followed at her master's side, her head high enough to rest her chin upon the table. Thorvald pointed to the mouth of the Fyriswater. "We stop him here, as she suggested, but not with an army."

"With what, then?" the king asked.

"Let me take a company of men," Thorvald said. "Strong men, the strongest I can find. Fighting men. We will plant stakes in the river—"

"A palisade?" Eric asked.

"Yes. We will keep his ships from ever entering the river. Styrbjörn is impatient. He won't take the time to tear down the stakewall. He'll leave his ships and march overland."

"And then?"

"I use my company as an axe to cleave away his army's limbs."

The king narrowed his eyes, and then he grinned. "I like this plan. My kinsmen and the other jarls may not."

"They won't accept it if it comes from my apprentice," the Lawspeaker said.

"It must come from the Lawspeaker," Thorvald said. "It must come from the gods."

"Which god?" Eric asked.

Thorvald thought for a moment. He had no idea where Styrbjörn stood now in relation to Asgard, but in his younger days, he had always favored Thor. That made the choice a simple one.

"Odin," Thorvald said. "When an impudent son rebels, it must be the father who puts him down and punishes him."

Next to Thorvald, Torgny nodded his approval.

Eric grunted. "Very well." He reached under the left sleeve of his shirt and pulled a golden arm ring down over his wrist. He handed the band to Thorvald. "Go with my authority and choose your men well. The Lawspeaker and I will speak to the others."

Thorvald bowed to the king, and then turned to his mentor. "I shall not fail," he said.

"Bring them the judgment of the Norns," Torgny said.

Thorvald left the council chamber and returned to the great hall, where the nobles waited in a mass near the throne. He said nothing to them, and met none of their eyes as he stalked through the throng toward the doors. The marshal stood near them, and when he saw Thorvald, the anger on his face showed that his earlier befuddlement had turned into a shame that demanded a reckoning.

"I would have words with you, skald," the marshal said, stepping into Thorvald's path.

"And I would have words with you." Thorvald stepped to the side to go around him. "But not today."

The marshal reached out his arm to block him. In an instant Thorvald had him twisted around, shoulder and elbow joints straining painfully behind his back, with a dagger at his throat.

Not his hidden blade, but an ordinary knife. The marshal winced, eyes open wide in shock.

"I go on the king's errand," Thorvald said, right into the marshal's ear. "You will not delay me. But I swear I will return, and at that time, if you still have cause against me, then we shall have words. Understood?"

The marshal nodded. Thorvald released him, and the man staggered away, rubbing his arm. Thorvald gave him a glare of contempt and marched through the doors.

There were warriors enough among Eric's war band for Thorvald to assemble his company, but he didn't want professional fighting men from Uppsala, and he was no longer sure of their loyalties if the marshal had been corrupted. Instead, Thorvald wanted warriors from the countryside who knew the land well, who loved the land, and would therefore fight all the more viciously to protect it. That meant he would seek his company from among those summoned under the *ledung* by the Bidding Stick.

He mounted Gyllir and rode south onto the plain of Fyrisfield to scout among the encampments there. He trotted past dozens of farmers, craftsmen, and common laborers, and occasionally, when he caught a spark of courage in a countenance, or saw confidence in the holding of a weapon, he stopped to ask a single question.

"If I could grant you one wish, right now," he said, again and again, "what would it be?"

The answers came easily.

A woman.

Ale.

Victory.

An honorable death.

But none of them gave the right answer.

He did not have much time to give this selection, and as the day wore on, he wondered if he should simply draw men from among the war band, after all. But then he spied a giant in a camp not far away, who stood heads taller and wider than any man around him. The kind of man who called to mind the children of the jötnar and their stolen human brides. Thorvald rode toward him at a brisk trot and dismounted as he neared the stranger's circle.

"Greetings," he said. "I come to you with the king's authority."

"You have it backward, friend," said a man missing several fingers. "You see, we're all here by order of the Bidding Stick, so I believe we come to *you* with the king's authority."

He laughed, and so did some of the others. The giant did not.

"You there," Thorvald called to him. "What is your name?"

"Östen," the giant said. "What's yours?"

"Thorvald," he said. "How do you earn your livelihood?"

Östen frowned. "Sheep. Why is that business of yours?"

"It is not my business." Thorvald raised his sleeve to reveal Eric's arm ring, and the sight of it forced the gathering into silence. "As I told your finger-deficient friend, it is the king's business."

Östen's frown softened, and he nodded. "How may I be of service to the king?"

Thorvald surveyed the giant's hands, his scars, his bearing, and did not need to ask if he could fight. Östen could fight very well. Instead, Thorvald asked the question he had asked of all the others that morning.

"If I could grant you one wish, right now, what would it be?"

"To go home," Östen said, without hesitation, as he touched a single thread tied incongruously around his thick wrist.

Thorvald smiled. That was the answer he had been waiting to hear.

CHAPTER ELEVEN

Natalya ran.

Not toward.

Away.

Her body wasn't hers. It belonged to her fear, and it carried her through the Forest, leaping over roots and dodging around the trees. Her mind wondered where she could run or hide in a wood that was the same in every direction, but her body asked no questions. It took the icy fuel of her adrenaline and filled her every muscle with it. It whipped her heart into such a frenzy she couldn't tell its beats apart. It numbed her to the scrapes and bruises acquired in her flight. It told her mind not to interfere. Her body knew what to do.

Owen ran beside her, and she tried to stay aware of him, even though she couldn't tell if he was aware of her.

The Serpent chased them. Its speed seemed impossible, blinding, as if the trees and uneven ground offered no obstacle. As if the Forest and the Serpent shared intent.

The monster gained on them, and then, with a sudden lunge, it entered the corner of her right eye. She turned toward it just as it struck, its mouth opened wide to reveal white flesh and ivory fangs as long as her legs. But the strike missed her by inches, and one of those fangs stabbed deep into the tree nearest her, and became embedded. The Serpent coiled up and thrashed, trying to tear itself free.

Guys? Monroe said. *Talk to me. What's going on?*

"A little busy right now!" Owen said, and then he called to her, "Are you okay?"

Natalya nodded, still bewildered.

"Let's go that way," he said, pointing in a new direction.

Guys? Monroe said.

"Not now!" Owen shouted back, sprinting away.

Natalya ran after him.

With the Serpent's attack, her mind had taken back some control. The Forest to either side and in front of her presented nothing but endlessness, a desert of trees. They couldn't outrun the monster, but they also couldn't hide. They couldn't even climb the trees to escape, because she was pretty sure the Serpent could reach them. She felt she had to be missing something.

As a memory, and a simulation, this made no sense. There had to be more to the collective unconscious than these two archetypes. There had to be something beyond them. The voice had said something about a path, and also fear, devotion, and—

Fear.

And Monroe had said that the Serpent archetype represented death and fear.

A few feet ahead of her, Owen skidded to a stop, and she almost ran into him.

"What are you—?"

"Shh!" he said.

She looked around him and saw the Serpent. Not its head. Just its huge, never-ending body, slithering across their path with the sound of a rushing river, disconcertingly unaware of them.

"Which way do we go?" Owen whispered.

They couldn't go back the way they'd come, unless they wanted another encounter with the Serpent's head. And it seemed foolish to turn to the left or right and follow its body if they were trying to escape from it. That meant they had to go over it.

"I don't get it," Owen said. "If this is all just a symbol, shouldn't there be a magic sword around here? Something we can use to kill it?"

"We have to climb over it," Natalya said.

"Wait, what?"

"It's the only way." She stepped forward, right up to the nightmare express of skin and scales rolling by. The snake's body was almost as tall as she was, and was smooth enough to gleam, which meant that climbing it, especially while it was moving, would be difficult.

"You're serious," Owen said, stepping up beside her.

"Can you think of another way around it?"

"No. But I also think this whole simulation is messed up."

Natalya couldn't argue with that. The Forest around them still seemed to twist and contort itself in the darkness just outside the edges of the dim light. The Serpent's body emerged from and disappeared into that same boundary. It felt as if they had become trapped in a moment, or a thought, that replayed itself on an infinite loop, and the only way to break the loop was to move ahead.

"So how do we do this?" she asked.

Owen looked around. "Maybe we climb one of the trees?"

She cast her gaze up with his, searching for a low enough branch to grab on to. None of the trees nearby offered one, so they walked along the path of the Serpent until they found a tree they could use.

From its side grew a branch just thick enough that Natalya could barely encircle it with her hands. She latched on to it, and with her feet against the trunk she pulled and heaved herself up until she rested in the branch's crook. Then she offered Owen her hand to help pull him up, and soon they were both safely above ground.

Natalya hugged the trunk of the tree and shimmied around it onto another, higher branch, and then another, until she reached one that stretched out far enough in the right direction and looked strong enough to support them.

"Here goes," she said.

Owen looked at her, looked down at the Serpent, and nodded.

Natalya lowered herself into a straddle over the branch and scooted out onto it several feet. Then she leaned forward to hug the branch, crossed her legs at the ankles, and allowed herself to swing over and around so that she was hanging by her arms and her legs. Then she inched along, hand over hand, making her way slowly outward until the branch sagged and complained, and she'd gone as far as she dared go. But when she looked down, she discovered she was suspended directly over the Serpent's body, not nearly far enough to make it to the other side.

"What now?" Owen asked, still clinging to the trunk of the tree.

"Um—" What else could she do? "I'm going to let my legs go. Then I'll hang on to the branch with my hands until I'm ready to drop onto the snake."

"Wait, onto the snake?"

"Yeah." She nodded toward the far side of the Serpent. "I'll try to fall off that way. You know, drop and roll."

"Yeah, good plan," he said with a shake of his head. "What if the snake doesn't want us to use it as a trampoline?"

The Serpent was so enormous, Natalya hoped that it might not even notice them. She reaffirmed her grip on the branch with her hands, took a deep breath, and muttered, "This better be worth it, Monroe." Then she let her legs uncross, and as they fell away from the branch, her body swung by her fingers and hands. But she didn't drop. Not yet.

It was hard to tell from her angle, but it seemed as if her toes now dangled about two or three feet above the Serpent's body. Not a problem at all, when she wasn't landing on a moving surface of reptile scales. But she felt her hands getting tired, and if she didn't go soon, she wouldn't be able to choose the moment for herself.

"Okay!" she called to Owen. "Wish me luck!"

He gave her a weak thumbs-up.

She let go.

A second later, her feet touched down, and she immediately dropped her body to all fours as the Serpent whisked her suddenly away, moving much faster than she had expected. She glanced back at Owen, up in the tree. His mouth hung open, and he grew distant until he disappeared into the woods.

She was supposed to fall off. Not go for a ride. But then she looked ahead and saw the trees careering by to either side, marking her passage through the Forest at exactly the speed of her terror. She felt the wind in her hair, and beneath her hands she felt smooth, hard scales, which were neither cold nor warm, but about the same temperature as the air.

She was riding a giant snake that had eyes like brass cymbals and fangs so large their venom wouldn't matter. A beast that had almost killed her only minutes before and probably wouldn't miss a second strike.

She was *riding* it. Keeping a grip on her fear, like Monroe had said to do.

She knew she should jump off, but she didn't want to. Not yet. This dangerous moment had captured her, and she wasn't quite ready to leave it. She and Owen could keep running from the Serpent, but for how long? This archetype seemed to fill the Forest, and it would find them eventually, but at least this way, she rode it by choice.

"Natalya!" It was Owen's panicked voice in her ear, in the same way as Monroe's. "Natalya, are you okay?"

"I'm okay," she said. "I'm here."

"You were supposed to fall off!" Owen said. "What happened?"

"I don't know. Where are you?"

"I'm on the snake with you! But now we can jump off together. Let's—"

"No," Natalya said. "Wait."

"Wait? What for, beverage service? Because I don't think they offer that on this thing."

Natalya didn't understand why she was hesitating.

"Natalya," Owen said. "We need to jump."

He was right.

"Okay," she said. "Get ready. We'll—"

But then it was there. The Serpent reared its head in front of her, looming out of the murk with its eyes upon her, flicking its forked tongue. Natalya felt the same all-consuming, mind-emptying panic she had when seeing the creature for the first time, and she lost the ability to move or speak. She could only watch as the Serpent eased into alignment with itself, bringing her directly toward its mouth.

She had to move. She had to fight it.

"Natalya?" Owen said. "Hello?"

"Jump," she whispered, straining and shaking.

"What?"

"Jump!" she shouted, and managed to tip herself to the side, rolling off the Serpent's back into a fall. She hit the ground hard, and her momentum tumbled her a few feet, slamming her back into a tree.

The Serpent's body continued to rush past her for a few moments, but she didn't spot Owen riding it, which hopefully meant he had listened to her and bailed out somewhere down-snake. She didn't dare call to him to find out, because even in that moment, the Serpent's body had slowed, and from every direction she heard the rasp and rattle of its scales against the trees. Then she saw one of its great looping coils slide into view. Then another, and another, until she was surrounded, and the whole Forest appeared to writhe with its impossible body.

Natalya cowered where she was, in pain, frozen in place as if already impaled against the tree by the Serpent's fang. At any moment, its silent head would slip around the tree she leaned against, and there would be nothing to do, and nowhere to run. Its mouth would open, and it would swallow her alive. The thought of it brought a scream to her throat, but she covered her mouth to trap it inside and stay hidden for just a few moments more. Just another moment or two of fear, fighting the inevitable.

Unless Monroe could pull her out before then. The simulation would end either way, with her death or with an evacuation. But she wouldn't have learned anything that could help stop Isaiah. He would still be unstoppable if he found the Trident.

Well, if she was going to fail, it might as well be on her terms, but it wouldn't be because she'd asked Monroe to save her. After all, the voice had said the path was *through* fear. So she accepted her fear, instead of fighting it. Against every instinct buried in the deepest corners of her mind, she stood up. Then she took several deep and even breaths, listening only to the sound of herself. When her hands stopped shaking, she closed her eyes for a moment, and then she stepped out from behind the tree.

The Serpent whipped its head toward her, tongue flicking, but she didn't run from it. In accepting her fear, she found it had actually vanished, for it no longer served a purpose. Now she stood her ground, calmly facing the enormous monster bearing down on her.

The Serpent closed the distance between them almost instantly, and Natalya closed her eyes, allowing it to happen when it happened. She felt the soft Forest floor beneath her feet, and high above the smell of snake she caught something light and fragrant. A blossom of some kind.

A shadow crossed her, blotting out even the meager light in the woods, and then she felt something flick the top her head, tossing her hair. The Serpent's tongue. After that came the monster's mouth, which pressed against her head and opened, sliding down over her face, soft and dry, smothering her. She remained aware of a painful squeezing at every point on her body that soon forced her mouth open to let the air out of her. She was in its mouth, about to enter its throat. She lost awareness then of where she was, and she felt herself slipping into nothing—

"Natalya!"

Her eyes shot open.

"There you are!" Owen called.

She looked down at her body, and discovered she was unharmed. The Serpent had vanished. She stood upon a path paved with red stone, a path that began at her feet, and the Forest around her had changed. Bright sunlight suffused it with a soft green glow that had banished the barrier of darkness. The path of red stone ran along the ground and around the trees in loops and whorls that made little sense, but away to the right it straightened out and proceeded confidently into the Forest.

"You found a path," Owen said, running up beside her. "Where did the Serpent go?"

Natalya looked again at the path, its regular stones laid close together like scales, much of its course a coiled knot. "I think . . . I think the Serpent *is* the path."

"What?" Owen looked down. "Really?"

"It ate me."

"What?" he blurted. "What do you mean it ate you?"

"I mean I felt it. I was inside its mouth. And then I was just . . . standing here."

Owen appeared to be tracing the path with his eyes, taking it in. Then he threw up his hands. "Sure. Why not? That makes about as much sense as anything else in this place so far."

"It does make sense. Sort of. When you think about what that light said." Natalya pointed to where the path straightened out. "I think we should follow it."

Owen agreed. "Maybe it leads out of the Forest."

"I think it does."

So they followed it, from the place where Natalya had accepted that her simulation would end, into a woodland still as thick and deep as it had been before, but which Natalya no longer found threatening. Instead, its vast distances called to her, enticing her to wander from the path and explore. But she resisted, fearing what it would mean for her mind if she became lost in this simulation.

"Monroe?" Natalya said.

Yeah?

"Just seeing if you were there," she said.

Oh, you mean you guys have time for me now?

"I don't think you realize how big that snake was," Owen said.

Big enough to turn into a path?

"So you are listening," Natalya said.

Of course I am. But like I said earlier, the Animus is having a hard time showing me what's going on. You guys are going to have to figure most of this out for yourselves. I'm actually starting to suspect that's the whole point.

"So what do we do now?" Owen asked.

Follow the yellow brick road.

"Right," Natalya said. "Maybe this path is *the* Path."

Man, I wish Joseph Campbell were here.

"Who?" Owen asked.

Joseph Campbell? Monroe sighed. *Let me put it this way. If you're on the Path, then Campbell has the map. But he's not here, so it looks like you're going to have to find your own way. So I'll leave you to it. Grace just walked in, and she needs to talk to me. But I'll be here if you need me.*

"Over and out," Owen said.

A large bird rose up from the trees to the right and flew over them, caressing the Path with its shadow, and a light breeze seemed to follow it. Natalya spied squirrels scampering up and down the trees, and smiled at the angry flip of their tails that accompanied their scolding chatter.

"If the last Forest had a giant snake," Owen said, "then this Forest definitely has elves."

Natalya agreed with him, but if there was an Elf or Fairy archetype inhabiting those woods, she never appeared, and after walking a distance that didn't seem measurable in miles, they glimpsed a break in the trees ahead. The edge of the Forest. As they drew closer, she saw a figure waiting in the road. It appeared to be quite large, but not human.

"What do you think?" Owen asked.

She shrugged. "I think we'll find out when we get there."

CHAPTER TWELVE

Grace waited until she was sure that David wasn't going to desynchronize, and then she left him in the Animus room to go for a walk so she could think.

It wasn't that she resented him for taking over the simulation. Even though she liked to tease him, she didn't feel the same level of personal rivalry that he did. He had to prove that he didn't need his older sister. Sometimes, it seemed as though he needed to prove it to her, and sometimes it seemed as though he just needed to prove it to himself. Either situation could be irritating. But watching him put that helmet on, and then knowing he'd left their world behind for a Viking one, had unsettled her and she wasn't sure why.

Maybe the vision had something to do with it.

The Piece of Eden in Mongolia had shown her the future

that most frightened her. The future she spent so much energy trying to prevent. It showed her a future in which David had done just about everything she had ever warned him not to do. He got older and ran with a bad crew, and got caught up in some really bad stuff. The vision showed her a David she didn't recognize, and it ended the night that he died. A night that began with two detectives knocking on the door, demolishing their family, and ended with the faces of her grief-stricken parents. A night of screaming and tears and anger so hot an inner part of Grace burned to ash.

After Isaiah had left with the dagger and the vision had ended, Grace had cried and hugged David so hard he probably wondered what was going on, but she hadn't told him then, and she still hadn't.

Now she needed some air, and some sky. She knew of a balcony next to the office that used to be Isaiah's, so she walked to the Aerie's main elevators and rode one of them to the top floor.

Outside, she found the day overcast with clouds that seemed the color and weight of cement. But even without the sunlight she'd hoped for, it felt good to stand in the open, surrounded by wind and mountains. For several peaceful minutes she just stood there, leaning against the balcony's railing, thinking of nothing.

But then she thought of David again, downstairs in the Animus.

That still bothered her. And it hadn't bothered her before. David had gone into simulations on his own, but something had changed since then, and the only thing she could point to was that vision. It scared her now to let him out of her sight, even into a virtual reality.

She had to get her mind off it somehow, so she went back inside, and, out of curiosity, she tried the door to Isaiah's office. It opened, which wasn't too surprising, since he had probably taken everything with him and there wasn't any reason for Victoria to lock the door. But she looked around anyway, and found the desk and its drawers empty.

There was a bookcase, however, and Grace thought reading might distract her and help her pass the time, if she could find something interesting. The titles she scanned dealt mostly with history, including a few biographies, most of it probably related to the Templars. There was a book on the Borgias, one about a guy named Jacques de Molay, and another called *The Journal of Haytham Kenway*, among many others. But she also noticed a couple of random books that didn't fit the pattern, one of them a book on Norse mythology.

Having just experienced the memories of Östen, she pulled that volume from the shelf, and then made herself comfortable in the big chair behind the desk. The first thing she decided to look for in the book was any mention of a magical dagger, because if the Vikings had a prong of the Trident, maybe there were legends about it. But after checking each of the mentions listed in the index, she concluded none of them fit. So she started just flipping through the pages, stopping to read anything that looked interesting, and realized pretty quickly the Norse gods were strange.

Especially Loki.

Here was a handsome half giant who could convince anyone to do just about anything, including getting Thor into a dress and a wedding veil, and he went and had three kids with a giantess. One of them was a half-dead girl they put in charge of the underworld, another one was a sea serpent, and the last one was the giant Fenris wolf. The gods kicked Loki's kids out of Asgard, which made the three of them into the mortal enemies of the gods.

That brought Grace to Ragnarök. The end of the world. Or at least the fate of the gods. In the final battle, Loki's wolf-son killed Odin, and the sea serpent killed Thor, which meant that, in a way, the gods had brought about their own demise. Grace turned the page to read on—

A folded sheet of paper fell out of the book onto the desk.

Grace set the book aside and picked up the paper, which contained a handwritten note. As she read it, she realized that it had been written by Isaiah, and her eyes widened in fear at his words. The situation was even worse than they had imagined. Much worse.

He didn't want to be a king. Isaiah wanted to destroy the world. He wanted Ragnarök.

Grace jumped up from the desk and ran from the office, back to the elevators, where she jabbed the button and fidgeted furiously until the elevator came, and she rode back down to the ground floor. She didn't trust Victoria or Griffin enough to go to them with this. That left Monroe, so she sprinted across the atrium toward the laboratories, and after searching several darkened rooms, she finally found Monroe seated at a computer terminal. Owen and Natalya walked in their Animus harnesses next to him, and he gave Grace a quick, perplexed nod as she came in.

"It looks like you're going to have to find your own way," he said into his headset, and she realized he was talking to Owen and Natalya. "So I'll leave you to it. Grace just walked in, and she needs to talk to me. But I'll be here if you need me." He touched a button on the display and then swiveled in his chair to face her. "Everything okay?"

She handed him the note without saying anything, and waited as long as she could to let him read it before speaking. "What is he talking about?" she asked. "Disasters? Cycles of death and renewal? Ragnarök?"

Monroe shook his head, then refolded the note and tapped it against his knee. "It seems that Isaiah has developed some peculiar ideas."

"Peculiar ideas?" Grace said. "He thinks the world needs to die!"

"To be reborn, yes. It's a common mythology around the world. First, a cataclysmic event occurs. It could be a great flood. It could be fire. But it wipes the slate clean, and, afterward, the survivors are left with a purified new world. That's a part of Ragnarök people sometimes forget. The cycle starts over. Apparently, Isaiah thinks we're long overdue."

"I—I thought he just wanted to conquer the world. Not kill everyone."

"Not everyone. I'm pretty sure Isaiah plans to survive. Then he can set himself up as humanity's next savior and ruler."

Grace remembered another detail from the note. "Who are the Instruments of the First Will?"

"Something I've only heard rumors about." Monroe held up the note. "Where did you find this?"

"In a book on Norse mythology. In Isaiah's old office."

"Have you shown it to anyone else?"

"Not yet. I don't trust Victoria, or Griffin."

Monroe gave her the note back. "You hang on to that, but let's keep it between us for now. I want to find out if Victoria knows about this. If she does, then I want to know why she's keeping us in the dark."

Grace nodded.

"Try not to worry. This doesn't change anything. No matter what Isaiah has planned, we're going to stop him."

She wished that reassured her, but it didn't. Grace now knew this was a doomsday scenario, and now that she knew that, she needed to do something about it that much more urgently. She looked at Owen and Natalya again, the hydraulics and machinery of their harnesses whispering as they strolled in place. Then she noticed a third, unoccupied Animus next to theirs.

"Could I go into their simulation?" she asked Monroe. "I want to help."

"What about your ancestor's simulation?"

"David's got it." And she couldn't let her fear for him stop her from doing what needed to be done. Besides, she told herself the dagger's vision wasn't real. He was safe, for now. "I can help Owen and Natalya."

Monroe looked over at the Animus machines and studied them for a moment. "It would be possible. But you should know it might be very dangerous in there. I'm worried about the risk to your mind."

"Owen and Natalya are in there," Grace said. "If I want to help them, it's my risk to take."

"True enough." Monroe rose from his chair. "I'll let them catch you up with everything once you're in there, if that's okay. It'll take me some time to tie this third Animus into the other two."

Grace found herself a chair of her own. "I can wait."

It did take some time, but eventually Monroe had the empty Animus ready to go. These three machines looked different from the others, more industrial, like they were stripped down to the bare hardware. Grace stepped inside the ring and climbed into the harness. Several minutes later, she stood blinking in the Memory Corridor, waiting to join the simulation. Monroe let Owen and Natalya know that she was coming in, and then he counted her down.

The world that appeared out of the gray void did not feel right, in a way that was hard for her to describe. It lacked a certain specificity. She stood on a path made of stone, but she couldn't say what kind of stone it was. A beautiful forest grew all around her, but she couldn't identify the types of trees. It wasn't that she lacked the knowledge. It was something about them that made them unidentifiable, like they were somehow *all* trees. They looked very real, as real as any rocks and trees she had ever seen, and yet, not real.

"Grace!"

It was Owen's voice.

She looked and saw him waving at her from farther down the path. Natalya stood next to him, and they waited as she jogged the distance to catch up. When she reached them, they seemed genuinely happy to see her.

"What is this place?" Grace asked.

Owen spread his arms. "This, my friend, is the Forest." Then he tapped his foot. "And this is the Path. With capital letters. You missed the Serpent." He pointed down the stone trail ahead of them, and Grace saw a distant figure in silhouette where it looked like the Forest ended. "We have something up there we're not sure about yet."

"This is a simulation of the collective unconscious," Natalya said.

"Oh, right." Grace remembered Monroe explaining that concept, back when they'd hitched a ride to Mongolia in an Abstergo shipping container. Now she took in her surroundings from a different angle, and its strangeness made more sense. "So these are archetypes."

"Yes," Natalya said, sounding a bit surprised.

Grace nodded down the path, toward the something. It looked like an animal of some kind. "So is that an archetype?"

"We don't know," Owen said. "We were on our way there when Monroe said you were coming in, so we decided to wait."

"And why exactly are we in here?" Grace asked. "Monroe didn't really explain the point."

"The collective unconscious and the Ascendance Event are connected to the Trident," Natalya said. "When we came in here, a talking light told us to follow the path through fear, devotion, and faith. We've already gone through fear, I think. We're supposed to go to the summit."

"With a capital *S*?" Grace asked.

Owen shrugged. "Probably."

"Then let's get to it," Grace said.

Owen and Natalya nodded, and the three of them set off down the stone Path. Gradually, the simulation seemed less strange to Grace, replaced by a vague familiarity, even though she had never been there before. It wasn't quite déjà vu, but it was similar to that. She assumed that's because archetypes were in some ways familiar to most people. That was one of their defining characteristics. As for the figure up ahead, it had begun to resolve itself, and it wasn't long before Grace could tell what it was.

"It's a dog," she said.

"A big dog," Natalya said.

"Maybe it's *the* Dog," Owen said.

The closer they got, the more likely that actually seemed. This dog was enormous, and had a wolfish appearance, with fur the color of dried blood, yellow eyes, and a thick mane around its neck. Grace had never been afraid of dogs, but this one was big enough to look her straight in the eyes while seated on its haunches. She felt a bit safer when it started wagging its tail, brushing it back and forth over the Path as the three of them approached.

"So what happens now?" Grace whispered.

"I don't know," Owen said.

"Well, what happened last time?"

"The Serpent attacked us—"

The Dog barked, startling Grace. She jumped, and so did Natalya and Owen. It had been single bark, very loud and very deep.

"Let's not talk about things attacking, okay?" Natalya whispered.

But then, with a soft whine, the Dog stood up on its four feet. Grace prepared to run, in case it charged at them. But it turned in the opposite direction from them and trotted away down the Path, past the edge of the forest, into the sunlight of the open countryside beyond. They watched it go, but the Dog soon stopped and turned back to look at them.

It barked again.

"What's it doing?" Owen asked.

"I'm not sure," Natalya said.

Another bark.

It looked to Grace as if the Dog might be waiting for them. "I think it wants us to follow it," she said.

Natalya looked again and nodded. "I think you're right."

So they left the Forest behind and ventured out onto a section of the Path that wound through a dry countryside of white rock, thick grass, and short, gnarled trees. The Dog led the way, quickly adopting a routine in which it barked and waited to see if they would follow, and when they did, it proceeded to the next spot, where it barked again. There was just no way of knowing where it was leading them or why.

Watching the Dog lope along made Grace think of the Fenris wolf, the monster she'd read about in the book on Norse mythology, which brought Isaiah's note to mind. She would not have thought that following a Dog would help in her in the mission to stop him, but this was important somehow, and she had to trust in that.

Just like she had to trust David.

Soon they'd traveled far enough into this new terrain that the Forest behind them disappeared over the uneven horizon. With each bark, the Dog sounded more desperate, and possibly even impatient with them.

"Let's try not to get lost in here," Owen said, looking over his shoulder. "I don't want my mind to be trapped in this place permanently."

That must've been one of the dangers Monroe had mentioned. Grace shuddered at the idea of her mind staying in this simulation while her body just kept walking forever like a zombie in the Animus.

"I think we'll be okay if we stick to the Path," Natalya said.

"I hope so," said Grace. So they continued following the Dog, trying to keep up with it, until it stopped and barked at something off the Path.

Grace looked for what it might be, and she spotted some kind of stone monument at the top of a green hillock nearby. When she and the others turned in that direction, the Dog barked one more time, and then shot away from them up the mound toward the structure, tearing a seam in the tall grass.

"I guess we go that way," Owen said.

"Didn't we just decide not to leave the Path?" Grace said.

"It's not that far," Owen said. "We'll be able to see the Path from up there. And we might even see more of the simulation."

"It still seems risky," Grace said.

The dog barked at them from the top of the hill.

"It also seems like that's where we're supposed to go," Natalya said. "But let's keep the Path in sight at all times."

They agreed, but Grace still didn't like the idea. As they left the Path and marched up the hill, the grass at Grace's knees, she looked back constantly to make sure the red stones were still there, charting a course through the collective unconscious.

The angle of the slope turned out to be steeper than it had appeared, and the three of them were soon breathing hard, while above them, the Dog continued to bark, distant and echoed. A few minutes later, they reached the top. The structure Grace had seen from below turned out to be a circle of high stones, each several feet taller than her and a few feet thick. They stood quite close together, with only a few inches between them, but the circle had an opening not far from them. The barking came from inside it.

They hurried through the opening, and within the circle Grace found the Dog sitting next to a man, whining and wagging its tail. The man sat on the ground, his back propped up against one of the stones, his rutted face turned heavenward, with his eyes closed. His gray beard and hair were long and unkempt, and he wore coarse clothing made of fur and animal skins. A long wooden staff lay across his lap.

Grace, Owen, and Natalya approached him cautiously. This situation, and this figure, seemed even less predictable than the Dog.

"Do you think he's dead?" Owen asked.

"I'm not dead," the stranger said, opening his eyes. "But I am dying. And I need you to do something for me after I am gone."

CHAPTER THIRTEEN

Restrained in the Animus, Sean could do nothing as Isaiah stalked toward him across the chapel, wielding the incomplete Trident of Eden.

"Until now I have only relied on your faith," Isaiah said. "But it seems I must also show you fear."

Sean didn't know what he meant by that, but before he could figure it out, an image tore through his mind, casting every other thought aside, more powerful than any simulation. It came from a time before the accident, a recurring fear he used to carry around before his life had become something completely unplanned and unimagined.

He was standing on the soccer field. His teammates had turned their backs on him to go congratulate their opponents on their win. A win that Sean had made possible by screwing up.

It didn't matter how he had screwed up. The fear came in all varieties. Not just soccer, but basketball and baseball, too. Whenever Sean had taken up a new sport, the image had changed to suit it. But the shame remained the same. The knowledge that the crowd and the team had watched him fail. That he had let them down. The fear of what they were thinking and saying about him when he wasn't around. The belief that they were right.

He wasn't talented.

He wasn't good.

In fact, he was terrible, and it wouldn't matter how long and hard he practiced. He should probably just quit and do everyone else a favor. He knew the coach and his teammates wanted him gone, but they were just too nice to say it. They only kept him on the team out of pity. His stomach hurt when he thought about having to go back into the locker room with everyone. They'd pat him on the back and tell him it was okay that he screwed up, but it wasn't. Rather than face that, he wanted the field to open up beneath him and suck him down where no one would find him and he could be forgotten.

He was worthless. More than worthless, he was the one holding other people back.

"Sean," a soothing voice said.

The image left, and Sean returned to the chapel. Isaiah stood before him. Sean's cheeks felt wet, and he realized he'd been crying.

"Whatever you just saw," Isaiah said, "I can free you from it. But only if you listen to me and do as I say. Your ancestor, Styrbjörn, was a stubborn individual, and I think perhaps that is rubbing off on you through the Bleeding Effects. But I need you to stay strong and resist him. I need you to remember why we're here, and how essential you are. I am very proud of you for what you've accomplished so far. You and I, we can do this together."

As Isaiah spoke, Sean felt the ground firming up beneath him. He realized there wasn't any reason for him to fear that he might fail. Not when he had Isaiah. It didn't matter what his teammates and his coaches had said or thought about him. However badly Sean had screwed up before, that didn't matter now, because he had Isaiah and he believed what Isaiah said.

"Are you ready to go back into your ancestor's memories?" Isaiah asked.

Sean nodded. "I'm ready."

"Excellent."

The chapel doors opened and several technicians swept into the room. They scurried over to the Animus, and very quickly had the simulation ready again. Isaiah placed the helmet back on Sean's head, and gave his shoulder a firm squeeze before throwing him back into the wild river of Styrbjörn's mind. Moments later, he stood between Palnatoke and Harald Bluetooth, shoulder to shoulder at the bow of his ship.

The calm waters of Lake Mälaren had granted his fleet easy passage, though the journey had not been as swift as he would have liked. They had stopped at several villages along the way to recruit men to his banner, but few had joined. It seemed that in his absence, honor had become a rarity among the Svear, but it was also said that cunning trolls had begun to stalk the forests, high in the trees, ready to slay anyone who supported Styrbjörn. Escaped bondsmen had been attacked, and the word had spread. But Styrbjörn didn't believe in trolls.

Superstition or not, it was no matter, for he had more than enough warriors and ships to defeat Eric, and would soon reach the mouth of the Fyriswater. From there, they would row up the river to Uppsala and to battle.

Palnatoke seemed as eager for that as Styrbjörn, as did all the Jomsvikings, whose covenant disposed them to war making. But to his other side, Harald's cowardice had become more pronounced with each passing league, and his hand never left the dagger he wore. It offended Styrbjörn that his sister had wed this Dane, no matter his power and the size of his kingdom.

"What is that?" he finally asked Harald, nodding to the dagger. "It is a strange blade. I can think of no use for it. And yet you hold to it as a suckling pig to its mother's teat."

An angry red entered the white of Harald's face. "It is nothing to you."

"If it was nothing to me, I would not ask."

"Then it is simply nothing."

"I doubt that very much. What is it to you?"

Harald shut his mouth and held it fast, the first sign of resolve he had yet shown, and in that moment Styrbjörn's curiosity about the dagger reached a point where it would not be denied. Sean had been waiting for a moment like this, for his ancestor to finally notice the Piece of Eden.

"I have a bargain I wish to make with you," Styrbjörn said.

Harald glowered at him. To his other side, Palnatoke listened and watched with a glint of amusement in his eye.

"Are you not going to ask about the terms of my bargain?" Styrbjörn said.

"I am not," Harald said.

"I shall tell you all the same." Styrbjörn turned to face Harald in full, with his arms folded. "I will release you, and your men, and your ships. Here. Now."

Harald looked at him then, as a fish eyes the bait on a hook.

"I swear it," Styrbjörn said. "If you pay my price, I will release you, and you are free to return to your wife, my sister, with your honor."

"And what is your price?" Harald asked with narrowed eyes. "I expect you want my dagger? But I shall not give it to you, not for—"

"No." Styrbjörn looked away, as if he momentarily found the distant shoreline more interesting than their conversation. "I do not want your dagger."

"Then what do you want?" Harald now sounded irritated, and Palnatoke leaned forward, as if he, too, were waiting for the answer.

"I want you to take up your dagger," Styrbjörn said, "and throw it into the waters of Mälaren."

Palnatoke laughed.

Harald did not.

Meanwhile, Sean felt a sudden panic at the possibility that the dagger might at that moment be lost somewhere at the bottom of a very deep lake, depending on how this memory played out. That would also mean the end of the simulation, but it couldn't be. He couldn't fail Isaiah.

"As I told you"—Styrbjörn smiled at the Dane-king—"it is a small price. Your freedom and your fleet in exchange for throwing away a simple, useless dagger that you claim means nothing. What do you say to my bargain?"

Harald's anger finally showed itself in full. The Dane actually quivered with it. "To your bargain, I say no. And to you, I say may the gods curse you."

"But you no longer believe in the gods," Styrbjörn said. "You have your White Christ. And now I know your dagger is much more than nothing, which is all I wanted you to admit. I am satisfied."

Palnatoke laughed again. "You gamble like a dying man, Styrbjörn."

"It was a ruse?" Harald shook his head. "A game? You made false promises—?"

"Not false," Styrbjörn said. "If you had thrown that dagger away, I would have kept my word. But I knew you wouldn't part with it. Now, tell me why."

"Why?" Harald blinked, appearing somewhat befuddled. "The dagger is a holy relic. A gift from the emperor, the Saxon Otto, delivered to me by the cleric who baptized me a Christian. It came to Otto from the Father of the Church in Rome."

"It is a relic of the Christ?" Styrbjörn said. "And for that you would trade your freedom and that of your men?"

"I would," Harald said.

Though this confused and even impressed Styrbjörn, Sean knew it to be a lie, or at least a partial truth. Harald may have received the dagger in the way he'd just explained, but Sean still believed that he also understood its true nature, which accounted for his refusal to throw it away.

"Perhaps you do have a kind of honor," Styrbjörn said, though he doubted it was the kind of honor that would keep Harald from betraying him, if given the chance.

After that, the fleet sailed on and soon reached the mouth of the Fyriswater, but the ships came to a swift halt when Styrbjörn discovered his route entirely blocked by a man-made stakewall. Tree trunks had been felled and driven into the riverbed, jutting from the water at all angles, thick as bramble and lashed together. There could be no doubt as to its purpose, and Styrbjörn's disbelief quickly turned to rage when he realized what Eric had done.

"Row the fleet ashore," he ordered, and that night some of the men made camp on land, while others slept on their ships. Styrbjörn held a council around his fire to discuss the next course for his army. In light of the barricade, the Bluetooth argued for a retreat, the mere suggestion of which confirmed to Styrbjörn that the man was a coward.

"This was supposed to be a surprise attack," Harald said. "But it is obvious that Eric is prepared for you. More prepared than perhaps you realized."

"It doesn't matter how prepared he is," Styrbjörn said. "I will not retreat, and he will be no more successful than you in standing against me."

Harald ignored the slight, and Styrbjörn wondered what it would take to finally provoke the Dane, who simply replied, "He outnumbers you."

"As did you," Styrbjörn said. "But his numbers will mean nothing when I slay him in front of his men."

"Your strategy is too single-minded," Harald said. "Listen to me. I have won many, many battles, and in some I claimed victory without ever needing to draw my sword, but do not listen to me as a king. I speak to you now as my brother, for you are the brother of my wife, and I would not see her grieve your death. There is cunning in those stakes—"

"There is cunning in *me*!" Styrbjörn roared.

Harald shook his head. "Not as much cunning as I think you will need."

Styrbjörn restrained himself, and Sean could feel just how difficult that was. "If you had married anyone but my sister, Harald Bluetooth, you would die in this moment, by my hand. You call me a fool?"

"No," Harald said very calmly. "I think you are quite cunning, in your way. But I think you are impatient. You will need more than your axe and your shield to take back your crown, Styrbjörn the Strong. You will also need time and opportunity, but I do not think you will wait for either."

"I will not," Styrbjörn said. "I have waited too long already."

He hurled a log into the fire, and it kicked up a cloud of glowing ash and ember. All the men except old Palnatoke backed away from the stone ring. Styrbjörn regarded him, hesitant to seek his counsel, for he respected the Jomsviking, and if Palnatoke should agree with Harald, then Styrbjörn might be forced to yield. But to ignore Palnatoke would be the greater mistake.

"What do you say?" Styrbjörn asked, looking at his friend.

Palnatoke glanced at Styrbjörn, and then Harald. "I think we should not underestimate Eric. I agree there is cunning in that stakewall, but I do not agree that we should retreat."

Styrbjörn nodded, encouraged. "Go on."

"The question we must answer is how we deal with the impasse. Do we leave our ships and march to Uppsala? Or do we clear the river and go by oar and sail as planned?"

"Clearing the river will take too much time," Styrbjörn said.

"It will take time." Palnatoke nodded. "But perhaps that is what Eric wants. To delay you."

"Or perhaps Eric is trying to force you into an overland march," Harald said, "in which you will be more vulnerable."

Styrbjörn found both strategies believable of his uncle, but one of them more so than the other, because he knew Eric to be a coward. Eric had poisoned Styrbjörn's father. It had never been proven, but Styrbjörn knew it to be true, just as he knew that poison was a coward's weapon. Eric had staked the waterway for the same reason. He was afraid. He knew that Styrbjörn was coming, and wanted to slow him down any way that he could. That made Styrbjörn's choice a simple one.

"We march," he said. "We march hard and swift. Pass word among the men. Make ready to leave at dawn."

The Jomsviking captains left to spread the order, but Palnatoke and Harald lingered.

"You have more to say?" Styrbjörn asked them.

"Only that we should prepare for further treachery," Palnatoke said. "It is a long march to Uppsala."

"We will be ready," Styrbjörn said. "I do not expect it to be easy. But nothing will stop us."

"Then I bid you good night, brother-in-arms." And Palnatoke withdrew to his own bed, among his men.

Then it was Harald's turn to speak. "I believe you are marching to your death, Styrbjörn. But since I can see that you won't be dissuaded, I will bid you good night as well."

"It will take more than a few sticks in the river to frighten me into retreating," Styrbjörn said. "I fight my battles differently than you."

Harald nodded and turned away, but just a bit too quickly, and something in his demeanor raised suspicion.

"Where are you sleeping tonight, Harald?" Styrbjörn asked.

Harald hesitated, and Styrbjörn heard treachery in the silence. "I will sleep on my ship, with my men," Harald said.

"So that you can sail away before dawn?" Styrbjörn asked. "Leaving behind what little honor you possess?"

Harald returned to the fire and faced Styrbjörn from across the flames. "Out of respect for my wife, and allowing for your youth, I have borne your insults. But I will not do so endlessly."

Styrbjörn rose to his feet and walked around the stone ring to stand over the Dane. "You wish to defend your honor?" Though posed as a question, Styrbjörn intended it as a threat, and Harald's step backward suggested he understood it as such.

"I will defend my honor in my time and in the manner of my choosing. Good night, Styrbjörn." Then he turned away again, but Styrbjörn grabbed him by the arm and spun him around.

"You will sleep here tonight," he said. "Next to my fire."

Harald shook his head. "No, Styrbjörn. I will sleep on my ship."

"I don't trust you to sleep on your ship. But I know your men won't leave without you, which means you will not leave my side until we're well into our march."

Harald sighed. "What assurance can I give you? Since it is apparently not enough that I am married to your sister."

Styrbjörn did not need to think long for an answer, and within his thoughts, Sean's anticipation grew. "Leave your dagger with me," Styrbjörn said.

Harald balked. "Never."

"If you don't leave your dagger with me," Styrbjörn said, "you don't leave."

Harald scowled and tried to push past him, but Styrbjörn grabbed him by the shoulders, lifted him off the ground, and hurled him against a tree. Not hard enough to kill him, but hard enough for him to know how easily he could be killed. Harald staggered to his feet, wincing, and wiped at the blood now running from a gash on his head. Styrbjörn could see the hatred burning inside him, and knew that one day Harald would try to kill him. But not today.

Instead, Harald reached down and unbuckled the dagger from his waist. Then he trudged up to Styrbjörn and shoved the weapon into his hands.

"When your sister mourns you, I will be there to comfort her," he said. "Know that." Then he stalked away from the fire and disappeared.

Styrbjörn looked down at the dagger. It truly was a strange weapon, with a curve to its barbed blade, and an unusual grip wrapped in leather. For a Christ relic, it certainly didn't impress, especially when compared to the hammer of Thor or Odin's spear. But it wasn't important what Styrbjörn thought of the dagger. It only mattered that he could control the Bluetooth with it. As he buckled it around his waist, Styrbjörn smiled, but within his memory, Sean laughed.

"Isaiah!" he said "I have it!"

Excellent work, Sean. We're almost there, but let's not get ahead of ourselves. We still need to find out what your ancestor did with the prong.

"Right." Sean worked to calm himself. "Of course."

I see that Styrbjörn is about to sleep. Let's accelerate the memory a bit, shall we?

"Okay," Sean said, and the simulation sped past him in a blur of fragmented dream images, trolls and dogs and chopped wood and floods, then darkness, but that panoply ended abruptly when Palnatoke awoke Styrbjörn, dragging Sean back into the depths of his ancestor's mind.

"What hour is it?" Styrbjörn asked, sitting upright. He felt for the dagger, and found it still at his waist.

"A few hours before dawn," Palnatoke said.

Styrbjörn growled. "Then why do you wake me?"

"It's the Bluetooth," Palnatoke said. "He and all his ships are gone."

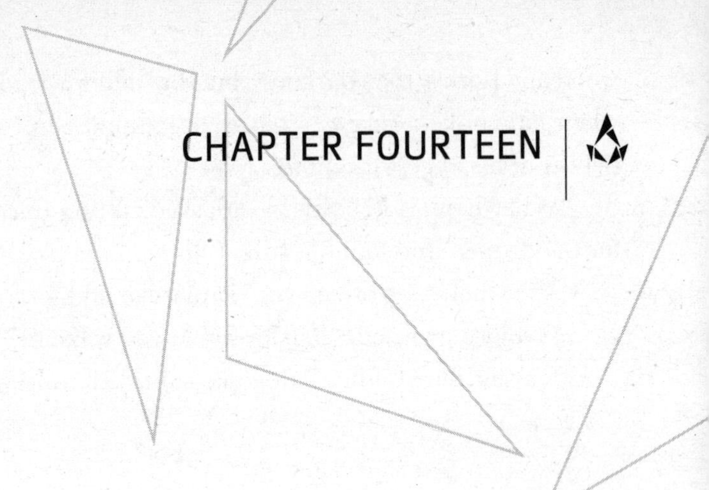

CHAPTER FOURTEEN

The dying caveman looked up at them with dull, watery eyes. Owen didn't know if he was technically a caveman, but that was what he looked like. He wore leather and fur, and no fabrics of any kind that Owen could see. His dark brown skin appeared almost corrugated, with black dirt deep in the folds and wrinkles, and he had pieces of straw in his long gray hair and beard.

"Can we help you?" Owen asked. "Are you hurt? Or sick?"

"You ask complicated questions," the man said.

They didn't seem complicated to Owen. He looked at Grace, and she gave a little shrug.

"You cannot prevent my death, if that is what you are asking," the man said. "After all this time, I have come to the end of my wanderings."

"What is your name?" Natalya asked.

"My name? I left that behind me on the Path many years ago. I had no use for it, and it only weighed me down."

His Dog seemed to have relaxed now that it had brought help to its master. It lay down next to him with a sigh and placed its heavy head in his lap, its yellow eyes rolling upward every few moments to look at its master's face.

"Does your dog have a name?" Owen asked.

"Oh, she is not mine."

Owen frowned. "But I thought—"

"She is not mine any more, nor any less, than I am hers." The stranger looked down and smiled, revealing a mouth of gray and missing teeth. He smoothed the fur over the Dog's broad head and scratched behind one of her ears. The Dog closed her eyes. "I suppose you could call her something if you like," the stranger said. "I just call her Dog. We've been together down the darkest of roads, and the most beautiful of roads, too."

"You're a traveler?" Natalya said.

The stranger seemed to think about that for a moment. "I think a traveler has a destination in mind. A place to arrive. I have had neither."

"So you just, like, wander around?" Owen said.

"I do." The stranger nodded, and then he wagged his finger at Owen, smiling again. "Yes, I am a Wanderer." He looked down at his Dog again, still scratching her ear, and his smile faded away. "Soon I shall wander where she cannot go."

"Are you sure you're dying?" Grace asked. "Maybe you—"

"I can't feel my legs," he said. Then he held up his right hand and flexed his fingers in and out of a fist. "I'm cold most everywhere else. I feel the life going out of me into the ground. Into this stone behind me. Into this hill."

"I'm sorry," Grace said.

"What for?" he asked. "I have beheld wonders and horrors and beautiful, everyday things. I have spent my life asking questions. Sometimes I found the answers, and sometimes I found more questions, and every so often, when I was very fortunate, I found the truth." He looked down at his Dog again. "There is only one question left for me to ask. But before that, a favor."

"A favor of us?" Owen said. "Is that why your Dog brought us here?"

"No. She is a Dog. She brought you here because she's worried about me. She knows that something is wrong, and she hopes you'll fix it. But now that you are here, yes, I have a favor to ask you."

"What can we do for you?" Grace said.

The Wanderer cleared his throat, and he paused. "After I am gone, will you find her a new companion?"

Owen had almost expected that, and he looked down at the Dog. One of her paws twitched, and her lip rippled, and he realized she had already fallen asleep, completely oblivious to what the Wanderer was saying about her. She was with him in that moment, which was all that mattered, and she was content. Owen smiled at her, but it was a sad smile. After her companion was gone, she wouldn't understand. She would be confused and all alone. In pain. And that wasn't fair.

"We'd really like to help," Natalya said. "But we don't . . . um, know anyone here."

"I see." The Wanderer scratched at his eyebrow with one of his thumbs, the nail chipped and worn down. "I . . . I worry what will happen to her."

A tightness gathered in Owen's throat, but he swallowed it down and said, "We'll take her."

Natalya and Grace looked over at him.

Owen knew this was only a simulation, and Monroe would say the Dog was a symbol, not a pet, but it didn't feel that way to him. He knew what she was about to face, and he couldn't leave her to do it alone. "We'll take her with us," he said. "We'll look after her until we find her a home."

"Thank you." The Wanderer closed his eyes again, and leaned his head back against the stone. "Thank you."

"You're welcome," Owen said.

"Not far from here," the Wanderer said, "there is a Crossroads. I think you will find someone for my Dog there, if you wait long enough."

"We'll go there," Owen said. "We'll find someone."

Grace and Natalya hadn't objected to this plan, but Owen could tell they felt unsure about it. They didn't smile and they didn't nod. Truthfully, Owen felt unsure about it, too. If they took this Dog and spent time waiting at the Crossroads, wherever that was, that would mean less time spent searching for the Summit and the key to this simulation. Less time figuring out how it could help them stop Isaiah.

The Wanderer leaned forward and laid his chest over the Dog in his lap, embracing her huge head. She woke suddenly and sat up, alert. Then she reached her nose toward his face, sniffing, and lapped his chin once with her tongue. She whined.

"You know," he said, exhaling. "You can smell it."

She rose to her four feet and stepped closer, licking his face again, insistently, urgently, his cheeks, his forehead, his nose, his lips. He closed his eyes and let her. Then he dug the fingers of both hands into the scruff around her neck and pulled her close, touching his forehead to hers.

"I know," he whispered. Then he leaned back against the stone, and looked up into the sky. "It is snowing. I will ask my question now."

But it wasn't snowing. It wasn't even cold. Owen looked up.

And then it was snowing.

Delicate white flecks found their easy way down from an ashen sky, and some of them touched Owen's face with their icy edges. The Dog whined again. Owen looked down, and he could tell the Wanderer had died. His body was empty. The Dog licked his lifeless face, waited and whined, and licked, and whined. She looked up at Owen, as if desperate for him to do something, and then she looked back at the Wanderer, who had left her. The snow gathered on her coat, white against her dark fur, and now she barked, sounding frantic, but not at anything, or anyone. Out of confusion and fear.

Grace looked at the Wanderer's body. "I know he's not real, and he didn't really die. But it's still hard."

"I'm not sure I know what real means anymore," Natalya said. "When the—"

The Dog let out a sound like a moan as she lay down next to her dead companion, placing her head in his lap as she had been doing only moments before.

"Poor thing," Grace said.

"Now you see why I couldn't leave her behind," Owen said. "You want to talk about what's real? For me, if it feels real, it's real. And I feel for that Dog."

"So do we," Natalya said.

The snow now fell heavily, and within moments white drifts

had gathered around the body of the Wanderer, slowly burying him with the Dog mourning at his side. Owen looked through the opening of the stone ring, and noticed that it didn't seem to be snowing elsewhere. Just the top of the hill, where the temperature had fallen quickly and suddenly.

"I think we should get back to the Path," Natalya said.

Owen agreed, and he called to the Dog, "Come, girl."

She didn't move. Didn't even look up.

Owen stepped closer to her, and tapped his leg. "Girl, come."

He saw her ears move, angling toward him, so he knew she was listening to him and just choosing to ignore him. With her size, he was still afraid to approach her, but he realized he would have to if he wanted to convince her to come with him. So he moved closer, one step at a time, watching her reaction to his presence.

"Be careful," Grace said. "I was just reading about a Norse god who got his hand bitten off by a wolf."

"Thanks, Grace, that's a great story," Owen said, taking another step.

"I'm just saying—"

The Dog growled, and if Owen had heard that sound while he was on a hike, he would have assumed it was a bear or a wolf. He would have taken off running, and he wouldn't have had a choice about it. That growl shook his bones. But instead of running from that hilltop, he stopped where he was and held his ground. The Dog turned her head slightly toward him, watching him with one eye, but she wasn't showing her teeth and the growling had stopped as he had halted. He slowly lowered himself to the snow where he was and sat down.

"What are you doing?" Natalya whisper-shouted. "Owen, come away."

"You guys go ahead," Owen said without taking his eyes from the Dog. "We'll catch up."

"Are you for real right now?" Grace asked. "You want us to leave you alone? In this simulation? With that thing?"

"She's just scared," Owen said. The Dog had started to pant, even though she was lying in the snow. "I'm just going to sit here for a while and see if she'll calm down."

"We don't have time for that," Natalya said with a bit of chatter in her teeth from the cold. "And I think that Dog can take care of itself just fine."

"That's not the point," Owen said. "And I told you guys to go ahead without me."

"I guess it's a good thing I came in here," Grace said. "Natalya needs someone with sense in their head."

"Owen," Natalya said, "stop and think about this. Think about where you are. Think about the risks."

Owen knew the risks, and knew he sounded ridiculous, but it didn't feel that way. This seemed important, and real, and he wasn't ready to give up. The snow had nearly buried the Wanderer's legs, with just the tops of his leather leggings poking through. The snow collecting on the Dog's fur had turned clear and icy around the edges.

"I'm serious, you guys," Owen said. "Just go. I'll be fine."

"It's freezing," Grace said.

"I'll be fine. I'm not leaving her."

Natalya shook her head, and then shrugged. "Whatever. Okay, fine." She turned to Grace. "Let's go, I guess."

"Guess so," Grace said.

They turned to leave, but Owen kept his eyes on the Dog, waiting. He wasn't sure what he was waiting for, but he waited.

The snow beneath him started to melt and soak into his clothes, and the cold finally got to him. He brought his arms in close to his chest, and pulled his legs up so that he was almost sitting in a fetal position. Over time, the falling snow clung to his eyelashes, and he felt its weight on his head and shoulders. When he shook like a dog to throw it off, the actual Dog raised her head and watched him. He imagined her judging his technique.

"I'm not good at that, am I?" he said.

The Dog laid her head back down, and she whimpered.

"I'm sorry," Owen said. Then he looked over his shoulder to make sure Natalya and Grace were gone. "I lost someone, too. It didn't make any sense to me. It still doesn't. I didn't even get to say good-bye, so you're lucky you got to have that." He rocked his body to try to warm himself with some movement. "But you can't just lie down. You have to keep going. That's what he would have wanted you to do."

The Dog looked at him as he talked, and then she yawned with a little whine, showing all of her many sharp teeth.

"Come, girl." He patted the snow-covered ground next to him, leaving an impression behind.

She watched him, but didn't move.

"Will you come?" He patted it again. "Come."

The Dog looked at the spot Owen had indicated, and he felt certain she understood exactly what he wanted. But still she stayed where she was. He'd begun to doubt whether she would ever voluntarily leave the Wanderer's side. He certainly couldn't pull her away, even if she decided not to hurt him as he tried. She was just too big.

Owen shivered now in a way he couldn't control. Violent convulsions seized his muscles and held them tight. It would still be easy enough for him to walk, or crawl, out of the stone ring, to escape the snow into the warm sunlight. But he refused to do that. Even if it meant he froze to death right here in this spot and desynchronized, he wouldn't leave the Dog. She had to know. She had to know that you can lose someone who means everything to you, and still keep going.

Besides, if she was devoted enough to stay by her companion, he could stay by her. So he stayed and stayed, hoping that if he did freeze to death in this simulation, it wouldn't do any permanent damage to his mind.

By now the snow had covered the Wanderer's legs and reached his waist. As for the Dog, Owen could still see the ridgeline of her back, as well as her neck and her head, but everything else lay buried.

He didn't know how long he had been there. He was trying to figure it out by watching the rate of the falling snow as it piled up, but before he got there his thoughts collapsed in a jumble and he lost track. He grew sleepy, and he'd read enough books and watched enough TV to know that was a sign of hypothermia. But he didn't care. He had made up his mind about staying until the end, and maybe going to sleep would make desynchronization easier.

That thought felt appealing. Simple.

Sleep.

"I . . . admire your . . . devotion," he said to the Dog. Then he flopped onto his back in the snow, staring up into the dancing sky. "Devotion," he said again, thinking that word was important, but he couldn't remember how or why. He closed his eyes, and he felt himself drifting up into the sky like a snowflake that gravity couldn't catch.

Higher he went.

Farther.

He could get lost up here in all the nothing. Just a speck floating away and—

Something hot branded his cheek. Something molten in the icy cold that burned him back into his body. He felt a gentle prodding, from his head to his knees. He felt something tugging on him, and heard a tearing sound, and then something jerked his whole body under his armpits, dragging him through and over the snow. He felt it sliding beneath him, its divots and swells, and he heard rough breathing in his ear.

It was the Dog.

As his mind came back down from the sky, he became aware of light falling against his eyelids, a warm wind across his skin, and the whisper of grass beneath him. When his body came to rest, he opened his eyes, squinting, and saw the head of the Dog directly above him. She looked down at him, panting, and then bent closer to lick his face.

"Okay, okay," he said, raising his hands to keep her at bay. "Good girl."

She backed away and stood there wagging her tail. Then she barked.

"I'm getting up," Owen said. But every part of him hurt as it thawed out, and it took him a while just to sit up, and even longer to struggle to his feet. His hair and clothing were soaking wet, and his favorite T-shirt hung loose and torn over his shoulder where the Dog had apparently used her teeth to pull him.

She had seen him collapse, and she had saved him.

And there he was on the hillside, a little unsteady, looking down at the Path below, while a dense bank of fog smothered the stone circle just above him. The Dog sat beside him, and Owen reached over to scratch behind her ear in the way he had seen the Wanderer do. Her fur was wet and cold with melted snow, and she smelled like any dog would, except maybe worse.

"Thank you," he said. "I want you to know that wasn't my plan. But if someone asks, I'm going to say that it was."

From his vantage, he could see the course of the Path as it wound away through the white rock bluffs and green hills. He scanned along it, but couldn't see any sign of Grace or Natalya. Off in the distance, he wasn't sure how far, it appeared that another road intersected with the Path, forming a crossroads.

"That must be it," he said, looking over at the Dog. "That's where we'll find you a new companion. Come, girl." He took a few slow and heavy steps down the hillside.

But she didn't follow him.

He looked back, and so did she, staring at the shroud of fog. She had saved Owen, but that didn't mean she was ready to leave her Wanderer behind. She whined and shifted weight on her paws, almost taking a few steps in place.

Owen sighed. He had nearly frozen to death for her. If that wasn't enough for the Dog to follow him, he didn't know what else he could do. Natalya and Grace were up ahead somewhere, and it might be possible to catch up to them. He still didn't want to leave the Dog, but now that she seemed to have broken out of her grief, at least enough to leave the Wanderer's side, he felt better about it than he had before.

"Come!" he called, one more time, putting as much command into his voice as he could, and then he turned away from her. He decided he would not look back. He would simply walk down the hill. She would either follow him or she wouldn't.

He was halfway down the hill before she barked. He kept going, slow and steady, without looking back. A few paces on, she barked again, and still he kept walking. But her next bark sounded closer. A few moments later, she barked directly behind him, and then she loped up alongside him, panting.

He looked over at her. "Good Dog."

She still appeared uneasy, walking with her head down, occasionally glancing back at the hill, but she kept pace with him until he reached the safety of the Path and set off in the direction they'd been traveling before. Hopefully, Grace and Natalya hadn't made it too far ahead of him.

CHAPTER FIFTEEN

It was difficult to be certain in the darkness, but it appeared that every Dane ship had broken away from Styrbjörn's fleet and now rowed back the way they had come. David and Östen marveled at how well Thorvald's strategy had worked. All the labor hewing and placing stakes in the Fyriswater had been rewarded, and Styrbjörn's army had now been greatly reduced before the fighting had even begun.

"Now our work begins in earnest," Thorvald said to his company. "But from this night it will be bladework."

There were thirty of them gathered around the skald, men he had chosen from among those gathered under the *ledung*. Östen had been the first, followed by Alferth and Olof, and from there they had moved from camp to camp across the Fyrisfield, taking with them only the strongest and fiercest they could find.

It had also been important to Thorvald that all of them were Svear and men of the land.

"In the coming days and weeks," Thorvald now said, "you may find your sense of honor challenged, for we will not meet Styrbjörn in the open. Not yet. We will strike, and then we will vanish, and then we will strike again. I have kept our number few, because we are not the axe and shield. We will be the knife in Styrbjörn's back, and it is very likely that many of us will not return to our homes. If you want no part of that, you may leave now and return to Uppsala. I will not hold it against any of you."

None moved to leave, but that did not surprise Östen.

Thorvald had proven to be a strange man, but a capable one. He was not large, but he was incredibly strong, and though he was a skald, he possessed a warrior's spirit. He also possessed a cunning mind the like of which Östen had never encountered.

"Rest for an hour," Thorvald said. "Styrbjörn marches tomorrow, and we must be well ahead of him."

"What if he orders the Jomsvikings to clear the river instead?" Alferth asked.

"He won't," Thorvald said. "Especially now that the Bluetooth has abandoned him. His rage will not sit still long enough to clear the river."

The skald had been right about Styrbjörn up to now. Östen trusted him in this, and moved to find a bed place and take what sleep he could. They had made no fire, and would leave no sign behind, nothing to betray their presence to the Jomsvikings. Olof and Alferth followed him, the three of them having formed a loose bond, and as they settled into their cloaks, Alferth spoke with a voice as low to the ground as a shadow.

"I don't like this."

"I'd prefer a fire as well," Olof said.

"No," Alferth said. "I don't like all this sneaking about. I'm not a thief or a murderer. When I kill, it is in plain view of the gods."

"You could have left just now," Olof said. "Why didn't you?"

"Because then I would have looked like a coward."

"Then you made your choice," Östen said. "The greater dishonor now would be to fail in it."

"Why are you here?" Alferth asked Östen. "We've all heard your name. This work does not seem fitting of your reputation."

The thread tied around Östen's wrist had somehow survived the previous day's labor in the water and mud, and though it was now crusty and soiled, it held fast. "And what reputation do I have?" Östen asked.

Alferth said nothing. He seemed caught in a net that Östen had not meant to cast, afraid to answer in a way that would offend.

Östen decided to let his friend escape. "I once fought for my glory and honor," he said. "But now I fight for my family and my farm, and I will defend them in whatever way brings victory to Eric."

"I respect you for that," Alferth said. "But Odin calls up the slain from the battlefield, not from the darkness and obscurity of ambush."

"My farm is not large," Östen said. "But it is mine, and Eric has never envied it. He has been fair in all his dealings with the landowners. Olof's land sits next to mine, and he also knows this to be true."

Olof nodded.

Östen continued. "Eric's brother was not so honorable. The assassin who poisoned him did a service to the Svear. If Styrbjörn returns, I fear he will take after his father, and we will return to the old ways." He paused. "If bladework in Thorvald's company means I give up my seat in Valhalla, it is so my family will keep our land when I am gone."

Alferth said nothing, but he nodded deeply.

In the quiet that followed, David felt pride in his ancestor, but also confusion. How could Östen stand so strongly for freedom, but have a thrall at home working on the same farm he fought to defend? It was a confusion that could desynchronize David if left unchecked, so he went back to what he had decided earlier. He didn't need to justify or agree with Östen to understand him.

"What is that?" Olof asked, a new, reddish glow against his face.

Östen looked southward toward its source, where great flames had erupted along the shore of Mälaren. From this vantage and distance, it was difficult to see what burned, but that close to the water's edge there was only one thing it could be.

"By Odin's beard," Alferth said.

"He burns his ships," Olof said.

Alferth sounded ready to laugh in disbelief. "He's a madman."

"No," Östen said. "The Jomsvikings covenant never to retreat from a battle. With this act, Styrbjörn has insured they keep their oath better than Harald Bluetooth kept his."

Olof nodded in agreement. "They will be more determined now."

Alferth grunted. "And I won't sleep now."

But Östen lay back down and closed his eyes. This changed nothing for Thorvald's company. The Jomsvikings would be a fearsome enemy whether Styrbjörn burned their ships or not.

Better to take what rest could be had, while it could be had. He closed his eyes, and not long after that, David entered a fragmented dream space within the simulation.

You are doing well, Victoria said.

"Thanks," he said. "How's Grace doing?"

She's fine. Monroe actually just let me know she's in the simulation with Natalya and Owen.

"Oh." David had imagined Grace waiting outside the Animus this whole time, watching for him to mess up in case she needed to step in again. He didn't know if he felt better or worse knowing she wasn't there. Maybe both.

I also heard from Griffin and Javier. You might be interested to know that Thorvald is Javier's ancestor.

"That's Javier?"

No, remember? Javier is in a separate simulation. But he is experiencing some of the same events you are from a difference perspective.

"We'll have to compare notes later."

Yes. In the meantime, I believe your ancestor is waking up.

David returned to Östen's conscious mind as Thorvald roused him, and even though David looked at the skald a bit differently now, he did nothing different about it. Östen sat up, wishing for another hour of sleep before they marched, but in the next moment he discovered it wasn't yet time for the company to depart, and that everyone else still rested.

"What is it?" he asked Thorvald.

"There is a task I must complete," he said. "I am leaving you in command."

"Is your task a solitary one?"

"It is."

"And you're going now?"

"I am."

Östen nodded. He did not want to ask what the task might be, preferring not to enter that far into Thorvald's purposes. But there were other, necessary questions. "What should we do in your absence?"

"Take the company north," he said. "When you reach the Mirkwood, I want you to lay traps."

"We can't trap an entire army," Östen said.

"Of course not. You will simply lay enough traps, in enough places, to slow the army down. If Styrbjörn's men are searching the trees for signs of danger, they're taking their mind from their march."

"I see." Östen thought about his own experience fighting. "If we injure one man in two dozen, that should—"

"Kill," Thorvald said. "Not injure. You must kill one man in twenty."

"That will be difficult."

"Not with this." Thorvald pulled a small bundle of oilskin out of his pouch, which he carefully unwrapped to reveal a fine bottle of glass filled with a viscous pale liquid. "This poison is extremely potent. A few drops will kill a man." Thorvald looked up at Östen. "Though perhaps not a man of your size."

"How should I administer this poison?"

"It will kill quickly if eaten or it gets into a wound. So lay your traps to injure, and this will do the rest. It can still kill if it touches the skin, but more slowly. Also, water won't destroy it, but whatever you apply it to must be dry." He rewrapped the bundle and handed it to Östen. "I suggest you wear gloves when you handle it, and then take care with those gloves."

"I understand," Östen said, tucking the bundle away.

"If your task is well done, the Jomsvikings will make camp for the night in the forest, to tend their poisoned brothers. You and the company will use the cover of darkness to harry them in their sleep. Strike from the trees, deliver a blow—a killing blow if you can—and then vanish. Offer them no respite."

This plan was not only cunning, but merciless.

"I'll find you when my task is complete," Thorvald said. "But if I should fail, continue north to the Fyrisfield with as many as yet live."

Östen nodded.

"Farewell." Thorvald pulled a hood over his head, concealing much of his face, and he turned to leave. But he had only an axe at his belt and nothing else.

"Where are your weapons and shield?" Östen asked.

"I have all that I need for my task," Thorvald said, and then he was gone.

Östen woke Olof and Alferth, and the three of them got the company under way, racing north much faster than Styrbjörn's army could march. Not long after sunrise, they reached the southern edge of the Mirkwood that lay between them and the Fyrisfield. Its expanse of towering spruce and pine stretched east and west far enough that Styrbjörn would have no choice but to march through it.

Olof organized their company into smaller parties, and then sent them off in all directions to lay snares and traps among the ferns, brush, and moss-covered stones. They armed their traps with thorns and splinters of wood. Östen went around to each of them and applied a few drops of the poison to the barbs and sharp points, and when he had finished, the company hurried on a good distance and did the same again. In this way they proceeded north, turning the forest as they went into a place where death might be waiting around every tree and at every step.

Östen worried about the many farms and villages the Mirkwood touched. The poison would kill a Svear out gathering wood or berries as easily as a Jomsviking. But the people of the countryside knew of Styrbjörn's coming, and Östen could only hope they had already sought refuge elsewhere.

Toward afternoon, the company stopped to take some food and rest near a marshy meadow on the Fyriswater. The flowers growing there reminded Östen of his daughters, who would plait each other's hair with them.

"Styrbjörn must have entered the Mirkwood by now," Olof said. "Which means the unluckiest of his men are already dying."

"Let us hope," Östen said. But he realized they needed to know for certain if, and how well, their strategy had succeeded, especially if they were to attack the enemy camp that night as Thorvald had ordered. "I will go back to see where they are," Östen said. "The rest of you remain here."

"Be careful you don't get poisoned by one of our own traps," Alferth said.

Östen nodded, and then he left the company, heading south into the woods. He traveled as quickly as he could, leaping over fallen trees and streams, using the brush and terrain as cover to keep himself hidden. The traps he had just poisoned were still held in his mind, so he was able to avoid them easily enough. But the farther he went, the slower he had to go, to make sure he didn't end up a casualty of Thorvald's cunning.

As evening approached, Östen finally heard something up ahead. He ducked behind the wide trunk of a tree, listening and waiting.

They were men's voices. The Jomsvikings. They called to one another through the trees as they moved through the forest, sometimes shouting that they'd found another snare and rendered it harmless, and the way was clear. But sometimes one of them would cry out in alarm and pain, and Östen counted each of those as a death.

The enemy's ranks moved slowly, as Thorvald had predicted they would, allowing Östen to stay ahead of them, and hidden. But he prayed to the gods that the Jomsvikings would at least reach the end of the snares and traps before making their camp. It would not be wise for Östen and the company to go raiding at night through poisoned woods. A short while later, the gods answered him, and the Jomsvikings halted their march in safe territory.

Östen returned to the meadow where he had left the other men, and after reporting the location of the enemy encampment and what he had observed, Olof again assisted by dividing the company. Then, when night had fallen completely in the Mirkwood, Östen gathered them all to give them their orders.

"Let none of you think you fight for your honor," he said. "In this night's bladework, you are nameless. You are an apparition. You appear from the forest, you strike, and then you vanish. Our purpose is to leave confusion and fear behind us. This is what Thorvald ordered."

"Thorvald isn't here," said Alferth. "And I am not a thief in the night."

Östen marked him with a nod, but continued. "If you tarry, if you think to stay and look your enemy in the eye to watch the life go out of him, I hope your honor will comfort you in your death."

Alferth folded his arms, appearing unsatisfied, but Östen

could not force him to understand. Each man had to fight in his own way.

"Return here while the sky is still black," Olof said, at Östen's side. "We leave at the first sign of blue."

"Pray to the god you favor," Östen said. "Then do the work of trolls."

The company disbanded, and each party stalked away into the night. Östen led three men, including Alferth, along the Fyriswater toward the western side of the Jomsviking camp. The night gave them little guidance, save the stars reflected in the water, but soon they smelled wood smoke and spied the yellow flicker of firelight off in the trees. They crept forward, slowly and silently, and chose the nearest of the fire rings. Each man drew his weapon, whether axe, sword, or knife, and at Östen's whispered command, they charged.

The trees flew by, nothing more than black stripes as the fire grew nearer and brighter. Östen kept his eyes from looking directly at the light, and focused instead on his target, a man sitting on a small rock, his knees up near his chest.

When Östen burst from the trees, some of the Jomsvikings looked up in surprise. But that's all they had time to do. From the edge of his sight, he glimpsed Alferth and the other two men rush in behind him. Östen neared his target, caught him hard in the head with his axe, and continued running, quickly leaving the circle of light behind him. The first shout of alarm didn't rise up until he and his three men had regrouped some distance away, watching the results of their sortie from the darkness.

Östen's man lay dead or unconscious. So did another. Two more men staggered, while several of their companions rushed to give them aid, shouting and cursing. Two men ran from the fire, deeper into the encampment, no doubt to raise the wider alarm.

Then they heard similar, distant shouts from other points in the forest, and Östen could feel the chaos rising.

"Again," he whispered.

Then he and his men rushed the same fire ring. The Jomsvikings were better prepared for this attack, and they clashed with them, but only briefly. Östen struck one of the men already injured, and he went down. Then Östen returned to the forest.

His companions were slower to join him, but eventually freed themselves of the firelight. Östen now saw three Jomsvikings on the ground, with two more wounded.

"Let's move on," Östen said.

They crept back toward the river and followed it a little farther south, until a different campfire came within view. Most of the men around it looked to be wounded already, lying on the ground or leaning against the trees.

"Poisoned," Alferth said.

Östen nodded. "Focus your attacks on the men tending them."

Then he led the first charge, and the second, until the fire ring held more dying men than it had but moments before.

The sounds that echoed throughout the forest spoke of disarray in the Jomsviking encampment. But that tide would turn soon. Order would be restored. Östen sensed they only had one more raid before their enemy would be too prepared, and he selected another campfire farther south than the last.

They charged, and Östen's axe bit hard to both sides as he

tore through the enemy ring. He had crossed the border, back into darkness, when a towering figure burst into the red light. He was a young man, a strong man, and he exceeded even Östen in height.

"Styrbjörn!" someone roared.

On the other side of the camp, Alferth leapt out of the forest, and Östen could do nothing to stop him.

The fight lasted only a few moments. Styrbjörn laid waste to Alferth's body. Östen had never seen such ferocity and power, and he could only hope that a passing Valkyrie had witnessed the end of his friend. The other two warriors in Östen's party then rushed from the shadows, apparently thinking to attack Styrbjörn simultaneously. An arrow struck one of them in the neck, shot by an archer just emerging into the light. Styrbjörn dealt with the second man as easily as he had Alferth.

As Östen watched this, his rage grew into something almost unstoppable. He tightened his grip on his axe and prepared to charge. But then he felt the gentle tug of the thread around his wrist. He could barely see it in the darkness, but it was still there. His talisman calling him home. He thought of his wife and his children, and he lowered his axe, even as Styrbjörn stood over the bodies of three good men of Thorvald's company. Men who—

"You out there!" Styrbjörn bellowed. "I know you can hear me! I demand safe passage to Uppsala! If these attacks continue, I will burn this forest to the ground! If you set any more snares, I will burn this forest to the ground! If I cannot rule this land, know that I will surely destroy it!"

It wasn't a ruse. Östen knew he spoke the truth, and thought again of the farms that touched the Mirkwood, the fields and pastures that grew near it, and the lives that depended on it. What would a victory over Styrbjörn matter if the Svear lost the very land they were trying to protect?

They would have to let Styrbjörn pass.

But Östen vowed in that moment that one day he would exact revenge on Styrbjörn. One day, he would show Styrbjörn the true meaning of ferocity.

CHAPTER SIXTEEN

Javier knew the giant was David and Grace's ancestor. But they weren't sharing the simulation, so it wasn't David or Grace that he spoke to as he gave his orders and left the company in Östen's very large hands.

Styrbjörn's ships burned in the distance, even as those of Harald Bluetooth retreated back to Jutland. Thorvald could guess what had happened to bring both events about, but he needed to know for certain, if he was to plan his next moves. It would be easy enough to sneak into the Jomsviking camp and kill Styrbjörn, but that might be a mistake if the Jomsvikings felt honor bound to exact revenge, to say nothing of the nobles who secretly supported Styrbjörn's return. Before Thorvald acted, he had to know more.

He raced through the night, using his Odin-sight to leap

through trees and over boulders in the darkness, until he drew near the Jomsviking encampment on the shores of Mälaren. He became one of the shadows and moved inward undetected, listening and watching, until he reached the council ring of Styrbjörn. Then Thorvald became as silent as a burial mound, and he observed the discussion from a position near enough to smell the salt cod on the breath of the Jomsvikings.

Styrbjörn had grown mighty since his banishment, standing taller now than Östen or any man Thorvald had seen before. At his right hand, an older warrior spoke to those gathered.

"I supported the burning. It was necessary after the Bluetooth's betrayal, lest any of our number believe we might also retreat."

"And what of the oaths we swore to you, Palnatoke?" one of the Jomsvikings said. "Years ago, when we entered Jomsborg. Do you remember? Were those not enough? Are the years we have fought for you not enough to convince you of our honor?"

Thorvald knew the name and reputation of Palnatoke, but had never seen the man. Though gray-haired and battle worn, he remained straight-backed and broad shouldered, plainly still a deadly fighter, and able to command.

"I don't doubt the honor of anyone standing here, Gorm," Palnatoke said. "But our numbers have grown, and the youngest among us are not so steadfast—"

"Then name the men you doubt." The man Gorm spread his arms. "Let this be in the open."

"I will not," Palnatoke said. "Now is a time for unity."

Gorm looked hard at Styrbjörn. "And yet you divide us by allowing this Svear to burn our ships."

"This Svear?" Styrbjörn smiled, but it held no amusement. "Have you forgotten my name?"

"No," Gorm said. "But I do not honor your name, and that is no secret. We follow Palnatoke."

"Then cease talk of this matter," Palnatoke said. "It is done. We were sworn to this before the burning of the ships, and we are sworn to it now. We march for Uppsala, and—"

"Palnatoke!"

All of them turned as two warriors approached the council ring, a woman marching between them. She wore ring armor, and carried a sword at her side, marking her a shield-maiden. Though not a beauty, she was closer to pretty than she was to plain, with blond hair braided tight across her head, and a fine nose. Javier smiled inwardly at Thorvald's attraction to her.

"Who is this?" Styrbjörn asked.

"A Dane woman," said one of the men escorting her. "Her countrymen left her be—"

"I was not left behind," the woman said, her voice steady and clear. "I chose to stay."

Styrbjörn stepped toward her, slowly, until he stood almost directly over her. "Why?"

The shield-maiden kept her eyes forward, and if Styrbjörn's presence intimidated her, she did not show it. "Because I will no longer fight for a raven starver. My devotion to Harald has broken."

"And your oaths?" Styrbjörn asked.

Now she looked up at him. "I swore no oath to him."

"No oath?" Palnatoke said.

"He never asked it of me," she said. "He assumed my loyalty."

"That was his mistake, it seems," Styrbjörn said. "Will you swear yourself to me?"

She cocked her head and looked Styrbjörn over, from his boots to his brow. "If you are an honorable man, I will swear to you when you are king, and not before."

Styrbjörn laughed. "What is your name?"

"Thyra," she said.

"Harald mentioned you," Styrbjörn said. "He offered you to me when—"

"I was not his to offer," she said. "As you would have learned had you accepted."

Styrbjörn laughed again. "Of that, I have no doubt. But now we must discuss what is to become of you. You stayed when your king and countrymen left. Do you intend to fight with us?"

"I intend to fulfill the oath Harald swore to you." She looked around the council ring. "I want it known that there is honor among the Danes."

"No," Palnatoke said. "The Jomsvikings permit no women."

"You permit no women into Jomsborg," Styrbjörn said. "We are not in Jomsborg. Besides which, you permitted my sister."

"Your sister was the daughter of a king," Palnatoke said.

"So am I," Thyra said.

Her declaration surprised Thorvald, which Javier knew to be an unusual experience for his ancestor. The others in the council ring appeared equally stunned, and for several breaths no one spoke except for the fire.

"Who?" Styrbjörn finally asked. "Whose daughter are you?"

"I am Harald's daughter," she said. "My mother was a shield-maiden."

"Has he claimed you?" Styrbjörn asked.

"No," she said. "And I have never desired it."

"Why not?" Palnatoke asked.

She turned to him and scowled. "Would you?"

Now Palnatoke joined Styrbjörn in laughing, and both men agreed that Thyra would join their ranks, and as a member of the council ring, which soon resumed its discussions of their coming march. Thorvald listened until the council separated, and then he crept out of the encampment to a distance from which he could observe the army's movements and plan his own.

It seemed that while Styrbjörn did not have the loyalty of the Jomsvikings, he had Palnatoke's sworn support. That meant Thorvald had to consider what Palnatoke would do if Styrbjörn were assassinated. Given the reputation of the Jomsvikings, their honor-bound answer would be swift and brutal. Thorvald decided that killing Styrbjörn was not yet an option, and turned his strategies instead to robbing Styrbjörn of support, to weaken him.

When the sun appeared, the Jomsvikings massed into ranks and marched. Thorvald stayed ahead of them, and later in the day, when they reached the Mirkwood, he went up into the trees.

Östen had already led the company through, and Thorvald could see the hidden snares they'd left behind. He waited to see if the first of the Jomsvikings would detect the traps, but they didn't, and when those traps sprang, men took injuries. If Östen had used the poison as ordered, those men would die later that day, but until then, the Jomsvikings felt no significant threat, and even laughed at the Svear and their harmless snares.

Thorvald leapt and climbed from tree to tree, staying high above the ground, following the army, and it was some time before the injured Jomsvikings noticed the first effects of the poison. By that time, many more of them had been tainted, and upon realizing the danger surrounding them, Styrbjörn ordered his force to a halt.

His roaring reached Thorvald high in the trees. He assailed the cowardice of his enemies for using poison, his immense anger entirely by Thorvald's design. It was poison that had slain Styrbjörn's father, after all, and the memory of that would infect Styrbjörn's judgment as surely as this new poison infected his men.

The simplicity and effectiveness of his ancestor's plan awed Javier. One cunning Assassin with thirty men had managed to halt an army. Perhaps not for long, but the Jomsvikings had lost all momentum.

After that, they slowed their advance through the Mirkwood, pausing to check for traps and disarm them, but they didn't find them all, and each subsequent injury only increased Styrbjörn's rage. Eventually, some of the men who had already been poisoned volunteered to lead the way through the forest, to spare their companions. Their deaths already assured, they felt no fear, and Thorvald admired their sacrifice and loyalty.

By evening, the number of dying men, and the danger of moving through the poisoned woods in the darkness, forced the Jomsvikings to halt their march and make camp for the night. Thorvald watched them settle down among the trees, the smoke from their dozens of fires blooming from the ground like fog. He climbed along the branches and trunks until he found Styrbjörn's fire. Thyra sat with him, while Palnatoke went through the camp to check on his men and bid farewell to those soon to die.

Thorvald settled to wait for nightfall, which fell with suddenness in the Mirkwood. He heard no laughter from around the campfires. The Jomsvikings seemed to have been hardened by their casualties, and they didn't know what to do with an enemy they couldn't see. They would be looking for a place to lay their anger.

Thorvald planned to give them one, and Javier found himself marveling once again.

A few hours went by, and after midnight, when those who could sleep had done so, and those who couldn't sat lost in their fears, a distant cry of alarm went up to the north. Östen and the company had begun their raiding.

Styrbjörn and Palnatoke leapt to their feet.

A second cry sounded from a different direction, and then a third. After the fourth and fifth, it seemed the entire camp had fallen under attack, and Thorvald smiled from his hidden perch.

"Fall back and form ranks!" Palnatoke shouted to those who could hear him. But many could not.

Styrbjörn's anger had reached the point of madness. Thyra tried to steady him, and warn him against rashness, but he ignored her and took up his sword and his axe. Then he charged away into the darkness, blindly seeking an enemy.

"That fool will get himself poisoned," Palnatoke said.

"Should I go after him?" Thyra asked.

"No," Palnatoke said. "He won't listen to you. It falls to me."

He gave a few last orders, and then ran after Styrbjörn. Thorvald left his position and gave pursuit, free-running through the trees in a gradual descent to the ground, waiting for the right moment.

Palnatoke ran in and out of firelight, asking the men in each camp which way Styrbjörn had gone. When he entered a place thick enough with darkness, between campfires, Thorvald fell upon him from above.

But somehow, the old Jomsviking deflected his hidden blade and threw him off. Thorvald rolled away and jumped to his feet, his axe and blade ready.

Palnatoke strode toward him, his sword drawn. "A hood to hide your face? Are you ashamed of what you do?"

"I bring the judgment of the Norns," Thorvald said. "You've reached the end of your skein."

"Try and cut it, then."

Palnatoke seized the first strike, but Thorvald ducked the blow and came around with his axe. Palnatoke leapt clear, more agile than he seemed, and the two men circled each other. Palnatoke could easily have called for help from one of the nearby camps, but he didn't. He couldn't. Not without risking loss of respect from his men.

The Jomsviking lunged, but it was a feint, and it almost threw Thorvald off-balance. He blocked Palnatoke's sword with his hidden blade, barely, taking some of the impact with his forearm, and managed a swing of his axe while Palnatoke had come in close.

The older man grunted, but the wound was shallow. It may have broken a rib, but not likely. "What is that little knife you wear?" he asked.

"You will find out soon enough," Thorvald said.

Palnatoke came again, harder, and without deception, trusting in his strength. Thorvald dodged and parried, waiting for an opening, but his opponent offered none. It was time for him to seize the attack. He ran for a tree, and then sped up its trunk, using his weight to launch himself over the Jomsviking, catching his enemy's shoulder with the beard of his axe.

The metal bit hard, and pulled Palnatoke backward. The Jomsviking planted his feet and spun, tearing his shoulder free of the axe, but Thorvald was ready with his hidden blade, and with a lightning thrust, the old man died, almost instantly.

Now Thorvald ran west through the forest, toward the river, using the sounds of battle and his Odin-sight to guide him. He heard a man shout Styrbjörn's name, and he raced toward it, arriving in time to see Alferth fall. Two more of his company followed and died. It would take a dozen of the finest warriors to stop Styrbjörn in his rage.

Another figure moved nearby, and Thorvald saw Östen not far from him in the trees. For a moment, he worried the giant would also charge Styrbjörn, but he didn't, and Thorvald crept toward him.

"You out there!" Styrbjörn shouted. "I know you can hear me! I demand safe passage to Uppsala! If these attacks continue, I will burn this forest to the ground! If you set any more snares or traps, I will burn this forest to the ground! If I cannot rule this land, know that I will surely destroy it!"

Thorvald considered attacking Styrbjörn then. But in the moment he took to plan his approach, he noticed a strange weapon at his enemy's side. A dagger. Its shape seemed familiar, but also sinister, and it stopped him. He heard Torgny's words counseling wisdom, and patience, and cunning.

Javier saw the dagger for what it was, the first glimpse they'd had of it in this simulation. Their race against Isaiah and Sean had now begun in a way it hadn't a moment before. The urgency had changed.

Östen moved toward the river, and Thorvald decided to follow him, leaving Styrbjörn for another day. When they had reached a distant enough point from the encampment, he called out, and Östen turned.

"Thorvald?"

"Follow me," he said, and led Östen to the Fyriswater. "Is anyone else with you?"

"They fell against Styrbjörn."

"Their fate is theirs. Where is the rest of the company?"

Östen pointed north, and Thorvald let him lead the way along the cold boiling of the river. Gradually, the sounds of chaos in the encampment faded until they couldn't be heard. They traveled then through the tranquility of a night forest, accompanied by the scent of pine and the lonely call of an owl.

Eventually, they reached a meadow on the river, where they found eleven men waiting. Thorvald had hoped to find more, but Östen informed him they had given the company until blue light to return. So they waited.

"Did you complete your task?" Östen asked him.

Thorvald nodded. "I completed a task."

"What task?" asked one of the others.

Thorvald considered how to answer, and decided to give these warriors the truth. Their labor over the last days had earned his trust. "I slew Palnatoke, leader of the Jomsvikings."

The men went quiet.

"Why him?" Östen asked. "Why not Styrbjörn?"

"Have my strategies failed?" Thorvald asked. "Have I led you astray?"

"No."

"Then let that be your answer."

"That is not enough," Östen said. "Good men are dead."

Thorvald sighed. He knew Östen meant no challenge, nor dishonor, and he did not want to return either to him. "Styrbjörn has no army without the Jomsvikings," he said. "But they are not sworn to him. They follow Palnatoke. So in killing Palnatoke, I have severed what bond they had to Styrbjörn. Come morning, they will blame him for the death of their captain, and we shall see if he has an army after that."

Östen nodded. "And what of Styrbjörn's threat to burn down the forest?"

"We must take him at his word," Thorvald said. "We must—"

A group of five warriors emerged into the meadow. Among them was Olof, who reported that the Jomsvikings had rallied and killed or captured many of their company. He did not believe that any more would come, and as the sky had finally turned, it was time to march. Thorvald ordered the men north, to Fyrisfield, their number reduced by half.

"So we'll let Styrbjörn pass through the forest?" Östen asked.

"We will," Thorvald said. "If the Jomsvikings follow him, we will let them pass through the forest as well."

"Have we reduced their number by enough?" Olof asked.

"No," Thorvald said. "But do not lose heart. I left designs for a war machine with the Lawspeaker. If Styrbjörn brings the Jomsvikings to Fyrisfield, death awaits them there."

CHAPTER SEVENTEEN 

Natalya kept looking back down the Path as she and Grace walked slowly away from the hill. She expected to see Owen running up behind them at any moment, possibly with the enormous and frightening Dog. But she saw nothing, even after walking for quite some time, and she began to worry that they had made a mistake leaving him behind.

"I thought he would be right behind us," she said.

Grace looked back. "He was smitten with that Dog."

"I don't think it was about the Dog," Natalya said. "And I think maybe the Dog is a part of what we're supposed to be doing in here."

Grace stopped walking. "You think we should've stayed with him?"

"I don't know. I think that was something he had to do. Or

something he thought he had to do. He wasn't going to leave, I know that, and I'm not sure he wanted us there."

"So what should we do now? We could stop and wait for him, I guess."

"We could." Natalya looked forward down the Path, and she glimpsed a small boulder directly ahead. "Let's keep going for now. I want to see what's up there."

Grace nodded, and they resumed their slow walk through a countryside of white rock ledges and green turf. The landscape felt both old and new at the same time, like a deep layer of earth that had only recently risen to the surface. The Path remained very much the same as it had been, and the wind smelled faintly of sage.

As they got closer to the stone, which turned out to be about the size and shape of a pig, Natalya saw that it sat by a crossroads where a dirt trail intersected their Path. Carvings covered the stone with geometric shapes, spirals, and figures of men and extinct animals. This was the Crossroads the Wanderer had mentioned, where Owen could find a new owner for the Dog.

"Maybe we should wait here," Grace said.

"I was just thinking the same thing," Natalya said, and they sat down on the boulder back-to-back.

Even though this part of the simulation felt more open than the Forest had, it had its own kind of boundary. The endless rolling hills closed them in and kept the horizon from view. It still felt to Natalya that if she left the Path she could get lost here, maybe forever, just on a larger scale.

But in another way, this simulation didn't bother her like the others had. Here she was herself, and she could make her choices. She wasn't trapped by the past and what her ancestors had done.

She didn't have to shoot anyone with a bow or fight anyone. She was glad to be here instead of the Viking memories.

"How is David doing?" she asked Grace.

"He had a hard time synchronizing, but he's got it now."

"Is that why you came in here?"

"Well, I wasn't going to sit around doing nothing," she said. "After I read—" She stopped and looked away.

Natalya wondered what she had just left unsaid, and she was about to ask when Grace pointed down the road.

"Is that Owen?"

Natalya looked, and it was. He trudged along the Path with the Dog trotting next to him.

"Looks like he's brought man's best friend with him," Grace said.

"I'd rather have that Dog as a friend than an enemy," Natalya said.

She got up from the stone and walked a few steps toward Owen to wait for him on the Path. As he got closer, she noticed his shirt was torn at his shoulder, but she saw no blood, and he didn't seem to be injured. He smiled at them.

"You okay?" she called.

He nodded. "I'm good." Then he pointed behind Natalya. "You guys found the Crossroads."

"We did," Grace said, rising from the stone.

Owen reached them, and the Dog stepped forward, wagging her tail, looking back and forth between Natalya and Grace. She was panting a little, with her tongue hanging out, and except for her size, she seemed like any other dog. But her size was enough to keep Natalya uncomfortable.

"You got her to come with you," Grace said.

"Yeah." Owen looked over at her. "I had to trick her into saving my life, but she came. Thanks for waiting for us, by the way."

"Saving your life?" Natalya asked.

"It's a long story," he said. "Between me and her."

"So what happens with her now?" Grace said.

Owen looked in each of the Crossroads' four directions and then he shrugged. "I guess we wait here for someone to come along?"

Grace sighed and took her seat back on the stone.

"You guys can go on if you want," Owen said. "Really."

"No," Natalya said. "We'll wait. I think this is a part of what we're supposed to do."

"It is," Owen said. "I realized this is the devotion part of the Path."

That made sense to Natalya. She took a seat on the stone next to Grace, and Owen sat down on the grass next to them. The Dog lay down on the warm red stones of the Path and went to sleep; while they waited, the three of them talked. Not about the simulation, or about the Trident, or about the Templars and Assassins. They talked about stuff that was unimportant, but still mattered, like the shows they liked to watch, and the music they hated, and stupid things they'd seen online. They talked about home, and their pets, and what they had been doing before all this started. But then at once they all fell silent.

Owen pulled up a handful of grass and threw it into the breeze. "It seems kind of ridiculous to think about going back to regular life, doesn't it?"

Grace nodded. "Yes, it does."

"But I hope we can," Natalya said. "I'll take my ridiculous, regular life any day."

"Sure," Grace said. "But regular life for some people is—"

"There's someone coming," Owen said, rising to his feet.

Natalya turned. A figure approached them, following the dirt trail as it rose and fell with the swells of grass and land. The three of them said nothing as they waited, all previous conversation lost. The stranger appeared tall and broad, and more details took shape with each of his steps. Unlike the Wanderer, he wore wool and woven fabrics studded with beads and shells, but like the Wanderer, he had dark bronze skin. His black hair and beard were long, but trimmed and clean and free of gray. He walked with a spear tipped with black iron, and when he reached them his eyes went straight to the Dog.

"That is a fine creature," he said without any greeting, his firm voice an imposing wall that kept others back. "Is she yours?"

Natalya wasn't sure what to think of this man, any more than she had known what to think of the Wanderer. Did these archetypes represent people? Actual people who had lived? Or were they ideas of people, just symbols in the same way the Serpent had been a symbol?

"She is mine," Owen said.

The stranger nodded. "I would have use for a Dog like that."

"Use?" Owen asked, stepping between the stranger and the Dog.

"Yes, of course," the stranger said. "To watch my tower. It stands on the other side of that hill. No one would dare steal my gold or my silver with that Dog standing guard. I assure you, she will be treated well. I'll feed her the finest meat from my table, and I'll give her a bed of clean straw."

Owen studied the man for several moments. Then he shook his head. "I don't think so."

"Perhaps you misunderstand me," the stranger said. "I will buy her from you. I will pay you handsomely—"

"No," Owen said. "She's not for sale."

The stranger scowled, and Natalya noted his spear again as he stared hard at the Dog. It almost seemed that he was thinking about taking her by force, but Natalya hoped he wasn't that stupid. Who would try to steal a Dog big enough to think of the thief as dinner? In the end, he lifted his glare from the Dog to Owen, and then he went on his way down the trail, presumably toward his tower, without saying another word.

"What happens now?" Grace asked after he was gone.

Owen sat down next to the Dog, and she rolled over to show him her belly, which he gave a rub. "We keep waiting," he said.

So that's what they did, talking very little now. Natalya wasn't sure how long they waited, because the time of day didn't seem to change here. They might have even sat there for hours, but the sun stayed where it was overhead, just a bit off center. An afternoon sun. But eventually, another stranger did approach, this time coming from the direction the previous man had left. As this new traveler drew near, Natalya saw that he was a short, round man with a balding head, wearing woolen clothes, and walking with one of those shepherd's staffs that had a crook at the end of it.

"Greetings!" he called, smiling, his voice creaking with the softness of an old leather coat. "It is a fine day to be on the Path, is it not?"

"Yeah," Owen said. "A fine day."

Natalya already liked this man more than the last, but it was Owen who had to like him enough to give him the Dog as a companion.

"But it's always a fine day on the Path, isn't it?" the man said as he came to a halt near them. Then he leaned on his staff, and he puffed air out of his red cheeks. "What are you three doing here at the Crossroads?"

"Waiting," Owen said.

"Waiting?" the man asked. "What for?"

"Just waiting," Owen said.

"Nonsense. We're always waiting for something." He looked at Natalya with strange blue-and-gold eyes. "Perhaps you have all been waiting for me, and I've been waiting for you."

"Why would we be waiting for you?" Grace asked.

"I wouldn't know," he said. "You haven't told me."

"That's because we're not waiting for you," Owen said.

"And yet there you are, and here I am." The stranger then looked down at the Dog, and his eyes opened wide, as if he hadn't noticed her until that moment. "What a magnificent animal," he said. "A breathtaking piece of creation." He looked up. "Does she belong to one of you?"

Owen nodded. "She is mine."

"That is wonderful." The man gave Owen a tight-lipped, knowing smile, as if Owen had done something he should be very proud of. "Wonderful, indeed." He looked down at the Dog again, and his smile loosened. "How very fortunate you are. I am not so fortunate, for I am in need of a dog."

"Need?" Owen said.

Natalya thought that was an improvement on having a "use" for the Dog.

"I need a dog to guard my herds and my flocks," the man said. "There are dangers at the borders of my pastures, and I can't protect my animals every moment of every day."

“What dangers?” Grace asked.

“Great dangers,” the man said. “Unspeakable dangers.”

“So you need a guard dog?” Owen said.

“Yes,” the man said. “But not only a guard dog. There are times when a lamb or a calf goes missing. They might get frightened by a storm, or they might fall into a ravine. I need a dog to herd them. To keep them together and safe.” He looked down. “A dog such as this.”

Owen scratched his chin without taking his eyes off the man, and seemed to be giving this offer more thought than he’d given the first, which surprised Natalya. If they were looking for someone to take the place of the Wanderer, a shepherd and a rich guy were both the wrong choice. Neither life would be like the one the Dog had known.

But Owen turned to Natalya and Grace and asked, “What do you guys think?”

Not only had Natalya thought this was Owen’s thing to decide, the decision seemed fairly obvious.

“I don’t think this is the guy we’re waiting for,” Grace said.

“But what about my herds?” the man asked. “My flocks are in danger. Why are you taking away the very thing they need for their safety?”

“He’s not taking anything away,” Grace said. “To take something away from you, it has to be yours to begin with.”

The man’s eyes narrowed at Grace for a moment, and with a *tsk* he turned toward Owen. “My need is true and just. I believe you surely see that.”

“Maybe I do,” Owen said. “But I’m still not giving you my Dog.”

“I see.” The man turned away from them, shaking his head.

He took a few steps, and then he looked back. "I do hope you will not be punished for this choice."

"Punished how?" Grace asked.

"When the Path brings you misfortune, you will know." Then he continued walking and was soon lost over the rise of a hill.

Grace snorted. "I'm pretty sure this Path is guaranteed to bring misfortune at some point, but it won't be because of that guy."

Owen sat down next to the Dog, and she inched closer to him and placed her huge head in his lap, just as she had done with the Wanderer. Owen scratched behind her ears, and then he looked at the rip in his shirt. "I think you guys better make the decision the next time, though."

"Why?" Grace asked.

"I don't think I can choose." He stroked the top of the Dog's head, and she closed her eyes. "I don't want her to go to anyone, really. But she has to. I know we're supposed to find her a new companion."

If the Dog had really saved Owen's life, at least inside the simulation, Natalya could understand why he would find it hard to part with her. But Natalya had also come to believe he was right. This was something they were supposed to do. An objective in the collective unconscious.

"Sure," she said. "We can decide."

Grace agreed, and they both sat down near Owen in the grass while the Dog slept, and more time passed without any way to mark it. Natalya found herself growing drowsy in the endless afternoon as she listened to the slow and easy breathing of the Dog.

"This feels like . . ." Natalya tried to find the words. "I don't know. Like we're in a story. A folktale or something."

"Maybe we kind of are," Owen said.

When a third figure appeared in the distance, Natalya almost didn't notice, but Grace did, and then Natalya stood up too fast. She shook her head to clear the rush and focused on the newcomer, who she could already tell was a woman.

The stranger strode with slow purpose on the Path ahead of them, and the narrow foot of her plain walking staff echoed against the stones. She was young, of the same dark complexion as the other travelers they had met, with curly bronze hair pulled back into several braids. She wore leather clothing, and as she walked, her gaze roamed the land and the sky.

"Hello!" Natalya called to her.

"Hello," the woman said. But she stopped short of them, near the stone, and she walked around it. She seemed to be studying the carvings that covered its surface, perhaps reading them, and Natalya wondered if the rock was some kind of signpost.

"Are you lost?" Natalya asked.

The woman paused as though she had to think about the meaning of the word. "No. I'm where I want to be. Why do you ask?"

"I saw you looking at the rock, and I just thought . . ." But Natalya didn't know how to finish that sentence.

The woman looked at the stone again, appearing confused. Then she asked Natalya, "Are *you* lost?"

Next to Owen, the Dog had woken up and taken note of the new stranger, her ears perked forward as she sniffed the air.

"We know where we are," Natalya said. "But we don't know where we're going."

"If that's what it means to be lost," the woman said, "then I think we all are."

"Where are you traveling?" Owen asked.

"Where?" The woman frowned, as if once again she didn't understand the question. "I'm just walking the Path."

"So you're wandering," Grace said, eyeing Owen, and Natalya knew in that moment they were all thinking the same thing.

"Yes, wandering," the woman said. "That's a fair word for it, I suppose."

That was when Owen finally got to his feet, the Dog at his side, as if he meant to say something. But he didn't, and several silent moments went by. The woman's gaze traveled from the three of them to the Path beyond the Crossroads, and she seemed ready to move on. But she hadn't even asked about the Dog, and it seemed as though Owen was just going to let her walk away.

"We, uh—we met a Wanderer, like you," Natalya said. "This Dog was his."

The woman regarded the Dog then and smiled. "She's beautiful."

And that was all she said.

Owen just nodded.

"Have you ever traveled with a dog?" Grace asked.

The woman shook her head. "No. I don't have a use for a dog. Or a need for one."

Natalya had no idea where to go from that.

"I'll be moving along now," the woman said.

But she couldn't leave yet. Not without the Dog, unless Owen planned to bring her with them for the rest of the simulation. He might actually want that, but Natalya still believed they had to do this before they could move on. She just didn't know how.

The stranger walked between Natalya and Grace, bowing her head, and then passed very close to the Dog, who looked up and wagged her tail for the woman.

She smiled at the Dog, and then said, "Safe journey to you—"

"Wait," Owen said.

The woman turned toward him.

"Do you—do you want my Dog?"

The woman craned her neck toward Owen. "Do I want her?"

"I can't keep her," he said, and cleared his throat. "She was really only mine until I could find a companion for her. And you're the only person we've met who I think should have her. She belongs with you."

The woman stood there for a moment, frowning, and it definitely seemed as if she wanted to say no. But then her frown relaxed, and she took a step toward the Dog with her hand outstretched, braver than Natalya had been. She first let the Dog smell her fist, and then her fingers and palm, and then she scratched the Dog's fur under her chin. That's when the Dog sat down and leaned against her with a contented sigh, thumping her tail, and the woman raised an eyebrow.

"She really is beautiful," the stranger said.

"Will you have her?" Owen asked. "I want to give her to you."

The woman paused, and then replied, "Yes. I think I want to have her with me."

Owen let out a very long sigh. "Thank you."

Natalya believed that to be the right decision, and the right end to this story they had just played out. But it meant that Owen now had to say good-bye.

He did so by digging his fingers into her scruff, and scratching behind her ears. The Dog seemed to be smiling at him, and she licked his face until it was time for her to leave with the new Wanderer, who had already started down the Path.

"Come!" she called.

The Dog glanced at her, and then looked at Owen.

"Go on," he said. "It's okay."

The Dog cocked her head almost sideways.

"It's okay." Owen waved his hand. "Go."

"Come!" the Wanderer called again.

This time, the Dog took a few hesitant steps toward her new companion, yellow eyes still fixed on Owen, and she whined.

"You're a good girl," he said. "Keep going."

"Come!"

The Dog took a few more steps, and a few more, until she finally broke into a trot that caught her up to the Wanderer, who reached out and gave her neck a pat. After that, the two of them grew smaller together on the Path, until they were gone.

Owen just stood there, watching, even after there wasn't anything more to see. He didn't say anything. He kept his face blank, and his eyes stayed dry. Natalya didn't know what to do for him, because she still didn't understand what had happened with the Dog, probably in the same way Owen didn't understand what had happened with the Serpent.

"You ready to go?" Grace finally asked.

He nodded. "Sure."

"You okay?" Natalya asked.

He shrugged. "The important thing is we just took care of devotion. If that voice at the beginning of all of this was right, that just leaves faith."

Grace walked up to him and gave him a hug. He seemed surprised for a moment, but then he hugged her back and said, "Thanks."

Then the three of them faced the Path ahead, but as they took their first steps beyond the Crossroads, the sky darkened, diving from gloaming to cold midnight with a suddenness that made Natalya gasp. It was as if someone had doused the sun.

"What is it with this place?" Grace asked.

"Maybe that guy was right," Owen said. "Maybe we're being punished."

CHAPTER EIGHTEEN

Grace shivered as they walked, the sky bright with stars that looked wrong, even though she couldn't say how. She didn't know a lot about the night sky, but she could identify a few constellations her dad used to point out when she was younger, and here in the simulation, those shapes seemed askew. The moon shone with a cold radiance, like a flashlight through ice, illuminating the Path ahead of them.

Their surroundings had changed, too. The easy rolling hills had steepened and sharpened, and the white stone bluffs had become gray rock cliffs. The Path found its way by staying low, changing course with the basins and the bottoms of the ravines.

Owen hadn't said much since giving the Dog to the new Wanderer, but that didn't surprise Grace.

"I had a cat when I was about three," she said. "His name was Brando."

"Brando?" Natalya asked.

"After Marlon Brando," Grace said. "My dad picked it. He said the cat walked around like the Godfather, which he did. But I loved that cat." She could still remember the way his nose tickled her ears when he was purring.

"What happened to him?" Owen asked.

"We found out David was allergic. So Brando had to go."

"Oh," Owen said.

"My parents got this older couple to take him. The day they came to pick him up, I locked myself in the bathroom. My parents were trying to get me to say good-bye, but I thought if I refused to say good-bye then Brando couldn't leave. When I came out of the bathroom, he was gone."

She hadn't thought about that cat or the day he'd left in years. But watching Owen say good-bye to the Dog had brought it all back, and she was surprised that it still hurt.

"I'm sorry," Owen said.

"Thanks," Grace said. "And just so you know, that Dog didn't even compare to Brando."

Natalya chuckled and Owen laughed.

"Since I never met Brando, I'll have to take your word for it," he said.

"Trust me," she said.

A moment later, Natalya shivered and looked up at the sky. "It's so clear. You can see the Milky Way."

The three of them walked in silence after that, staring up at the stars. The Path stretched on and on, without any branches, forks, or crossroads. It had only two directions: forward and backward, and they had already seen what lay behind them. Unless they wanted to hold still and do nothing, they had only one choice, so they kept moving.

The night seemed as timeless as the day had felt. The moon and stars held fixed positions, and they looked closer to the ground than they were supposed to be, as if they could dress themselves in clouds. The three of them walked and walked and gradually the high hills closed in, becoming a canyon with sheer walls to either side that pinched off their view of the sky near the horizon. But something up there caught Grace's eye.

She thought it was a star at first, but it was very bright, and she realized it was too bright. It sat in the wedge formed by the canyon, and as they walked closer to it, the light brightened, and Grace realized it wasn't in the sky at all. It sat at the top of a mountain.

"Is that the light you guys saw at the beginning?" she asked them.

"Maybe," Natalya said.

"I'd say that's probably the Summit, though," Owen added.

Grace glanced up at the rims of the canyon, projecting forward ahead of them, and assumed that was where the Path led.

"It's a long way away," Owen said.

But it turned out it wasn't. Their journey brought the mountain and its summit closer much more quickly than Grace had expected. Either the distance wasn't as great as it seemed, or they walked faster than she thought they did, or maybe it was just the odd way time ran here, because they soon reached the end of the canyon, where an enormous human figure loomed over them.

It had been painted or burned against a sheer rock face on the mountainside, a giant's simple shadow, without detail or gender. It stood at least a hundred feet tall, but maybe more. It was hard for Grace to gauge the distance from where she stood, and the darkness hid most of the mountain above. She also couldn't see the light at the Summit anymore.

"I hope that's not a self-portrait," Owen said.

Grace looked over her shoulder at the moon. "It seems like in this place, it could be."

"Where do we go?" Natalya asked. "The Path ends here."

Grace looked and saw that she was right. The Path stopped at the giant's feet. But to the figure's right, she noticed a narrow channel cut into the rock. It zigzagged up the mountain as high as she could see, and she guessed even higher than that.

"Hey, there's a rope over there." Natalya walked in a different direction than Grace was looking, toward the figure's left.

She and Owen followed her, and they did find a rope descending from the darkness. Next to it, someone had chiseled a very narrow, steep staircase. It climbed vertically, straight up the mountain, each stair no more than a few inches deep. It was practically a ladder. Grace felt queasy just looking at it.

"Do we have to climb this?" Owen asked.

"I think we do," Natalya said.

"Uh, there's a path over there." Grace pointed to the figure's right. "Not *the* Path, but a path. It might be safer than this way."

They crossed to the giant's other side and looked more closely at the path Grace had seen. It didn't have stairs, and was just a little over a foot wide, but not nearly as steep as the rope climb, because it switched back and forth.

"I don't like either of these," Owen said.

Grace agreed with him.

"I think we have to pick one of them," Natalya said.

Grace did not want to agree with that. She didn't like heights. She had never labeled it a phobia, but it was definitely a fear, one she had always thought healthy.

"Maybe there's another way?" she said, even though she knew there wasn't. The canyon stopped where the mountain began, enclosing them on three sides, and the only way out was up, or back.

"I don't see another way," Natalya said. "If we want to get up there, and that's clearly where we're supposed to go, we have to climb one of these."

Owen looked at the path, and then stared off to the right toward the rope. "I think I'm leaning toward Staircase of Doom over Trail of Death."

"Why?" Natalya asked.

"Look at this thing," he said, gesturing toward the path. "It's barely wide enough, and there isn't anything to stop you from falling. You're just on your own. At least with the rope, you have something to hold on to."

Natalya nodded. The two of them returned to the staircase, and Grace followed them, unsure whether she agreed.

"See?" Owen grabbed the rope. "You just hold on to this."

Grace looked up. "Yeah, but we don't know where that goes. We don't know what it's attached to, or how old it is. What if it snaps? Without that rope, you fall."

Owen looked up, and then he let go of the rope. "Good point."

"So that's what we have to decide," Natalya said. "Use the ladder and pray the rope holds, or take the path and hope we don't need the rope."

Grace still didn't like either option. It didn't even help to tell herself it was only a simulation. But it was a simulation that held unknown dangers, and she wasn't sure what falling to her death would mean in here. There were apparently some ways her brain just refused to compromise, and looking up at the path and the rope, she felt herself falling already. What if her mind couldn't recover from that?

"I'm taking the rope," Owen said.

"I think I am, too," Natalya said.

Grace did not think so. If she had to choose, she would choose the option where she didn't have to trust a mystery rope. The path told her everything it could, which wasn't much, but she hoped it would be enough.

"I'm going to take the path," she said.

The other two looked at her.

"Don't you think we should stick together?" Owen said.

"Maybe," Grace said. "So come on the path with me."

"I think the rope is safer," Owen said. Then he looked up. "Maybe we should ask the giant which one is best."

Grace believed for a very brief moment that might be possible, because why not? This was a simulation of the collective unconscious. Who knew what the rules were? But when she glanced up, the massive figure didn't move, or speak, or seem to notice them at all.

"I don't think we should split up," Natalya said. "I don't think I can use that path. I need something to hold on to."

The three of them looked at one another.

"Okay," Grace said. "So we hold on to each other, if we need to."

Owen and Natalya looked at each other, and when it seemed

that they'd come to some unspoken agreement, they both inhaled and nodded.

"Okay," Natalya said. "Okay, let's do this."

Grace sighed, and then made herself walk to the path. She knew that once they started up it, there would be no going back. They wouldn't be able to turn around, or climb down backward. They would achieve the Summit, or they would fall.

"I think I can," she whispered to herself, and Owen chuckled.

"So who goes first?" Natalya asked.

"I will," Grace said.

Otherwise, she worried she would lose her nerve. So she took the first step, and felt the grit of the mountain's stone beneath her shoe. She took another step. And another. And another. She leaned a bit toward the mountain, so that she could reach out with one of her hands if she needed to steady herself.

Natalya came behind her, followed by Owen. After Grace had taken a few dozen steps, she reached the first switchback, and she pivoted with the path, an inch at a time, until the mountain had moved to her other side, and for a moment she could see Natalya's and Owen's faces. They both looked grim, focused, and determined.

Grace took more steps, dozens of them, to the next switchback, where she changed direction again. She repeated this several times, and, with each fold in the trail, the climb up the path seemed to be getting easier. Even routine. But then she looked down.

Vertigo seized her gut and her head, nearly tipped her into open air, but she threw herself against the mountainside, her hands splayed against the ice-cold rock.

"Are you okay?" Natalya asked.

They had climbed very high. As high as the giant's shoulders, Grace guessed. The ground seemed very far below, the path little more than a red ribbon. The wind had picked up, too, and it was a freezing wind, with gusts that whispered in her ear that she would die.

"I'm okay," she said, clenching her teeth against the chatter of the cold and her fear.

She took several deep breaths, and then resumed her climb. One step, then another, and another. One switchback, then another, and another. She kept her eyes rigidly straight ahead, but every so often, she risked a quick backward glance, just to make sure Natalya and Owen were still there. Together, they made steady progress up the mountain, leaving the giant far below.

"Hey, guys," Owen said. "Look down."

"Owen," Grace said, "whatever energy my feet aren't using, I'm spending it trying *not* to look down."

"But the ground is gone," he said.

A moment later, Natalya said, "He's right."

Grace stopped. Then she very carefully lowered her eyes, and this time when she looked down, she saw nothing. The view below them had turned darker than the sky, and Grace stared into an abyss. She wasn't sure what would happen if she fell into it, but it looked as if the plummet might never end, and she would be trapped in her terror.

"How much farther is it?" Owen asked. "Can you guys see the top?"

Now Grace steadied herself with her hand and looked up. The sheer rock wall faded into the night, the Summit still hidden somewhere above it. "I can't see it," she said.

"Me neither," Natalya said.

Owen sighed. "Just making sure."

Grace resumed her careful climb, but not long after that, she felt the first twinges of fatigue in her thighs. Each step after that kindled a slow fire in her muscles, until they burned hot and red. But the top of the mountain remained out of sight, and she wondered for the first time whether she could even reach it. Not because of falling, but because it was just too high, and she physically couldn't do it.

"Is anyone else getting tired?" she said, breathing hard.

"I am," Natalya said.

"I'm slowing down," Owen said.

"Should we stop for a rest?" Grace asked.

The other two agreed, so they halted their climb and very carefully sat down on the path. Grace wedged herself into a position as securely as she could and faced the night sky above, and the abyss below, with her feet hanging over the edge. She was too tired to talk, and since Natalya and Owen didn't say anything, she figured they felt the same way. The three of them just sat there, resting their legs and catching their breath.

At first, it felt good, and reassuring. Her legs stopped quivering, her heartbeat slowed, and her breath came easier. But then the wind found her as it rushed up the mountainside, and it turned her to ice where she'd been sweating only moments before. It whispered to her again, turning her mind toward doubt, and she began to wonder.

What if there wasn't anything up there? What if that light they had seen at the Summit was some kind of optical illusion, and they climbed toward an empty promise? What if it didn't matter if the light was real, because they would never reach it? It was too high, and the path was too narrow, and they would fall before they ever got close to it.

At first, it seemed these thoughts came from within Grace, but she soon realized they called to her from the abyss as she stared down into the heart of it. It promised her open arms, and told her how easy it would be for her to simply push off from the ledge. Not much effort, and then she would need no effort at all. If they would never reach the Summit, or if they did, and they found nothing there, why make the climb at all? Why cling to an indifferent mountain that kept silent in the face of her struggles? The abyss heard her, asked nothing of her, and waited to receive her.

One little push. That's all it would take. Just lean a little, and then a little push with her hands—

Grace gasped and looked up. Thoughts of her brother wrenched her sight and her mind away from the abyss. The stars and moon hung low and gleaming, almost closer now that they had climbed so far. Natalya and Owen seemed lost in their own thoughts.

"Guys," she said.

They didn't respond.

"Guys, listen to me." She reached out and touched Natalya's arm. "We have to keep moving. If we sit here, we won't make it."

Natalya swung her head toward Grace slowly, as if anchored to the abyss. "I'm beginning to think we never were going to make it. This is impossible."

"No," Grace said. "No, you're wrong. That's not what you think, Natalya. You're the one who beat that Serpent, remember? You helped Owen find the Dog a new companion. We can make it."

"How do you know?" Owen asked. He'd been listening to them, apparently. "How do you know we can make it?"

Grace didn't have an answer for that question. She didn't know they would make it in the way Owen asked the question. But she believed they would make it because she had confidence in herself and in them.

"I just know," she said to Owen.

Natalya sighed and shook her head. "I think I'm done with this."

Grace saw her lean forward, and in the second that she saw it and realized what Natalya was about to do, she reached out her hand and grabbed Natalya's wrist.

"No!" she shouted.

But Natalya pushed herself off the ledge, and Grace braced herself as she held on.

Natalya dropped as far as she could until her wrist and her arm yanked her back around and into the mountain, almost pulling Grace over the side. But she lay down flat on the path, one arm hanging over the edge, and held on.

"Owen, help!" Grace shouted. She looked down into Natalya's open eyes and saw terror. Whatever had prompted her to jump, that spell had broken.

"Don't let go!" Natalya screamed.

"I won't," Grace said. But she couldn't hold on forever. "Owen!"

"I'm here!" He scrambled up and reached one of his hands over the edge to grab Natalya. "Okay," he said. "We've got you. We're going to pull you up."

"Hurry," Natalya said.

Grace looked at Owen. He gave a nod, and they pulled at the same time, lifting Natalya closer.

"Give me your other hand," Owen said, and as soon as Natalya raised it high enough, he seized it.

After that, Grace and Owen hauled her up, each grasping one of her hands, until Natalya was able to get a knee up on the ledge. A few moments later, all three of them sat on the path with their backs against the mountain. Natalya had her eyes shut tight, chest heaving.

Grace looked past her and scowled at Owen, breathing hard. "What took you so long?"

"I don't know." Owen shook his head and looked downward. "I don't know."

But Grace knew, and she wasn't really mad at Owen. She was just scared at what had almost happened.

"I'm sorry," Natalya said.

"It's okay," Grace said. "But we have to keep moving."

"Okay." Natalya opened her eyes and nodded. "Okay."

They rested just a few minutes longer, until they had caught their breath, and then they resumed their climb. The abyss was still down there, calling for Grace's surrender, but she refused to listen to it. She also still had doubts about what they would find at the Summit, and she continued to fear that they might fall before they reached it. But instead of dwelling on those questions, she focused on the placement of each foot with every step she took.

Hundreds of steps.

Maybe thousands.

It became a kind of meditation in which she became lost, and up they went, until suddenly, without warning, there was no more cliff wall beneath her hand. Grace pried her gaze from the path and looked around, blinking. They weren't at the Summit of the mountain, but they had reached the top of its sheer face, and the path led them away from the abyss, along a glacier that glowed blue in the moonlight. Its ice filled a gap between two ridges, and atop the taller of them, Grace saw the light, though it wasn't as bright as it had looked from the canyon. But it was there.

It emanated from within a huge, shimmering dome that rose out of the mountain like half of a giant pearl. Beneath it, cut right into the rock, was a doorway, and their path led them directly toward it. Grace continued to lead the way, and they walked the glacier's edge until they stood beneath the entrance.

"I think this is the end," Owen said.

"It has to be," Grace said. "There's nowhere else to go."

With that, they went inside.

CHAPTER NINETEEN

Even though Sean held the Piece of Eden in his hand, it felt impossibly far away, separated from him by hundreds of years and who knew how many miles. And the hands weren't actually his. They were Styrbjörn's, and the Viking still didn't understand what he had. But he carried the dagger around, and he studied it, because he suspected it possessed some significance that went beyond its holiness as a relic of the Christ.

"You should destroy that dagger or throw it away," Gorm said. "It offends the gods."

"And how do you know what offends the gods?" Styrbjörn asked. "Do you speak for them? Are you now a seer?"

They sat in the morning light around the embers and ashes of the previous night's fire, still camped in the Mirkwood. Thyra kept to Styrbjörn's right hand, while Gorm and several other Jomsviking captains faced him angrily from across the ring. They had not yet spoken of retreat, but Styrbjörn knew he was in danger of losing his army. He could feel it. If but one of the captains suggested they abandon their purpose, the rest would follow.

"Palnatoke is dead," Gorm said. "I do not need to be a seer to know the gods are displeased."

Styrbjörn raised his voice. "Palnatoke knew the length of his skein was set. He faced the end of his life in battle, instead of hiding in Jomsborg. This dagger had nothing to do with it, and you take away the honor of his death by claiming otherwise."

Gorm said nothing in reply.

"I honor Palnatoke," Styrbjörn continued. "And so I will seek vengeance for his death. But I wonder what you will do."

"Do not pretend you fight Eric for Palnatoke's honor," Gorm said. "You fight for—"

"I do not think he pretends," Thyra said. "I think Styrbjörn is as angry as you are at Palnatoke's death, just as he is angry at his uncle. Can he not fight for both? For his crown and also the honor of his sworn brother? If you speak against Styrbjörn, you speak against Palnatoke."

She forged her words with the calm and steady assurance of a blacksmith's hammer, and Gorm said nothing against them. The Jomsviking lowered his head under Thyra's gaze, as though she were a queen, rather than a shield-maiden. Styrbjörn was surprised at how quickly he had come to admire Thyra and value her presence at his side. But now was not the time to weigh it.

He pressed Gorm further. "I am still wondering what you

will do to honor Palnatoke. How you will fulfill the oath you swore not to retreat."

Gorm looked up. "We will fight. But know this, Styrbjörn. We fight for vengeance. We fight for our oaths and our honor. We do not fight for your crown."

Styrbjörn nodded. In the end, it did not matter why the Jomsvikings went to battle. It only mattered that they fought. "Prepare your men. We march for the Fyrisfield."

Gorm bowed his head, but there was no love or respect in it. Then he and his captains left the fire ring, and when they had gone, Styrbjörn turned to Thyra.

"Thank you for your counsel."

"I spoke only the truth," she said.

"I think you changed the tide of Gorm's mind."

"But not my father's, or he would still be here as well." She looked at the dagger Styrbjörn wore at his waist. "I'm amazed Harald left that behind."

Styrbjörn looked down at it, and Sean focused more intently on the memory's current, as he always did when the dagger became the focus of the simulation. "It seemed to be more than just a relic to him," Styrbjörn said.

"It always did. I've thought many times there must be power in it."

"What kind of power?"

She tipped her head sideways, looking up into the trees, and her green eyes captured sunlight. "I would say that it drew others to him. Enemies would leave his presence devoted to him. But only when he wore that dagger."

Sean knew exactly what she had observed. That was the

power of this prong of the Trident. But Styrbjörn still looked at the weapon with suspicion, even as he kept it at his side.

A short while later, the Jomsvikings stood ready with their spears, swords, axes, and shields. Those too injured or weak from poison remained behind, while the rest marched that day toward Uppsala. Styrbjörn led them through the forest, at the head of their army, to show them that there were no more poisoned snares, and none of Eric's warriors to harry them. They came within sight of the Fyrisfield in the later afternoon, where Styrbjörn expected to see Eric's army mustered on the plain.

But it lay empty.

No warriors. No encampment. Just an open expanse of grass and marsh.

"Where are your countrymen?" Gorm asked. "Surely Eric sent out the Bidding Stick."

"He must have gathered them north of here, at Uppsala," Styrbjörn said.

"Near the temple?" Gorm asked. "Why would he risk a battle there?"

"Perhaps he thinks the gods will save him," Styrbjörn said.

Before they entered the plain, they fanned out and formed ranks, and then Styrbjörn marched the Jomsvikings forth at the spear point of their wedge. They emerged from the Mirkwood beating a steady rhythm on their shields with their axes, like drums. They chanted and marched, sweeping northward. To the west, the Fyriswater flowed down into Mälaren, and to the east, the marshes lay dank and reedy. Ahead of them, the green land swelled and dipped like the loosened sail of a ship billowing in the wind. It had been years since Styrbjörn last walked here, the land of his fathers, where he ran as a boy. Years spent in exile, waiting to avenge his father's murder and claim his crown. At last his time had come. He could feel his rage and thirst for battle rising.

"What is that?" Thyra asked.

Styrbjörn looked at her. "What?"

"Listen," she said.

At first, he heard nothing over the sounds of the Jomsviking march. But then he felt a rumbling in the ground beneath his feet, and he heard distant thunder, though the sky was clear.

"Something is coming," she said. "Eric's army?"

"No," he said, listening. "It's something else."

He searched the horizon as the sound grew louder, and nearer. The Jomsvikings ceased their chanting and shield-beating to listen. They halted in their march at the base of a low, broad rise, and they waited, weapons ready.

"You're right," Thyra said. "That is no army."

"Whatever it is," Styrbjörn said, "we will kill it, or destroy it."

Thyra didn't nod, or agree. She simply looked at him with a blank expression he didn't understand, and then returned her attention to the plain. Styrbjörn tightened his grip on his axe, Randgríð, and then he smiled at what was about to begin.

A moment later, a huge beast appeared over the distant rise. It charged down toward them, bellowing, and at first Styrbjörn didn't understand what he was seeing: a solid, many-legged mass bristling with horns, spears, and swords that spread almost the width of the Jomsviking line. Then Styrbjörn realized it wasn't a single thing, but many, a herd of cattle hundreds of animals long and three or four deep. They had been yoked and tied together so that they moved as one, studded with weapons, a living war machine, unstoppable, meant to trample, crush, cut, and impale. Styrbjörn had never seen anything like it.

It was an army breaker.

Any warrior caught in its path would be maimed or killed, and Styrbjörn knew what was about to happen to the Jomsvikings. They couldn't retreat southward, because the cattle would run them down. If they fled to the east, the marsh would simply mire them. That left but one route of escape.

"To the river!" Styrbjörn ordered, waving his axe over his head, then blowing on his war horn.

The Jomsvikings heard him, then turned and raced west to get clear of the behemoth. Thyra ran with them, and when Styrbjörn was sure she would make it to safety, he turned and sped directly toward the oncoming storm. The Jomsvikings' eastern flank would not have time to get clear before the cattle slammed into their line. Styrbjörn had to find some way to break up the beasts.

They stampeded toward him with wide, rolling eyes, and frantic bellows, mindless with fear. He returned Randgríð to his belt as the distance between him and the war machine closed. When the cattle were but yards away, he launched himself into the air using all his strength, sailing high enough to clear the first spears and horns.

But as he came back down, a sword slashed his thigh, and he tumbled sideways onto the heaving shoulders of a bull. The beast threw him, and he nearly slipped through a gap between two oxen. His legs dangled among the pounding hooves, and the rushing ground snagged his heels, trying to pull him down the rest of the way to his death.

Styrbjörn grabbed on to a heavy yoke and hauled himself up, using the rest of the wooden framework for support. His thigh bled heavily, and he had only moments to act.

He pulled Randgríð from his belt and went to work hewing, splitting, and sundering the ropes and wood around him that made this herd into a weapon. Soon the thundering line of cattle fractured, and then it broke in two.

But that wasn't enough. Styrbjörn balanced and jumped along the surging backs of the animals to another joining, where his axe work made a second break.

The war machine now charged in thirds, the gaps between them widening, the remaining tethers weakening. At least some of the Jomsvikings could now make for the openings that Styrbjörn had made.

He turned and leapt from the rear of the war machine, landing in a hard roll behind it. Then he got to his feet and watched the cattle charging away from him toward his men, and a moment after that, the air shattered with the sound of impact. Shields tore, and men screamed, and metal rang. Some of the Jomsvikings made it safely through the gaps, but far too many went under, and they were spat out from under the cattle, broken and dying, as the machine rolled mindlessly onward.

Styrbjörn raced through the muddy, shredded turf toward his men, but before he reached them, he heard a new sound coming from the north, this one familiar. He turned and saw Eric's army charging down, coming to slay those that had survived the stampede.

"To me!" Styrbjörn bellowed, raising Randgríð, and he blew the command on his war horn. Then he turned to face Eric's army, and moments later, ranks of Jomsvikings formed around and behind him, among them Thyra and Gorm.

"Shield wall!" Styrbjörn ordered, blowing again on his horn.

"They outnumber us at least four to one," Gorm said.

Styrbjörn pointed to the west. "The sun will set soon. All we have to do is last. Today we show them how hard they have to work to kill us. Tomorrow we show them how hard we will work to kill them."

Around Styrbjörn, and in other pockets across the plain, those Jomsvikings who could still lift a shield fell back together, shoulder to shoulder, shields and spears outward. Thyra stood next to Styrbjörn, and she noticed his thigh.

"Is it bad?" she asked.

Though he felt blood pooling inside his boot, he said, "It is nothing."

She gave him a fierce and eager smile that surprised him, and which he returned.

Then Eric's army fell upon them.

It was close bladework after that, thrusting with spears and swords, pushing back against the enemy with their shields. But Eric's men were farmers and freemen summoned under the *ledung*, many of them inexperienced in battle, while the Jomsvikings were men sworn to raiding and war. For every blow one of Styrbjörn's took, they returned five on Eric's. Thyra proved herself skilled and deadly, and as the day wore itself out, the shield walls held, and as evening fell, Eric's army withdrew across the Fyrisfield to their camp.

The Jomsvikings gathered their wounded and their dead,

and returned to the Mirkwood, along the boundary of which they found the remains of the cattle war machine. Many of the animals had died upon impact with the trees, and those that hadn't appeared to have run deep into the woods. The men butchered several cows and ate beef that night, as much meat as their bellies could hold, and afterward, Gorm came to Styrbjörn at his fire.

"I wish to swear to you, Styrbjörn," the Jomsviking said. "I and all my brothers. We saw all that you did. Forgive me for doubting your honor."

"You are forgiven," Styrbjörn said as Thyra sat by and stitched the wound in his thigh.

Gorm continued. "They will sing songs about your feats this day, and tomorrow the Jomsvikings will fight and die by your side, to the last man if the gods will it. This is the oath we will take."

As Sean observed this memory flowing along, it struck him that Styrbjörn had acquired the unwavering loyalty of the Jomsvikings without using the power of the dagger.

"Oaths tomorrow," Styrbjörn said. "For now, there are wounded and dying warriors who need their captain. Go to them, Gorm, and you and I will talk again."

Gorm bowed his head, this time in sincere devotion, and left Styrbjörn's fire ring. After he had gone, Styrbjörn stared into the flames, into the deepest, hottest hollow among the logs and coals. He would need a strategy for the next day's fighting. Eric still had superior numbers, and he had yet to send his personal war band into battle.

"This wound was far worse than you let on," Thyra said.

"I said it was nothing. And that's what it was."

She shook her head, frowning.

"What are you thinking?" Styrbjörn asked.

"I am thinking that I would have you for my husband," she said.

He whipped his gaze toward her. The fire cast its light against her red cheeks, and into her hair and eyes. "Are you mocking me?" he asked.

"No," she said. "Why would you think so?"

He looked away from her, flustered and unsure of himself.

"Do you plan to marry?" she asked.

"I will marry," he said. "When I have avenged my father and claimed what is mine, I will marry."

She nodded, but with a slight frown. "You are the first man I have met who I think worthy to be my husband. And I think I am the first woman you have met worthy to be your wife."

She spoke with plain confidence, and she was right about the way he saw her, but he had kept those thoughts apart from the rest of his mind until he could properly consider them. Because this was not the time for those thoughts. He had a war to win, and an uncle to kill.

"I think we should wait to discuss this," he said.

"I don't think we should wait," she said. "I would marry you tonight."

"Tonight?" He stared at her then, shocked by her boldness, but also admiring of it. "Why tonight?"

"Because after tomorrow, you will be a king, and I don't want you or anyone to think I marry your crown. I don't marry Styrbjörn the Strong. Years from now, when our grandchildren sit at your feet, I want you to tell them of this night. You will tell them that I wanted you even in your exile. I wanted to marry Bjorn."

Styrbjörn liked hearing her say his true name, and had no wish to correct her. He regarded her for a long while, and she said nothing more, apparently intent on giving him time and space to think. It was true that he wanted to marry one day, and it was also true that he would want to marry Thyra above any woman he had ever met. But tonight? Must it be tonight?

When looked at from a certain angle, there seemed to be madness in her words. Yet from a different angle, she made more sense than anything else he had encountered in this mad world.

"In what way would you wish to marry?" he asked.

"In the old way," she said. "Witnessed by the gods."

"And what of the bride price? The traditions?"

"I don't care about any of that."

He nodded, and he gave it more thought, until he reached a decision that in fact he had already made without knowing it. "I will marry you tonight," he said. "But I must ask something of you that you will not like."

She smiled, and when he looked at her then, he decided with finality that she was beautiful.

"What?" she asked.

"I ask you not to fight tomorrow," he said. "You must leave the battlefield."

"What?" Her smile vanished. "No husband of mine would ask me—"

"I may die tomorrow," he said. It was the first time he had spoken those words to anyone, including himself. The only reason he considered them now was out of love, not for Thyra, though he believed he would love her, but for Gyrid, his sister. "I do not want to die," he said. "But the Norns have already cut my skein, and if I am to reach the end of it tomorrow, then I would ask you to bring word of me to my sister. She will be your sister, too, and I ask you to comfort her, and take my place at her side."

Thyra looked at him with the same blank expression he had seen earlier that day, and he wondered if he would ever learn to read it, and if so, how many years it would take.

"I know that I can't make you go," he said. "And I would not try. But I do ask it of you. Will you grant me this?"

Thyra didn't answer him for a very long time, but he knew better than to press her.

"I will," she finally said. "Though I didn't think I would."

He laughed. "Neither did I." He nodded toward the forest. "And now I have a shrine to build."

So they walked away from the camp together deeper into the Mirkwood, and soon they came upon a great boulder twice as tall as Styrbjörn. It bore a crack right down the middle of it, as though it were a frost giant's head that Thor had struck with his hammer, and they decided they would make their vows before it. Styrbjörn gathered pale stones in the twilight and piled them up against the boulder to make a shrine, and though they had no honey or grain, he placed a golden ring upon it. When it was complete, Styrbjörn gave his Ingelrii sword to Thyra, and vowed to be her husband, and to honor her above all others, and to let no one speak against her. Then she gave her sword to him and swore the same oaths, and thus they sealed their marriage before the god Frey, who was the father of all the kings of the Svear.

"Now the blood sacrifice," Styrbjörn said. "I will find us an animal—"

"No." Thyra looked at his belt. "We already have an offering that will please the gods."

Styrbjörn looked down, and then he pulled the Bluetooth's dagger from its sheath. He studied it for a moment, and then he placed it on the shrine, and dedicated the offering of the Christ relic to Thor. He asked for aid from the sky god in the coming battle. Then he shoved the dagger within the split in the boulder and he piled the stones up higher against it, to hide it from the view of passersby.

When that was complete, Styrbjörn and Thyra returned to the camp as husband and wife, leaving the dagger in its resting place. If it was still there, then Sean could easily find it.

"Isaiah," Sean said. "Can you hear me? Did you see that?"

Yes, Isaiah said. *Excellent work, Sean. Excellent.*

"Do you have the location?"

We do. I can pull you out of the Animus now. Styrbjörn's memories are about to end, at any rate.

"They are?" Though Sean had fulfilled the purpose of the simulation, he wasn't quite ready to leave his ancestor behind. "Why?"

It seems that Styrbjörn will shortly pass on his genetic memories, when he conceives a child with Thyra. We don't have DNA of his memories after tonight.

"So he didn't have any more children?"

No, of course not.

"Why of course not?"

I—I thought you knew, Isaiah said. *It is a matter of history that Styrbjörn died during the battle of Fyrisfield.*

CHAPTER TWENTY

Owen stood in a corridor unlike anything he had encountered in the simulation thus far. Where the Forest and the Path had seemed old, or primitive, this place seemed advanced. The gray walls to either side appeared to be made of a metallic stone, veined with a network of thin, golden lines that spread like circuits. Ahead of them, the hallway ended at the entrance to what appeared to be a bright, cavernous room.

"I don't think this is an archetype," Owen said.

"There's still only one way for us to go," Grace said.

So the three of them listened and walked carefully down the corridor, which seemed to pulse and shimmer at the edges of Owen's vision, but not when he looked directly at the walls. Their footsteps made very little noise, even as a deep, resonant sound filled the space around them as constant and noticeable as a heartbeat.

When they reached the end of the corridor, they crept to one side and peered around the corner, into the chamber, and found they were now beneath the dome they had seen from outside. Its shimmering curvature spanned a vast vaulted space suffused with a pale blue light. Directly under the dome, several large platforms bore strange objects and equipment that Owen didn't recognize or understand. It might have been machinery, or computers, or simply sculptures. Crystalline walkways, staircases, and conduits linked the platforms together into a structure that looked almost molecular. It climbed up into the space beneath the dome, and descended into a silo that had been hollowed out of the mountain beneath them.

"What is this place?" Owen asked.

"Maybe it's an archetype for a mad scientist's lab," Grace said.

"Something like that," Natalya said. "I think this is the key Monroe is looking for. The Pieces of Eden came from an ancient civilization, right?" She nodded toward the middle of the chamber. "That looks like it was made by an ancient civilization to me."

YOU ARE CORRECT, said a strange voice.

Owen turned toward it as a figure walked up from below. She had long dark hair, and her pale skin seemed to glow from within. She wore a silver headdress that might have been a helmet, and her white robes nearly touched the ground. As the stranger approached them, she spoke with the same voice they had heard at the beginning of this simulation.

WHAT YOU ARE SEEING DOES BELONG TO AN ANCIENT CIVILIZATION. MY CIVILIZATION. She turned away from them. **COME.**

Owen, Grace, and Natalya followed the stranger to one of the crystal staircases, which they ascended, stepping out over the seemingly bottomless chasm below. Owen gripped the cold handrail tightly.

"Who are you?" Natalya asked the stranger as they climbed.

I AM A MEMORY OF ONE WHO CAME BEFORE, the stranger said, and that was all.

She guided them from staircase, to walkway, to staircase, up into the highest reaches of the dome, until they attained a platform near the peak of the structure. A kind of bed waited there, its contours shaped and molded from the same metallic stone. It reminded Owen of an Animus, and upon it lay a woman, with the same copper complexion as the archetypes they had encountered. A sheet covered her body from the shoulders down, and she appeared to be sleeping.

I AM KNOWN BY MANY NAMES, the stranger said. **BUT YOU MAY CALL ME MINERVA.**

"Like the goddess?" Grace asked.

MY PEOPLE ARE THE SOURCE OF YOUR MYTHS, AND I HAVE HAD MANY NAMES. The stranger spread her open hands to either side. **ATHENA. SULIS. VÖR. SARASWATI. WE WHO CAME BEFORE REIGNED OVER HUMANITY FOR THOUSANDS OF YEARS.**

The voice of the stranger, Minerva, entered Owen's mind with such power it blurred his vision, and the figure of her wavered, and grew large, and burned with light.

TO THAT END, WEAPONS AND DEVICES WERE FASHIONED. THE TRIDENT WAS MADE TO RULE WITH PERFECT

AUTHORITY. She waved her arm, and overhead the dome darkened. Then images filled it, and chased one another across its surface. Scenes of battles, and fields strewn with thousands and thousands of dead bodies. **MY PEOPLE. WE FOUGHT OURSELVES. WE FOUGHT YOU, OUR CREATIONS. WE DESTROYED OURSELVES, BECAUSE WE MADE A MISTAKE.**

She walked over to the contoured bed, and she touched a part of it that looked no different from the rest. But at her touch, pulses of light began to travel the golden veins within the substance of the platform, illuminating it, and this light flowed into the sleeping woman. Minerva then looked back at Owen and the others, and he waited, saying nothing.

Owen wondered if they were supposed to do something, or say something. He looked at Grace and Natalya, who both appeared equally confused.

YOU DO NOT ASK ME WHAT MISTAKE, Minerva finally said, sounding weary, and Owen got the feeling that they had just failed a test they didn't know they were taking. **MY PEOPLE BUILT A CIVILIZATION OF UNPARALLELED STRENGTH AND BEAUTY. WE BENT THE CHAOS OF NATURE TO OUR WILL. WE UNLOCKED THE CODE OF LIFE ITSELF, AND BECAME ITS MASTERS. WE DID ALL THAT AND MORE, AND YET WE, THE ISU, DESTROYED OURSELVES, AND YOU DO NOT THINK TO ASK ME HOW? ARE YOU SO SURE THAT HUMANITY CANNOT ALSO FALL?**

"How?" Natalya asked. "How did you destroy yourselves?"

Minerva now paced about the platform, shaking her head, periodically casting glares at them that seemed almost disappointed. PERHAPS I HAVE FAILED. PERHAPS I HAVE MADE A SECOND MISTAKE.

"Please," Grace said. "We've come a long way."

I KNOW YOU HAVE. Minerva stopped pacing. I LAID THE PATH MYSELF. AFTER THE CATACLYSM OF THE FIRST DISASTER, AN EJECTION FROM THE SUN LEFT OUR CIVILIZATION IN RUINS. AS I SPEAK TO YOU NOW, FROM THE PAST, MY PEOPLE ARE ALMOST EXTINCT, AND I AM SHORTLY TO JOIN THEM. HUMANITY WILL SURVIVE US, AND WHEN WE ARE GONE, I FEAR YOU WILL BE LEFT WITH OUR LEGACY. OUR WEAPONS.

"The Pieces of Eden," Owen said.

THAT IS WHAT HUMANS CALL THEM. Minerva stepped toward them. IF I COULD DESTROY THE TRIDENT, I WOULD, BUT IT HAS DISAPPEARED. I KNOW IT WILL NOT STAY HIDDEN FOREVER, AND WHEN IT IS FOUND, HUMANITY WILL SUFFER. THAT IS WHY I HAVE BROUGHT YOU HERE.

She returned to the contoured bed and stood beside it. Then she gestured with an open palm toward the woman lying upon it.

I FASHIONED THE WHOLE OF THIS COLLECTIVE MEMORY IN MY FORGES, AND I INSTALLED IT DEEP IN THE MINDS AND CELLS OF A FEW HUMAN

BEINGS. I READ THE BRANCHES AND POSSIBILITIES OF TIME, AND I PREDICTED AND INTENDED THAT THEIR ANCESTORS AND THE TRIDENT WOULD BE DRAWN TOGETHER, DOWN THROUGH THE CENTURIES, AND I FORESAW THE DAY THAT HUMANITY WOULD NEED MY HELP. AND HERE YOU ARE.

"But what does this mean?" Owen asked, still bewildered by everything Minerva had said. "How do we stop the Trident?"

IN COMING HERE, YOUR MIND HAS RECEIVED A SHIELD SO THAT YOU CAN DO WHAT I COULD NOT AND DESTROY THE TRIDENT.

"But how?" Natalya asked. "How does this collective memory help?"

THE WAY OF THE PATH IS THROUGH FEAR, DEVOTION, AND FAITH.

Owen thought about the Serpent, the Dog, and the third part, which had to be the cliff they had climbed. "But what does that mean?" he asked. "How is that supposed to help?"

YOU ARE ONLY HUMAN, AND WOULD NOT UNDERSTAND. BUT THIS MEMORY HAS UNLOCKED YOUR POTENTIAL, AND WHEN THE TIME COMES, YOU WILL HAVE WHAT YOU NEED.

Owen didn't feel any different, and he didn't know how this simulation could have possibly changed anything for him.

"You never did tell us how you destroyed yourselves," Grace said.

WE FORGOT, she said.

"Forgot what?" Owen asked.

WE FORGOT THAT WE WERE A PART OF THE UNIVERSE, RATHER THAN APART FROM IT. WE FORGOT THAT WE STOOD NEITHER AT THE CENTER OF CREATION, NOR OUTSIDE IT. WE FORGOT THAT DANGER AND FEAR ARE NOT THE SAME THING, AND WHILE WE FOUGHT AGAINST OUR FEARS, WE FAILED TO SEE THE TRUE DANGER. WE FORGOT ALL OF THIS UNTIL THE UNIVERSE PUNISHED US WITH OUR OWN SUN, REMINDING US OF OUR PLACE. Minerva waved her hand in a wide arc over her head, and the dome opened like the widening pupil of an eye, revealing the night sky. **DO NOT REPEAT OUR MISTAKE. DO NOT FORGET.**

"We won't," Owen said.

Minerva nodded. **YOU HAVE REACHED THE END OF THE PATH I LAID FOR YOU. REMEMBER EVERY STEP YOU TOOK.** She waved her hand once more, and then she vanished.

The platform fell away from them, along with the rest of the structure and the dome around it, splintering and fragmenting into the pit at the heart of the mountain. Owen remained suspended in the night sky next to Grace and Natalya, surrounded by stars and facing a commanding moon. But those lights slowly faded and died, until he hung in total darkness, unable to even see his friends nearby.

Something tugged on his head. He flinched and reached up

to fight it off, but he felt human hands, and the Animus helmet, and then the helmet lifted away.

He stared, confused, and then squinted and blinked. He was back in the Aerie lab. Monroe stood in front of him, and then clapped him on the shoulder. Grace and Natalya hung in their Animus rings next to him.

"What happened?" Owen asked. "Did we desynchronize?" It didn't feel as though they had. It was the smoothest exit from a simulation he had ever experienced.

"No," Monroe said. "You didn't desynchronize. The memory just . . . let you go."

He helped the three of them disconnect from their harnesses, and then step out of their rings. Owen rubbed his head and his eyes, and went back through his memories to make sure the simulation was all there, and not fading like the dream it almost seemed to be. But the memories stayed, and in some ways, that made them even harder to understand. The earth apparently had an entire history that no one knew about. An ancient, mythical race had gone extinct. If anyone but Monroe had sent them into that simulation, Owen would have suspected the whole thing was fake.

But it was real.

"Everyone okay?" Monroe asked. "No adverse effects?"

Owen shook his head.

"I feel fine," Grace said.

"Me too," Natalya said.

"Good." Monroe sighed. "In that case, you can tell me exactly what you saw in there. Let's have Natalya start, and then you two can fill in any details she misses."

So they all took seats, and Natalya walked Monroe through

the entire simulation, beginning with the Forest and the Serpent, and ending with Minerva, and the shield she claimed to have given them. Owen filled in what had happened with the Dog while the other two had gone ahead, and Grace spoke more about their experience climbing the mountainside. Monroe said very little, only stopping them to ask brief questions. When they'd finished, he sat there with his arms folded across his belly, covering his mouth with one of his hands, apparently thinking through everything they'd told him.

"This is extraordinary," he finally said. "You three have just answered some of the biggest scientific questions that I have ever asked. And to top it off, you've had indirect contact with a Precursor."

"A Precursor?" Grace asked.

"The Isu. A member of the First Civ. Those Who Came Before. We have several names for them." He shook his head. "But that doesn't mean we can comprehend them. Think about what it would take to create a genetic time capsule meant to open at a specific time tens of thousands of years later."

"But Minerva didn't open it; you did," Grace said.

"It seems that way . . ." Monroe said, but left off the rest.

"Is what Minerva said true?" Natalya asked.

Monroe uncrossed his arms and leaned toward her. "Which part?"

"All of it," she said.

Monroe nodded. "More or less. It all happened tens of thousands of years ago, so we don't know exactly what happened. What we do know is that we have the Pieces of Eden. We have found some Precursor temples. Others before you have had contact with the Isu in different ways, including Minerva. Their civilization did exist, and it was incredibly advanced. We believe they were destroyed by a coronal mass ejection known as the Toba Catastrophe. So, yes, what Minerva told you is basically true." He turned to Grace. "There are even some who want to bring the Isu back."

"The Instruments of the First Will?" Grace asked.

Monroe nodded.

"Who're they?" Owen asked.

Monroe gestured to Grace in a way that gave her the floor, and she pulled a folded-up piece of paper out of her pocket.

"I found this in that book of Norse mythology," she said. "Isaiah wrote it."

"What does it say?" Natalya asked.

"It says he doesn't want to rule the world." Grace held up the paper. "He wants to destroy it."

"Wait, what?" Owen had assumed Isaiah wanted to be another Alexander the Great. "Why?"

"He thinks the earth needs to die to be reborn," Grace said. "It's a cycle. He says we've been preventing this cycle from happening, and there should have already been another great catastrophe. But there wasn't, because the Assassins and the Templars stopped it. So now Isaiah wants to make it happen another way."

Owen knew that could easily be accomplished with the Trident. Not only could Isaiah use it to create an army, but he could turn other countries against one another, with their nuclear weapons and bombs.

"So who are the Instruments of the First Will?" Grace asked.

"I've only heard rumors," Monroe said. "But within the Templar Order there is supposedly a secret faction trying to restore another Precursor named Juno to power. From Isaiah's writings, it sounds like he was aware of them. Maybe even a part of them for a time. But if he was, he isn't any longer. He's decided that *he* wants the power, not Juno." He rose from his chair. "I'm going to go check on the other two simulations and see how David and Javier are doing."

"What should we do?" Grace asked.

Monroe glanced around the lab. "You can hang out here, or you can go back to the common room and wait. Then I'll know where to find you."

"What about me?" Owen asked. Before he had agreed to go into the simulation of the collective unconscious, Monroe had promised to show him the real memories of his father's bank robbery.

"This isn't the time," Monroe said.

"You promised—"

"I promised I would help you, and I will. But I think you know there are more urgent matters we need to take care of first."

Owen's impatience turned to irritation. "But all we're doing right now is waiting around for Javier and David to find the dagger."

"Which might happen at any moment." Monroe strode toward the door. "Besides, I'd rather have your mind clear for what lies ahead."

"Why wouldn't my mind be clear?" Owen asked.

Monroe gripped the door handle and paused. "If you have to ask that question, I wonder if you're ready to get what you're asking for." With that, he exited the room, leaving the three of them alone.

CHAPTER TWENTY-ONE

Thorvald stood next to the Lawspeaker in the king's tent. Eric sat in a dark wooden saddle chair, with Astrid at his side, but they were otherwise alone. Javier still hadn't grown accustomed to the presence of the huge house-bear, and she startled him whenever his ancestor encountered her. A brazier offered orange light and white smoke, which gathered in the peak of the tent before escaping.

"The cattle killed a third of the Jomsvikings," Thorvald said. "Those that survived held their ground behind their shield walls. The battle ceased with the setting of the sun."

"Styrbjörn?" the king asked.

"He lives." Thorvald did not see a need to tell the king what Styrbjörn had done to stop the cattle. Not yet. Thorvald could hardly believe it himself, and for the first time since this engagement had begun, he wondered if their enemy could win. "His army pulled back to the Mirkwood."

Eric nodded. "Your strategies have been very effective. I commend you both, and I wish to reward you." He produced two small leather pouches from within his tunic and handed them to Thorvald, who tucked them away.

The Lawspeaker bowed his head. "We serve our people that all might live free."

"And how would you serve them now?" the king asked slowly, his question weighed down by the words he didn't say, but fully intended. "Has the time come?"

"Yes," Thorvald said. "As it came for your brother."

"I've told you." Eric turned and looked at Astrid. "I don't want to know anything about that."

Javier felt Thorvald's struggle to restrain his anger. The king wanted the bladework of the Brotherhood on his behalf, yet protected his own sense of honor by refusing to speak openly about it, as though he could convince himself it had nothing to do with him. But everyone in that tent except the house-bear knew what he meant and what he asked of them.

Even so, the Lawspeaker did not appear angered by the king's weakness. "Thorvald will go tonight, and tomorrow we shall see what the dawn brings."

"Do not wait until dawn to inform me," Eric said. "Wake me if you must."

"As you wish," the Lawspeaker said.

Eric nodded, and then Thorvald and the Lawspeaker left the king's tent.

Outside, they walked through the encampment surrounded by the sounds of steel against grindstone, and the ringing of blacksmiths' hammers. They heard laughter, and smelled meat cooking over fires, and the mood about the camp felt high and confident. Their numbers were greater than the Jomsvikings, and Eric's war band would join the battle the next day. Victory seemed inevitable.

"Take nothing for granted," the Lawspeaker said, seeing right into Thorvald's mind with his blind eyes. "Whatever these warriors believe, any battle can turn with the beat of a raven's wing. Think of the dagger you saw. If it is what you fear, we may have already lost this battle, regardless of our cunning or our strength."

"I understand," Thorvald said.

"The time has come to bring Styrbjörn the judgment of the Norns. He must not ever again take up his sword or his axe."

"He won't."

Torgny nodded. "If you find this dagger, bring it to me."

Thorvald grasped his mentor's hand. "I will."

With that, he left the Lawspeaker in the war camp and made his way southward over the Fyrisfield. The moon had not yet risen, which meant he could avoid being seen, but raced through darkness. He had to rely on his Odin-sight, sensing more than could be had by his ears and eyes alone, following the contours of the land and avoiding its pitfalls and marshes.

As he came upon a clutch of low boulders and leapt over them, his Odin-sight caught a glimmer near the ground, and he stopped to investigate it. A thick coat of moss covered part of the rock there, and as he peeled it away, he found a small piece of hack-gold encrusted with dirt. Thorvald stared at it for a few moments, puzzled, but then he remembered the story of Hrólf, who scattered his gold across the Fyrisfield to distract his enemies while he escaped. It seemed there might be truth to the legend, after all, and it gave Thorvald an idea. One final cunning strategy, perhaps the simplest of them all.

He pulled out the pouches the king had given them, and inside he found a small trove of silver Arab dirhams. Hrólf would not have scattered such coins as these all those generations ago, but Thorvald did not believe that detail would matter to the Jomsvikings. He arranged the coins over one of the boulders, and then he pulled out another vial of the same poison he had given Östen. Very carefully, he laced each piece of silver with death, and after the poison had dried, he scattered the coins as he traveled the rest of the way over the Fyrisfield.

When he reached the Mirkwood, he climbed up into the branches, and once again ran freely from tree to tree, passing unseen over the sentries, until he reached the heart of the camp. The cattle had done tremendous harm to the Jomsvikings. Many lay broken and dying, and though their brothers tended them, they would not live through the night. And yet the camp did not seem so different in spirit than Eric's. After all of their casualties, the courage and will of the Jomsvikings had not yet broken, and Thorvald admired them for it.

He eventually found Styrbjörn in council with a Jomsviking captain, while a shield-maiden dressed a wound in his thigh. The sight of the woman surprised Thorvald, because Jomsvikings allowed only men in their ranks.

"They will sing songs about your feats this day," the captain said, "and tomorrow, the Jomsvikings will fight and die by your side, to the last man if the gods will it. This is the oath we will take."

It seemed the courage and strength that Styrbjörn had shown now bound the Jomsvikings to him, with the loyalty that their code and their honor demanded. They truly would fight to the last man, which meant that Eric's army would be left with no choice but to destroy them all.

Thorvald watched as Styrbjörn dismissed the captain, and after some moments of silence, fell into conversation with the shield-maiden. The two of them spoke in low voices on the subject of marriage, surprising Thorvald once again. When they moved away from the encampment into the forest to make their vows, he followed them through the trees, observing from a distance.

Eventually, they came upon a large, sundered stone, and Styrbjörn built a shrine before it, and offered up a gold ring from his arm to Frey. As he and the shield-maiden exchanged their vows and their swords, Thorvald considered striking them both down. It would be a simple enough task, distracted as they were by each other. But the Tenets that Torgny had taught him held him back.

He did not know this shield-maiden. She could be no Jomsviking. Perhaps a Dane? She might even be an innocent, and if she was, the Creed of the Brotherhood forbade Thorvald from shedding her blood. Before he struck, he had to know who he would be killing.

"Now the blood sacrifice," Styrbjörn said below. "I will find us an animal—"

"No," the shield-maiden said. "We already have an offering that will please the gods."

Thorvald wondered what she meant, but then Styrbjörn pulled out his strange dagger and placed it on the shrine. In dedicating the offering to Thor, Styrbjörn called the weapon a relic of the Christ, which meant the dagger might be what Thorvald feared it was. But if that was true, why would Styrbjörn offer it up on the eve before a battle? Why would he give away the very thing that could secure his victory?

After Styrbjörn had finished at the shrine, he placed the dagger inside the crack in the stone, piled up a few more rocks, and then he and the shield-maiden left in the direction of their camp.

Thorvald waited a few moments to be certain they had gone, and then he descended from the trees to the boulder and the shrine. The golden arm ring held no interest for him, and he pushed it aside along with the smaller stones until he'd uncovered the large crack, and the hidden dagger within.

Javier felt a thrill. "I have it," he said to Griffin.

Good. Very good. Stay with Thorvald. Let's see where it goes from here.

"Of course."

This is a whole branch of the Brotherhood I didn't know about, Griffin said. *It's incredible. With your heritage, your blood, I know you have it in you to become a truly great Assassin.*

Javier didn't know what to do with that. He liked hearing it, but he also fought against it within his mind as he dove back into the memory.

The dagger was not an ordinary weapon. Thorvald could see that plainly. But that didn't mean it was an ancient weapon of the gods. He had never held an Aesir blade before, so he couldn't say for certain whether this was divine or not. But he believed it was, which meant that he needed to get it safely into the hands of the Lawspeaker.

Styrbjörn's death would have to wait.

Thorvald ascended to the treetops once more, and he made his way back through the Mirkwood, and then over the Fyrisfield, where his silver glinted weakly in the starlight. The Lawspeaker had left his hovel near the temple and taken a tent within Eric's encampment, and as Thorvald approached it, he found Torgny sitting outside near the fire with his chin buried in his chest, snoring.

"Mentor," he said, touching the Lawspeaker on the shoulder.

Torgny looked up, inhaling deeply through his nose. "You have already returned? How long have I been in contemplation?"

"Only you would know the answer to that." He touched the dagger's pommel and grip against the Lawspeaker's hands. "I believe it is what I thought."

Torgny accepted the blade, and though he could not see, he turned it over and over in his hands, and Thorvald worried he would cut himself, but he didn't.

"I believe you are right," the Lawspeaker said.

"Can you tell what power it possesses?" Thorvald asks.

"No. What of Styrbjörn?"

"He lives," Thorvald said. "He married a shield-maiden in secret as I watched. To kill him would have required killing her, and I don't know her."

"You were wise to stay your blade," the Lawspeaker said. "Better that our enemies go unharmed than we risk doing harm to our Creed."

"Eric will not be pleased."

"But we have this." Torgny held up the dagger. "I think it will please the king."

"You're going to give it to him?"

"Not in the way you think. Let us go to him."

The Lawspeaker rose from the fire, and then Thorvald led him through the camp, which had grown much quieter as the warriors there labored at sleep, until they reached Eric's tent. Two guards posted at the door allowed them entrance, but immediately inside they faced a huffing, snorting Astrid.

"Steady," Thorvald said to the mass of brown fur shambling toward him. "You know us."

"Eric," Torgny said loudly and forcefully, and the king stirred with a snort.

"What is it?"

"Your house-bear," the Lawspeaker said.

"What? Oh." He first sat up, and then climbed to his feet, his furs and blankets falling away. "Astrid, to me," he said, tugging on her chain.

The bear stopped her approach, but not her noisemaking, and turned to lumber over to the king, where she sat herself down and leaned against him.

"Is it done?" the king asked.

"No," the Lawspeaker said.

"No?"

"We have something better." He extended the blade toward the king, and Eric took it, frowning.

"What is this?"

"That is a Christ relic," Torgny said. "Styrbjörn took it from Harald Bluetooth, who received it from the great Christian Father in Rome."

Now Eric's frown turned to a sneer of disgust. "And why would I want this?"

The Lawspeaker turned to Thorvald. "Tell him what you saw."

It became clear then that Torgny intended to wield the dagger as a symbol, so Thorvald said, "Styrbjörn thought he could obtain the favor of Thor by offering that relic to the sky god. But Styrbjörn was careless, and I have taken it from the shrine. If you were to offer this Christ relic to Odin, and dedicate tomorrow's battle to him—"

"I thought I was not to fight Styrbjörn," Eric said.

"That is still true," the Lawspeaker said. "You are not to

fight him. But your army will, and with Odin's favor, their victory will be assured."

"The Jomsvikings have now sworn to Styrbjörn," Thorvald said. "It will go better for your rule if Styrbjörn is defeated on the battlefield, in the open, rather than in the shadows. Let it be known among your army that you have Odin's favor."

"But will Thor not be angry?" the king asked.

"The offering was poorly done," Thorvald said. "Thor's displeasure will fall on Styrbjörn."

"And if Styrbjörn challenges me?" Eric said.

"He must not be given that chance," the Lawspeaker said. "You must stay away from the battle."

"No." Eric shook his head, his cheeks glowing red. "I am no raven starver. I will not cower in my tent. I will fight with my people, even if it means my death."

"That speaks well of your honor," Torgny said. "No one doubts your courage. But the people of this land need you to rule for many years hence."

And Thorvald knew that the Brotherhood had spent too many years establishing Eric's rule for him to die the next day on the battlefield. And die, he would. Thorvald had seen Styrbjörn fight. The king would be no match for his nephew's size, strength, and youth. There were few men who would be. But Thorvald thought of one.

"The people of Svealand need me to lead them," the king said. "On this, I swear your counsel will not sway me."

Thorvald could see that was true. "Then lead them," he said, "but choose a champion. One who will fight Styrbjörn for you if it comes down to single combat. There is no dishonor in that."

"Perhaps no dishonor," Eric said. "But neither is there honor."

"It must be this way," the Lawspeaker said.

"There is a giant in your army," Thorvald said. "His name is Östen—"

"By tradition, my marshal is my champion."

Javier remembered the way the marshal had tried to prevent the Assassins from entering the king's war council, and so did Thorvald, who shook his head. "I know him, and he will surely fall. There is only one man among all the Svear I would send against Styrbjörn."

Eric laid a hand on Astrid's head and scratched her fur as he studied the dagger. "A strange blade for a relic," he said. "I will never understand these Christians. They offend me."

"They offend the gods," the Lawspeaker said.

"Then let us appease them," the king said. "Let us offer this thing to Odin."

So they left his tent, and the three of them walked through the encampment at the midnight hour, with Astrid tethered by her chain to the king. Then they left the camp and traveled to the temple at Uppsala, where they entered that hall by the light of a single torch. Astrid came into the temple with them, and she sniffed the air, peering into the darkness outside the torch's reach, where gods and heroes stood as sentinels, in silence.

Torgny knew this place without torches, and without sight. He brought them before the wooden pillar of Odin, which had been carved into the trunk of an ancient ash tree and raised at one end of the hall. The Allfather stared out with his one eye, armed with his spear, Gungnir, which he would wield in battle against the Fenris wolf at Ragnarök.

By torchlight, the Lawspeaker took the king through the blót ritual. They called on Odin to listen to their plea, and they asked for his favor in battle, but instead of offering up the life and blood of a horse, or a pig, they gave the dagger, and in doing so they pledged their worship to the Aesir over any other false god. The king took oaths, and swore his life to Odin, vowing to enter Valhalla ten years from that day. He dedicated the next day's battle and all its dead to the Allfather. The mute figure of Odin towered over them in the quiet, darkened hall, half in shadow, and gave no sign that they had been heard.

At the end of the ritual, Torgny guided the king from the temple without speaking, and behind them, Thorvald secretly recovered the dagger. After the three of them had returned to the king's tent, Eric said to Thorvald, "Bring Östen to me. I would meet this champion." Then he and Astrid went inside.

"I'll wait here with Eric," Torgny said, moving toward the tent's entrance.

Thorvald left the Lawspeaker and went in search of his company. The men he had chosen to thwart and harry the Jomsvikings had remained together, even upon rejoining the rest of the army. He found their fire a short time later and easily spotted Östen's sleeping bulk among them. Thorvald approached him loudly enough to wake him, and then called his name.

Östen rolled toward Thorvald, his eyes only half open. "What is it, skald?"

"Come with me," Thorvald said. "You are needed by the king."

Östen's eyes opened the rest of the way and he rushed to his feet, again surprising Thorvald with his speed, given his size. "The king asked for me?"

"Yes," Thorvald said. "And I can think of no one better. Bring your weapons and your shield."

They returned to Eric's tent, and Thorvald led Östen inside. The Lawspeaker waited there with the king and his house-bear, and Östen bowed his head upon entering.

"You have need of me, my king?" he asked.

"Yes," Eric said. "Though it is not by my choice. I've summoned you according to the counsel of others." He turned to Torgny. "Skald?" he said, suggesting that the Lawspeaker should explain, and then he sat himself in his saddle chair.

Torgny smiled. "Though I cannot see you, Östen, I can tell that you are a man of uncommon honor."

Östen bowed his head again. "I thank you for that."

"And a man of renown," Torgny added.

"Perhaps when I was younger," Östen said.

Thorvald stepped toward him. "Tomorrow we battle Styrbjörn to the end. It is likely that he will seek out his uncle, the king, on the battlefield."

"To challenge him," Östen said.

"Indeed." Torgny placed his hands together behind his back. "As another man of uncommon honor, the king would of course accept such a challenge—"

"He should not," Östen said.

The king leaned forward in his chair. "And why is that?"

It must have seemed a dangerous question, for Östen bowed his head low, and dropped his shoulders, but still he seemed to brush the roof of the tent with his hair. "You would die, my king," he said. "Forgive me for saying it, but I have seen Styrbjörn fight. You would not leave the battlefield, and Svealand would be lost."

Eric narrowed his eyes, and then leaned back in his chair. As Thorvald watched and listened to the exchange, he felt grateful that Östen had confirmed all the reasons for choosing him.

"And you?" Torgny asked. "Would you fight Styrbjörn?"

Östen turned toward him, and for the first time since Thorvald had met the giant, he saw fear at the tightened edges of his eyes. Östen didn't answer the question at first. Instead, he looked down at the skein still tied around his wrist. Thorvald didn't know what that thread might mean, but it clearly held significance.

"I would fight him," Östen said, firmly, but quietly.

"If you stood beside your king in battle," the Lawspeaker said, "and Styrbjörn rushed toward him, what would you do?"

"I would engage Styrbjörn in bladework," Östen said, "before he could reach the king to challenge him."

Torgny nodded. "It is as I said. A man of uncommon honor."

Thorvald clapped Östen on the back, glad to have judged him rightly. "From this moment forward, you will be the king's spear and shield. You will remain at his side until this storm has passed. Do you accept this honor?"

Östen took a deep, rumbling breath, sounding much like Astrid. "I accept."

"Odin will be with you," Torgny said. "So let the morning come."

CHAPTER TWENTY-TWO

A low fog lay in wisps over the Fyrisfield in the hours before dawn, gathering more thickly in the folds and dips, and covering the grass with dew. Östen followed the king, who led his house-bear by her chain until he reached a stone enclosure. Someone had planted a heavy stake in the middle of it, and the king fixed Astrid's chain to that stake. As they left the house-bear there, and closed the gate behind them, Östen grew curious enough to ask a question, one that David had wondered about also.

"Would she fight in battle?"

"Astrid?" The king looked back over his shoulder, toward the enclosure. "Yes, if I commanded it, she would."

"But you don't want her to?"

"I captured her as a cub," the king said. "I raised her up, and

I trained her. I've had her for ten years now. So, no, I would not command her to fight. Every warrior on the battlefield would want to kill her, and she means too much to me to let that happen."

"She seems to have grown accustomed to her chains."

"They are there for her sake. Without them, she might wander and kill livestock, or a hunter might take her."

Östen had killed bears. In the summer, their fat tasted of the berries they foraged. They gave fierce competition to the wolves, and a strong pack could sometimes bring a bear down. But it was hard for Östen to decide which animal lived a better life. Astrid safe in her chains, or the wild bear risking death.

"When we left my tent this morning," the king said, "did you notice that large raven in the yew tree?"

"I didn't."

"Then it was a sign for my eyes alone." He smiled as they walked back through the encampment, which had fully awoken to arm itself for battle. "Odin is watching over us. My offering was accepted. The Lawspeaker was right."

"He is very wise," Östen said. "And Thorvald is very cunning."

"Both offer me valuable counsel," the king said.

At his tent, they gathered their weapons and shields. In addition to his ring mail, the king donned the golden-scale armor of a defeated Grikklander, and then they were joined outside by the elite housecarls and the captains of the king's war band. Some of those seasoned warriors looked at Östen with suspicion, especially the king's marshal, who cast him glances sidelong, but none dared voice their misgivings.

The king gave his captains their orders. The strategy was simple, because the king knew exactly what Styrbjörn would do.

The Svear would offer the Jomsvikings a solid front to attack, and Styrbjörn, ever defiant, would attempt to break their line with a wedge to reach the king. But then the center of Eric's front would feint backward, to draw the Jomsvikings farther in, while at the same time, the Svear clans at the flanks would extend and entirely surround the enemy. Now that the size of Styrbjörn's army had been reduced, the Svear could trap and crush them.

"Also spread word of this," the king said. "Last night I made an offering to Odin, and this morning I have been given a sign. The Allfather is with us, and victory will be ours."

The captains left to take those words and the king's command to the clans they would lead into battle. Östen and the king found a vantage to watch the sun rise over the plain, first a spark, then an ember, then a flame. Its warmth thawed the rime and banished the mist.

Not long after that, Östen glimpsed the Jomsvikings coming over the horizon, and almost in that same moment, the Svear horns sounded. He and the king left their vantage and raced from the camp out onto the open field, joined by the marshal and a company of one hundred housecarls.

The clans massed their ranks along the Fyrisfield, thorny with spears and flapping banners, roaring their battle cries and banging on their shields, drowning out whatever howling the Jomsvikings already sent their way. The king raised his own spear and gave the order to march.

Horns blared down the line, and the front advanced. Östen kept pace with the king at his right hand, while the marshal kept to Eric's left, and the housecarls and standard-bearers marched before and after them, their pace disciplined and unwavering.

The smell of turf in the air, and the dew of the Fyrisfield that wet Östen's boots, reminded him of his fields back home, and he wished he could wash his face in the cold spring as he did most mornings. He looked down at the thread tied around his wrist, and then he kissed it.

Before long, the Jomsvikings broke over a hill ahead of them, like a wave crashing over the bow of a ship, and on they came.

The king gave his next command, and the horns sounded. The housecarls prepared to fall back while fighting, and Östen readied his axe and shield.

The Jomsvikings launched their charge, boots all a-thunder, as though they truly had the favor of the sky god. Östen could see fury in their eyes and their teeth as he searched their line, finding Styrbjörn near the front, at the point of the wedge. The sight of him, and the memory of Alferth, fanned the embers of his own anger into flames.

The enemy stormed closer, devouring the ground before them until very little distance remained. At the final moment, the king then gave the third command, and the horns sounded.

The housecarls formed a shield wall, and when the Jomsviking wedge rammed into it, the Svear gave ground like a willow branch, bending without breaking. The maneuver gave no signal of retreat, but incited the Jomsvikings to press harder. Swords and axes fell hard on shields, and spears stabbed into the gaps.

Östen stayed at the king's side, behind the line, watching Styrbjörn, who tore through all in his path as housecarl after housecarl stepped forward to bar him.

"Your men die for you," the marshal said.

"I know it," the king said, his voice strained.

"You could end this with single combat," the marshal said. "Surely you could defeat your nephew."

Östen looked hard at the man, who had voiced no objections to the strategy until now, waiting until this moment of battle rage to press the king. There seemed to be something sinister in that.

"The king has already decided what he will do," Östen said.

The marshal smiled. "I would never presume to speak for the king."

"Peace, *stallari*," the king said. "Östen is right, though I loathe it. He is here at my call, to fight for me when the time comes."

The marshal lost his smile then, and he glowered at Östen with open hatred. "So you are now the king's champion?"

"I am," Östen said.

In that moment, the Jomsvikings managed a sudden, renewed surge, and the housecarl shield wall nearly broke, sending warriors backward into Östen and the king. Östen managed to keep his footing, and after a quick glance found Styrbjörn a safe distance away. But the marshal had moved, and as Östen turned to look for him, he found him at his side and glimpsed the flicker of a blade thrusting toward his ribs.

He spun to block it, knowing he couldn't.

But the blade never reached him. It fell to the ground from the marshal's limp hand, and Östen saw shock on the marshal's face.

The man stood with an arched back, staring just over Östen's head, eyes wide and mouth open. Thorvald stepped out from behind him as the marshal's whole body collapsed, and Östen noticed a strange and bloody blade on the skald's wrist.

Thorvald gave him a nod, and Östen nodded back. From a few yards away, the king looked down at the body of his former marshal as though it were a pile of dung, and then returned his attention to the battle.

The feint continued for several hundred yards, until Östen heard the distant horns of the flank clans signaling that they had executed the pincer maneuver and begun their rear assault.

The king blew on his own horn, and the housecarls dug in, their shield wall first holding fast against the press of the Jomsviking line, then pushing back against it, driving the Jomsvikings before them.

The faces of the enemy showed surprise, and anger, and finally realization as their own horns bellowed from behind.

Östen stepped over the wounded and dying, both Svear and Jomsviking, and as warriors fell, others leapt into their place. He had to restrain his own urge to join the fray, and it appeared the king did as well, judging by the way he held his spear. Thorvald and his wrist-blade had vanished.

"Where is the skald?" he asked the king.

"He goes where he will," Eric said.

A housecarl next to Östen cried out and looked down, where a wounded Jomsviking on the ground had stabbed his calf through with a long knife. Before Östen could act, the king leapt past him and thrust his spear into the enemy's throat. The wounded housecarl pulled the knife from his leg, wincing, and stabbed the dead Jomsviking with it.

"Can you still fight?" Östen asked him.

He nodded and pulled off one of his belts, which he used to bind his leg tightly to stanch the bleeding. After that, the rear housecarls finished off any wounded Jomsviking yet living.

For hours they clashed. The Jomsvikings refused to die easily, but the housecarls pressed inward, their bladework slow, steady, and hard-won. The invaders' horns continued to sound from the rear, calling for reinforcements, but there were none to be had. Östen maintained his watch on Styrbjörn, who fought ferociously and raged, unable to stop this tide from turning.

"The day is ours," Eric said.

"Not yet, my king," Östen said.

The Jomsvikings had sworn to fight to the last man, and it seemed they would fulfill that oath, but at what price? How many Svear lay dying or dead? How many families waited at home for someone who would never return?

"Eric!" Styrbjörn shouted, loud enough to be heard over all the other sounds of war.

Östen readied himself and waited.

Styrbjörn threw his shield aside and grabbed the top of the housecarl's shield in front of him, but rather than pushing against him, he yanked on it, pulling the man off-balance, and threw him to the ground. Then he stepped on the man's back and used it to leap into the air, right over the heads of the housecarl line.

He landed swinging his axe, and the Svear fell away from him in shock. "Eric!" he shouted again. "I challenge y—"

"I challenge you, Styrbjörn!" Östen stepped in front of the king. "Single combat!"

As the battle continued behind him, Styrbjörn pointed his axe toward Östen. "My quarrel is with my uncle! Who are you?"

"I am the friend of a man you killed, and I seek retribution!"

Styrbjörn strode toward him, and Östen could see a wound in his thigh bleeding through his leather and ring mail. "You would fight me?"

Östen readied his own weapon. "Yes."

"Then let us not delay!" Styrbjörn rushed him, almost faster than Östen could raise his shield, and landed a blow that rattled the marrow in the bones of his arm.

Östen fell back, but was ready for the next attack, deflecting it deftly. He tried to counter, but Styrbjörn leapt aside easily and swung again, almost striking Östen's head. Never had he fought a man so quick, or so strong. Having seen what Styrbjörn did to Alferth, Östen had expected a fearsome opponent, but had trusted in the gods that he would prevail. Now, facing this enemy, Östen believed he may have reached the end of his skein.

Styrbjörn struck again, and again, and the second blow shattered Östen's shield. He tossed the splintered wood and twisted metal aside, and now both men fought with axes alone.

"Is this what you want, Uncle?" Styrbjörn asked.

The king stood by with his spear, watching the duel.

Styrbjörn waved his arm toward the ongoing battle. "All these men fighting me in your place?" He laughed. "Where is your honor?"

"His honor is his own," Östen said. If this was to be the end of his skein, he would meet it fighting, without fear. "My honor claimed you first."

"So be it," Styrbjörn said. "But you die for nothing."

He swung his axe, and as Östen ducked the strike, Styrbjörn bashed his face with the side of his metal armguard. Östen staggered away, blood filling his mouth, but had no time to recover before Styrbjörn was on him again.

Östen used his axe to fight off three blows, as though he fought with a sword. After the third, he seized an opening and rammed Styrbjörn hard in the chest with his shoulder, sending the other man sprawling backward.

Östen didn't wait for his enemy to hit the ground before leaping after him, and his axe bit deep into Styrbjörn's arm, right in the elbow joint of his armor. Blood poured instantly from the wound at a pace that might soon be fatal, but Styrbjörn ignored it and attacked again.

After several repeated slashes that Östen managed to dodge and block, the tip of Styrbjörn's axe caught him in the side, opening a gash through armor and flesh. Östen struck Styrbjörn in the throat with his fist and fell back to check his wound, relieved to find the blade had cut through his skin but not all the way through his muscle.

Styrbjörn choked and took a shambling step toward Östen, wobbling on his feet. It seemed the loss of blood had begun to weaken him. He blinked and took another step, but then dropped to one knee, his head drooping.

"The silver," he said, shaking his head. Then he spat. "Coward."

Östen stepped toward him. "You name me coward? Now? After I have—"

"Not you." He looked at the king. "My uncle. He has poisoned me, just as he did my father."

Eric stepped forward. "I did not poison my brother, and I have not poisoned you."

Östen knew who had done it, even if he didn't know how, and he wondered how Thorvald had accomplished it.

"Eric the Coward." Styrbjörn laughed. "Whether you did it or you ordered it done, it is the same." He looked up at Östen. "Let's finish this."

"You cannot fight. I won't—"

"Finish this!" Styrbjörn shouted, and then grunted and growled his way to his feet, his arm and axe hanging loose at his side. He nodded toward the Jomsvikings still fighting for their lives. "I will die on my feet with them. Now finish this."

Östen did not know which would be more honorable. To let Styrbjörn leave the battlefield and suffer until his death by poison, or strike him down now in his weakness.

"Östen!" the king shouted. "Kill him!"

But even then, Östen hesitated. He couldn't kill a man this way, and within his memories, David felt himself in perfect agreement with his ancestor.

Styrbjörn took a step toward him. "I will decide this for you."

"Stop," Östen said.

But Styrbjörn took another step and very slowly hoisted his axe over his head. "If you do not finish this, I will finish you."

Östen took a step backward, but raised his axe. "I didn't want this."

"I know that," Styrbjörn said. "You have more honor than a king." He staggered forward another step. "I've lost too much blood anyway. If the poison didn't kill me, your blow would have. I would rather my death be yours. Not Eric's."

Östen looked Styrbjörn in the eyes and saw his pupils quivering, going in and out of focus. The former prince took another step, and came within striking distance of Östen. Then his axe moved, and Östen reluctantly raised his own with hands that wanted no part of this. That was when he noticed that the skein was gone from his wrist. That delicate, blood- and mud-soaked thread had finally broken away, lost somewhere in the chaos of the battle. In that moment, the only thing Östen wanted was to have it back. He would have traded a golden arm ring as thick as his thumb to have back that ordinary, filthy piece of string from Hilla's loom.

"Styrbjörn!" a woman shouted.

Östen turned as a shield-maiden charged at him, sword drawn. But before she could reach him, three housecarls set upon her. Her blade flashed, and her shield rang as she fought them, holding her ground, returning blow for blow with blinding speed and agility. But no warrior could last forever, and even now, several more housecarls closed in.

"Thyra," Styrbjörn whispered, and dropped once again to his knees. "No."

"Who is she?" Östen asked. "Tell me quickly."

"My queen," he said.

"She's your wife?"

"Yes."

Östen sprinted toward the melee. "Halt!" he shouted. "Halt!" But they ignored him.

He grabbed one of the housecarls from behind and hurled him away. When the other two turned toward him, the shield-maiden tried to seize the opportunity to kill one of them, but Östen blocked her with his axe.

"Halt, Thyra!" he bellowed.

At the sound of her name, she stopped, shoulders heaving.

Östen pointed. "Go to him. While you can."

She looked from Östen to Styrbjörn, and then she raced to her husband's side. Östen held out his hands to make certain the housecarls would stay back, and then went to stand near her. He couldn't hear what they said to each other over the sounds of the Jomsvikings' destruction, but he could tell the moment Styrbjörn died by the way Thyra bowed her head low, though Styrbjörn remained upright on his knees, hunched over, his lifeless body leaning against her.

In that moment, Eric raised his spear, and he strode toward what was left of the Jomsviking army.

"I sacrifice you!" he shouted. "The dead! The dying! And

the yet-to-die! I dedicate your blood to Odin! The Allfather, who granted me victory!" With that, he hurled his spear into the heart of the Jomsvikings.

Not one of them fled the Fyrisfield.

To a man, they stayed and died.

At the end of the battle, Eric bound Thyra, and summoned Östen to walk with them. They left the Fyrisfield, where the housecarls and captains sought out the living among the fallen of their clans, and they walked through the war camp. Then they left this behind also, and eventually reached the stone enclosure where Astrid waited on her chain. The house-bear rumbled and got to her feet at the sight of Eric, and Östen could see deep scratch marks in the dirt around the stake.

Thyra stared at Astrid with her jaw set and her chin high, but her hands shook.

Eric said nothing.

"Why have you brought this woman here, my king?" Östen asked.

"I have not yet fed Astrid," Eric said.

Thyra's lips parted, but she didn't gasp, and she didn't look away from the house-bear.

"My king," Östen said, "you cannot mean to do this."

"Why not? She is the wife of my traitorous nephew. He who would have murdered me for my crown and taken Svealand for himself. He who threatened to destroy this land if he could not rule it."

"That was Styrbjörn," Östen said. "Not her."

"But if I let her live, will she not seek to avenge him?"

"I will not," Thyra said. They were the first words she had spoken since the death of Styrbjörn. "I wish only to go home."

"To Jutland?" Eric asked. "You are a Dane?"

She nodded.

"You would return here with the Bluetooth," Eric said. "Or perhaps you would go to Jomsborg, and bring more Jomsvikings—"

"I will not," she said again.

"You are a shield-maiden!" Eric shouted. "You fight as well as three of my housecarls together. I cannot believe that you will leave me in peace—"

"You must not feed her to your house-bear, Eric," said the Lawspeaker, appearing suddenly beside them with Thorvald. Östen hadn't heard them or seen them approach. "There are some who will secretly mourn Styrbjörn among your own nobles. If you do this thing to Styrbjörn's wife, you will make bitter enemies of them."

"Then what am I to do?" the king asked.

The Lawspeaker regarded Östen with his milky eyes. "Give her as a thrall to your champion. The man who slew her husband."

That suggestion angered Östen, who had not slain Styrbjörn, and did not want his widow as a thrall, and it angered David, who still hated that his ancestor owned slaves.

"That would be seen as both fitting and just," Thorvald said.

Eric looked at Östen. "Even though you faltered at the end," he said, "you fought well." Then he turned back to Thorvald. "What of my marshal?"

Thorvald bowed his head. "Forgive me for not warning you, but I had no time. He was about to kill Östen."

Again, Östen bowed his head in gratitude toward the skald.

"Why?" Eric asked.

"So that Styrbjörn might kill you," the Lawspeaker said. "The marshal sought your downfall, and we believe he was not alone. In time, we will find the den of these vipers. Until then, do what you can to avoid turning anyone else against you."

Eric looked at Astrid for a few moments, and then he handed Thyra's tether to Östen, who accepted it without offering any thanks. The king entered the stone enclosure, where he separated his house-bear's chain from the stake, and then he led her outside, past the others, and set off in the direction of his hall.

"I will go with him," the Lawspeaker said. "He will need my counsel in the coming days."

The old man shuffled away, calling to Eric, who stopped and waited for him to catch up before he and Astrid lumbered on. Östen watched them go, the house-bear chained to a king, and the king chained to a man far wiser and more cunning by links he couldn't see.

Thorvald turned to Östen. "How bad is your side?"

Östen looked down. "It will need attention, but it didn't open my gut."

"Then you should leave at once. Get her out of here before there is more trouble." He gave Östen a handful of hack-silver, a small fortune. "Leave your things, and pay for what you need on the road."

"I do not want her," Östen said.

Thorvald took his arm and led him a short distance away. "Then do not keep her," he whispered. "Only get her to safety first." He then pulled out a strange dagger, and even though Östen didn't recognize it, David did. "I want you to take this blade and hide it well," Thorvald said. "Far from here."

"Why?" Östen asked.

"It may not look it, but this dagger is dangerous," Thorvald said. "It must never be used, not even by me. For that reason, it cannot stay in Uppsala, and you are perhaps the only man in Svealand with whom I would trust it. Do not show it to that Dane woman."

Östen accepted the dagger, and tucked it away out of sight within his tunic.

"You are an uncommon man," Thorvald said loudly. "I doubt our paths shall cross again, but I am honored to have known you."

"The same to you, skald," Östen said. "You will write a song about today?"

"Of course," Thorvald said. "Too many heard Styrbjörn call him 'Eric the Coward.' That cannot stand. He will be Eric the Victorious, because that is what Svealand needs him to be."

Östen shook his head. "I will leave you to your word craft," he said, preferring that to Thorvald's poison craft, or the narrow blade concealed at his wrist, and they bade farewell.

Östen led Thyra from Uppsala, to a ford over the Fyriswater, which they crossed, and then traveled slightly south of east, along the empty market roads. Along the way, they used the silver Thorvald had given them to buy what they needed from villages and farms, but rarely did they speak at all. Östen kept her bound, not because he wanted to, or because he feared her, but because word of them might spread, and they were not yet far enough from the king.

It was not until days later, when they crossed the border of his land, that he cut her binding completely. When they reached his farm, his family rushed to greet him. First, he gathered Hilla up in his arms, and he kissed her and squeezed her until she complained about his smell, and then he embraced Tørgils and Agnes and Greta. Arne the Dane then came with Stone Dog, who reached up to lick Östen's fingertips.

"The farm looks well, Arne," Östen said. "I haven't forgotten my promise." Then he introduced Thyra to his family, and he called her a guest, rather than a thrall.

That night they ate well, and afterward Östen walked by moonlight with Stone Dog up to the spring, where he took an icy bath in the only water that could make him feel clean after the battle he had fought. Then, with Stone Dog as his only witness, he wrapped Thorvald's strange dagger in an oilskin and buried it next to the spring, afterward covering the spot with a small cairn of stones.

Alongside Östen's mind, David took note of the location, the features that wouldn't change as much, even after centuries. "That's it," he said. "We've got it."

We've got it, Victoria said. *Good work, David. If you're ready, I'll bring you out—*

"Not yet," David said. "If—if that's okay. I just need to see something."

There was a pause.

All right, a few more minutes.

David rejoined Östen's mind and memories, and as his ancestor returned to his hall, he found Thyra standing outside, gazing up at the moon. Östen tried to walk past without disturbing her, but she called to him and asked him to join her, which he did.

"You are a fortunate man," she said, "to have a life such as this."

"I would die to protect it," he said.

She looked down at the ground, no doubt thinking of her dead husband, and he realized he'd chosen his words poorly, but didn't know how to repair them.

"I thought he would surely do it," Thyra said. "At Uppsala, I thought Eric would feed me to his bear, no matter what the Lawspeaker said."

"Why?"

"The power of symbols," she said, "and the meaning of my husband's name. Styrbjörn, the wild and unruly bear, and I, his widow, eaten by a bear on a chain."

Östen fell silent. "I hadn't thought of it."

Their exchange recalled to Östen's mind his own question on the subject of bears, and whether it was better to live on the king's chain, or to live free and risk death at the hands of hunters or the cruelties of the savage winter. Eric had made his choice, just as Styrbjörn had made his. For his own part, Östen knew what he would choose, and what every man deserved.

"My thrall is one of your countrymen," Östen said.

"Yes, I know his village."

"I intend to free him. You may stay or go as you wish, of course. But there is still plenty of Thorvald's silver left. I thought you might take it and go with Arne back to Jutland."

This was the moment David had stayed to see. Not because he needed to. Because he hoped to.

Thyra turned toward Östen, her pale face as blank and unreadable as the moon above. "Thorvald was right. You are an uncommon man." Then she looked back up into the sky. "I will speak with Arne, but I am not of a mind to leave just yet."

Östen frowned. "It will be dangerous for you to stay. Why would you risk it?"

She looked down at her right hand. “When Eric had me bound, one of the housecarls took Styrbjörn’s Ingelrii sword from me. It was the blade he gave me with his wedding vows.”

Östen began to understand, but now he worried even more. “You seek to recover it?”

“I do.” She laid her sword hand against her stomach. “I will have need of it one day.”

David? Victoria said. *It’s time.*

But he didn’t want to leave. He wanted to know what happened to these people, to Östen, and his children, and their children. He wanted to know if Thyra got Styrbjörn’s sword back, and if Arne the Dane went home, and—

I need to pull you out, David. Remember why you’re in there. Think about Isaiah.

He didn’t want to think about Isaiah. But he knew he had to. “Okay,” he said, and sighed. “Okay, I’m ready to leave. Let’s go save the world.”

CHAPTER TWENTY-THREE

Natalya waited with Owen and Grace in the common room. It was nighttime outside, turning all the Aerie's windows into mirrors, and she'd just eaten a second bag of barbecue potato chips, not because she was hungry, even though she was, and not because she liked barbecue potato chips, because she didn't, but because she was anxious and had nothing else to do. The two empty bags stared at her, asking *now what?*

"So how do you think the shield is supposed to work?" Grace asked.

Owen slumped low in his chair, his feet up on the table. "I've been wondering that, too. I don't feel any different."

Natalya sat forward, her elbows and forearms flat on the

table. "Well, we followed the Path through the simulation, right? The first thing we met was the Serpent in the Forest. I'm guessing that's the fear part. The next thing was the Dog, which was probably devotion."

"And climbing that mountain was faith," Grace said.

"Exactly."

"Right," Owen said. "We know all that. But I hope Minerva's big message wasn't just a summary of what we had already done. How is that a shield?"

Natalya had no idea. But since the prong Isaiah had used in Mongolia caused fear, and the other two caused devotion and faith, it had to mean something that they lined up with the archetypes in the simulation. But that insight still didn't explain where the shield would come from, or how they could use it to resist the power of the Trident.

"Maybe the collective unconscious is broken," Grace said. "Monroe said it's really old, right? What if Minerva's genetic time capsule went bad before it got to us?"

Owen closed his eyes, as though he was aiming for a nap. "I don't think that's how it—"

The door opened and Javier walked in, followed by David. Then Monroe, Griffin, and Victoria entered the room. Owen's eyes popped open as he got his feet off the table and sat up in his chair.

"Everyone staying hydrated after their simulations?" Victoria asked.

"Yeah," Grace said, restraining an eye roll, and looked at David. "Did you find it?"

He gave her a nod and a smile.

"We found it," Victoria said. "The Piece of Eden changed hands several times, but we now have our best estimate for its final location."

"So let's go get it," Owen said. "And then we figure out how to take the other two from Isaiah."

"I'm afraid it's not as simple as that," Victoria said. She took a seat at the long conference table. "The Templars have been trying to find Isaiah using more conventional means. They tracked him to an old Abstergo facility that was never completed, on the Isle of Skye near Scotland. They lost contact with the first strike team they sent in, and the second team found the site abandoned."

"What happened to the first team?" Grace asked.

"It seems they joined him," Victoria said. "That's the power of the Trident. Any force we send after Isaiah will only build his army and make him that much stronger."

"Isaiah is like a black hole," Monroe said. "If we get too close, he'll suck us in, and we'll become one of his followers."

"You mean slaves," David said.

Javier tipped his head toward him. "I was thinking zombies."

"Whatever you call them," Monroe said, "let me ask you, do you like the idea of Griffin fighting on Isaiah's side? Against us?"

Natalya did not like that idea at all. She had seen what Griffin could do to those he considered his enemies. But beyond that, she didn't like the thought of any of them losing themselves to the power of the Trident. They had already lost Sean to it, and Natalya still planned to get him out, somehow.

"That's why we can't just charge off to Scandinavia to find the Piece of Eden," Griffin said, standing near the table.

“Do we know where Isaiah is now?” Grace asked.

“Somewhere in Sweden,” Victoria said. “That’s as close as we can get.”

“No, it’s not,” Javier said. “We know Sean was in the memories of Styrbjörn, right? And the last time he saw the dagger, it was hidden in a shrine in the middle of the forest. I was there. We know where that is. And even if Isaiah realizes it’s not there, the only other place he’ll look will be Uppsala. We know where that is, too.” He glanced at David. “Isaiah will never guess that my ancestor gave the dagger to a giant farmer.”

Griffin nodded. “Javier is right. And that gives us at least some idea of the perimeter we’re talking about.”

Victoria nodded, and then she tapped and swiped at her tablet. “The location from David’s simulation is over forty miles from either Uppsala or the forest.”

“Is that enough of a buffer?” Monroe asked. “If Isaiah realizes you’re there, he’ll be within striking distance.”

“I think it’s as good as we’re going to get,” Victoria said. “I’ll arrange an Abstergo jet to fly us—”

“Wait a minute.” Monroe held up his hand, looking at the table. “Before you do that, how do we know you can trust anyone from Abstergo at this point? Or the Templars?”

“What are you—” Victoria wrinkled her brow. “I’m not sure what you’re suggesting. I told you, you’re all perfectly safe here.”

“That’s not what I mean.” Monroe pressed his index finger against the table. “How do we know Isaiah doesn’t already have zombies, or slaves, or whatever you want to call them, *inside* the Order?”

“That’s impossible,” Victoria said.

"Impossible is a pretty big word," Monroe said. "Are you sure it applies? Are you sure the Order doesn't have some housekeeping to take care of?"

Natalya knew he was talking about the Instruments of the First Will, and Isaiah's connection to them. The question was whether Victoria knew about them. But instead of answering his question, she set her tablet on the table, frowning, and said nothing.

"It sounds like you know something, Monroe," Griffin said.

"I do." Monroe hadn't taken his eyes from Victoria. "The question is, does she?"

Victoria still said nothing, her face unsettlingly serene. Griffin took a step toward her, and the tension in the room escalated to feeling almost dangerous. Natalya knew Monroe wasn't going to budge, and it didn't look as if Victoria would break. Someone else would have to end the stalemate, and quickly, before they wasted any more time.

"We know about the Instruments of the First Will," Natalya said.

Monroe swung a disbelieving glare in her direction, trying to silence her from across the table, while confusion cracked the veneer of Victoria's serenity. Little creases appeared at the corners of her lips and between her eyebrows.

"What do they have to do with this?" she asked. "And how do you know about them?"

Natalya turned to Grace, and she pulled the paper out of her pocket.

Monroe threw up his hands and swore. "So much for keeping any of this between us."

"I found this in a book," Grace said, ignoring him. "Isaiah

wrote it. It seems like he was a part of the Instruments of the First Will."

"May I see it?" Victoria asked.

Grace hesitated for a few seconds, but then shrugged, and passed Victoria the paper. As she read it, the creases on her face seemed to deepen with her confusion. When she finished reading it, she passed the paper to Griffin.

"I had no idea Isaiah had ever been connected with the Instruments," she said. "I suppose he shares some of their objectives. But I can assure you, they are being dealt with. Internally."

"So you didn't know about any of that?" Natalya asked, nodding toward the paper in Griffin's hands.

"I knew about Isaiah's motives," Victoria said. "He sent me a similar document before he left for Mongolia. I honestly didn't think his reasons would make a difference to us and our plans. But he made no mention of the Instruments of the First Will to me."

"Now do you see why I was suspicious?" Monroe asked.

Victoria nodded. "If Isaiah was once allied with them, it's possible he would have spies and followers even without the power of the Trident. But *with* the Trident . . ."

"Now you see why we can't go to the Order." Monroe looked at Griffin. "Or the Brotherhood. We're on our own. The only people we can trust are in this room."

"That's better anyway," David said. "You already said that agents and strike teams won't help us here. In fact, they'll make it worse."

"Right," Victoria said. "Then I guess I need to arrange for a plane to Sweden."

Natalya looked around the room. "All of us?"

"Why not?" Owen asked.

"Because if something goes wrong," she said, "and Isaiah takes over our minds, there won't be anyone left to stop him."

"A smaller team will also stand a better chance of going undetected," Griffin said.

"Right." Victoria picked up her tablet. "So who's going?"

"This is in my wheelhouse," Griffin said. "I'll go."

"I'll go," said Javier.

"Nope." Monroe shook his head. "I don't think we should send any of you kids."

"Kids?" Grace said.

"But we're the ones with the shield," Owen said. "We're actually the best ones to send." And then he added, "As long as it works."

"I actually agree with Owen," Victoria said. "But Javier and David haven't been through the collective unconscious simulation, so they'll stay here. Monroe can run them through it while Griffin takes a team to Sweden."

"I'll go to Sweden," Owen said.

Natalya weighed her choices, but made up her mind when it occurred to her that Sean might also be in Sweden. "I'll go," she said.

Griffin nodded.

"I'll stay here, if that's okay," Grace said, and looked over at David.

"I need all hands on deck," Griffin said. "Your brother will be fine."

Grace bit her bottom lip, and then she nodded.

"I'll buy four tickets on the next available commercial

flight," Victoria said. "I can't charter an Abstergo plane without drawing attention, but I can use a corporate credit card."

"Commercial," Griffin said. "That means no weapons."

"I'm afraid so." Victoria focused on her tablet. "Isaiah left no weapons behind anyway. The only thing left here at the Aerie are some tools and devices used for pest control. At any rate, it's highly unlikely that Isaiah has the ability to monitor commercial air travel, so this is the safest option to avoid detection. To be on the safe side, you'll be traveling with fake passports."

"We will?" Owen said.

"Of course." Victoria smirked, then tapped the screen. "You can't land in Stockholm. That would create unnecessary ground travel, and depending on which route you take around the lake, it could put you too close to Uppsala." She tapped again. "Ah, this will work. There's a flight leaving for Västerås in eighteen hours. The airport there is only fifteen miles from the prong's location."

"No sooner flight?" Griffin asked.

"No," Victoria said. "But everyone needs rest anyway, after their simulations." She looked at David, and then the others. "The Animus keeps your mind stimulated, but your body is active and it still feels the effects of fatigue, even if it hasn't set in yet."

It occurred to Natalya that she didn't even know what time it was, just that it was late, and she suddenly felt exhausted, as if Victoria had just flipped a switch by mentioning it.

Monroe pushed himself up out of his chair. "I'll go see what I can cook for everyone. Then you can all get a good, long rest. You've earned it. I'm proud of you."

"So am I," Victoria said. "It's too late at night to call your parents, but you should all make a point of doing that in the morning."

As soon as she mentioned that, it was like she flipped another switch, and Natalya suddenly felt very, very homesick. She wanted her own bed, or better yet, her grandparents' sofa, where she sometimes slept better than anywhere else, and woke up to the noxious smell of buckwheat porridge on the stove, which she would gladly eat right now if her grandmother put it in front of her.

Monroe headed for the door. "Meet back here in twenty or thirty minutes if you're hungry."

Natalya decided to just stay put and wait.

"My mom still thinks I ran away," Owen said.

"Mine too," Javier said.

"Why?" Natalya asked.

"Because that's what I told her," Owen said. "I couldn't make up a story about being at a special Abstergo school. We were with Griffin."

Javier hung one arm over the back of his chair. "It's closer to the truth than what you guys tell your parents."

Natalya was too exhausted to argue with him; besides which, he had a point.

"So what's this Instruments group that you were all talking about?" Javier asked.

"Oh, right," Grace said. "You guys weren't there. It's kind of hard to explain, but basically, the Instruments of the First Will is a group of Templars who want to bring back the civilization that created the Pieces of Eden."

"And that would be a bad thing?" Javier said.

"Probably," Owen said, "since they destroyed themselves."

"Why do they want to bring them back?" David asked.

"Because they're Templars," Griffin said.

"I object to that statement," Victoria said. "The Instruments seek to restore Juno as their master. They believe humans should be *slaves* to the Precursors."

"Slaves?" David asked.

"Yes," Victoria said. "The Instruments are *not* true Templars."

"Or are they the truest Templars?" Griffin asked. "Maybe they're just the logical result of what the Templars started. The whole reason we have the Animus is because the Templars wanted to find Pieces of Eden. Your Order went digging for Precursors, and once you start down that road, where does it end?"

Victoria's lips thinned, and she offered no response.

"Sounds like it ends with the Instruments," Javier said.

Victoria rose from her chair. "I'm not hungry, and I have to arrange your flights. I'll see you all in the morning." With that, she swept from the room.

Griffin's argument echoed much of what Natalya had been thinking since this ordeal had begun. She didn't think anyone should have the Trident. Yanmei was dead because Natalya had tried to keep the others from finding the second piece of it. Once you allow yourself to use a power like that, where does it end?

How does it end?

Natalya shook her head. Griffin was wrong. "I don't think it ends with the Instruments," she said. "I think it ends with Isaiah. He doesn't want to bring Juno back. He wants to be the master. He wants to destroy and enslave the world."

The room went quiet after that, and it stayed quiet until Monroe wheeled a cart into the common room carrying plates and a big pot.

"Isaiah took most of the nonperishable provisions with him," he said. "The perishables have all gone bad. So for dinner we have buttered noodles with some garlic and thyme." He looked around the table. "Where's Victoria?"

"She doesn't like where things have ended up," Griffin said. "I think she's feeling a bit defensive of her Order."

Monroe nodded. "Can't say I blame her for that." Then he stuck a serving fork into the pot and dropped a pile of noodles onto one of the plates. "Who's hungry?"

Owen raised his hand. "Me."

Monroe passed him the plate, and then dished up noodles for everyone else. They all ate, and Natalya thought it actually tasted pretty good. Several minutes went by without anyone speaking, but then Monroe put his fork down.

"Of course, to be fair, the Assassins have been guilty of their own excesses. Haven't they, Griffin?"

Griffin stopped chewing.

"What excesses?" David asked.

Monroe picked his fork back up. "It's hard to say for sure, since the Brotherhood likes to keep everything in the dark. Especially their mistakes. Abstergo historians blame the burning of Constantinople on a man named Ezio Auditore, one of the most revered Assassins in history. Countless innocent deaths during that disaster. And then of course, one of Javier's ancestors, Shay Cormac, became a Templar after he caused an earthquake, and blamed the Brotherhood for it. And then there was Jack the Ripper."

"He was an Assassin?" Grace asked.

"No, he wasn't," Griffin said, his hands in fists on either side of his plate. "Not a true Assassin."

"Or was he the truest?" Natalya asked. "Assassins kill people. Once you start down that road, where does it end?"

"And who gets to say who's true and who's not?" Monroe asked.

"No one does." Griffin now rose to his feet. "Our Creed speaks for itself. Anyone who violates it is not an Assassin." He turned away and stalked toward the door, but before he left the room, he turned back and said, "Assassins *stopped* Jack the Ripper. We clean our house."

Then he was gone, and after he'd left, everyone finished dinner quickly. Natalya had pretty much lost her appetite with the mention of a serial killer, and only took another couple of bites.

"You all head to bed," Monroe said. "I'll clean up."

Natalya felt very heavy as she tried to get out of her chair, and her feet dragged a bit as they all walked to the Aerie's dormitory wing. She found her room and fell into her bed still dressed, and when she opened her eyes again, it was light outside, and she hadn't moved at all during the night.

She climbed out of bed, feeling sore everywhere, and trudged from her bedroom to the common room. David and Javier were there, and they seemed a lot more alert than she felt. Grace sat in an armchair, staring blankly, and Owen hadn't appeared yet.

Natalya shuffled over to Grace, and winced as she lowered herself into the armchair next to her.

"You too?" Grace asked.

"Yeah, what's the deal?" The Animus sometimes took a toll, but mostly in the form of headaches. A simulation had never left her feeling this beaten-up the next day.

"I don't know." Grace pointed her chin at her brother. "He was in for a lot longer than me, and he was practically skipping this morning."

"Javier looks fine, too." Natalya decided that the difference must have something to do with the collective unconscious, and she hoped that meant the simulation had worked after all.

A few minutes later, Monroe strolled in carrying a tray of biscuits he'd managed to bake up, along with some peanut butter and jelly to spread over them. The biscuits smelled like butter, and Natalya finished three of them before she stopped to wonder how many she should eat.

"Save some for Owen," she said.

The others all looked down at their plates, and then at the tray. There was one biscuit left.

"He'll be fine," Javier said.

That biscuit was cold by the time Owen stumbled into the room, and not long after that, Victoria appeared with their passports and plane tickets. Natalya went back to her room and took a shower, which helped soothe her sore muscles, and then she changed into a fresh set of Aerie-issued sweats and hoodie. By the time they left for the airport in an Abstergo van, she felt slightly closer to normal.

Monroe drove them down the mountain, with Griffin in the front passenger seat. Neither man spoke to the other for almost the entire drive, but as they pulled up to the airport curb, Monroe lifted the gear into park and twisted in his seat to face the Assassin.

"Listen, what I said yesterday about the Brotherhood . . . I was talking about it as a whole. Not about you."

Griffin nodded. "I appreciate that."

"And you do keep a pretty clean house," Monroe added. "Considering."

"Considering what?" Owen asked with a grin.

Monroe shook his head. "Get out of the van, you little punk. And stay safe. All of you. Don't take any unnecessary risks."

"We won't," Grace said.

They all piled out, and Monroe pulled away. Griffin led them through security without setting off any alarms, which meant he had either left his hidden blade back at the Aerie, or he had found a way to make it truly hidden, and they boarded their flight. Victoria had bought them first-class tickets, something Natalya had never experienced before, and probably never would again. But as she took her wider, softer seat, her sore body felt deeply grateful for Abstergo's corporate card.

She sat by a window, next to Griffin, and as the plane lifted off, he leaned back and closed his eyes. "See you in Sweden," he said.

Natalya looked out the window at the shrinking buildings and roads. "See you in Sweden," she whispered.

CHAPTER TWENTY-FOUR

They landed in the early afternoon. Grace had slept for part of the flight, but she'd also watched a couple of movies, and that had been a weird experience. With everything going on, movies seemed completely trivial, and even worthless, but what else was she going to do while she was stuck on a plane? One was a superhero flick, and the other was a comedy, and both had actually done a pretty good job distracting her from the reason she was stuck on that plane to begin with. Maybe that's all movies needed to do.

The city of Västerås looked lovely from the air, situated on Lake Mälaren, with a river running through it and a few small islands offshore. Once they'd landed at the small airport outside of town, Griffin rented an SUV, and then drove to a hardware store. He went in alone, and came back out with two shovels, which he threw in the back of the car. Then he drove them into the countryside, passing numerous farms, with barns and silos, ponds, grain fields, and pastures. They traveled through small stands of trees as well, but it wasn't until they were several miles from the city that they reached true forest.

When Grace thought of Hansel and Gretel getting lost in the woods, she imagined it to be a place like this. Huge pine trees and oak trees kept much of the forest floor in shadow, which felt oppressive in one moment and comforting in the next. Its depths both beckoned and threatened her.

"It's like the Forest," Natalya said.

"Without the giant snake," Owen said.

Grace rolled her window down, and cool, pine-scented air blew across her forehead. Above the car's engine, she heard a variety of birdsong coming from the trees, and then suddenly, as they came around a bend, she glimpsed a moose just off the road. The back half of its huge body stood in the shadows under the trees, while its head and broad antlers caught the sun. She'd never seen a moose in person before, and whipped around in her seat to get a second look, but it had already disappeared into the woods, probably startled by their SUV.

"The location David identified is on private property," Griffin said. "We don't have time to get permission from the owners, so we're just going to not be seen. Owen and Natalya are fairly proficient at not being seen." Grace could see his eyes in the rearview mirror looking at her. "What about you? You had an Assassin ancestor in New York, right?"

Grace nodded. "Eliza."

"Did you pick up anything from that experience?"

"Some," she said. Owen's ancestor, the Assassin Varius, had

trained Eliza, and the Bleeding Effects had given Grace some of her ancestor's hand-to-hand combat skills, and some free-running ability. "I'll try to keep up," she said.

Griffin drove them another few miles, and then turned the SUV onto a rutted forest access road, where a short distance in he stopped and killed the engine. "We'll walk from here."

They all climbed out, and Grace looked up into the trees and the filtered green sunlight, breathing the air in deeply. This place felt right to her, familiar, and she realized that she had been here before. Not this spot, specifically, but this land that her ancestor knew so well. She hadn't spent much time in Östen's memories, but it had apparently been enough to leave an impression.

"It's weird to do this without any weapons," Owen said. "No crossbow. No grenades."

"What about your hidden blade?" Natalya asked Griffin.

He held up his right forearm and tapped it with his other hand. "Ceramic. You guys get these." He handed Owen and Natalya one of the shovels each, and then he pulled out a phone. "Hang on while I pull up the location on GPS."

But Grace didn't need GPS. Östen always knew his way home. "It's that direction," she said, pointing off into the woods.

Griffin looked at her, then at the forest, then at his phone. "You're right. How did you know that?"

"Bleeding Effect," she said. "You're in my house now."

"Your Viking house," Owen said.

Griffin slipped the phone back in his pocket. "Lead the way."

So that's what Grace did, guiding them through the woods past boulders she recognized, though the streams they crossed flowed differently than she remembered. They didn't come across another moose, but they did see a small boar that bolted away, and through Östen, Grace knew that it was a young sow, and shy, and normally hard to spot.

They came at Östen's old farmstead from behind, walking up the backside of his hill where a cell tower now stood. The sight of it bothered Grace, but she knew it would probably bother her more to see what had become of Östen's land on the other side. There wasn't anything she could do to change it, though. It was just the passage of time.

"Let's be as quick as we can about this," Griffin said as they came over the top of the hill.

But Grace knew instantly there wouldn't be anything quick about it.

Below them, what looked like a small factory occupied the space where Östen's farmstead had once stood. A chain-link fence surrounded it, enclosing the spot that should have been Östen's spring. But instead of the spring, Grace saw a small brick building with a thick pipe running from inside it down the hill to the factory.

"It looks like they're bottling the water," Natalya said.

"That's exactly what they're doing." Griffin pulled his phone back out. "I don't understand. This wasn't listed."

"Look at all the dirt." Owen pointed at several places around the site of the factory where the turf and the trees had been cleared. "That's all fresh. I think they just built this."

Griffin pointed at the brick building. "That springhouse is sitting right on top of the Piece of Eden."

"So what do we do?" Owen asked.

"I'm thinking," Griffin said. "You do the same."

Grace tried hard to see the place through her ancestor's eyes, hoping it might give her an idea. She remembered Östen digging out a pool around the spring, to collect more of the water before it ran away to join the streams and the lakes. The rock had been hard, and the labor difficult. To build that new brick springhouse, they would have dug out even more, which meant they might have disturbed the dagger.

"When they were building this place," Grace said, "what do you think they did with any historical stuff they found?"

Griffin raised an eyebrow. "Now there's an idea."

Grace looked down at the factory. "I think we should ask if they give tours."

"Right," Griffin said. "Owen, Natalya, you stay here and keep out of sight. Grace and I will go down and check things out."

They set off down the hill, walking around the chain-link fence to the plant's front entrance, where Grace saw the company name and logo.

"You gotta be kidding me," Griffin said.

The logo bore the unmistakable image of one of the Trident's prongs in simplified silhouette, with the word *dolkkälla* written over it. "Can you translate the name?" Grace asked.

"Dagger Spring," he said. "I'm pretty sure that's what it means."

Grace almost laughed. "Hide in plain sight, right?"

Griffin shook his head. "Let's go see what's inside."

They hurried past the sign, up the driveway, to the plant's main entrance, its name and logo everywhere they looked. Through the front doors, they entered a modest lobby that smelled of fresh paint and carpet. A receptionist looked up from his desk, smiled, and said something in what Grace assumed was Swedish.

Griffin shook his head, and in that instant he lost all the casual menace he normally projected, and became a mild and embarrassed tourist. "I'm sorry," he said. "We're from the U.S."

The receptionist's smile changed, very subtly, taking on a shade of impatience and condescension. "Of course. What can I do for you?" he asked with only a slight accent.

"We were just driving and saw your plant," Griffin said. "Do you offer tours?"

"Not at the moment," the receptionist said. "We opened very recently. Perhaps one day."

"Where does your name come from?" Grace asked.

"That, I am happy to say, I can show you." He rose from his chair and came around from behind the desk, and then led them across the lobby to a glass door. The room on the other side of it was dimly lit, with glowing display cases. Some held fragments and small objects Grace couldn't identify from this far away. Some cases were empty. But at the far end of the room, by itself under a warm spotlight, the Piece of Eden sat on display.

"There have been several farms on this site going back many hundreds of years," the receptionist said. "We worked with scientists to preserve what we found. Most went to a museum, but we arranged to display these. That is the dagger. They found it buried next to the spring. Very strange, yes?"

"Unbelievable," Griffin said. "Can we go in?"

"No, I am sorry, the museum isn't ready. They are still adding to it." The receptionist then folded his hands in front of his waist and gazed through the glass door as if he never got tired of the view. "You are the second American to see this today," he said.

Grace looked at Griffin, the back of her neck prickling. Griffin looked at the receptionist.

"Is that right?" he said. "Where was he from?"

"She," the receptionist said. "I didn't ask where she was from. She read about us in the paper yesterday, and came from

Uppsala to see." He pointed toward his desk. "I have the article if you want to read it."

Grace tried to convince herself it was just a coincidence, but did a poor job of it. It was possible that the woman who came to see the dagger had nothing to do with Isaiah, but why take the risk? It would be smarter to simply hurry and get out of there.

"This was interesting," Griffin said. "But we better get going. Thank you for your time."

"You're welcome," the receptionist said. "Please come back when the museum is open."

"I wish we could," Griffin said. "But we aren't here for very long."

"Then you have a reason to come back to Sweden." The receptionist gave them a broad smile.

"That's true," Griffin said, nodding. Then he looked toward the front doors. "Well, have a nice day."

"You as well," the receptionist said.

Griffin waved a good-bye, and guided Grace through the lobby, then back outside. They walked as fast as they dared down the driveway, trying to avoid drawing attention, but once they reached the fence, they veered to the side and raced back up the hill. At the top, they found Owen and Natalya waiting where they'd left them.

"Well?" Owen asked.

"You're not going to believe this," Grace said. "They have the prong in there."

"How do you know?" Natalya asked.

"Because I saw it," Grace said. "It's just sitting there. On display."

"This plant is called Dagger Spring," Griffin said, and

Grace noted that his usual menace had returned. "They dug up the prong when they were excavating."

"So what's the problem?" Owen asked. "We just break in tonight and grab it."

Griffin stared down at the plant. "The problem is Isaiah. Someone else was here today asking about the dagger. He might already be on his way."

"Then maybe we shouldn't wait," Natalya said. "Could you steal it right now?"

"There aren't any guards," Griffin said. "I could easily force my way in and walk out of there with it. But they think it's a national antiquity. They'll be looking for it, and for me, which will make it harder for us to get it out of the country."

"So what do we do?" Grace asked. The prong was right there, within reach. But any option for taking it came with risks.

Griffin looked down at the ground and rubbed his shaved head. "We wait until this evening. As soon as that place shuts down, I go in, grab the dagger, and then we get the hell out of here." He looked up at them. "Agreed?"

Grace nodded, and so did Owen and Natalya.

"Okay." Griffin lowered himself to the ground and sat down. "Might as well get comfortable."

Grace did the same, and the four of them soon sat in a circle on the hilltop, surrounded by forest, waiting for evening to come. The fluffy clouds overhead shuffled along in their slow tumble, threaded by the occasional bird, and in the stillness, Grace thought of David. She hoped he was doing okay in the collective unconscious simulation, reminding herself that he would be safer there than she was here. No one said much, but the silence didn't feel awkward or empty. At least not to her.

Maybe it did to Owen. After they'd been there for a while, he cleared his throat. "If I get cancer from this cell tower, I'm holding all of you responsible."

"Cell phones don't give you cancer," Natalya said.

"Oh, really?" Owen said. "Do you hear that buzzing?"

"I think it's relaxing," Griffin said. "When I was a kid, I lived near a busy railroad track. You get used to having noise in the background."

"You were a kid?" Owen said.

Griffin nodded, smiling. "Believe it or not."

"Do they make onesies with little Assassin hoods?" Grace asked. "What was your first toy?"

"A switchblade," Griffin said, his voice flat.

For a few seconds, Grace couldn't tell if he was joking, and she looked over at Owen and Natalya, who had both stopped smiling. But then Griffin cracked, and he chuckled. "You guys almost believed that."

"No, we didn't," Owen said.

"Sure you did." Griffin leaned toward them. "Listen, I have to be honest with you guys about something. I didn't think you'd make it this far."

Again, silence followed, and Grace wondered if this was another joke. "Um. Thanks?"

"No, just listen," he said. "When I found out Monroe had dragged a bunch of kids into this, I assumed it would come to a quick, bad end for everyone. But here you are. It's impressive, that's all I'm saying. You've impressed me."

"Thanks," Owen said. "You're pretty nice for a ruthless killer."

Griffin fake-lunged at him.

"Smart-ass," the Assassin said.

"What time is it?" Natalya asked. "It feels late, but it doesn't look late."

"We're practically in the land of the midnight sun," Griffin said. "This far north, at this time of year, the sun stays up for a lot longer." He checked his phone, and then got to his feet. "But they'll probably be closing up shop soon. At least in the lobby."

Grace, Owen, and Natalya all stood up, too. Grace peered down at the plant and saw that the parking lot was mostly empty.

"Okay," Owen said. "So how are we doing this?"

"We aren't," Griffin said. "I am."

"Why?" Owen asked. "You just said we impressed you. We can help."

"This is a one-person job. More than that will just complicate it." He looked at Grace. "Tell him how simple this is."

"It's basically right there when you walk through the front doors," Grace said.

"The only hitch might be a security system, but I can deal with it." Griffin set off down the hill, but pointed back at them. "Stay there, Owen."

Owen scowled and folded his arms.

Grace kept her eyes on the Assassin the entire way as he skirted along the fence, seeming to move much more quickly than he had when she'd gone with him. A couple of times she even lost sight of him, as if he'd just vanished in the daylight. But then he appeared again, some distance on from where she'd last seen him. Her heart was pounding, even though Griffin had appeared perfectly calm and confident. When he reached the edge of the fence, he ran up the drive, and was lost to Grace's view.

"Now we just wait," Natalya said.

A few minutes went by. Then a few more minutes. Grace almost expected alarms to start going off at any moment, but realized that was stupid. This wasn't a government facility. It was a bottled water plant with a one-room museum. So no alarms went off. But Griffin didn't come out, either.

"It's taking longer than I thought it would," Natalya said.

"Maybe the security system is tougher than he thought," Owen said.

Grace watched, and listened. More minutes passed.

The she heard something. A distant, familiar whumping sound. She looked over at Natalya and Owen, and from their wide eyes, she knew they could hear it, too.

"Helicopters," Owen said.

"Hide!" Grace said.

They ran from the open hilltop back to the tree line, where they hid in the shadows, watching as two helicopters swung into view. They were large and black, emblazoned with the Abstergo logo, and similar to the ones Isaiah had escaped in from Mongolia.

"What about Griffin?" Natalya whispered.

The helicopters hovered low over the plant for a few moments, and then doors opened up suddenly in their sides, spilling coils of black rope. Abstergo agents in paramilitary gear then emerged from inside, and one by one they slid down the ropes.

"What do we do?" Natalya asked.

Grace didn't know. She felt helpless. They had no weapons, other than the two shovels.

"We've gotta do something," Owen said. "We can't just—"

Gunshots echoed up the hill, sounding distant and muffled, as if they came from inside the plant. Grace knew that sound, and it pierced her stomach.

"Seriously, what do we do?" Natalya asked.

Owen took a step forward. "I'm going in—"

"No, you're not." Grace grabbed him and held him back. "That's suicide."

"Well, I can't just stand here," he said.

"I'm not letting you go in there," Grace said. "I don't care how good you think you are. You aren't—"

More gunshots, these sounding louder and clearer, and Grace ducked her head involuntarily. Those had come from outside, and much closer.

"Look!" Natalya said, pointing.

Down below, Grace spotted Griffin sprinting behind the plant, then up the hill along the main pipe. Three agents chased him, pausing to aim and shoot. But Griffin kept moving, erratically, and managed to avoid getting hit. As he reached the springhouse, one of the helicopters dove at him, and three more agents leapt to the ground, on the side of the fence near Grace and the others.

"He's trapped," Natalya whispered.

"Screw this," Owen said. He snatched up one of the shovels and charged away before Grace could stop him.

CHAPTER TWENTY-FIVE 

Grace watched Owen as he raced to help Griffin. A second later, she grabbed the other shovel and did the same, and before she really stopped to think about it, she was closing in on the first agent. They were focused on Griffin, so they didn't see the attack coming. Owen reached them first, swinging hard. Grace heard the metal impact of the shovel against the agent's helmet, and she spun almost 180 degrees before collapsing.

The other two turned toward Owen, but then Grace was there. She jabbed the shovel two-handed, like a spear, at the nearest agent's knee, and his leg buckled. Then she spun the shovel and brought it down on the agent's head, driving him to the ground.

From the corner of her eye, she saw the third agent raise his gun in her direction, and she raised the shovel reflexively, like a shield. A shot, a *clang*, and the shovel flew from her hands. But then Owen hit the agent from behind, hard.

With that, all three were down.

Grace looked and saw that Griffin had reached the fence, but he was struggling to climb it, and at the top, he simply rolled his way onto the other side, falling hard to the ground.

"He's hit," Owen said, sprinting toward him.

Grace ran, too, feeling like Östen, and Eliza, and herself, all at once.

The agents were still shooting, and bullets struck the ground around her as she and Owen helped Griffin to his feet.

He pressed something into Grace's hand, and she realized it was the prong, wrapped in a towel. She shoved it into one of her pockets.

"Get to the forest," Griffin said. "Go deep. The helicopters can't land. You'll lose them."

"You're coming with us," Owen said.

"No!" Griffin said, wincing. "Listen to me. I'm not going to make it. You have to move. Now."

But he couldn't stop them from staying at his side, and he kept limping along as they helped him up the hill. Grace looked back and saw six agents rushing after them, but they reached the trees first, where Natalya waited for them.

"What now?" she asked.

"We have to lose them," Owen said. "And get back to the car."

"Which way?" Natalya asked.

Grace paused, and let Östen step more fully into her head. She thought about the forest, which she knew well, and found a way. "There's a wash over there." She pointed to their right. "It'll keep us out of sight. We can follow it out of here."

"Sounds good to me."

Griffin grunted, like he meant to say something, but didn't.

They stumbled and raced through the woods, trying to hide behind the trees, until they reached the wash and clambered down its grassy embankment into a shallow, icy stream. Shouts echoed behind them from the Abstergo agents searching the woods.

"Let's go," Grace whispered.

She led them down the gully, Owen and Natalya on either side of Griffin, splashing through the water as the helicopters circled above. But Grace could barely see them through the trees, which meant that they would not be seen. Soon, the shouts grew more distant, as did the drone of the helicopters.

"Do you think they're giving up?" Owen asked.

"No," Grace said. "They know we have the prong. There's no way they're giving up. They're just looking for us in the wrong place, but they'll figure it out eventually. We have to keep moving."

"Griffin is bleeding pretty bad," Natalya said.

Grace looked over, and saw the Assassin's side was covered in red, and so was Natalya where she leaned up against him for support. His head wobbled, and his eyelids fluttered, even as he somehow managed to stay on his feet. Even with her very limited knowledge, Grace could see he needed urgent medical attention, but she had no idea how he could get it.

"Let's get him to the car," she said.

So they pressed ahead, staying low, listening. The frigid water turned painful, and she walked up on the mud and rocks when she could, knowing that eventually they would have to leave the wash to get to the car, and that would be the most dangerous leg of their escape.

"What?" Owen said.

Grace turned toward him, and saw him leaning his head toward Griffin.

"Hang on," Owen said to Natalya. "He's trying to tell me something." So they halted, and the stream gathered around their ankles. "What's that, Griffin?"

"Give—give my . . ." The Assassin's voice was a ragged, wheezy gasp. "Give my blades to Javier."

"No, man," he said. "No, those have to come from you. So you gotta stay with us."

Griffin shook his head. "Tell . . . tell him he—he earned them."

"You tell him," Owen said. "He's not going to believe me if I tell him that."

Griffin's mouth formed a thin smile. "Owen," he said. "Owen . . ."

"Yeah, Griffin, I'm right here."

"It doesn't matter," the Assassin said.

"What doesn't matter?"

"It doesn't . . . matter," Griffin repeated.

Owen looked at Grace, and said in a hushed voice, "I don't know what that means."

"Let's just keep moving," Grace said.

They resumed walking, and they made it another hundred feet before Griffin's legs gave out and he slumped into the stream. Water gurgled over his face, and they rushed to lift him up.

"Griffin," Grace said. "Griffin, stay with us."

But he didn't move.

Owen knelt down in the stream, his face right in front of the Assassin's. "Griffin," he said, shaking him. "Griffin."

Still no response.

"Help me," Owen said, grabbing Griffin by one of his arms. Grace and Natalya took the other, and together they pulled the Assassin's heavy body out of the stream. Then Owen dropped to his knees again and started CPR, counting off chest compressions and offering mouth-to-mouth.

Grace could see it wasn't working. Nothing could work, because Griffin was already gone, and there wasn't anything anyone could do. But Owen kept at it for several minutes, and Grace let him go for a while before she knelt down beside him and put a hand on his back.

"I'm sorry," she said.

Owen kept counting and pushing.

"Owen, he's gone."

"No," he said. "It would take more than that to kill him."

Grace looked up at Natalya, and she knelt down on his other side. They both put their arms around him, and gradually the compressions ceased, and he just leaned over Griffin with his hands pressing against the middle of the Assassin's chest. They stayed that way for several moments, saying nothing as the water behind them warbled on, which seemed wrong, as if the stream should have stopped.

Grace couldn't make sense of this.

It was a matter of minutes.

Only minutes.

Minutes ago, they were sitting on the hill, talking about Griffin as an Assassin baby. Now, minutes later, they were kneeling in a stream, with Griffin's blood on their clothes, and he was dead. She couldn't figure out how this had happened.

Owen sat up straighter, and Grace and Natalya lowered their arms from his back. Then he reached across Griffin to his right arm, and he pulled up his sleeve. There on his wrist was his hidden blade, this one ceramic. Owen undid the straps and slid it over Griffin's hand. Then he placed it on his own wrist.

"Just until I can give it to Javier," he said.

"His phone!" Natalya said, and she searched his pockets until she found it. But the stream had found it first, and the phone wouldn't do them any good now.

Grace didn't want to be the one to mention his wallet, but they were going to need money. They were stuck in a foreign country with fake passports, no cell phone, and a Piece of Eden. Without saying a word, she reached under him, found his back pocket, and then she pulled his wallet out. Owen and Natalya saw what she did, but they didn't say anything, either, and the three of them sat in silence.

Silence.

Something was missing.

"Do you hear the helicopters?" Grace asked.

Owen craned his neck. "No."

"I don't, either," Natalya said.

Grace didn't believe Isaiah had called off the search. Not when he knew someone else had taken the final prong of the Trident. But the helicopters weren't in the air anymore, and she couldn't hear anything in the forest except for what was supposed to be there.

"I don't want to leave him here," Owen said, looking at Griffin's body.

Grace didn't like the idea, either. But they'd left the shovels behind during the chaos at the bottled water plant, so they had no way to dig him a grave. And they also had to keep moving. They had to find a way to get the prong away from here, and away from Isaiah.

"He wouldn't want you to worry about him anymore," Natalya said. "You know that. He'd want you to escape, and get the dagger away from Isaiah."

Owen nodded, looking down at the hidden blade he now wore on his wrist. "Let's get moving. It's not going to get any easier by sitting here."

Grace and Natalya looked at each other and gently nodded. Then the three of them got up, and Grace led them forward down the wash, and it was suddenly a harder journey. Physically harder, as if she felt the weight of Griffin's lifeless body on her shoulders. But she persisted, refusing to look back, hoping that burden would lessen with distance.

It didn't.

But eventually they reached that place in the wash where they would need to climb out of it and cross through a stretch of woods if they wanted to get to the SUV. Grace listened for the helicopters, and still heard nothing. She couldn't hear any agents moving through the forest. But she didn't trust that silence.

"I think we should wait here for a while," she whispered.

"What for?" Natalya asked.

"Something doesn't seem right," she said.

"Something isn't right." Owen picked up a stick from the ground. "Griffin just died."

"No," Grace said. "Not that."

"Then what is it?" Natalya asked.

"Where did Isaiah go?" She looked up into the trees. "I don't like not knowing where he is, and I think we should wait here, just in case, until it gets dark. Then we go to the car."

Owen shook his head and snapped the stick. "Fine," he said.

Natalya just reached out and laid her hand on Grace's arm.

So they stayed there in the wash, wet and shivering, listening for any sound that might indicate Isaiah's return. After Grace had been sitting in the same position for a while, she moved her legs, and felt the dagger in her pocket, which she'd almost forgotten about. She pulled it out, wondering where Griffin had found the towel he'd wrapped around it, and as she unwrapped it, she noticed his blood on the fabric. The red-brown spot trapped her eyes and held them until she broke free of it and brought out the dagger.

The prong of the Trident. The Piece of Eden.

"So that's it," Owen said. "That's what this is all about."

Her ancestor, Eliza, had carried one of the daggers from New York City to General Grant on the battlefield. But Grace had never held one before. Its edge was still sharp after thousands and thousands of years, and even without its power, it would be deadly. Isaiah had demonstrated that when he used one to kill Yanmei.

"Put it away," Natalya said. "Please."

Grace wrapped it back up in its towel and slipped it into her pocket. Not long after that, she noticed that the forest had grown darker, and the blue in the sky had deepened. Evening had come, and soon that turned into twilight without any sign of Isaiah. If they were going to try for the SUV, now would be the time.

"Let's go," she said.

They climbed up out of the wash, over the embankment, and darted into the trees. In the gloom, Grace found that Östen's memories gave her an advantage. She knew this land, and that allowed her to run swiftly, which allowed Owen and Natalya to follow her.

They encountered no Abstergo agents as they made their way, and Grace heard no helicopters. The closer they got to the SUV, the more she thought she had been worried over nothing.

"I think I see it," Owen said.

He was right. Up ahead lay the forest access road, and the SUV was still there, its windows black and empty. They had made it.

"I'll drive," Grace said as they rushed up to the car. She reached into her pocket, and then she stopped, and almost didn't want to ask. "Who has the keys?"

Neither of them answered, and Grace felt her breath grow heavy in her lungs, pressing down. They had left the keys with Griffin's body. She tried the driver's side door, hoping that maybe it was unlocked, and that maybe Griffin had left the keys inside. But it wasn't unlocked.

"We have to go back?" Owen asked.

It had been hard enough for him to leave the first time. Grace didn't want him to relive it in the dark. "I'll go," she said. "I know my way. You guys stay here."

"I don't think we should separate," Natalya said.

Grace didn't like the idea, either, but if they all went, it would take more time than she felt they had. "I'll be fine," she said. "Just stay here and—"

A blinding beam of light smacked Grace in the face, and she held up a hand to shield her eyes. Then another light switched on, and another, and another, coming from all sides and closing in.

"I must say," said a familiar voice, "you kept me waiting so long, I had begun to wonder if this was even your car."

It was Isaiah.

Grace almost bolted, in panic and reflex. But her mind kept her feet in check, because she knew they were surrounded, and she wouldn't get far. It wouldn't have mattered if they had remembered the keys.

"Where is the Assassin?" Isaiah asked, a tall silhouette in the spotlights.

No one answered him.

"It was a fatal shot, then," Isaiah said. "So which one of you has the dagger?"

Still no one answered him.

"Let's dim those lights," he said. "Perhaps that will help them see this situation more clearly."

The spotlights swung their beams toward the ground, and Grace could now see the agents holding them, and between them, an even greater number of agents silently aiming their guns. Isaiah stepped closer, wearing Abstergo paramilitary gear, his green eyes somewhat paled by the artificial glare.

"You notice I don't have the Trident with me," Isaiah said. "You don't have to die tonight. I certainly don't wish it."

"You want your own Ragnarök," Owen said. "You want everyone to die."

"No," Isaiah said. "No, I don't want that at all. But many people must die for the world to be reborn in a better form. Do you mourn for the dead flakes of skin shed by the snake? Do you grieve the loss of the caterpillar after it has become a butterfly?"

"I think my history teacher would call those false analogies," Grace said. "The earth doesn't shed, and humans aren't its skin. And the caterpillar doesn't die to become a butterfly."

Isaiah nodded, almost approvingly. "I'm reminded of how exceptional you all are. More reason to spare you, because I don't actually wish for specific people to die any more than an exterminator wishes death on specific ants." He stared at Grace. "Does that analogy meet with your approval?"

"Where is Sean?" Natalya asked.

Isaiah smiled. "Your loyalty and devotion are admirable."

"Where is he?" Natalya asked again, but it was clear to Grace that Isaiah wasn't going to answer.

"What are you going to do with us?" Grace asked.

Isaiah snapped his fingers, and a group of the Abstergo agents closed in tighter, guns still raised.

"I had planned to simply leave you here," Isaiah said. "After I recover the dagger, of course. But I believe I may take you with me. You might be useful, given your lineages. But if you fight back on either score, I will have you killed, and while I do not wish for your deaths, believe me when I say I will not regret them."

Grace's legs had begun to tremble, from the cold and from her fear, but she hoped Isaiah couldn't see that. This was the closest she had ever come to death, and it was right here, just minutes or seconds away, like it had been with Griffin, and it was staring at her down the barrel of a dozen guns. The agents aiming their weapons looked at her as though she was nothing but a target. She might as well have been made of cardboard, and whatever shield Minerva had given her, it would be useless against bullets.

"You have the dagger, don't you, Grace?" Isaiah said.

She couldn't feel her body. She thought of David, and her parents.

"Cole, check her pockets."

One of the agents approached Grace, and she recognized the woman by her codename, Rothenberg, a Templar mole who had helped her escape from the Aerie with Monroe. But when the woman looked at Grace now, she didn't seem to care about any of that.

Javier was right. More zombie than slave.

"Don't move," Cole said, and even though Grace didn't want to obey, the part of her mind most driven to survive held her still. Cole reached into Grace's pocket and pulled out the dagger, which she handed immediately to Isaiah.

He shook the dagger from the towel, into his open hand, and closed his fist around the grip. "Were you as amused as I was by this prong's location?" he asked.

They had lost.

They had lost *everything.*

Isaiah had all three pieces of the Trident now, the very thing Minerva had feared all those thousands of years ago.

"You're forgetting about something," Owen said.

"Highly unlikely," Isaiah said. "But tell me."

"The Ascendance Event." Owen actually smirked, and made it convincing. "Monroe figured it out, and it can stop the Trident. Your superweapon is worthless."

What was Owen doing? Trying to intimidate Isaiah? Bluff their way out of this somehow? Or just showing the only card they had?

"The Ascendance Event?" Isaiah cocked his head and bent

down to look Owen in his eyes, their faces very close together. "You're lying."

"No," Owen said, returning Isaiah's stare, "I'm not."

A few seconds passed, and then Isaiah leaned away. "So Monroe finally did it. After all these years."

"Yes, he did," Owen said. "So like I said, your Trident—"

"Not to worry," Isaiah said. "I've taken care of that. Without Sean, you have no Ascendance Event." Then he nodded to himself. "You've changed my mind, Owen. You're not useful at all. In fact, I think you might be a danger to me." He turned away from them. "Cole, line them up."

"Yes, sir."

The woman waved over a few more agents. Two of them took Grace by the arms, high up near her shoulders, and they half dragged, half lifted her along and placed her in the middle of the main road. They brought Natalya and Owen over the same way to stand next to her, and then Isaiah asked for a gun.

"You're going to do it yourself?" Owen asked. "I'm surprised."

"That's because you still don't understand what I am." Isaiah strode toward them, now armed with a pistol. "I am the Fenris wolf. I have come to swallow the sun, and the moon, and I do not turn away from the task before me."

"I think there's probably a name for what's wrong with you," Owen said.

Grace wondered where he found the will to be defiant. She wondered where her will had gone as she felt the seconds ticking by, like her life was a thread, and she had come to its end.

CHAPTER TWENTY-SIX

"You disappoint me, Sean," Isaiah said.

"I'm sorry," Sean said. "So sorry." He wanted desperately to please Isaiah, and he had been trying, spending endless hours in the Animus, reliving the same memories again and again, searching for any detail, or hidden clue that might reveal what had happened to the dagger after Styrbjörn left it at the shrine.

"There must be something you are missing," Isaiah said. "We have searched every inch of ground within three hundred meters of that rock, and the dagger isn't there."

"It must be," Sean said. "That's the only place it could be."

"Obviously not," Isaiah said. He turned to the technicians. "Prepare the simulation. We'll run it again—"

"No," Sean said. "Please. Let me out."

"I believe I have shown you what happens when you tell me no," Isaiah said.

"I know, I know, but please. I can't."

The inside of his skull felt scraped and raw. He'd been hanging in the Animus for what seemed like days, but he couldn't be sure because so much of that time had been spent in the simulation, where time flowed differently. Even during those moments when Isaiah let him out of the simulation, Sean experienced uncontrollable Bleeding Effects that terrified him. Viking warriors appeared out of nowhere and charged at him with their axes and spears. Giants and gods strode over him, threatening to crush him under their feet. A giant wolf lunged at his throat with its mouth full of teeth. Crashing waves filled the room, and the water level rose by inches until it covered his mouth and touched his nose, soon to drown him. Each of these and many other visions felt utterly real, and Sean found it more and more difficult to maintain his grip on what was him and what was not. Clarity rolled in and out like fog.

"When you find the dagger, you will be free," Isaiah said. "I want that for you. I do. But that is not mine to give. It is yours to earn."

Sean raised his head, and Isaiah was smiling, revealing a huge, rotten tooth that worms had eaten through and blackened. Sean blinked, and Isaiah was Isaiah again.

"The simulation is ready," one of the technicians said.

"Good." Isaiah reached for the helmet. "Don't fight this, Sean. You know it goes worse for you when you fight it."

He couldn't. Sean couldn't do it again. His mind had been reduced to cobwebs, its structure long gone, barely recognizable for what it once was. He felt certain another round in the Animus would wipe him away completely like a broom.

"Please," he said, whimpering.

"Try to relax," Isaiah said, lowering the helmet. "You will—"

"Sir!" A shield-maiden burst into the room carrying a dead raven, which she threw at Sean, and he screamed as the dead bird clawed and pecked at his face.

"Is he okay?" the shield-maiden asked.

"Pay him no mind," Isaiah said. "Where have you been, Cole?"

"I went to Västerås," she said.

The bird suddenly flew out a window, and Sean recognized the shield-maiden now.

"Västerås?" Isaiah said. "Why?"

"I read an article in the newspaper about a new company selling bottled spring water. Apparently, when they dug up the area during construction for their plant, they uncovered a unique dagger. The article had a photo."

"And?" Isaiah replaced the Animus helmet on its hook, which meant that he might not put Sean back in the simulation, after all, and for that, Sean sighed with relief.

"I wanted to be sure before I brought it to your attention," she said. "So I went to the plant. Look at this." She held up her phone for Isaiah to see. "They have it on display."

"This is extraordinary. You've done well, Cole. Very well."

"Thank you, sir. There's something else. I've been using Abstergo's network to monitor CCTV feeds. Mostly airports, for security. Earlier today I believe I saw Owen, Natalya, and Grace arrive in the country in the company of an Assassin."

"Prepare two helicopters and a strike team. They might catch up with us at any moment, and I will take no chances. We leave as soon as possible."

"Yes, sir." Cole turned and left the room.

"She found the dagger?" Sean asked.

Isaiah was smiling to himself, and that lasted for a few moments. Then he looked over at Sean, a bit suddenly, as though he had just heard him. "Did you say something?"

"Cole found the dagger?" Sean asked again.

"Yes. She did."

"So I don't need to go into the simulation anymore?"

"No, Sean. You don't."

"Thank you," Sean said, his whole body sagging with relief, and he waited for Isaiah to undo the clasps and straps that held him in the Animus armature. Since it wasn't powered up yet, the framework couldn't move, locking Sean in place. But Isaiah made no move to free him.

"Can you help me?" Sean asked.

"Help you?" Isaiah said.

Sean felt his mind returning as the fog receded. The old barn where he had spent so much time the past few days had grown warm around him, coaxing the aroma of wood smoke from the timber walls, which meant it was now afternoon. He still found this an uncomfortable place for the Animus, but there hadn't been time to make a dedicated structure near the location site of the dagger, and Isaiah had utilized an existing building instead.

"Help me out?" Sean said.

Isaiah acted as though he hadn't heard Sean, and turned to leave.

"Wait," Sean said, jostling his arms against the restraints. "Please."

But Isaiah continued to ignore him as he strode toward the barn door, and Sean didn't know what to say. Everything had stopped feeling completely real a long time ago. The last time he had really been himself, without any fog or pain or fear, was back at the Aerie. But ever since leaving that place, he had entered into a strange, parallel-feeling existence, as if the real him might still be out there, but somewhere else.

As Isaiah reached for the doorknob, Sean panicked and raised his voice. "You can't just leave me here like this!"

That stopped Isaiah. "Yes, I can," he said. "That is what one does with broken things for which there is no longer any use."

His answer rendered Sean speechless for a moment, but in that moment Isaiah left the barn without saying another word, and the technicians followed silently after him, leaving Sean alone.

Even then, he struggled to decide if this was really happening or not, or if this was all part of a Bleeding Effect hallucination. Those tended to come in waves and clusters, so he inventoried everything else around him: his wheelchair; the huge bale of rusted wire in the corner; the horse stalls, one empty, one containing a small pile of rags; the pitchfork hanging on two nails on the nearest wooden post; the old-fashioned bicycle with the ridiculously huge front wheel.

It all checked out, the same as it had been for days.

So that meant this was happening. Isaiah had just abandoned him here, still hanging in the Animus, his arms outstretched like a bird. Forever. But that couldn't be. Isaiah wouldn't do that. Sean had faith in him.

The minutes passed. Quite a few of them.

He heard the whine of two helicopter rotors gearing up outside, and then the full-throttle beating of the air as they took off. He caught sight of one of them through the gaps in the barn's roof, and a little while after that, he couldn't hear them anymore.

Silence gathered around him, and the shadows drifted out of the corners of the barn like smoke. He tested the Animus restraints a few times but knew it would be impossible to free himself.

After he'd hung there for an hour or so, the longest he'd spent in the Animus without being able to move, his shoulders and elbows began to itch. Then they began to ache. After another hour had gone by, they demanded that he move them, but he couldn't. He tried, straining against the straps and buckles, but nothing brought relief. All he could do to escape the claustrophobia pinning his body down was move his fingers, which he did constantly, making his hands into tight fists and pumping them like he'd done for the nurses who drew his blood in the hospital.

Time passed.

More time.

Hours.

Hours that Isaiah had left him there, and as that time passed, his faith in Isaiah faded until he knew that no one would ever come back for him. It felt as though Sean's worst fear had come true. He had failed. He was worthless, after all.

He hung there, his head throbbing, and his body screaming and shivering, robbed of the ability to do what bodies were made to do. He had never known torture like this, and he realized he needed to distract his mind from it, or he would either burst into flames or twist himself into a knot he'd never get out of.

He tried thinking of home and his parents. He wondered what they knew, if anything, about where he was, and vaguely remembered talking to them on the phone, on more than one occasion, with Isaiah sitting right next to him.

Next, he tried singing songs to himself. Then he tried shouting and screaming songs to himself. Then he heard shouting and screaming, as if it was on a loop. He decided to recite the alphabet. He recited the alphabet again. And again. The letters took on meaning that had nothing to do with their sounds, as though he wove a spell, summoning a fog that settled over his eyes and his mind, carrying him away.

Black and swollen *draugr* clustered at his feet, listening to his magic as he hung from the goalpost. The stands were empty, and a vicious wind swept across the field, stretching the yards into miles.

But in the distance, a figure approached, drawing closer, and closer, seeming undisturbed by the wind, or by the undead warriors who would suck on his bones if they could. He came up through their midst until he stood below Sean, and Sean recognized him.

It was Styrbjörn.

"That is a strange tree you are hanging from," his ancestor said. "Why do you not come down?"

"I can't. I'm tied up."

"Break the cords, then."

"They're too strong."

"But you are strong, are you not?"

"Not as strong as you," Sean said. "Nobody calls me Sean the Strong."

"Perhaps they should," Styrbjörn said. "This tree is as nothing if you command it to be so. Break the bonds! Go on, break them!"

"I can't."

"Break them! Now!"

Sean closed his eyes and pulled against the restraints, every muscle and cord in his neck, arms, back, shoulders, and chest strained close to tearing.

"That's it!" Styrbjörn said.

Sean roared, and Styrbjörn roared with him, and the wind howled, until Sean heard a loud groaning, and a snapping, and the goalpost began to buckle and bend.

Styrbjörn nodded his approval, and without bidding farewell, he returned across the field the way he had come, and then the wind began to shear away pieces of the *draugr*, taking limbs, and teeth, and eyes, until they had been stripped away, and Sean raged alone. He pulled and pulled and pulled—

Something hit him.

Or he hit it. And when he opened his eyes, he was lying at the foot of the Animus, under the safety ring. He was free. Parts of the armature were still strapped to him, but most of it hung above him, dangling, twisted, and broken. He didn't know exactly what had happened, or how he had done that, but he was free.

After pulling off all the Animus parts still strapped to him, he crawled across the floor of the barn to his wheelchair, which he lifted himself into, and then rolled himself to the barn door. Outside, he saw the massive stone where Styrbjörn had married Thyra, and the grid of rope all around it on the ground that Isaiah had ordered to aid in the excavation. A few agents, technicians, and guards still patrolled the site, and Sean wheeled himself through the camp as quickly and quietly as he could, trying to avoid being seen.

When he reached the parking area at the edge of the camp, he smiled. Isaiah had left in the helicopters, and hadn't taken any of the vehicles.

There was Poindexter. Sean wheeled toward the SUV, and at his approach, the door opened and the ramp descended.

"Hello, Sean," the car said.

Sean heaved himself up the ramp, and then maneuvered his chair into the back of the vehicle. "Hello, Poindexter."

The ramp lifted back into place, and the door closed. "Where would you like to go?" Poindexter asked.

Sean didn't know. He just knew he needed to get away, while his head was still clear. He was in Sweden, he knew that much. Isaiah had gone to a place called Västerås to get the dagger, and he worried that Victoria might catch up to him at any moment. That probably meant that one of the others, Owen or Javier, or someone, must have had a Viking ancestor as well. Maybe Isaiah was right, and they were in Sweden, too, and if they were, it might be possible to contact them.

"Poindexter," Sean said. "Are you still connected to Abstergo?"

"No," the vehicle said. "Communications systems are off-line."

"Can you bring them back online?" Sean asked.

"Yes," Poindexter said. "One moment . . ."

Sean waited, periodically glancing out the windows to make sure no one had spotted him, hoping he could figure this out before another wave of Bleeding Effects disoriented him.

"Communications systems online," the vehicle said. "Is there someone you would like to contact?"

"Can you reach the Aerie facility?" Sean asked. "Or Victoria Bibeau?"

"Yes. Connecting to the Aerie Facility . . ."

Sean looked at the small monitor in the console in front of him, where simple icons showed a dashed line traveling between a car, a satellite, and a phone. A moment later, Sean heard a dial tone, and then a few moments after that, the screen switched to an image of Victoria. He almost couldn't believe it. She was right there, staring at him through the monitor. She was the first real thing he felt like he'd seen in weeks.

"Sean?" she said. "How—?"

"Victoria," Sean said. "Thank God. Listen, I've escaped from Isaiah, but I don't know exactly where I am, or where I need to go. I need you to tell me what to do."

"Sean?" she said again. "I—I can't believe this. Okay. Are—are you hurt? Are you okay?"

"My head's not right," he said. "Too much time in the Animus, I think. But it comes and goes."

"Okay, we'll take care of that. You're going to be okay. I—I can't believe you called me. Griffin is there in Sweden with Owen, Grace, and Natalya, but I've lost contact with them. No one is answering the phone. I see you're in a vehicle. Would you be able to go to their last location? You can't . . . can you drive?"

"I have a car that can drive," Sean said. "Just say where you want me to go. Poindexter, listen up."

Victoria read out some coordinates, and the vehicle locked them in. "Estimated arrival time in forty-seven minutes, thirteen seconds," Poindexter said, shifting into gear.

With that, Sean was on the road, leaving Isaiah's camp behind, driving through a dense forest. The sunlight flashed repeatedly through the leaves and branches, strobing his eyes, and Sean covered his face to shut it out. But when he did that, he saw another forest, this one full of poisoned thorns, and rampaging bulls among the trees, and when he opened his eyes, the animals were still there, charging down the road after him.

"Victoria?" he said. "Are you still there?"

"I am," she said. "I'm not going anywhere until I get all of you back safely."

"You're a psychiatrist, right?" he said.

She paused. "I am."

Without warning, Sean felt his voice crack. "I think I need help."

CHAPTER TWENTY-SEVEN

Owen felt as if he was going to throw up. But he kept going, because there wasn't anything else he could do, and he wasn't going to do nothing. Natalya and Grace had fallen silent, and he thought they might be in shock. He wanted to wake them up. He wanted them to fight, even if they couldn't win.

"Seriously?" he said, even though Isaiah now stood in front of him with a gun. "You just compared yourself to a Norse myth? Hey, Grace, what happens to that wolf in the end?"

Grace looked over at him, but she didn't say anything. Owen waited, suddenly feeling alone and exposed. But then she cleared her throat.

"One of Odin's sons kills him," she said. "Rips his jaws apart."

"Right." Owen gave Grace a little nod. Then he turned back to Isaiah. "So if you're really that wolf, I guess you have that to look forward to."

Isaiah didn't react, either with anger or amusement. Instead, he placed a hand on Owen's shoulder in a paternal gesture, and Owen recoiled and shrugged him off.

"Don't touch me," he said, even though he knew how ridiculous that sounded when Isaiah held the gun. But Owen did have the hidden blade. The only problem was, as soon as he used it on Isaiah, all those agents would open fire, killing Grace and Natalya, and him.

"Do you remember the simulation I showed you of your father?" Isaiah asked.

After just losing Griffin, the question about Owen's dad landed an emotional blow to his gut, and his confidence doubled over. In spite of the way he'd been mouthing off, he was barely keeping it together. He couldn't deal with Isaiah bringing up his dad. Not right now.

"Surely you've figured out that I manipulated that memory, yes?" Isaiah said.

Owen refused to say anything back. He couldn't lose control.

"Would you like to know what I saw in the real memory?" Isaiah bent down again and looked Owen in the eyes, but this time, Owen refused to look back. Whatever Isaiah was about to say, he didn't want to see it, and he didn't want to hear it. But he couldn't stop it. "There was no Assassin there," Isaiah said. "Your father—"

"Shut up!" Natalya said, the first thing she had uttered since Isaiah had captured them. "Just shut up and leave him alone."

"Why are you picking on him like that?" Grace added. "You already got the gun. Whatever you were about to say just makes you pathetic."

Isaiah took a few steps backward from the three of them, tapping the barrel of the pistol against his thigh. Owen was glad to have Grace and Natalya back, even if this was it.

But Isaiah didn't point the gun at them like Owen expected him to. Instead, he just paced in front of them for a few moments, looking down at the road.

"Back in Mongolia," he finally said, "I saw it all. What the Trident showed you, it showed me also." He pivoted to face them. "Before I killed that Assassin with the prong, I saw what she feared more than anything else. Would you like to know what it was?"

"No," Natalya said, a guttural sound of rage.

"She feared her own father," Isaiah said. "The things he did to her. She relived them all. She died with that in her mind—"

Natalya made a choking sound, and Owen looked over. She was crying softly.

"Shut your mouth," he said. "Just do what you're going to do."

But Isaiah ignored him and walked up close to Natalya, his back straight, looking down at her. She didn't look up.

"Yes," he said. "Her death is your fault, just like that nightmare in which your grandparents are murdered. There will always be something you could have done differently."

Natalya's shoulders heaved once, twice, with her crying.

"Don't listen to him," Owen said. "Natalya, it's not real." But even as he said it, he realized it was the wrong thing to say. Yanmei's death had been very real.

Isaiah turned toward Grace, and strolled down to stand

before her. "And you. Know this: you can't save your brother, no matter how hard you try. After this, I'm going to go to the Aerie to find him."

Grace lunged at him, but Isaiah stopped her by raising the pistol to her forehead. She held up her hands and backed off, but the rage-glare didn't leave her eyes.

"If you hurt him . . ." she said.

"Oh, do finish that thought," Isaiah said. Then he waited.

But Grace said nothing more, and Isaiah turned away to face Owen, who knew exactly what was coming. He tried to prepare himself for it as Isaiah came closer. He tried to tell himself it wasn't real, and it wasn't true.

"As for you, Owen," Isaiah said. "What can I tell you that you don't already know? You just won't admit it to yourself. But your father did it all. Alone. In cold blood." He leaned in closer. "I'm talking about your father's own memories of what he did, of course. He actually sat and watched that security guard bleed out. He was surprised at how quickly it was over."

Owen bit down so hard he thought his teeth would shatter. But he offered Isaiah no other reaction. No other satisfaction. Isaiah was lying about his dad. His dad was innocent.

He was innocent.

He was innocent.

He was innocent.

But even as Owen told himself that once again, for the millionth millionth time, his mantra, it felt empty. He realized he didn't know who he was trying to convince. He realized he didn't know if he believed it anymore. He wasn't sure he had ever believed it, and thought that maybe this whole time, he had been angry at the wrong people, and blamed them for his own mistakes.

His mother wasn't weak.

He was.

His grandparents weren't wrongheaded and stubborn.

He was the fool who had lied to himself, and now he didn't know what to do with the truth.

Isaiah stepped away again, backing up to look the three of them over, a surveyor measuring impact craters. Then he raised the pistol, and Owen knew this was his last moment, but Isaiah stopped partway, and Owen heard the sound of a vehicle coming.

The sound of it stirred him up.

He looked to his left as two bright headlights sliced around a bend in the road, and then a large white SUV came barreling right for them. He reached out with both hands, grabbing Natalya's arm with one, and Grace's arm with the other, and dragged them backward so the vehicle would pass between them and Isaiah. Owen had thought maybe they could use the distraction to escape into the forest on the other side of the road.

But instead, the SUV screeched and stopped right in front of them. The side door opened, and there was Sean.

"Get in!" he said.

Natalya's mouth gaped. "Sean?"

"Hurry!" he said.

Owen jumped into the front passenger seat, and Grace and Natalya climbed over Sean into the back. Then Owen saw the empty driver seat.

"What the hell?"

Gunshots exploded, rocking the SUV with their pinpoint strikes. But apparently the car was bulletproof.

"Poindexter," Sean said. "Drive. Fast."

"Yes, Sean," said a computerized voice. The SUV floored its own gas, and the car gunned it down the road, pulling Owen deeper into his seat as the forest became a blur of black and gray in the darkness.

"A self-driving car," Grace said, sitting next to Sean.

"Yeah," Sean said. Then he raised his voice slightly and said, "Victoria? Are you still there?"

"I'm here," Victoria said, her voice coming through the car's speakers.

"I have them," Sean said.

"Oh, thank God," she said. "Is everyone okay? Can I speak to Griffin?"

Sean glanced around the vehicle, as if he had only just then realized that Griffin was missing. He looked at Grace.

She raised her voice a bit and said, "Victoria, Griffin is dead."

The line went quiet. "How?"

"Isaiah's agents," Owen said. He looked down at his wrist. "They shot him."

Saying it out loud like that made it real in a way it hadn't been just moments before. The SUV speeding them away from Isaiah was also speeding them away from Griffin's body, which was back there in the woods next to the stream, where it would stay.

Owen had learned a lot from Griffin. They had disagreed on things, but he respected Griffin, and even admired him. Griffin had put his own life on the line to save Owen's several times, and he'd given up the most important thing in his life—the Brotherhood—to stop Isaiah.

"I'm sorry," Victoria said. "How are you all holding up? Are any of you hurt?"

"We're fine," Grace said. "Just . . . shaken."

"I can only imagine."

"Isaiah has the third prong," Natalya said from the far back seat.

The line went silent again. "I've chartered a jet," Victoria said. "You're heading there now, and it will bring you back here. We need to hang up so you can take the car off-line. Otherwise, Isaiah can track you. So stay together, stay safe, and I'll see you soon. All right?"

"All right," Grace said.

"There's one more thing," Owen added. "I, uh, I told Isaiah that Monroe had figured out the Ascendance Event. I told him it could stop the Trident. I think Isaiah may be heading to the Aerie. I'm sorry."

"Then we have work to do," Victoria said. "I'll see you all soon. Don't forget to go off-line. Good-bye." The call ended.

"Poindexter," Sean said.

"Yes, Sean."

"Take communications systems off-line."

The car responded to the command, and then Natalya leaned forward from the back.

"Okay," she said. "Now you can tell us what happened to you, and what you're doing in this car."

Owen twisted around in his seat to listen.

"Well," Sean said, scratching his temple, "the thing is, I don't really know. I mean, I know, but I don't know if I can trust what I think I know, you know—?" He cut himself off and shook his head. "Okay, that sounded confusing."

He was behaving differently than he had back at the Aerie. He was twitchy, and seemed disoriented.

"I spent way too much time in the Animus," he said. "Isaiah made me do the same thing, over and over. The Bleeding Effects are bad." He paused, nodding his head. "Really bad. And Isaiah used the Trident on me, which . . . made me not feel like myself."

"Oh, Sean." Natalya leaned forward and put a hand on his shoulder.

Owen tried to imagine going through something like that, but he couldn't. "How did you escape?"

"Isaiah left me in the Animus to go look for the third prong. Somehow I—I broke out. Then I got in Poindexter and called Victoria. She basically took care of everything after that."

"Well, you're safe now," Grace said. "You're back."

"I'm coming back," Sean said. "But I still don't feel right. Victoria says it'll take time, but she'll help me."

Natalya gave his shoulder another squeeze from behind, and Sean smiled. The vehicle got quiet after that, and as the surprise and excitement settled, echoes of everything Isaiah had said came back and found Owen just as vulnerable to them as he was before. It was possible Isaiah had lied again. In fact, that was probably likely. But there was a doubt in Owen's mind now that had never been there before, or at least, he'd never openly acknowledged, even to himself. But now that he knew it was there, he couldn't ignore it. More than anything now, he wanted to get back to the Aerie. It was time for Monroe to let him learn the truth, whatever that truth might be.

A short while later, the car pulled onto a private airfield. Owen scanned their surroundings, and saw no sign of Isaiah, or any Abstergo agents. Instead, three planes waited on the tarmac, two small propeller planes, and one larger jet. The pilot, a middle-aged woman with golden-blond hair, waited for them with two flight attendants at the foot of a mobile staircase.

"Is it just me," Grace said, "or are you guys suspicious of everyone now?"

"It's not just you," Owen said. One of the flight attendants wore a fitted scarlet shirt with a black tie, while the woman next to him had on a navy blue skirt with a white blouse. Either of them, or even the pilot, might have been compromised by Isaiah. That was possible, and that's all it had to be for Owen to worry.

The car pulled up near the jet, and after it stopped to let them out, the side door opened and a ramp descended.

"Good-bye, Sean," the car said.

"Good—good-bye, Poindexter," Sean said, then quickly rolled himself down the ramp, toward the plane.

The pilot and flight attendants greeted them, and then helped everyone on board. The cabin looked almost exactly like the private jets Owen had seen in the movies. Plush seats with plenty of room ran down each side, with a wide aisle between them. Owen wondered how much this flight had cost Abstergo, but decided he didn't want to know. He was just grateful Victoria had arranged it. They all found seats, and a flight attendant pushed Sean's wheelchair to the rear of the plane for storage.

The crew brought them all Abstergo-issued changes of clothes, and shortly after that, they were airborne. Not long after that, Sean was asleep. It took longer for Owen to get to that place. His mind kept jumping back and forth between his dad and Griffin. But eventually, he grew drowsy, and he let himself close his eyes.

Victoria was waiting for them when they landed, and Owen was glad to see her. Grace and Natalya seemed to feel the same way, and Victoria even gave Sean a brief hug. Owen guessed she probably felt a different kind of guilt over what had happened to him than she felt toward the others.

At the bottom of the stairs, they all climbed onto a shuttle cart that rolled them across the tarmac, and soon they arrived at a helicopter pad, where a large helicopter waited for them. That was another first for Owen, and between the noise and the tighter space, he much preferred the private jet. Not that he would ever in his life have to make that choice.

The helicopter carried them toward, and then over, the mountains, and as they came in for their landing, Owen got to see the Aerie complex from above. It sprawled over the peak, but not in an aggressive way. Instead, it seemed to have insinuated itself very subtly into the surrounding forest, its glass corridors snaking through the trees, and much of its structure in shade. Upon landing, they pushed through the strong wind stirred up by the helicopter's blades, and entered the Aerie's main atrium.

Owen was surprised at how good it felt to be back, and next to him, Sean grinned as he wheeled himself across the open space. They went to the common room and were soon joined there by Monroe, Javier, and David, but Griffin's absence kept the room somber.

Javier and David had completed the simulation of the collective unconscious, and as far as Monroe could tell, it was basically the same simulation Owen, Grace, and Natalya had experienced. The same genetic time capsule. But Owen still didn't see how it would help them or shield them from the Trident or anything else.

"It didn't protect us in Sweden," he said.

"Did Isaiah use the pieces of the Trident on you?" Victoria asked.

Owen shook his head. "Not directly. But he tapped into the fears we all experienced in Mongolia. He even knew what they were, and he used them against us. I didn't feel like I had any protection from it at all. No shield."

Monroe turned to Grace and Natalya. "What about you two?"

"Same," Natalya said.

"Pretty much," Grace said.

Monroe frowned, and rubbed the heel of his palm against the whiskers on his chin. "Let me take Sean through, and then we can work on figuring this out."

"I don't think I can recommend that," Victoria said. "Sean has been through a tremendous amount of psychic trauma."

"Then I think it's even more important that we leave the decision to Sean," Monroe said.

Sean looked back and forth between them. "If it's something everyone else has done, then I'll do it. I'm already feeling better."

"Good man. I think it's important that you experience it. All of you. It seems that's how it was designed."

"Watch him closely," Victoria said.

Monroe gave her a thumbs-up, and then he and Sean left the common room.

"As for the rest of you," Victoria said. "You have a decision to make. It is very likely Isaiah is on his way here right now. The

Ascendance Event was always an obsession of his, and now we know why. He will come for Monroe's work, because he knows it poses a threat to him. The choice you have to make is whether you wish to be here when he arrives." She set her tablet on the table and folded her hands together next to it. "Griffin's death is a reminder of what we are dealing with. I have said this to you before, but I will say it this one last time. If any of you wish to leave, you may. I won't force any of you to stay."

Owen only had to give that a moment of thought. "I think we know what we're dealing with," he said. "Isaiah made that pretty clear back in Sweden when he pointed a gun at us and told us he was going to eat the sun and the moon. Now that he has the complete Trident, he can call himself Fenris wolf or whatever he wants, because he'll be unstoppable. I'm not sure what good it would do to go anywhere else. So I'm going to stay to fight him."

"Me too," Natalya said.

Grace and David looked at each other, and they seemed to be going through that same wordless tug-of-war they'd gone through since Owen had first met them. David wanted to stay and fight, and Grace wanted to protect her little brother. David refused to leave, so Grace decided she had to stay, and that was that.

"It looks like we're all in," Javier said. "This is for Griffin."

Owen turned to his best friend. He didn't know if now was the right time, but he also didn't know if there ever would be a right time, with Isaiah on the way. He pulled up the sleeve of his hoodie, and he undid the straps on the hidden blade.

"Is that what I think it is?" Javier asked.

Owen nodded. "He wanted you to have it. He said to tell you that you've earned it."

"He did?"

Owen slid the blade off his arm and handed it to Javier. "Those were his words."

Javier took it and looked hard at it, his brow deeply creased. "But I haven't earned it. I'm not an Assassin."

"I'm just telling you what he said, and I'm giving you what he wanted you to have. I guess you have to decide what you're going to do with that."

Javier nodded and set the blade on the table.

Victoria raised an eyebrow at it. "I'm going to pretend I don't see that. Instead, we need to come up with a plan."

CHAPTER TWENTY-EIGHT

Isaiah will come at us with every weapon at his disposal," Victoria said. "Not just the Trident. He'll bring every Templar agent he has managed to gain control over, because he'll assume the Aerie is guarded."

"When, really, we're on our own," David said.

Victoria sighed. "Yes, precisely."

"So how do we do this?" Natalya said. "We don't really stand a chance, do we?"

"The odds are not in our favor," Victoria said.

"Then let's even the odds," Javier said. "It's like the battle in the Viking simulation."

"Right." David had begun to nod along with him. "We just need to slow them down and take as many out as we can. Like Östen and Thorvald."

"How?" Grace asked.

Javier turned to Victoria. "We already know the Aerie has some defenses. We broke in once before. So the question is, how do you think Isaiah will attack?"

"By helicopter," she said.

"Then the first thing we have to do is make sure the helicopters can't land," Javier said.

"Some of Isaiah's forces will be driving up the mountain," Victoria said.

"Then we close the roads," David said. "We force them to climb the mountain on foot."

"And we lay traps in the forest," Javier said. "We keep as many of them as we can from reaching the top."

Victoria nodded, grinning. "It worked for your ancestors, I suppose."

"So we have a lot of work to do," Javier said.

The first thing they did was open up the Aerie storage and drag every heavy box and crate they could find out onto the helicopter pad. Then they stacked them up at random intervals, covering the surface with enough debris to make it impossible for any helicopter to land there. The trees that covered the rest of the mountain left no other openings large enough, which meant that if the helicopters wanted to land, they would have to do it pretty far from the facility.

Next, they drove with Monroe down to the base of the mountain, and he used a chain saw from the Aerie's tool supply to cut down several large trees, aiming them to fall across the road. As its deafening motor bellowed, and fragrant woodchips flew, Owen worried they wouldn't be able to hear any approaching helicopters. But before long, they'd downed three modest trees, enough to keep any vehicle except for maybe a tank from climbing to the Aerie by road.

That left the traps they planned to lay in the forest.

The Aerie still had its sentry system, which had been easy enough for Griffin to bypass that Owen didn't think it would slow down Isaiah and his team much at all. But Javier had another idea, something else he'd drawn from his experience in the memories of his Viking ancestor.

The Aerie still had a supply of pest control devices, including M-44 cyanide bombs. When Owen saw one, he realized it wasn't really a bomb as much as sprinkler head. Abstergo used the devices to cut down on predatory animals like coyotes and foxes around their facility. Isaiah had likely left the M-44s behind because he didn't consider them a useful weapon. But cyanide could be very effective at slowing down or even stopping any agents trying to climb the mountain. So the last thing needed to prepare for Isaiah's arrival was to plant the M-44s at periodic intervals in the forest, ready to poison anyone who passed by with a cloud of toxic gas.

After that, they could do nothing but wait.

Sean completed his time in the collective unconscious, and it actually seemed to help him recover somewhat from the abuse Isaiah had inflicted on him. But Owen assumed it would be a long time before he was really back to normal.

With preparations complete, they all gathered in the common room to discuss additional strategies. Monroe stood at the head of the table.

"When the helicopters aren't able to land," he said, "there's a good chance any agents on board will rappel down. Those are the ones we have to worry about first. The blocked roads and the traps we set will keep the ground troops occupied."

"So what do we do about the ones dropping down on us like spiders?" Natalya asked.

"We fight," Owen said.

"Griffin had a few weapons in his gear," Javier said. "Some grenades. EMP devices and some sleep bombs. If we use them effectively, we could do some damage."

"We need to pick a central location as our fortress," Victoria said. "I would recommend the garage below ground. There are a limited number of entrances, and no windows. With our smaller numbers, I think we need to force the enemy into a bottleneck."

"Agreed," Monroe said. "Everyone get what you'll need, and let's load it down there."

Owen didn't have much, but upon scrounging around the Aerie, mostly in the tools, he did find some objects that he could use as weapons even more effectively than he'd wielded a shovel back in Sweden. Then he loaded it all into the garage with everything else they'd found, and they worked at barricading the doors.

The last thing Monroe brought down was the Animus core containing all the data for the Ascendance Event. That was what Isaiah wanted, and he would have to fight for it if he hoped to claim it. After that, they gathered together once again in the common room to wait, and this time, no one spoke. Instead, everyone listened for the sounds of helicopters.

They had done everything they could. Owen doubted it would

be enough. But he was ready to face the enemy, just the same, still unsure of how Minerva's secret package would help them.

They waited.

And waited.

And eventually, they heard exactly what they had expected to hear. The distant thrum of helicopters. Isaiah had come for them.

"Battle stations," Monroe said.

Without speaking, they all rose from the table and marched from the common room, out to the main atrium. A few minutes later, helicopters circled overhead, having apparently taken note of the compromised landing pad.

"Get ready," Victoria said.

Owen pulled out the one EMP grenade he had, and then he remembered the first time he had encountered an Abstergo helicopter, outside Ulysses Grant's home at Mount McGregor.

Owen looked up at the aircraft overhead, examined the device in his hand, and glanced at Javier. "I'm going up to the roof," he said.

Javier looked at him a moment, and then nodded, realizing what Owen meant. "Let's do it."

They took off at a run, and Monroe shouted after them, but they ignored him. They skipped the elevators and went right for the stairs, bounding up them three and four at a time, climbing each floor of the Aerie until they reached the highest balcony.

They paused at the door before charging outside. The moment they appeared, they might get shot at.

"Are you ready?" Javier asked.

Owen armed the grenade. "Count me down."

"In three, two, one—"

Javier shouldered the door open, and Owen leapt through in a roll. As he came up, he found the nearest helicopter, hoping it would be the one carrying Isaiah, and he hurled the EMP grenade at it.

The second it left his hand, he heard the first shots, and dove back inside with Javier as bullets struck the cement balcony with sparks and chips and dust.

"Did you hit it?" Javier asked.

Owen didn't know, but he turned to look, and saw the blades slowing on the helicopter he had targeted. "I hit it," he said.

The EMP pulse had knocked out the helicopter's electrical systems, and the aircraft was going down in an uncontrolled spin, forcing the other helicopter to dodge away from it.

"Nice job," Javier said.

The disabled aircraft careened overhead, its tail swinging dangerously close to the Aerie's windows, and it occurred to Owen that the helicopter could very well crash into the building, which was something he hadn't considered.

"We better get back to the others," he said.

So they raced back downstairs, flying down the steps much faster than they had climbed, and found Monroe still furious. But the rest of them had also noticed the helicopter, and they watched it through the atrium's glass ceiling as it came closer, and closer, until it became clear how it would finally lose its tug-of-war with the ground.

"Run!" Victoria shouted.

They all sprinted toward her, and toward the garage, where they'd planned to hole up, just as the ceiling above them exploded in a glittering shower of glass, and the building shrieked from torn girders. Then an entire helicopter dove right into the atrium, nose first, its blades tearing up the building as it fell.

The others managed to get out of the way before it made an impact with the floor of the atrium, but they were on the other side of it from Owen and Javier.

The helicopter's blades struck the floor, causing an explosion of tile and subflooring, and a huge piece of one blade snapped off and went flying, slicing the air above Owen's head. He and Javier dove, and then dove again to get out of the way as the body of the helicopter smashed into the ground and rolled through the glass walls of the conference room, the lobby, and lodged itself in the front doors.

"Go!" Javier shouted.

He pushed Owen, and the two of them ran to join the others just as the first ropes from the remaining helicopter uncoiled through the now-opened ceiling. A moment later, agents descended through the breach, guns already firing.

Owen and Javier reached the rest of their team as they fled from the atrium, racing down the corridors until they reached the glass tunnel that would take them partway down the side of the mountain to the entrance of the garage.

"That was incredibly stupid!" Monroe shouted.

"But I took out a helicopter!" Owen yelled.

"You took out most of the building!" he said. "And you almost took us with it!"

Inside the tunnel, Owen had a better glimpse of the forest, and through the glass he could faintly hear shouting and gunfire from the Aerie's sentries. Whether the M-44s were doing their job, he had no idea, but he wasn't about to go out in that mess to find out.

A few moments later, they reached the garage, and they took up their positions guarding the doors in groups with the few weapons they had. Owen had one more EMP, and Javier had a sleep grenade. The others had their own weapons, also taken from Griffin's equipment.

"Get ready!" Victoria shouted.

Owen listened to the distant sound of what had to be the first helicopter exploding. Any moment now, the first agents would find them. His body had gone numb with the adrenaline of it all, but he kept himself alert and ready.

"If they come to your door, you know what to do," Monroe said, Sean in his wheelchair nearby, Natalya standing at his side.

Several moments later, he heard the sound of footsteps approaching, and voices over radio sets. He and Javier prepared themselves, and when the enemy came into view wearing Abstergo's enhanced paramilitary gear, they both attacked. Owen threw his last EMP grenade, knocking out the systems in their helmets for communication and visual enhancement.

Then he and Javier threw themselves into hand-to-hand combat. Owen drew on every experience, every Bleeding Effect, and laid into his enemies with his fists, his feet, and a length of a steel bar he had found among the tools, laying out as many of them as he could before retreating back through the hallway into the garage.

Across the large, open room, Monroe and Natalya had taken on a group of agents, and Owen wanted to go help them, but that would leave his door unguarded. A few seconds later, he was glad he hadn't given in to that temptation, because another wave of Templars came at him and Javier.

Without an EMP grenade, the only tool they had was Javier's

sleep grenade, which he tossed into the hallway. But its effects weren't immediate enough, and some of the agents made it through. Owen knew they weren't going to be able to hold out as long as they would need to.

Another group of agents ripped through the door Victoria, David, and Grace had been guarding, and now Owen went into defense, using every twist and dodge to try and disarm the agents of their guns.

"Fall back to me!" Monroe shouted.

This battle had turned to a losing one faster than Owen had expected. He and Javier first joined up with Victoria, David, and Grace. Victoria held her own well against her former allies, and David and Grace had both clearly gained their own Bleeding Effects from their simulations.

But it was hopeless.

Even if they beat them all, Isaiah hadn't even appeared yet.

And with that thought, as if summoned, Isaiah stalked into the room, wielding the complete Trident.

"Finish them!" he shouted.

"No!" Sean screamed, loud enough that Isaiah could hear. "I want you! I challenge you, Isaiah!"

"Halt!" Isaiah bellowed, and his agents ceased all their aggression and attacks within seconds. "After all your failures, you would challenge me, Sean?"

"I do challenge you!" Sean replied, wheeling himself forward.

"Do you still think you're Styrbjörn?" Isaiah asked.

"No," Sean said. "But I don't need to be to stop you. And I know that's what you're afraid of. That's why you're here."

Isaiah scoffed. He wore a sleek, white armored suit, and the Trident of Eden bore all three of its prongs in wicked formation atop a long metal staff. Owen now saw it not only as a source of power, but as a weapon capable of inflicting injury and death.

"The earth's renewal begins now," Isaiah said. "It begins with your deaths. You have brought this on yourselves."

"Actually," Owen said, taking a step toward him to stand beside Sean. "It begins with—"

Isaiah slammed the base of the Trident into the floor, as if planting it there. It cracked the cement floor beneath it, and the metal sang, filling the garage.

Then *fear.*

Owen closed his eyes, holding his head against the storm. He had been here before. He had seen this before. The worst of everything ever said about his father all made true. He knew the others now experienced their own versions of this hell. But for Owen, it had become something else since the last time he'd seen it. Monroe had always questioned whether he was ready to see his father's memories, and Owen hadn't ever understood what he meant.

But now he did.

Before, Owen had never considered the possibility that his father's memories would reveal anything other than his innocence. But Monroe was able to ask what would happen if the memories showed something different. Something Owen wasn't prepared to see. To be ready in the way Monroe asked, Owen had to accept that his greatest fear might be confirmed. He had to accept that his father might be a murderer. He had to accept that his grandparents were right.

He had to *accept* it.

That was the true opposite of fear. It wasn't courage, or bravery. He could be brave and afraid at the same time. But if he stopped fighting his fear, and accepted it, the fear lost its power. The way Natalya had accepted that the Serpent would eat her.

Was that what Minerva had given them? Not an immunity, but a way to deal with the effects of the Trident?

Owen looked directly at the vision the Piece of Eden showed him.

And he accepted that it might be true.

He accepted that he didn't know what his dad had done, and that he might never know, and maybe he didn't even need to know. He could move on, and live his own life.

With that, the vision fled, taking the fear, and Owen opened his eyes.

The others staggered under the weight of their visions, and Owen called out to them.

"You need to accept your fear!" he shouted. "Remember the Serpent, and step into its mouth!"

One by one, his friends opened their eyes as they escaped their own terrors, standing up straighter, blinking away tears, finally understanding the shield the ancient Minerva had given them.

"Listen up!" Javier said. "We charge him at once. Use everything you have. Every Bleeding Effect and every skill."

"No!" Isaiah shouted, and he struck the floor again.

This time, Owen felt his mind bombarded by wave after wave of awe, emanating from Isaiah.

"I offer you a better world!" Isaiah said. "Don't you understand? Don't you see? The earth is weak and diseased, kept alive for too long. It must be allowed to die to be reborn. I offer you this. The new earth will be your inheritance, if you but join me!"

Isaiah burned with radiance, drawing Owen toward him, and Owen wanted to serve that light. He wanted only to be near it, to feel its warmth. But he forced himself to close his eyes and shut out that brightness. He returned to their next stop on the Path, the Wanderer they had met, and the Dog who had traveled with him in complete devotion. And when Owen had to find a new companion for that devotion, he did not choose the rich man in his tower, or the shepherd with his flocks. He chose another Wanderer and seeker of truth.

Isaiah deserved no devotion, because his light was a lie.

Owen opened his eyes, and the glow around Isaiah tarnished and went cold. Then Owen took another step toward him. The others did as well, finding their own answers in Minerva's gift.

Isaiah's face now showed his rage, and he struck the ground a third time with the Trident. The cold flood that now poured over Owen's mind was a tide of despair, pushing him toward an abyss that beckoned him to embrace its oblivion.

Over its siren call, he heard Isaiah saying, "None of you can see what I see. None of you understand what I understand. But I can lead you from this fallen earth. I can carry you into a world of hope and rebirth."

Owen felt the abyss pulling on his mind, and there he was, back on the mountain, the wind clawing at his face, the Summit impossibly distant. On one path, Isaiah offered him a rope to hold on to. The promise of safety. But on the other path, Owen would instead rely on himself. No rope. Just his own strength. His own hands. His own will.

He turned away from the abyss, and he turned away from the rope that Isaiah offered. He would instead place hope and faith in himself.

With that, the torrent of despair washed away, and when Owen opened his eyes a third time, he stood only a few yards from Isaiah. The others had almost reached him as well, as they climbed their own mountains, but Owen decided not to wait.

He charged, letting his Assassin ancestors rise up through him. Varius, and Zhi, two different warriors from different times and different parts of the world. Both of them working in the darkness to serve the light. But Isaiah was prepared, and even though the Trident no longer had any power over Owen's mind, its deadly edges now sought his flesh.

Isaiah leapt away, spinning the Trident around his body, making it difficult for Owen to get close. But gradually the others joined him. Javier, and David, Natalya, and Grace.

The rage Owen had seen on Isaiah's face had become fear, and that made Owen laugh. Now Isaiah finally understood the Ascendance Event.

Isaiah flipped the Trident around and leapt at Owen, but the others joined in the battle and defended him, without weapons, instead fighting hand-to-hand. Isaiah proved to be a more formidable fighter than Owen would have expected. He spun and leapt and thrust and slashed, but Owen and the others countered his every move, and he began to slow.

Monroe and Victoria stood by, waiting and watching, as did Isaiah's agents, as if they understood that the challenge had to play out.

But the end had almost come. The battle was almost over. Owen and the others pressed Isaiah, throwing punches and kicks, until they finally began to land. Isaiah grunted, and flinched, and staggered as they launched assault after assault, until they disarmed him at last and flung the Trident away.

Isaiah watched it abandon him, and as he reached for it, Javier was there with Griffin's hidden blade.

One thrust, and it was over.

Isaiah slumped to the ground, and no one moved or said a word for a long time. They all stood around his body, breathing heavily.

Gradually, the hold he had over the Templar agents seemed to fade, and they looked at one another in confusion. Victoria ordered them all from the garage, while they were still dazed and off-balance, and then hurried toward the Trident.

But Natalya beat her to it.

She picked up the weapon, and gripped it tightly, with purpose.

"Natalya," Victoria said. "Please. Give me the Trident."

"No," Natalya said, her voice both calm and strong.

"Natalya," Victoria said. "I will not ask again. Give me the—"

"You know as well as I do you can't take it from her," Monroe said. "Though it would be interesting to see you try."

Victoria raised her voice. "You have no stake in this, Monroe. You walked away from the Order. From everything. But I didn't. I am still committed to making this world what it ought to be."

"Like Isaiah?" Natalya said. "Where does it end, Victoria?" She looked down at the weapon in her hands, and then she looked at Owen. "Minerva wanted us to do something else. Something only the six of us can do." She held out the Trident, and they all came together to grasp it.

Upon touching it, Owen felt an exhilarating surge of power that rippled the muscles in his arms and reached his heart, which began to race. But that power seemed to summon something else from deep inside him. He felt a presence ascending within his mind as though he were in the Animus, a consciousness so unknowable and vast he couldn't find the edges of it, or even make sense of it.

Then he heard Minerva's voice tolling loudly. **THE TIME HAS COME. YOU HAVE ALL BROUGHT ME HERE, AND NOW I WILL DO WHAT I SHOULD HAVE DONE EONS AGO.**

The power within Owen moved back out from his chest, down his arms, and into the Trident. Its staff and blades began to vibrate, mildly at first, but soon grew stronger, and stronger, until Owen didn't think he could hold on to it anymore. He looked at the others, and they were all gritting their teeth, holding fast, the Trident almost a blur in their hands, until suddenly it felt as though something gave way inside it. A fault line finally cracked, releasing all the stored-up power and energy it contained, which radiated outward in a shock wave. In its wake, the Trident had been rendered nothing more than a simple piece of metal.

Exhausted, Owen let go. The others did, too, and the Trident clattered to the ground.

"What have you done?" Victoria asked.

Natalya turned toward her. "We saved the world," she said.

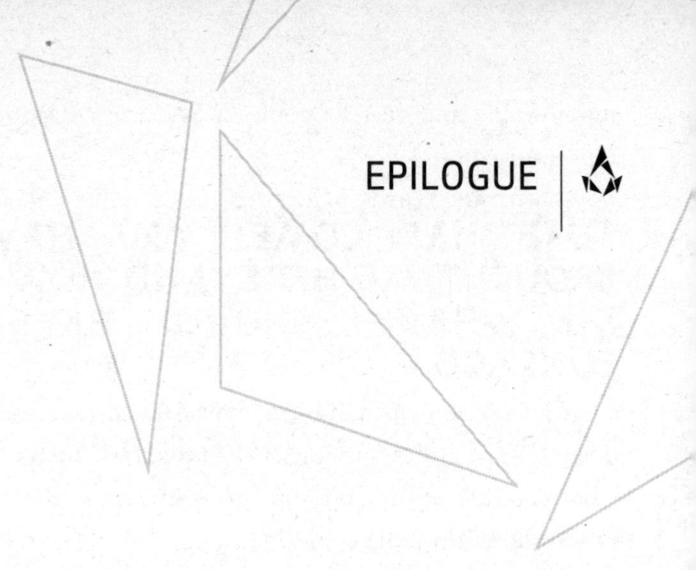

EPILOGUE

The town car turned onto Grace and David's street, and she felt a strange uneasiness about being home. In some ways, it was the same place it had always been, but in other ways it felt completely different. She knew things now that almost no one else knew. She had done things no one in her neighborhood had done. Victoria had told them all it would probably take some time to adjust to this new normal, but they would, eventually. She had also promised that the Templars would leave them in peace, so long as they did nothing to draw the Templars' attention. That promise felt a bit hollow to Grace, or even empty. It meant they were probably being watched. But she had no intention of entering the world of the Order and the Brotherhood ever again, so she told herself she had nothing to worry about.

The car pulled up in front of their house, and, next to her, David let out a sigh.

"Here we are," he said.

"Here we are," Grace said.

"I'm glad Victoria sent us in the car," he said. "Dad would have flipped out when he saw the crashed helicopter in the middle of the Aerie."

"Speaking of Dad," Grace said, "we agreed we're not telling him or Mom anything, right?"

"Right."

Grace looked hard at him.

"What?" he said. "I'm not going to tell them anything."

"Good," she said.

"You don't have to worry about me anymore," David said.

"I know I don't," she said. "But that doesn't mean that I won't. You're going to do what you're going to do, and I've accepted that. But that doesn't mean I won't black your eye if you step out of line."

"You won't always be there, Grace. That's what I've accepted. And that's okay."

She gave him a little shove. "Hop on out. Let's go inside and let them know we're here."

"Okay."

He opened the car door, and they got out and walked up to their porch together. Their mom opened the door for them before they'd hit the top step, and Grace could smell her banana bread baking inside.

Natalya opened the door to her grandparents' apartment and walked inside. She didn't smell anything cooking on the stove or in the oven, but that was okay, because the only thing she wanted was a hug, and when her grandmother met her at the door, Natalya reached her arms around her and squeezed a little too tightly. But her grandmother was a strong woman, and she could take it.

"It is good to see you, Natalya," she said. "So good to see you. We've missed you coming around. Are you home from that school now?"

"I am," Natalya said. "Home for good."

"You did well at this school?"

Natalya smiled. "I did."

"Then why did they send you home?"

"They sent everyone home," Natalya said. "They ended that program."

"That's too bad."

They walked into the living room, where her grandfather sat in his recliner reading the newspaper, his reading glasses sitting so low on the tip of his nose, Natalya wondered how they stayed on.

"Natalya!" he said, folding the newspaper to set it aside.

She walked over to him and leaned into a hug. "Hello, *dedulya*."

"What is wrong with this school that they send you home?" he asked.

"Nothing," she said. "It was only a temporary program. It's over now."

"Ah," he said, looking at her over the rim of his glasses. "Well, you're too good for them. You hear me? Don't you worry about it."

Natalya smiled. "I won't," she said, and she put her arm around her grandmother. "There are a lot of things I'm trying not to worry about anymore."

Owen had the car drop him off a couple of blocks away from his grandparents' house. He wanted a little extra time to think about what he would say when he walked in. They thought he had run away, and there would be lots of questions about that. There would be lots of doubt and suspicion at first, and Owen understood why. He accepted that.

His grandpa would probably want to take him for a drive to get ice cream, to see if Owen would tell him something he wouldn't tell his mom or his grandma. His mom would come into his room that night for the same reason. But Owen wouldn't tell them anything beyond what he had already decided, which was to be honest.

He had gone looking for information about his dad.

They would want to know where, and if he had found anything.

He would tell them he had been looking in the wrong place, and that he hadn't found anything. Monroe had made good on his promise, and offered Owen the simulation of his father's memories, but in the end, Owen had decided not to. If he needed so badly to know the answer to those questions, then the answers would have too much power over him, no matter what the answers were. Owen had decided he didn't want that.

He wanted to be okay not knowing. He wanted to accept that his father might have done those things Isaiah had talked about. But Owen also wanted to hope that his father hadn't. That was a strange place to be, sitting right in the middle, without answers. But it was the best place to be for Owen to move forward. Like his dad would have wanted him to.

Eventually, his slow walk brought him to his grandparents' door, and he tried the knob. It was locked. So he knocked on the door, and he took a deep breath.

He was home.

Javier sat in his bedroom with the door locked. Alone. Finally.

It had taken hours for his mom to calm down, but she had, and she accepted that he didn't want to talk about where he'd been for now. She wasn't going to let it go, and he knew that, but at least she allowed him some privacy for the moment. His brother wasn't going to let it go, either. His dad would just let his mom and brother do the work of hounding him, but he would want to know, too.

Mostly, they were all just glad to have him home safely. They worried about him more than they needed to, but Javier understood why. There were still places where it wasn't safe to be himself, openly. But that was getting better, too.

He sat on his bed and looked at two things. The first was the ceramic hidden blade that Griffin had given to him. The second was a phone number.

He hadn't asked Monroe for it. But Monroe had given it to him, and told him not to tell Victoria under any circumstances. Javier was to simply hold on to that number and use it when he knew what he wanted to do. Who he wanted to be.

He looked at the Assassin gauntlet for another moment, and then tucked it into a shoebox under his bed. Then he memorized the phone number, and tore up the piece of paper. Javier had always had the best memory of anyone he knew. Now that he had that number saved in his head, he'd never lose it. He didn't know exactly who would answer, but he had a pretty good idea. He could call it if he decided to.

But deep inside, he knew it wasn't actually a question of if.

It was when.

Sean sat in the waiting room, flipping through an uninteresting magazine he'd picked up without thinking about it. He and the receptionist had already finished their normal exchange. He'd told her school was going well. That he was feeling better. Then she had gone back to answering phones, and Sean had wheeled over to an open space between two of the chairs.

Before he reached the last advertising pages of the magazine, the door opened, and Victoria called his name.

"Good to see you," she said.

He let the magazine fall with a slap onto the chair next to him. "Good to see you, too."

She held the door open while he wheeled through, and then she led the way through the downtown Abstergo offices to another door with her name on it. She opened it, and Sean wheeled inside.

Victoria sat down in a white leather armchair, crossed her legs, and held her knee with interlaced fingers. "Any visual hallucinations this week?"

Sean wheeled his chair over to face her, parking himself about six feet away. "No."

"What about auditory?"

"I still hear some things. When I'm falling asleep. But I can't really make it out like I used to."

"That likely means they're fading, too."

"I hope so."

She pulled up her tablet and tapped at it a few times. "Your neurovitals have certainly improved. They've almost returned to normal parameters. You've been doing the meditation exercises?"

"Yup. Except when I forget."

She frowned, but it felt more like a smile. "And how often does that happen?"

"Oh. Just weekdays and weekends."

"Sean. You know how important they are."

"I know." Meditation was supposed to promote "mindfulness" and connect Sean to his body, but he didn't feel as though he needed to do that three times a day for twenty minutes. He was feeling better.

"As soon as you've fully recovered," Victoria said, "we can get back to the work Abstergo started on your prosthetics. You're almost there."

"I know."

She looked at him, tapping her lip with her stylus, and then put her tablet aside. "Do you not want a prosthetic that might help you to walk?"

"No, I do," he said. It would be great if he could walk again. How could it not be? That would certainly be more convenient than his wheelchair. There were still a lot of places that weren't accessible to him, like some stores and restaurants that weren't up to code.

"Then what is it?" Victoria asked.

"I'm . . ." Sean shrugged. "I'm just not in a hurry, I guess."

Victoria nodded. "Well. I'll take that as a good sign of your recovery. You'll be back to your old self soon."

"No," Sean said. "I'm going to be better."

Monroe had disappeared once before, and he could do so again. The Ascendance Event had shown him that his work wasn't done, but he wouldn't be able to pursue that work in cooperation with the Templars or the Assassins. They would never be able to see past their ideologies. He would have to find his way alone, just as he'd been doing when he found Owen and the others.

The headlights of the sleek Abstergo car he'd stolen reached ahead of him as he drove along the dark highway. His Animus core and what was left of the Trident sat in the back seat, also stolen. Natalya had insisted all the power had gone out of the Piece of Eden, but Monroe wasn't convinced the relic had given up all its secrets, and he planned to study it as soon as he found somewhere safe enough to proceed.

He also suspected that he wasn't quite finished yet with the teens. As with the Trident, their DNA held profound secrets that Monroe had only begun to unravel.

But for now, they deserved a long rest.

And, as always, their freedom.

YOUR FUTURE LIES IN THE PAST— EXPERIENCE THE EPIC ADVENTURE FROM THE BEGINNING!

"THE FASCINATING, FREE-WHEELING BLEND OF SCIENCE, HISTORY, AND ACTION-ADVENTURE WILL MAKE THIS A SURE HIT, EVEN FOR THOSE WHO HAVEN'T PLAYED THE VIDEO GAMES."
—*KIRKUS REVIEWS*

"THE TARGET AUDIENCE WILL REJOICE THAT THERE IS FINALLY SOMETHING FOR THEM IN THIS THOUGHT-PROVOKING HISTORICAL FICTION SERIES."
—*SCHOOL LIBRARY JOURNAL*

scholastic.com

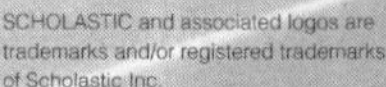

ACLASTDESC